TO

IT ALL

TO CAP IT ALL

G. D. TALKIN

ISBN 978-1-9998262-0-8

IT DESIGN STUDIO

DESIGN – PUBLISHING – MANAGEMENT

'for far away young farmers and their families'

Chapter 1

The rain ran down his back, but did little to cool the burning in his shoulders.

They had tied his hands behind him around a vertical scaffold pole then pulled the boards away so that he looked down passed his feet - now supported only by a horizontal component - to the pavement five floors below. They said they would be back but he doubted it. This was just a reminder that they really did want him to change sides, after all, apparently they had already told the other side he had – most unhelpful.

There was a noise again.

This time he was certain it was not the wind. Someone was stealthily approaching from his left. He peered along the walkway, looking down and to the side in an effort to improve his night vision, but all he caught sight of was the end of a solitary scaffold board, which still protruded over the void at his feet. Not fully withdrawn as its partners, it extended from his right half way across the centre of the gap, the end unsupported.

He heard nothing more for sometime then suddenly she was there, the smile that had mesmerised him playing around her lips, relieved and triumphant at her find. She was not beautiful it was something else, she was arresting. He could never have imagined she would have been interested in such a mediocre man as he, but he had certainly never complained.

The break in the cloud continued for another couple of seconds and he saw the black eyes flash as she withdrew a long bladed knife from the sheath at the small of her back. Then before he could speak, she leapt cat like onto the single scaffold board between them.

He would always recall the spray as the other end of the board hit the walkway above instantly halting its rise, but it was too late. She had slid sideways off the slippery dipping board, grabbed in vain for a hand-hold, then plunged below, once with a metallic ringing striking her head on a horizontal support before smashing into the ground with a sickening thud.

Throughout she made no sound, but then nor did he. Gingerly leaning forward he looked down and in the diffused light through the thinning cloud he could see her body sprawled on the pavement incongruously resembling a lifeless human Swastika.

She was gone.

"Was that all rain or did you piss yourself up there?"

The man was not a nice man, but then he supposed few senior keepers of 'life and liberty' were?

"She would have gutted you like a kipper and fed your giblets to the cat."

The commingled simile and physiological disarray seemingly no problem for the bald guardian of their shores.....

"I think I've done enough now, I can't see how I can do anything now they all know who I am?"

"Bullshit!" and the phone went dead.

It was worth a try, but he didn't really believe they'd let him off that easily.

"So if you pick the truck up tomorrow after the morning rush hour and as long as you're in Dusseldorf by lunch time the next day to pick the 'boys' up from the airport, they'll be happy."

He was receiving the week's itinerary from his boss and the 'boys' manager.

".......and then you can have a few days off as long as you look in each lunchtime to make sure everything is OK and they've got all they need."

'Looking in at lunchtime' of course guaranteed that the 'few days off' would not be spent in the sunny mid February Caribbean but in a freezing back street hotel in Dusseldorf. He should not really complain however as the boss was not a nasty man, just a little neglectful until it came to his 'boys'.

But then given their ten per cent probably paid for the new limousine every year – not to mention a month in the afore mentioned sunny Caribbean – you could not really blame him.

The 'boys' themselves were also not nasty, just thick as shit - which did not stop them being a successful rock band, but had led to his somewhat embarrassing involvement with Her Majesty's Customs and Excise.

Subsequently the 'boys' had been very sorry that he had been the one driving the truck when it had been pulled by customs, but then who else would it have been - it was his job. And they were positively remorseful that the customs people had been difficult. But then again that might have had something to do with the kilo of cocaine that had been discovered hidden inside one of the speaker cabinets. The 'boys' were pleased everything had turned out OK though and expected that it was just one of those things and were really pleased everything was 'alright now' and he had got the 'gear' through.

The problem was everything was not 'alright now', not for someone who had been offered a choice of 'assisting the authorities' in return for an acceptance of his ignorance plea, only to find that the 'assistance' amounted to spying on his recently acquired incredibly attractive girlfriend. Regrettable for his then new found self-esteem, he discovered it was not rudimentary Casanova attributes with which the dusky mid European maiden had been smitten, but the truck. It was she that had convinced the 'boys' to 'run' the drugs and also insisted that he was not made privy to the plan, convincing them that it is always better if the 'mule' is kept in the dark.

The 'boys' were to be paid in 'kind' and he was to remain oblivious, his new girlfriend no doubt would be around all the time the truck made its regular trips to the continent. Who knows, perhaps if things had continued he might even have got married - and she again.

Alas, having assumed that the dummy run had been successful, a large shipment had been attempted and this time had been intercepted by customs and there had been a number of arrests in the UK and on the continent, but not his girlfriend. She had gone missing.

As instructed he had feigned a last minute illness, a substitute driver had been used and he had ostensibly not been involved. He had assumed this would be an end to the matter, but on his last trip to Holland he had been approached by 'associates' of his girlfriend's crowd who were keen he should provide a similar service for themselves now that the others were 'indisposed' – he had refused.

Indisposed meant locked up. The bald man had delighted in informing him that it was in fact his new girlfriend's husband that was the ring leader and would continue to be locked up for a considerable length of time and that he should be careful.

"These Romany Slavs or whatever the bleeding 'ell they are, don't take kindly to having their men shut up, she'll probably try and chop your balls off."

It was this that had been at the forefront of his contemplation following his return from Holland when he had been waylaid on the way to the corner shop to buy some milk. It was dark and true it had begun to rain, but it was at this point his trousers had been dampened in the fashion to which the bald man had alluded - long before he was attached to the scaffold and his ex-girlfriend came calling. He had been escorted into the old warehouse - soon to be the luxury river-view dwellings of some young city slickers – and as they climbed the inside staircase it had all been explained to him. He should not worry - this was merely a demonstration of how earnestly they wanted him as an employee. His only concern should be that until he agreed they would be unable to offer him protection and rumour had it that there was a young wife he knew searching for him.

She was under the impression he had 'sold out' her husband to remove him from the romantic triangle – they were very confident about what she believed because they were the ones that had told her. He was to reconsider things under the cooling rain and ascertain how high up he was and how easily it would be to slip next time, although they hoped there would not need to be a next time – they would be in touch.

He would always try and convince himself that she had come to free him, that the knife was to slice his bonds and not his balls and they would escape together to start anew. And he would have made it, if not for the break in the clouds and the flash of those eyes, irritating how often the bald man was right.

Her body had been found by the police officers that had been sent for him following an anonymous phone call as to his whereabouts and predicament. He had been arrested but soon released following the telephoned intervention of the bald man, but he still did not like him.

Following the telephone call and his release he had gone to meet the bald man at their normal rendezvous.

"You do the same as last time, it's just a different bunch of arse 'oles that's all."

He pleaded that he had already kept his side of the bargain and fulfilled his obligation.

"Double Bubble son, double bubble, can't let it go by, can we? Mustn't look a gift horse in the mouth, must we? Same again and you're home free."

'Home free' he thought, indeed a pleasant concept'.

An only child, his parents had been killed in a car crash when he was seven and he had been raised for as many years again by his Grandmother until her death, when he had been placed 'in care'. The next two years defeated the efforts of the previous fourteen and he had learnt to lie, steal and fight – and that was just to stay alive and unmolested 'in care'.

Lying he was good at. It required a good memory and serenity and it was always his first option. Stealing he disliked and fighting was his weakest suit. Being a coward was obviously a disadvantage and so he had changed his attitude to this facet of self-preservation from fighting to winning – a subtle but important modification. Should there be any doubt as to the outcome of any fair contest, triumph unfairly. If one was unsure as to the result of a Queensbury Rules bout for example, creep up from behind on the way to the ring with a fire extinguisher or chair leg.

He was neither ashamed nor proud of the dubious trinity that had kept him whole whilst institutionalised and satisfied his conscience by pleading he used his nefarious talents exclusively for defence and hoped that if there were ever to be a final analysis this would be taken into consideration.

He now lived alone in a 'flat' under a railway arch that he rented from a landlord who officially listed his 'home' as light industrial and insisted he keep a lathe in the entrance space for fear of enquiring eyes. Thus he tended not to have visitors or hanging baskets and was away a lot so there seemed little risk of a problem with the council and the neighbours minded their own business in common with most arch enterprises – 'dodgy' car body shops and 'funny' book suppliers – all very discrete.

He was away a lot because of his job, which he had come by, by default. He had answered an advertisement for a sound engineer for a rock band but had not been chosen, he had however become aware that the band were looking for a full time road manager and so had swallowed his pride and asked if he might be considered. He had explained that he knew the business, had experience travelling abroad, no family ties and most important, he needed the money. Somewhat surprisingly he had been given the job then and there and everything had gone well until he had happened upon a beautiful dusky maiden and the rest was recent, damp, disagreeable history.

He collected the truck from its security lock up on the Isle of Dogs, was in Dover by lunchtime and after doing a little shopping, boarded an evening ferry to Calais. It was nearer to go to Oostende or Zeebrugge, but for the sake of the odd extra fifty or so miles he preferred the shorter sea crossing and there were more sailings should there be a problem. He didn't expect a problem until he got there, but you never know. He also liked to practice his French.

His Grandmother that raised him was Belgium, but from the French speaking region and had insisted he learnt her native language. At first he acquiesced out of reverence for his benefactor, but soon found an interest and a talent and although his spoken French was impaired due to lack of use, he maintained the ability to understand from regularly listening to French radio stations.

He drove through the night taking advantage of the quieter roads and after stopping for diesel and a midnight breakfast, passed out of France, through Belgium and on into Germany without incident. Soon afterwards he forked south of the industrialised centres of Duisburg and Essen and entered Dusseldorf just as dawn was lighting the wintry sky and traffic clogging the wintry roads.

It was cold and had been snowing but he was able with surprising ease to find the theatre in the middle of town to which he had been directed. After a considerable amount of horn blowing, he was able to attract the attention of the booking office staff and allowed entrance to the rear car park and loading bay. He backed the truck as tight as he could to the theatre rear wall to at least make it difficult for any thieves, locked it and returned to the booking office. Here he politely asked for the keys to the car that the theatre was due to loan the 'boys' for the week of their engagement.

The booking office knew nothing about a car. His German only ran to asking for the car, not to arguing for it and so he tried in vain once more and then asked if they could arrange a taxi to take him to the airport. This they were happy to do and the taxis deposited him at the airport arrivals hall half an hour or so later to wait for the 'boys' flight from London. He found a quiet spot away from the main hub of activities near the observation windows and sat in a line of seats facing out across the tarmac. He knew he would have a while to wait so had brought a book with him in which to become immersed and had succeeded adequately until a voice said quietly,

"So she nearly got you even though we called the ol' bill?"

He looked up and could see in the partial reflection of the glass that two men had taken the seats on either side of him in the row behind. The speaker leant forward enabling a reduction in his voice level, whilst the other sat bolt upright appearing twice the size of his associate and stared straight ahead with what could best be described as an oriental inscrutability.

"I won't ask you how you managed ol' son, but this little job should be a push over after that an' my er...... sponsors shall we say, pay a lot better than them pikeys from the Balkans or wherever the bleeding chavs come from."

It was amazing, if he closed his eyes and ignored the differing timbre it could have been the bald man. It seemed whatever part of the world the villains came from there was always someone from the east-end in there somewhere - and another one trying to catch them.

"We've even made it simpler for you, all you do is drive the truck back and park it over night where it says on the paper we'll leave in the glove box."

"We'll handle the loading during the week, you just make sure the trucks left open, OK? That's all you have to do, OK?"

Then again, "I can't hear you.......OK?"

In the reflection from the window he watched the associate's head turn towards him and better expose the Mongoloid countenance. 'Slant eyed git,' he could well imagine the bald man's assessment, but slant eyed or not he was big and although to be fair, it may have been the distortion in the glass, the Mongol did not look particularly sympathetic. He nodded.

"Can't hear you….."

The bored, slightly whining appeal was more intimidating than the far-eastern hulk.

"Yes I understand, I leave the truck unlocked and park it where it says when I get back, but I can't do this again, I've had it…….and the police must be aware of me after what happened in town."

"'Course they are ol' son, that's why this is the last thing they will expect," the tired rationale continued, "an' in any case, this is just a 'tester,' just enough to pay for next year's bubbly so to speak, next time we'll make it really worth while…….and for you of course, so let's have no more of this can't do it nonsense."

He had been gazing down at his hands to avoid the slant-eyed stare, but when he looked up they had both gone, the eyes and the mouth, there was no one left to hear any continuing plea.

Chapter 2

The 'boys' arrived all bouncy and full of whiskey and coke, but the drummer did at least have the decency to carry an example of the distinctively shaped bottle so suggesting their bliss was liquid based, but he doubted it.

He escorted them from the airport to the taxis rank explaining the absence of any car, but they were not really interested and would never have used a vehicle anyway, experience taught him they would spend their time between the hotel, the theatre and powdered oblivion.

Thus the week passed as others beforehand. He was called upon to fetch and carry a little, but mostly for sound checks. Each lunchtime - soon after the 'boys' had risen and while they could still think as far as they could of course - they walked the short distance to the theatre.

Following his appointment as road manager he had been asked to help out with regard to the duties relating to the sound engineer - the job he had originally applied for - which it appeared that since his appointment as road manager there had been a distinct lack of effort in filling. He did not mind, it made his life a little more interesting and it eliminated the obligation of having someone travel with him – but more money would have been nice.

Every morning he tuned the guitars only to watch the 'boys' fiddle with the tuning pegs to ensure everything was nicely discordant and then they would go through the 'balancing the mics' routine. There were three singers, one sang flat, one sang sharp and one did not sing at all, but obviously wanted the microphone for the photos.

'Balancing' was a ruse in the perpetual endeavour by all three – presumably it effected the photographs as well – to ensure each individual's microphone was louder than the others.' This was in keeping with the general philosophy of most bands of the day, that they wanted 'everything louder than everything else'.

He fiddled with the volume sliders, raising one as its corresponding microphone was tested and surreptitiously restoring it to the original position when the respective performer was satisfied he was ahead in the fanfare stakes.

"Testing, testing. One…two…three…" Rarely did you ever hear four and he was never sure whether it was an acoustic aberration or arithmetical – after all it was one more than the chords that would be used.

He himself, had played in a band for nearly a decade, but either what he played was wrong or the record buying public was, so he had retired from the fray and found work on the periphery - hence his familiarity with the stratagems of the tone deaf and the profoundly so.

Eventually the week was over and having escorted a tired but happy 'band of boys' back to the departure lounge – he had put them in a cab once but they had got lost in the airport and missed the flight – he returned for the truck. It had been left unlocked as instructed and he had kept well clear of it for most of the week, only visiting once for a replacement set of guitar strings – apparently the originals 'sounded flat'. Now he manoeuvred the vehicle as to make best use of the loading bay, painstakingly stored all the equipment in the rear, threw in his personal luggage and was soon on the autobahn, heading west.

He had so far deliberately avoided looking in the glove compartment in a pathetic charade of distancing himself from matters of the day and this he maintained until only a few miles from the port, after he had stopped for diesel and something to eat. When he returned to the truck, a cursory glance identifying no evident signs of surveillance, he locked the doors from the inside and opened the glove box.

Sure enough there was a folded piece of plain paper with a London street and 'between house nos. 29 and 34' written on it – nothing like being exact when parking contraband – but also a ferry sailing time that was different from his scheduled crossing. Presumably he was to miss his planned boat and wait for the other. In itself it was not a problem, it had happened before when there had been delays due to weather or accidents. The only problem being if there was not sufficient space on the unreserved boat, but at this time of the year there should be no difficulty. The truck also normally travelled on the car decks or to be more precise the car and caravan decks, it being no bigger than the large motorised camper vans the Germans delight in producing so that you can take your 'three bed semi' on tour. He was certain there would be no problem, he just had three or four hours to kill and as long as he timed his arrival at the port to coincide with the ferry loading it should be plain sailing.

It was.

He first returned to the restaurant of the service station for another meal – living alone meant he could always eat for tomorrow as well – and three hours later pulled into the terminal in time to make his apologises, have his papers endorsed and drive up the ramp onto the ferry. Breathing a sigh of relief, he turned off the engine and squeezed out of the drivers door, locked it and made note of the number of the deck exit and staircase that took him to the bar for a well earned pint.

It was not the first thing he saw when he entered the bar, but that is how it would be remembered. The Mongol stood at the bar every bit as big as he his reflection in the window at the airport. Ironically it was again a reflection in the mirrored wall behind the optics that for a split second gave the impression the man was staring directly at him, but no, it was just a reflection – he hoped they would only ever meet this way.

He walked to the bar and ordered a pint - albeit the beer he suspected would now taste distinctly flat – and was wondering what to do next, when the matter was taken out of his hands. The Mongol moved along the bar and with little attempt at discretion, placed a similar piece of folded paper on the bar in front of him and left through the door to the duty free.

He carried his beer and the piece of paper to a table away from the bar by the window and sat for a time looking out as the ferry slipped its moorings. He visually marked a spot on the side of the beer glass and agreed with himself that when the level of the ale dropped to this point he would look at the paper, thereby convincing himself he retained some autonomy between the bent and the bald.

The point on the glass was lowered twice before he unfolded the single sheet of paper, but then you can always 'con' yourself, because 'you' won't tell – they did it in the music business all the time.

'Change of plan,' it read, 'take M1 north - fuel for Manchester'.

His first thoughts were that from where he was it would be hard to take the M1 any other way and why was he smuggling diesel to Lancashire?

Flippancy had been one of his favoured abstractions, but it was never enduring. There was no way he could disappear into the land of the northern hordes and still retain his job as conscientious road manager and what would the 'boys' do without him, who would make 'everything louder than everything else?'

Within the hour he retraced his steps along the companionway, descended the stairs and squeezed back into the truck. He had no idea what he was going to do, but began to feel a far from unknown mixture of fear and anger 'begin to simmer'. He eased the truck up the ramp from the 'roll on roll off' ferry and was quietly following the line of other vehicles towards the passport control when a small white car cut in immediately in front, causing him to brake. He had hardly began to mumble his opinion as to the driver's absence of male parentage, when the passenger deliberately turned to look out of the rear window, ducking his head so that he could more easily be seen, it was the Mongol. So, it was he that was to be escorted for a change.

The line of cars made sedate irregular progress towards the guardians of the borders of his homeland and as is normally the case if you have one too many bottles of whiskey secreted in your bags, there seemed to be far more customs officers than normal. He was now stationary half a dozen cars from the control point and already most of the officer's seemed to be focussed on the truck – but then they always did if you had that extra bottle.

He eased forward gradually allowing the gap between him and his malevolent mates to increase. By the time the small white car was being inspected there were fully four car lengths between them, clearly enough to irritate one driver further back in the queue who briefly sounded his horn. But only briefly, judging the distance and ensuring the steering was set 'straight ahead,' he ducked his head below the dashboard toward the centre consul and stamped down hard on the accelerator.

Traditionally diesels vans are not renowned for their acceleration, but to compensate the truck did have a fair amount of open space in front of it. Nonetheless it seemed to take a long time before anything happened apart from the mounting noise of the engine and he wondered if he had misaligned, missed his target altogether and was at present accelerating up the A2. A resounding crash and the dashboard striking him on the side of the head allayed his fears, but the panicked clamour from outside suggested he had other concerns.

He cautiously sat upright and wiped his forehead with the back of his hand which revealed some blood, but no where near as much as the Mongol would have produced if he had been able to get through the locked drivers door. It eventually took three burly port police officers to restrain the barbarian who was definitely disturbed at the damage done to his travelling companion's car, which though obviously considerable, was not easily calculable, as a sizeable proportion appeared to be under the truck. The two occupants of the remains of the small white car were eventually taken into custody and he too was led away, although happily to alternative albeit secure accommodation to wait for what he did not know, but which in the event was at least not long in arriving.

He had never actually seen someone apoplectic before. In fact he was not really qualified to make the diagnosis, but to the best of his knowledge and assessment the bald man was definitely apoplectic.

"All you had to do was to sit tight, we we're going to pull you, you stupid bastard."

He sat silently wincing as a lady customs officer tended albeit far from tenderly, to the cut on his head. He was relieved when she had arrived, as before then he genuinely did think the bald man might have a seizure and there had been a lot of language even he did not understand.

"You've blown months and months of work, you soppy prick, all you had to do was just sit there."

The bald man had apparently been waiting at the port and the plan had been to stop the van on the pretext of searching it, thereby isolating it from the escort and allowing him to receive new instructions. He felt it better not to mention he did not want any new instructions, but did risk asking when he would be allowed to go home.

"You're not going home."

He said he understood there would be certain procedures to go through and things to arrange, but ultimately, when did the bald man think he would eventually be allowed home?

"You're not going home….. Ever."

There were so many challenges he did not know where to start and before he could the bald man continued in his inimitable compassionate manner.

"Listen you dumb shit, you've got the remnants of one gang and the whole of another after your blood, you wouldn't last a month. They both think you ratted on them and if you have any doubts about that don't have, because the only way we can keep this show on the road and protect one of our real sources, is to tell 'em you were the little shit that 'grassed' 'em up…….and that's what we'll do if we haven't already. Your best bet is to take the offer that's coming your way and start again, what have you got to lose?"

The bald man continued warming to his assessment.

"You're a gofer for a bunch of weirdoes, you live in a railway shed, you've got no family, no friends and the first time some pikey tart bats her eyes at you, you piss your pants. If you take my advice, you'll listen very carefully to what the man has to say, although you might as well know, I've told him in my opinion you ain't worth the gamble."

With that the door slammed behind the bald man and he was left alone with an uncomfortable Custom's first aider.

"Technically I pissed my pants long before the pikey tart came on the scene."

She finished packing her first aid box and left obviously grateful she had worn the latex gloves.

He sat at the steel-framed table and gradually developed a headache. He was being held in one of the small rooms that are used for body searches, although he assumed in his case there would be no need to seek small quantities of banned substances in various personal orifices, as he had a van full of the stuff outside. According to the bald man, at the eleventh hour the gang had decided to skip the dummy run and go for the 'big one' straight away, hence the change of plans – everybody's!

He heard the sound of heavy vehicles as they towed away the remnants of his car wreck and wondered what the 'boys' would say about the damage to the truck and no doubt to some of the equipment. The guitars would definitely be nicely out of tune now and with any luck the sliders on the mixer desk would be fixed eternally on maximum – so they would really have nothing to worry about.

An hour went by and he was brought some tea by his earlier substitute medic and asked how he felt, but he noticed she had donned another pair of latex protectors so he could have felt better – not leprous for example.

The port boasted a heli-pad and he heard a couple of the noisy whirlybirds come and go when soon after the arrival of one there was a polite knock on the door and a slight man with rimless glasses entered and extending his hand declared,

"Hello, my name is Mr. Reece."

Mr. Reece wore a light gabardine raincoat and a porkpie hat and carried a black briefcase that folds the back over the front where it is buckled with two straps.

"We understand you are in some difficulty and believe we may be able to offer a solution. We have a job for you Mr. Wilkinson which we think you are well suited for and which we believe if brought to a successful conclusion, would be to our mutual advantage."

"My name is not Wilkinson."

"Ah, but it will be if you work for us." Mr. Reece continued albeit a little pained, "You see your present predicament requires, shall we say evacuation – we think elimination demonstrates an unfortunate attitude – and we believe we can offer you a considerably better alternative to er...eradication than that countenanced by your er...previous importation associates."

Mr. Reece brightened as if at the passing of a little indigestion,

"We will conclude any outstanding matters you have with the authorities as well as settling your affairs with your present employer, plus we will clarify the situation with any close personal connections you may have, although to date we must be frank, we have not identified any.....?"

There was a pause, but only a little one.

"Your er...'flat' will be cleared and any personal effects you specify would naturally be forwarded, subject of course to professional scrutiny for as you will obviously be aware by now, we are offering you the chance of a new life. In return of course we are asking you accept an endeavour, which although significant we believe to be well within your capability – not to labour the point, but we feel any alternative you may choose, shall we say, would be er...short lived. I shall leave you now to your deliberations and return in one hour to learn of your decision." With which Mr. Reece quietly let himself out.

He hadn't even said what the job was, but did it really make any difference. He quickly ran through the recommended system for making decisions, list the pros and cons, what would he miss.......a painful death, what would he gain.......some kind of life.......he had failed in his attempt to become a member of Mensa, but did he really need that high an IQ for this conundrum?

There was another knock on the door and he assumed Mr. Reece had been as swift in estimating the time needed for his evaluation as himself, but it was the young lady customs office again with more tea and this time without gloves. If working for Mr. Reece could produce results like this, it must be worth investigating.

He had finished his tea and was lost in thought when the door was once more gently rapped upon and Mr. Reece quietly re-entered and paused in anticipation.

He stood up from the table, extended his hand toward the ever polite intruder and resignedly declared,

“Hello, my name is Mr. Wilkinson.”

Chapter 3

The forerunner to the European Union was born out of the aftermath of World War II with the aim to prevent another conflict on the European mainland. To that extent it was successful, although many would feel the tensions and mutual dread by which the USA and the USSR held each others ability to destroy the world should any hostility ignite may have been more pertinent.

There followed trading treaties between the member states and much was made of the Common Market, but again there are those that question if the trade would not have developed regardless, after all it had existed beforehand. Furthermore each state continued to maintain significant trading partners outside of the Union, trade which also continued to develop despite the existence of the Common Market. Nevertheless, the vast majority of the political and commercial elite sought increasingly closer affiliation until a Confederation of European States with a single constitution became for many an overt aspiration.

By the end of the twentieth century however, it became clear that this political elite had failed to carry a majority of the people with them, despite promises of more prosperity in return for a diminution in national identity. Thus a stubborn fifty per cent of the populace desired no greater integration. Although half of the community numerically, this constituency existed largely in the rural areas across the continent, where the perceived threat to a cherished way of life was most feared and so the geographical land area where the European Union had become suspect was huge.

Regardless of political persuasion however, one aspect was beyond dispute, as an organisation the European Union was corrupt. From its inception it had never managed to provide accounts that any auditor would accept. Other than in general terms, no one knew where the money went and it was a very great deal of money. It was as if the wage earner gave the partner the wage packet at the end of the week and asked how last week's money had been spent, to which the partner replied that they did not know. If it had been a corner shop, it would have been closed down many years past and the proprietor would probably have been imprisoned – not providing annual audited accounts is a very serious business for companies and their executives.

Efforts were regularly made to bring some order to affairs and a department was created to specifically reduce the more blatant corruption abounding in Brussels and Strasbourg, but was eventually closed down due to the level of internal corruption within the said department.

One area where fraud is rife is within the Common Agricultural Policy, which is unfortunate, as this division represents over half the total expenditure of the Union. The main area for the misappropriation of funds is within the substantial and complex sphere of grants and subsidies.

There are grants for almost anything. Farmers can receive grants for growing crops, harvesting crops, destroying crops or not growing crops, for plant and machinery, for erecting buildings then dismantling them and of course, for doing nothing at all. For pigs until there are too many, then chickens until there are too many, then cows until there are too many, then tobacco that will not grow in the northern European climate and then for ploughing it back into the ground. In Holland there are grants for window boxes and Italy demands subsidies for her olive groves that in total area are greater than the entire landmass of the country.

With corruption at the top and idiocies at the bottom, what scope lies between?

"This is the one I think, plenty of land, house and farm buildings for renovation and well off the beaten track – they'll think you're a hermit as well as stupid."

He watched his 'interpreter' walk back to the estate agent and confirm in excruciatingly painful 'French' the client's decision to make an offer for the property they had just viewed. The agent instinctively responded with the need to pay the asking price to secure the purchase ahead of any other parties, but given the property had obviously been empty for a considerable time the 'interpreter' declined and confirmed his client wished to offer the asking price less ten per cent. They then retired to their respective cars - he driving the 'interpreter' having witnessed the man's driving skills as potentially more painful than his mastery of the French language - and were soon meandering their way back to the estate agent's office to complete the paperwork.

If all went according to plan and his offer was accepted, in three months he would be a French farmer.

It had been a busy month.

He had never returned to the 'flat', but had been taken that same night directly to a small country manor house he suspected somewhere in Hampshire, but had been advised not to take any account of the location – apparently it was another place he was ultimately intended never to return. The next day Mr. Reece, as polite as ever albeit a tad more businesslike, outlined what was expected in return for his new tomorrow – which was the first shock for it was estimated that the new tomorrow could be two or three years away – if all went well.

Somewhat disgruntled, he mentioned that he had not anticipated 'the endeavour' to be so protracted and that three years was a considerable slice of anybody's life – and what if all did not go well? Mr. Reece was confident that it would and what would have been the alternative – no slices at all?

A day later his personal effects arrived. They consisted of a new radio cassette he had recently treated himself to, his old but cherished acoustic guitar and a large suitcase. The suitcase was not his and he had had to 'sign for it' before he opened it to find it full of those clothes he had not taken with him to Dusseldorf, two framed photographs of his parents and grandmother, his personal papers file and some other odds and ends. Not much for nearly three decades on earth but at least he now might see a fourth.

Two more days passed quite quickly whilst he studied the pile of information that Mr. Reece had politely provided and then he was driven by the 'interpreter' further west where he was billeted on a beef farm with an elderly couple who lived far too well to be beef farmers. Nevertheless the couple were knowledgeable about their hefty charges and did their best to help him over his newly discovered fear of all things with four legs - or more.

After a week the 'interpreter' reappeared and this time they journeyed eastward to the Garden of England where he was deposited with a gentleman farmer who talked eloquently about apples and pears, strawberries and vines and grain crops – when he was not cleaning his vintage Bentley.

The next time the 'interpreter' arrived it was to actually act as an interpreter and to demonstrably mangle the language of his grandmother once they had crossed the English Channel and were deep into the French hinterland.

Apart from the 'interpreter' having a greater knowledge of exactly what type of property would best suit Mr. Reece's purpose, it was considered essential that from the start the language skills his grandmother had dutifully imparted be concealed. He would understand all that was said around him, but no one was to know he did. Thus the 'interpreter' dealt with all that was required while he impersonated just another dumb shit Englishman hoping to make a living in a foreign land where he knew not the systems, the culture or the language. What did all these semi-detached suburban dwellers hope to do, grow an entrepreneurial by-lingual brain whilst passing through the Straits of Dover? It wasn't his problem - he was just supposed to make it so.

What was his immediate problem however was what to do for the next three months until he took possession, but here Mr. Reece was his ever polite and helpful self.

Upon his return from France he was driven back to the manor house in Hampshire – the 'interpreter' felt he had to drive this leg as it needed to be assumed his charge did not know where it was – to find Mr. Reece awaiting his arrival and politely pleased with recent developments.

"Bravo Mr. Wilkinson, I am pleased to hear you have found a farm that suits you."

It of course had nothing to do with him, which was not unreasonable, as it was not his money, although he was apparently to be allowed to keep the property if 'the endeavour' was brought to a successful conclusion. This was to form part of the remuneration for the time he would spend 'endeavouring'. What formed the other parts he had not been told and conscious that no one knew how much time he would actually spend 'endeavouring', he did not know whether his was to be well paid or not – but then presumably nor did anyone else. Mr. Reece really was a master of ambiguity and loose ends.

"Now, you will be pleased to hear we have found a position for you for the next three months or so until matters concerning the farm are concluded - and we think you will find it both instructional and invigorating."

There were some words his time in institutions had taught him were not what they sounded and 'instructional and invigorating' were two such fists in velvet gloves.

"We have managed to obtain a position for you in one of the competition horse yards in the Newmarket area. We feel that it may well be that some experience with equines could be very useful as the Department in France in which you will soon be residing is renown as an equestrian region.......one never knows?"

True one never knows - and he certainly knew nothing about horses other than that they had four legs, which was exactly the number of legs the beef had that he had had so much trouble getting to know.

"You will be driven along tomorrow and we will be in touch 'as and when' with regard to the purchase, so have a fulfilling time and we will meet again before you depart these shores."

With a farewell smile Mr. Reece buckled his briefcase and was gone. There were obvious questions he would have liked answered but he had come to recognise that there were times when Mr. Reece would be forthcoming and times when he wouldn't and this was one of the latter.

They departed after breakfast the next morning and he insisted on driving. The 'interpreter' was a little miffed by the manifest lack of confidence in his driving skills, but allowed himself to be mollified by the ' bad passenger' ploy and compliments regarding language proficiency – his most favoured of the dubious trinity coming to the fore.

He drove steadily and was soon London bound on the M3, skirting west and north of the metropolis on the M25 thus avoiding any possible hold up at the Dartford Tunnel, heading north through Essex on the M11 eventually arriving via the A11 at Newmarket. After a brief stop for a cup of tea and a sandwich they followed the directions furnished by a fellow tea-breaking postman and after another fifteen minutes he pulled into the impressive premises of a successful race horse trainer and his new home for the next dozen weeks or more. There appeared to be nobody in the office but no doubt anticipating an early finish to the day, the 'interpreter' helpfully unloaded all his worldly goods and with a haste virgin on discourtesy, called something about 'seeing him anon' and was gone.

Earlier the recently 'signed for' suitcase had easily swallowed the few items he habitually took with him when travelling together with the shoulder bag he took them in plus the radio cassette. Thus it was only two pieces of luggage he hauled into the office, the huge suitcase and his guitar, snuggled in its even older canvas bag.

There was indeed nobody in the office and so he sat on the bench just inside the door and waited. He sensed their were people or some kind of life form around and just as he was about to venture outside a Range Rover came to an abrupt halt in front of the office door and a smart portly man descended. He burst into the office with that, 'the world will end if I don't open my mail' look mediocre middle managers have and glared,

"You're early."

He was not aware he had an ETA and said so.

"Carl won't be here for another hour, you'll have to wait."

He did not know who Carl was nor why he had to wait for him, but if that was what he had to do he would.

"Well?"

"OK, I'll wait."

"But you can't wait in here."

"OK, where would you like me to wait?"

"Outside."

"OK."

He gathered up his guitar and opened the office door wrestling his suitcase through and to the side then turning to shut the door. It had started to drizzle and so he pushed the suitcase tight to the wall next to the door so remaining within the shelter of the entrance canopy. No sooner had he sat on the case and leaned back making himself as comfortable as possible, then the office door opened and the portly man leaned out and exasperated pronounced,

"You can't wait there."

To which he replied without turning his head,

"Bollocks!"

There was a pause and then the door slammed shut.

Carl showed him his 'room' - which was the size of a disabled persons toilet cubicle, but not as clean - and was every bit as hospitable as his portly boss had been.

"I don't know why they're taking on more people, we've lost a couple of owners and there's 'ardly enough work to go round as it is."

He cautiously explained to Carl that he would not be there long, but was loathe to say too much as he was not certain of the actual arrangements. It made no difference, to Carl however who was lost in a world of labour surpluses and anticipated redundancies and so he bade the trouble man good afternoon but just as he was leaving Carl remembered,

"I'll give you a shout tomorrow morning, that's when the Gaffer said you're supposed to start."

Closing the door on local employment uncertainties, he opened his case and took out some of the literature he had gathered over recent weeks and began to read about cows and sheep and arable crops. He wondered if there was an evening meal available, but if there was he was obviously not invited as nobody came to call and so he finished his emergency supply of peanuts, crisps and chocolate and settled down for an early night. Hardly had he seemed to have closed his eyes then there was a loud knock on the door and a voice he recognised as that of Carl, told him it was 'morning stables' and he would be back for him in ten minutes.

When illuminated the face of his watch showed 5am and he wondered if it had been a dream, but the obvious sounds of activity from outside suggested otherwise. Ten minutes later – around about the time he would often be going to bed not leaving it – there was the promised knock on the door. He left his cubicle and followed Carl through the dimly lit yard and began to fetch and carry as instructed – this time bales and buckets, not basses and buffoons. It was cold and dreary, but his main concern was maintaining a safe distance between himself and the silent four legged creatures that had begun to be led about the yard on apparent bits of stout string that nevertheless did not look at all up to the job.

After breakfast, by which time he had completed half a days work - but which had at least revealed the whereabouts of the communal kitchen and rest room – he was shown his very own personal assignment for the forthcoming weeks, he was to 'muck out' a row of elderly stables. He was to shovel shit for a couple of months. Carl seemed quite disappointed that the newcomer was to be the lucky one, presumably preserving the chore to prolong the time before he was reacquainted with his P45, but the newcomer was less enthralled. Nevertheless for the next two days he bailed and bucketed until sunrise and shovelled shit until sundown. Nobody spoke to him or came near him until the third afternoon, when, just as he was thinking about finishing for the day, three of the stable 'lads' suddenly appeared behind his antiquated wheelbarrow.

He had noticed that all the other wheelbarrows on the property were plastic or some form of composite, but he had been allocated an obvious ex-builders barrow that was metal and heavy. He was not over bothered, he had pushed many like it before, but it did need to be respected if one wished to preserve undamaged shins.

'Lads' was the customary designation for his fellow workers although misleading to the uninitiated as the term was not age related, thus the spokesman of the trio was probably older than he, but they were all comfortingly small.

"There's an initiation ceremony for all new lads, alright?"

The words were almost spat out and it was evidently not the 'we hope you are settling in OK' speech he might have preferred and it continued,

"Well?"

The one word question seemed to be as popular with the staff as it was their portly gaffer. Regardless he politely explained that he was not really a 'new lad' and would only be staying for a short time so there was no need to worry about any initiation or their jobs for that matter. He had added the last comment in deference to Carl's anxiety, wondering if the palpable hostility had a similar root cause.

"We don't care how long you stay or where you come from, we just don't like you London tykes and will be glad to see the back of you."

The inherent contradiction posed the spokesman no vexation, so he felt it unkind to draw attention to the inconsistency and ruefully recognised the time for talk was expired.

"Well?"

Perhaps it was the East Anglia flatlands that induced this obsession with shafts sunk in the ground, whatever, it was obvious the brief negotiations were coming to an end as the three 'lads' began a belligerent fidget.

During the exchange he had desultory continued with his toil so as he turned to heap another shovel it was unremarkable, but as he turned back to the wheelbarrow the spokesman was totally unprepared for the shovel full of shit that hit him in the face. As indeed were the shins of the two associates that felt the full force of the overturned heavy wheelbarrow he kicked onto them with the sole of his foot. Not waiting for a reaction he swiftly swung the shovel in a low ark smashing the back into the knee of the shit-eating spokesman, producing a wail instead of a well.

One of the others made a half-hearted advance around the front of the wheelbarrow to which he responded by again aiming at the knee, jabbing the edge of the shovel blade hard just above the joint, halting the progress amidst a series of curses and hops.

"Please understand if you ever come near me again, I will ensure that you never sit on one of those stupid fucking creatures without a hoist."

His voice was breathless and intimidating, the words delivered through gritted teeth, but more bedded in self-preservation than menace. He stared at each of his protagonists in turn,

"Well?" when in Rome he thought or had he caught wet-rot?

"We wouldn't have hurt you."

Suddenly one of the others had a voice.

"Perhaps not, but I will hurt you if you come near me again, so please leave before we really fall-out."

He tried to make the reasonable politeness a threat in itself.

The spokesman was assisted to his feet and aided across the yard by the least injured of his accomplices and he wondered if they would be back, but he doubted it. Frightened people are always the most frightening and he had been frightened, it was where his courage came from or should it be termed panic?

He slept with the shovel that night and with a chair wedged against the door, but there were no attempted intrusions. At morning stables next day he noted a couple of 'lads' limping around one of the other lines of stables, but took no particular interest. It was not until he had finished breakfast, that the portly man entered the rest room to curtly announce that he was wanted on the telephone. He followed the waddling figure across to the office and lifted the receiver to hear the dulcet tones of Mr. Reece ask if everything was 'agreeable'.

He said it was.

"No problems then?"

"No."

"Fine then, we'll be in touch 'as and when'." And the line went dead.

He replaced the receiver and looked up to see the portly man staring at him with ill concealed antagonism so continued in a similar monotone,

"I know you don't want me here," he spoke resignedly but with conviction. "But then you would not have me here if you didn't have to, no more than I would be here if I didn't have to be, so why don't we just see the time out as best we can and then forget each other ever existed?"

"I don't have to have you here," petulant but resigned.

"Then pick the phone up and tell the nice man to come and get me."

The smart portly man suddenly did not look so smart and more 'pissed' than portly. It was obvious that there had to be some leverage that permitted his continued presence and although he did not know what reason Mr. Reece had for wanting him here he doubted it was for his health and wellbeing. He had also been unable to find anybody during the morning that had heard of any 'initiation ceremony' so presumed it had been a ruse to commence hostilities and perhaps engineer a spontaneous departure freeing the portly man of any embarrassment with the likes of Mr. Reece.

"Oh and by the way, I've learned how to shovel shit, now I want to learn how to ride one of those nags there's so much fuss about."

He deliberately let himself out of the office and walked even more deliberately back to the rest room - aping John Wayne, but probably looking more like Wayne Sleep. He really did not know why he had said it. It happened sometimes; keeping cool, calm and collected seemed at times to evoke from him proclamations of the most amazing stupidity. He was still considering his recklessness when Carl 'came a calling', only to be told in no uncertain terms that the shit shovelling days were over and he would not be 'coming out to play'.

He spent the rest of the day in continued study of the papers he had been given not least those appertaining to his personage. He was Mr. Timothy Wilkinson an only child and late of the northern Kentish Downs where his parents had farmed until their untimely demise in a car crash – nothing like the benefits of fabricating a story as near to the truth as possible. He was unmarried with no living relatives and the documentation established he had enjoyed a career in farming, was a registered young farmer and member of the National Farmers Union. More detailed examination of his passport indicated various trips across the channel to France where on the last visit according to the accompanying copy of an *'acte de vente'* he had contracted to purchase a farm. All documents appeared authentic as far as his non-professional scrutiny could determine, duly dog-eared and grubby as befitting a tiller of the soil, albeit he knew most to be counterfeit.

Just as his earlier imprudence had felicitously slipped from his mind there was another knock on the door, this time more discrete, but regardless when he opened it he was accompanied by his trusty shovel. There was no need and actually he felt a trifle silly answering the door dancing a tango with an upturned spade as his caller was a rather embarrassed looking young lady. The embarrassment was entirely unwarranted however given her ample femininity amply displayed by her jodhpurs and tight fitting sweater. Returning her smile and hoping she had not noticed it wasn't the first place he had surveyed he demonstrated all his recently acquired suavity and inquired,

"Yes."

"Mr. Mutt said I was to take you riding, if you still want to go."

She was very attractive despite the horse-shit on her boots and jodhpurs - and hands unless she held cigarettes between all fingers of both – and would probably 'wash up well' as his grandmother would have said, but was she attractive enough to get him on one of those half ton greyhounds?

"Well?" he heard himself mumble – he most definitely had contracted something! "I really don't think I have time at the moment, I've got rather a lot of work to do and……."

"It's alright, I know you don't ride, but you'll be alright really, I'll look after you - and it'd be one in the eye for 'Mutley'."

She was most persuasive, as indeed was the sweater.

"OK."

There it was again, the other time it happened in addition to endeavouring to stay cool, calm and collected; when waylaid by a lovely young lady – which he was sure she was with the shit washed off – another proclamation of amazing stupidity!

Chapter 4

"So, Mr. Wilkinson, what's to do?"

He sat opposite a jaunty Mr. Reece with a Mr. P to his left and a Lord S to his right. He was amused to find that even with the utilisation of alphabetic pseudonyms, one still kept one's title – presumably if the Monarch was also seated around the table with them, she would be appropriately addressed as Queen B.

"Discontinue the practice of betting on a horse to loose. It's far easier to stop a horse winning than to ensure it succeeds, the authorities would then only have to look for stimulants as before. There're so many ways or stopping a horse performing to expectations it could never be policed. Many techniques are perfectly mundane and could be classed as bad stable management - too much food or water at the wrong time is often probably enough – and if all else fails, just instruct the jockey not to try too hard. It's already happening on a regular basis."

There was an awkward silence and then the product of an accident of birth or Prime Ministerial patrimony turned to face him and loftily observed,

"I'm interested in the veracity of your opinions on horsemanship Sir, I was under the impression your riding experience stretched to something nearing three months?"

Personally he was not really bothered about the 'betting public'. His life experiences had tended to make him quite suspicious of Lady Luck, but if folk choose to place their hard earned 'buck' on the turn of a card or speed of a horse, he felt they should at least have the 'chance' that was advertised.

"I'm not basing my opinions on any riding experience."

Pausing, he considered his audience before continuing deliberately.

"When a champion jockey 'sits-up' half way round and looks over his shoulder waiting for the others to catch up, anyone that has ever been in an egg 'n' spoon race knows there's a bad smell around – and it's not the eggs."

He felt his summary would inspire no immediate honorary membership of the Jockey Club nor elevation to the Peerage, but he had done what he had been asked and why should he care about the British aristocracy, he was off to France.

True to her word the young lady had looked after him and he had leaned how to sit on a horse and not fall off, but unexpectedly continued to be still quite wary of the large beasts when on the ground. As a senior 'lad' she had been allowed to keep one animal of her own in the yard and it was on this that he had 'cut his teeth' - and his tongue following one of the more painful involuntary somersaulted dismounts. The animal was an accommodating sort however, unlike its more typical neurotic fellow boarders and he came to enjoy the experience – particularly when he stopped falling off.

One considerable additional bonus was that the young lady almost by accident had provided the information for which it had transpired Mr. Reece required his sojourn in the racing world – how were they stopping the winners? It turned out in principle it was nothing very clever, just as he had explained - basically the wrong preparation before the race.

There were of course other more obnoxious methods, but why take risks unless it was really necessary? Particularly as the authorities had little idea how much interference was being perpetrated if ostensibly everything appeared to be natural. Only abnormal activity on the off course betting exchanges and the odd stupidity of anxious jockeys no doubt concerned as to their health, wealth and longevity had indicated there was probable duplicity.

It had been easy and as proof of his gratitude he suggested he should take her to dinner to which she had readily agreed, then asked if her fiancé could come too? This had not actually been what he had envisaged for the night, but with an enthusiasm he did not feel, he agreed and in the event they had all had a pleasant evening. He also gleaned more information than he might have if the evening had proceeded in accordance with his original aspirations as the young lady did indeed 'wash up well'.

Nonetheless, he completed his time at the yard and had returned to Hampshire to prepare his report and was now reading from the one page document and generally 'pissing off' the 'man that had neglected a toilet break' and 'a north London cricket ground' – Mr. P and Lord S.

"Well gentlemen that appears to be about all we can help you with."

Mr. Reece seemed positively perky, "it's obviously now for you to effect your own deliberations and determination. I'm sure we are all grateful for the efforts Mr. Wilkinson has made with respect to this matter and he will now retire from the fray so to speak...er....... and is unfortunately unable to join us for lunch. Thank you Mr. Wilkinson."

Nothing like a polite dismissal and it was indeed nothing like a polite dismissal, but he was not over bothered, it was clear the two Jockey Club officials had a lot to think about and he doubted if his presence would have aided their digestion.

He returned to his room and continued with the study of his papers, literature and other information. It seemed he had done little else for months, but he knew it was important he be able to play the part as required although could have done without Mr. Reece's reassurance that 'you never know, it could be a matter of life or death'.

He was due to leave in a couple of days with the 'interpreter' plus two 'friends' in a Luton van that was to transport 'his furniture'. Mr. Reece wanted everything to look as normal as possible with regard to his emigration. Obviously it was felt that a man of his age should have acquired slightly more worldly possessions than could be stowed in a suitcase and so a second-hand amount of the typically absent items had been purchased on his behalf to disguise the deficit.

The two 'friends' would not only deal with the furniture, but in the two days they were scheduled to stay, hopefully improve the rudimentary facilities of the ancient farmhouse to a minimum level of accommodation, as well as make some other unspecified modifications. Amused, he looked forward to seeing what his new chattels amounted to.

It was late into the afternoon when Mr. Reece returned, neat and dapper as ever. He did not know why exactly, but the thought of Mr. Reece smoking or drinking seemed totally bazaar so an extended lunch had had no impact on the fastidious nature and application to duty.

"Now Mr. Wilkinson it is likely we will not speak for many months and alas my attendance is demanded in the capital thus I will not be present to bid you *bon voyage.*"

He saw an opportunity to further quiz Mr. Reece as to whom he worked for but was waived to silence as before with some vague reference to 'government department.'

"You must not concern yourself with such matters Mr. Wilkinson, if we are able to bring about a successful conclusion to our endeavours, as I have said before, all this will soon be a distant memory. Should of course remember that when your 'friends' leave the farmhouse you will be on your own. You have I hope committed to memory a number of means by which you could contact us in an emergency, but there is no rush, indeed to rush would probably be counter productive and dangerous."

Mr. Reece seemed positively perturbed at the notion.

"Please remember, for many involved – and there will be many involved, even if reluctantly - the stakes are high and although these people are perhaps not normally delinquent, that alone would render them unpredictable. They have the funds and should at any time they fear apprehension, will likely engage the assistance of others who most certainly would be villainous."

Smiling amiably Mr. Reece stood, buckled his brief case then turning at the opened door,

"I sincerely wish you good fortune in your endeavour Mr. Wilkinson and hope to see you in a couple of years or so."

And the door closed behind him.

"Actually we probably don't need to leave 'til five."

He gazed blankly across the table into the smiling face of the 'interpreter' not knowing whether it was a statement or question - and not caring. The smile dispersed into a smirk and the 'interpreter' chuckled,

"OK 4am it is lads."

The 'interpreter', his two new furniture 'friends' and himself were seated around the same table at which he had lost all hope of joining the honour's list, but there was one major difference, this time he was the boss. Apparently from the time they left the Hampshire Manor – including the time they left – it was his 'show', he was to take responsibility and his three associates were to look to him for instruction and executive decision. All slightly whimsical given he would be waving goodbye to them in a few days, but the 'government department' were sticklers for definitive chains of command, no doubt so that in the event of a reversal they knew who to Court Marshall or hang.

The 'Completion' of the purchase of the property in France was arranged for five o'clock in the afternoon when they would need to be at the 'Notaires' office to hear the contracts read, sign them, pay the man and collect the keys. At this point they would be free to visit the farm and see what remained after the previous owners had spent the last three months awaiting completion, removing everything that was not screwed down and a lot that once was.

He estimated it could take twelve hours to complete the journey, added one for contingencies and still hoped there would be no unforeseen delays – he certainly would not accept a later start. In the event, they arrived a little over an hour and a half before the rendezvous and had time for coffee and cake, but could easily have had a four-course meal as in accordance with national tradition formalities started nearly an hour late. There was no vendor in attendance, some form of power of attorney being invested in the Notairial office and so when things did get under way all went quite smoothly despite the 'interpreters' French. The Notaire was duly arrogant and he duly humble, plus ostensibly oblivious of all proceedings, in common no doubt with many of his countrymen before him who were devoid of any language skills.

He decided not to visit the farm that evening, but chose to book his quartet into a reasonable hotel and treat them to a decent meal, knowing the next few days would be hard for everyone. He paid for everything with his 'new' credit card and despite all that had gone before, was still quite surprised when it was accepted without query. Up until now he had been allocated cash when necessary, but prior to his move overseas he had been furnished with a bank account and a credit card – to go with the furniture. There were to be monthly credit payments into the bank account from which he was to draw his living expenses and if the confidential defences of the offshore account were breached, the payments would only be traced to a trust fund set up by his parents before their death.

Mr. Reece thought of everything - except the antacid.

The undercooked steak and the overcooked 'frits' guaranteed a restless night, but the breakfast was better and the 'café au lait' excellent, so they were in not too bad a shape when they arrived at the farm the next morning. He was pleasantly surprised that everything looked exactly the same as when he had seen it last, run down and over-grown, but at least it was still there.

The farmhouse consisted of four downstairs rooms, all roughly the same size and extending from front to back with three communicating doors giving access one to the other with two external doors from the two end rooms both facing south. Above was a large attic than ran the whole length and width of the building and was accessed by an external staircase and door.

He decided to concentrate on two of the rooms to establish a kitchen-diner and a bed-sitting room. Having made the decision he was impressed how fast his two 'friends' and 'interpreter' began to refurbish his new home.

Apart from the furniture the van had transported a host of materials which were soon cleaning, priming and painting their way across his walls, floors and woodwork.

That night they slept on a mixture of camp beds and mattresses, but by the end of the next day almost everything was in place and he again took his benefactors for something to eat, but this time he settled for an omelette. He slept well in his own bed of two days and next morning was beginning to enjoy life even as he watched the two 'friends' preparing to leave, when he was handed a smallish sports bag and informed that there were instructions inside.

He was to find somewhere close at hand to secure the valet and tell not a soul. Still unperturbed he stashed the bag inside his new wardrobe for the time being and returned outside to make his farewells.

Despite the fact that he did not know their names and had never met them before, he had enjoyed their company and they had laughed a lot – more than he had done for a long time.

"If it goes wrong we will probably be the ones to come and clean up, is there anyone you want informed – the office is s'posed to, but it sometimes slips their mind especially if there's a political aspect."

The 'interpreter' had just departed in his car to get fuel and meet up later with the van in the village; he had been taken to one side by one of his 'friends' while the other sat in the van with the engine already running. He stammered and shook his head.

"You sure, no one else is gonna ask you?"

He continued to shake his head, "No, there's no one."

"OK. Oh, one other thing, don't rely on that peashooter, get yourself a shotgun, even if you don't hit anything it makes 'em think about it, Good Luck."

He suddenly stopped enjoying life again and wondered whatever had made him start.

Chapter 5

She wore a small brimmed straw sun hat covering jet-black hair that appeared to have been chopped just below the ears with the aid of an upturned basin, round amber rimmed shaded spectacles and no make up. A smock styled mackintosh despite the season, buttoned under the chin and extending almost to her feet that were enclosed in heel-less mules.

It wasn't so much that she wasn't much to look at - it was just that there wasn't much to look at – especially for a wife.

A year had passed.

Not so much passed as flown. He had bought a car, a tractor, some chickens and goats, a horse plus a dog at auction. In reality he thought he was bidding for a hay-bailer and was duly surprised that the desired piece of farm equipment had been secured at such a reasonable price. Only to swiftly discover that it was not the bailer he had purchased for a few Francs, but the dog tied to it. Terrified, the emaciated creature growled at him from the rear of the car all the way home. It was weeks before he could even touch the animal, which still exhibited a significant fear of strangers.

Nevertheless it was all in keeping with the portrayal of a young, poor, foreign farmer, not speaking the language, struggling against economic adversity and in need of all the bureaucratic and financial help he could get. He had conscientiously filled in a number of applications for grants and subsidies, but nothing excessive, only enough to draw the authorities' attention to his existence.

Immediately upon his arrival in France he had applied to join the equivalent of the Farmers Union and had been readily accepted, all subscriptions being gratefully received by an organisation that was technically bankrupt – and practically would be when enough farmers reached retirement. He had duly received some nominal sums in respect of his goats and renovations, but the administrative paper trial would be the same for a little as a lot and it was his presence he wanted noted.

The renovation grant had included a contribution toward a septic tank, which had led to a WC and bathroom in the last of the four downstairs rooms, which was a great improvement on the chemical toilet over which he had previously squatted. Nothing else of any import happened during the period, he played with the tractor, fenced some paddocks for the goats and rode his huge Percheron – built for comfort, not for speed and as sage as his master's previous stable mates were neurotic.

He took occasional trips further afield where he was able to rehearse his French without risk of any locals becoming aware of his proficiency. He also briefly visited a couple of locations he had committed to memory before leaving Hampshire to ensure he would be able to find them in haste if necessary, but other than that he pottered around the farm.

Although alone, he began to enjoy life – always a bad omen.

"It's your cousin Rita, how are you getting on?"

"Fine, fine."

"Look we are thinking about coming over, between the 18th and 24th, your niece or whatever she is, is nearly four now and you haven't seen her for ages, I'll ring you again the day after tomorrow."

The phone call was in response to one he had made earlier in the week from the local post office and was not from his cousin Rita – he had no cousin Rita, which was hardly surprising as he had no relatives, in this life or the other. This did not bother him, it had always been this way and as he sipped his dry white wine in the warmth of the evening sun, in his mind he systematically deciphered the telephone call.

Equidistant between 18 and 24 was 21 an odd number, which meant the rendezvous, was to be at the first location. It was to take place at 4pm, the age of the child, the day after tomorrow, the promised day of the next call. All very cloak and dagger and he would have thought quite ridiculous were it not for a communication he had received through the post the week before.

It was marked for his attention and obviously had been addressed and delivered to the farm, but it also bore a company name that he did not recognise. More confusing, it was a request for further information in respect of a grant that had been applied for and of which he had no knowledge. This maybe what he had been waiting for, but now that it was here he was a little disappointed and more than a little anxious.

He arrived at the rendezvous point early, so walked around the adjoining shopping centre until it was time to enter the fast food restaurant, order his hamburger and fries and carry the tray to a seat by the window. "What more natural, than a young ex-pat taking advantage of a traditional 'pie and chips' amongst all that fish and *fois gras*." Mr. Reece had a way with words and was at times amazingly prophetic, he was indeed grateful for the efforts 'Donald the Clown' had made in convincing a food obsessed nation there was another way to parcel pyrosis.

It was not Mr. Reece's tray however, that soon accompanied his on the small table between them, but one of his 'friends' from a year ago – the one with disparaging views about peashooters. This had transpired to be a small revolver secreted in the valet he had been instructed to hide, together with two boxes of ammunition, instructions on its use and warnings not to use it – very useful? He had never opened the bag again and it now resided under the dog's wooden box in the kitchen, but as advised he had invested in a shotgun and as also speculated never hit anything. On the one occasion he had attended a local clay shoot, he was not certain whether he had made anyone 'think about it', but he had certainly made them 'laugh about it'.

"At least this is better than the crap I had on the way down."

Evidently not a lover of *nouvelle cuisine* he watched his 'friend' demolish two 'Big Macs' and a correspondingly big box of fries, before quietly enquiring of him what they were to discuss.

"Nothing much really, Reece wants you to know he is pleased there has at last been a development and to impress on you that things must now be taken seriously."

Hardly worth his journey - let alone the 'friend's' trip from England,

"But what about following it up, I can't ask questions and pursue matters while at the same time pretending I don't speak French – it's just silly."

"Oh yeah, that's the other thing, you gonna get a wife."

He had been thinking about trying a cheeseburger, but was suddenly more concerned with holding on to what he'd already had.

"I can't get a wife, I don't know anyone, and anyway I don't want a sodding wife!"

"Calmly, calmly, everything is taken care of, Reece is sending someone out next week, here's the paperwork. You supposedly advertised in one of the farmer's 'I need a wife' magazines and she's what's come up."

A crumpled magazine was pushed across the plastic topped table toward him,

"She speaks French, can pass as one of those far easterner types and knows her way around – she's 'on loan' if you see what I mean, but apparently she's alright."

"But she'll have to live with me."

"Yeah, that's what wives do and anyway, you never know, there might be some fringe benefits."

His 'friend' grinned luridly, but he had his mind on other things.

There was not room, there was no corridor, each room opened directly into the other, the bathroom was at one end and the kitchen the other and there were the animals to consider.

"I really think this is not necessary and that I should discuss it all with Mr. Reece.......I really do not need a wife."

Slowly his 'friend' put down his coffee and stared at him across the table, smile still in place, but all humour evaporated.

"It would be silly in the extreme to think that after all the time and money that has been expended on this operation that Mr. Reece is likely not to do it the way he chooses."

He noted it was suddenly Mr. Reece now.

"You also need to reflect on the potential jeopardy your situation may be subject to as developments ensue, having a trained operative around could keep you intact – even alive – but as I say, you do not have a choice, believe me, be sensible."

All thoughts of additional burgers now extinguished, he studied the other papers lying on his tray. There was a copy of an agreement from an agency with his signature on it which he had never signed, some details of a young woman whose photograph was as hazy as it was out of focus and the time and flight number of her arrival.

"Stay cool."

His 'friend' stood and calmly walked out of the diner, leaving him to attend to the post meal debris along with his own – empty hamburger cartons and imminent domesticity.

He worked on the extra room everyday, converting it from his store and over spill to a second bedroom. He made a couple of trips to a second-hand furniture market for a few pieces, but the important items had come over with the other furniture the year before so he already had a spare bed, wardrobe and dressing table that there was never room for in the lounge. Most of the work was cleaning and decorating which he did as best he could in view of the limited time, but in the end he was not displeased with the results – if she wanted it any better, she would have to do it herself.

And really this was at the heart of his discomfiture.

He poured another glass of wine, red this time and gazed across the pastures in the fading orange sunset, he was to collect her tomorrow off the lunchtime flight from London. Obviously he did not know the woman or anything about her and recent romantic involvement, albeit eighteen months or so ago now, had left him bruised and uncertain. Romance had never been his strong suit and most of the girls he had known, after being taken into 'care' he would rather not have. The women he met around the music business again were very much an acquired taste and it wasn't his.

His grandmother had told him there was a girl for every boy and he was happy to believe it as a pre-pubescent schoolboy, but now he was not so sure. Still, looking on the bright side, always a more dangerous ploy in practise than anticipation, perhaps his 'bride' would be a paragon of eastern quiescence and cook him curry and egg fried rice everyday.

But then there was Dog.

Although not the most inventive of names it was a marked improvement on all those that he had utilised in the first few weeks of their relationship, but Dog still did not like strangers. Being a cattle-herding dog with the corresponding size to ensure bovine deference, it was better if Dog liked you. For example Dog did not like the postman and so quite sensibly the postman never got out of the mail van, but one could not reasonably expect Mrs. Full of Eastern Promise to lock herself in her room all day, however nice the paint job. How would she get to cook the curry?

Dog would have to sleep outside for a while and perhaps even be chained – he could not really see Dog taking to that, but then they would all have to make some concessions, after all he was expected to embrace matrimony. Puzzled to find himself smiling at his flagrant flippancy, he reached for the bottle and realised the source of his temerity, the bottle was empty – and it was not the first.

"Mr. Tim?" she enquired softly.

A mere formality as he was holding a card with the words printed on it in large letters.

"Yes," he smiled, "can I take your case?"

"No, it will be fine."

He turned and led the way out of the airport concourse pausing at the parking ticket machine to pay and receive his barrier exit card. Once in the car he attempted some polite conversation, but when it became obvious it was not to be reciprocated, he subsided into silence, which was how the balance of the two-hour journey was accomplished.

At the farmhouse he led the way through the kitchen then the lounge where he slept into the recently completed third room leaving her alone on the pretext of making some tea. Before he reached the kitchen however, he heard the door shut behind him and quietly cursed Mr. Reece for his thoughtfulness.

He was stepping carefully back into the lounge with a cup of steaming tea in each hand when the door into the third room opened and she stood framed by his recent paint work. All timidity gone along with the hat, hair, glasses and raincoat, she stood with hands on hips in a black leotard matching the colour of her hair, which under the wig was severely cropped close to the scalp. She still wore the flat shoes, but even so her eyes stared levelly into his, seemingly the same colour as her hair and glowing with latent hostility.

Her voice was now strong and hard with no accent, not at all like the few words he had heard her speak so far,

"Let us get one thing straight, if you ever touch me I will kill you."

Although perhaps not an archetypal Englishmen he could not totally disregard his heritage of polite manners and good form. Thus, calling upon all the spirit and intrepidity that had at one time annexed much of the world he responded to the threat as any true blue would when faced with intimidation from 'Johnny Foreigner',

"Do you take sugar?"

Chapter 6

He received no reply to his enquiry regarding complimentary sweetener. Thereby carefully placing the two cups on a chair-side table, he sat down and smiled as pleasantly as he could manage across the room into the large dark eyes.

"Is that the 'pop star's' smile that had the little girls tossing their knickers in the air?"

She had not changed her stance or her manner.

"No, it's the smile for when my grandmother told me I was a good boy."

She moved languidly to the settee opposite and sank into the soft upholstery, slowly crossing her legs and forming a steeple of fingers under her chin.

"And why can't your grandmother wet nurse you now?"

It was provocative and he suspected deliberately so - and far more than the tightly sheathed calves and thighs. She must know at least the basics of his situation and history; she was the professional; she would have been briefed.

He sipped his tea and returned it to the table gesturing to the other cup. She deliberately shook her head and sustained her stare. He felt the hollow sensation in his stomach and the anger start to build, but he leaned forward and spoke in the most reasonable tone he could muster,

"I have spent the last eighteen months in the hope that I can achieve a solution to somebody else's problem so that I may be released from my obligation and return to what for me counts as a normal life – this is what I have been promised. On a more mundane level, I've worked hard for over a week to provide accommodation so that your stay here would be as comfortable as possible."

He felt his little soliloquy was going well, but had begun to hear the 'tell tale' alteration in the pitch of his voice.

"I have also thought about how, accepting the very peculiar and difficult set of circumstances, we might live together with a minimum of embarrassment and conflict."

No one could say he hadn't tried, "But let's get another thing straight," Too late now, "I wouldn't touch you with a ten foot fucking barge pole!"

There had been no immediate reaction.

She had maintained her stare for a number of seconds and then quietly stood, returned to her room and shut the door. His anger dissipated while he drank the second cup of tea and just as he was about to take the empty cups back to the kitchen, the door opened and she re-entered the room dressed in jumper and jeans and carrying a file,

"We need to go through these papers, commit much to memory then some will need to be destroyed, my documents will obviously be kept with yours and it would be better if we compare the two to ensure that there are no glaring inconsistencies. Your people assure me there will not be a problem, but I would feel better if I check for myself and it will also help us familiarise ourselves with our story."

"They are not my people."

He sounded like a spoiled child, but it did not seem to matter as she totally ignored his grouchy interjection.

"I then need to know what level of physical support you would be able to offer and I believe you have an armament which I shall take charge of please."

Politely he drew attention to the dichotomy; one minute he was to be terminated if he touched her and now she wanted physical support, but she ignored the feeble attempt at brevity,

"Can you fight, Timothy?"

No one had ever called him that before and he was for a moment lost for words.

"Well?"

It seemed the whole world was stuck in a hole in the ground.

"No."

"Your people say you can."

"They're not my people and they're wrong."

She sighed with exasperation and demanded, "Where is the gun?"

"Oh, it's a gun now."

"Yes Timothy, it's a gun. A gun that was brought out by road for your protection a year ago which is fortunate, as it is very difficult to smuggle firearms on aeroplanes these days and no less so into friendly states where if you're caught, considerable embarrassment will be encountered by our Lords and Masters."

"They are not my Masters."

She sighed, "Perhaps not, but I'm sure whatever they are you do not wish to exchange them for jailers."

So she did have knowledge of his situation.

"Now, where is the gun?"

"Dog's got it."

She sighed again and at once he was tired of the verbal sparring,

"I keep it under the dog's wooden box which is normally in the kitchen, but I moved him into one of the stables as he doesn't like strangers."

She sighed again, "So where is the gun now?"

"Under Dog's bed, I left it there, no one could get near it, as I say, he doesn't like strangers."

This time she did not sigh, quite the opposite, she took a long breath instead.

"So if the house was encircled you'd ask permission to visit the dog locked in the stable to procure your firearm so you could defend yourself and perhaps even let the dog loose as well, as he doesn't like strangers?"

Apparently his weariness of repartee was not universally shared, but she did have a point.

"It's only been for today and I shall be very happy for you to take charge, but we must be careful with the dog."

He moved to the door but she remained where she stood,

"What's its name?"

"Dog."

"You named a dog, Dog?"

He shrugged - wait 'till she met the horse called 'Perch' - she slowly shook her head.

"What sex is it?"

"It's a boy er.......male."

"You're sure?"

He did not answer, but he was sure – the vet had told him when he had had it vaccinated. Just because it said farmer on the paperwork did not mean he had absorbed a lifetime's knowledge of animal biology overnight.

"Bring him in on the lead and let him see me, I will sit at the table in the kitchen, let him smell me and then let him loose, don't fuss or fidget and don't panic, if he senses you're unhappy he may think it's me."

As he walked to the barn he felt if that was Dog's inference the canine would not be far from the truth, but he continued as he was bidden. Dog entered the kitchen pulling on the end of his lead rope, barked twice at the interloper, sniffed a few times and then was content to be fondled and wagged his tail appreciatively. It was most irritating – he thought the dog might at least have taken a lump out of her arse.

"I take it you don't have a lot of experience with dogs Timothy?"

She was smiling at Dog and laughing at him, it was a wonderful smile, but the laugh was without sympathy.

"Nah, you don't get to keep a lot of pets in Borstal."

As soon as he had said it he was instantly enraged with himself. He never said things like that - he never even thought them. What was, was – there was nothing to be done about it.

"So we gonna get the popgun or what?"

An edge to his voice he was unprepared for. He led the way to the stables and retrieved the valet from the twelve inch or so space below the actual bed of Dog's box while the dog stood next to his new found friend panting and wagging his tail - so much for loyalty and male solidarity. He carried the bag back to the kitchen – she was busy skipping about with the dog - and placed it on the table, returning for Dog's box, there obviously now being no need for the animal to sleep in the stable. By the time he got back to the table there was in progress a slight of hand show amidst the clicks and snaps of slides and clips.

"You have played with this?"

"No."

"Do you know how to use it?"

"No."

"Have you used the shotgun?"

He only hesitated a little, but long enough for her to continue, "It's leaning up against the wardrobe in the corner of the next room." He hadn't even had to ask the question.

"Yes."

"Hit anything?"

"No."

She repacked the valet and ironically laid it in Dog's bed and returned to sit at the table.

"So why would I be told you can fight if you can't?"

It was his turn to become exasperated.

"Look, I don't know what all this is about, but I am led to believe we are interested in substantiating that there may be some administrative duplicity with regard to certain moneys that are paid on behalf of the European Union. Simplistically, a fiddle to do with the farmers and their grants. I understand 'my people', as you quaintly refer to them, believe that at some point there maybe some irritation which could lead to aggravation with the locals, but this ain't the fucking Alamo!"

She held his eyes but there was no hostility anymore, perhaps just a little peevishness, "Now, now Timothy, I would be grateful if you could desist from the use of profanity."

He looked at the face across the table that could pass as having some kinship with the far-east, but he was sure did not -

and from the quality of the English language a profound knowledge was transparent. Yet there was a trace of an accent of that he was now certain, but unable to identify.

"Tell me where you come from."

"No."

"Tell me where you fucking come from and I won't fucking swear."

The little peevishness began to surrender to its previous more antagonistic emotion, "You can't shoot, can't fight and even your dog would have a conflict of devotion, are you sure it is wise to be so unreasonable."

"Perhaps I can fight, you've been told I can?"

It was unbelievable, she had only been on the premises an hour and he was having a 'pissing' contest with her that he knew he could never win. He jumped up from the table - which he was gratified to see, produced a small defensive response - and walked to the door,

"Whoa, whoa, whoa." He turned and said this was all silly, they had other concerns, "I will do my best not to swear and all I would ask in return is that you do not call me 'Timothy'."

"What should I call you then?"

"I don't know."

"Well a prospective wife should at least know how to address her betrothed, 'Tim' perhaps?"

He had lost.

He would have liked to ram the sugary reasonableness down her throat, but he would probably have lost that one as well and so he mumbled something about 'doing the animals' and walked out the door.

'Doing the animals' took over an hour. The chickens took flight, the goats took to the woods and Perch took the skin off his instep in the rush to get to the water basin he had forgot to replenish before leaving for the airport. Thus his mood had definitely not improved by the time he returned to the house and encountered a most unexpected surprise, the smell of cooking.

"I'm preparing some spaghetti."

He muttered that he did not have any spaghetti.

"I know, you don't seem to have much of anything, but I always travel with some emergency supplies and we can top up tomorrow."

He had to admit it smelled as if it had the edge on peanuts, crisps and chocolate, but there was always a catch.

"I suggest you prepare the food one day and I will do the next, now what are these 'thoughts' on how we are to live together with a 'minimum of conflict and embarrassment' and why are they not working?"

One had to hand it to her she really did have a way of getting 'right up his nose'. Nonetheless he controlled his irritation and began to explain some basics.

"The bathroom is at the other end of the house, there is an internal door that leads directly from your room plus an external one."

He went on to explain that he would exit the kitchen door and walk along outside the house to external door thereby avoiding the need to pass through her room. He had fitted a lock on the inside of her internal door to the bathroom so that any visitors that might use the bathroom could not gain access to the rest of the house – they would also be obliged to use the external door. All she had to do was to make sure he was not in the bathroom before she entered from the door to her room and he would do the same from outside, although there was a bolt on the inside of the external door should she choose to use it.

Satisfied, he sat back and appreciatively watched his plate heaped with spaghetti and a sauce he was unfamiliar with but had that novelty value in common with the rest of the meal, it was hot – most of his food came out of the fridge and the bread bin.

"I understand, but there is no lock on the door into the other room."

He thought it was too good to be true.

"There's no need. Dog sleeps in the kitchen and I sleep in the lounge."

"Just as long as you do not acquire a barge pole longer than ten feet."

He wanted to smile despite everything, but would not give her the satisfaction.

"Don't worry, you'll be perfectly safe."

"Oh I know I'll be safe, it's just you I'm concerned about."

He enjoyed the meal regardless of the friction and remained seated while she washed those utensils she had soiled and replaced everything as she had found it. She then collected the file from the table and the valet from the dog bed and yawning said,

"I think we will leave this until tomorrow. I have recently had a series of long flights and am suddenly tired, so if you will excuse me, Goodnight Tim."

With that she walked out of the kitchen, through the lounge into her room and closed the door.

Eventually he finished the bottle of wine gazing once more upon the remnants of the sunset. He had had it all to himself as his guest did not drink, but at least there had been no evident condemnation for his fondness for a glass of wine. He might be able to control his tongue, but he did not see why he should deprive it and what kind of detectives or undercover agents were they producing these days, no profanity, no booze, no sex, it was enough to make you turn in your 'double O' number.

He chuckled to himself, but he knew it to be the mollifying effect of the wine. He didn't really have anything to laugh about.

Chapter 7

The next morning they studied the information in her file.

In the afternoon she read through the papers he already had in his possession and they tested each other's knowledge. She was immaculate he made two mistakes.

They then ate a burnt omelette with baked beans that he had prepared for dinner. She made no comment on the meal, but insisted they go shopping the next day and then retired to her room. He again finished a bottle of wine staring into the diminishing dusky radiance and reflected on the day.

Although she had a supposed far-eastern name she had a British passport. This it was felt would make formalities easier with regard to residency – after their debacle in Vietnam which is often overshadowed by the American failures that followed - the French were highly suspicious about any oriental name and a British passport still stood for something - even in the European Union.

It was also felt that a 'catalogue' far-eastern wife would likely be considered artless and no threat to any future bureaucracy they were likely to encounter. Ostensibly he would not understand the language so could not argue, she might understand, but be too subservient to argue – Dumbo and Dum, just another pair of denuded English immigrants.

He was to call her Sun.

According to her papers her name was more complicated, but she believed that this was an understandable diminutive.

"Sonny, yesterday my life was filled with pain."

He had tried the line from the song as an engaging aside, but she had just stared through him and suggested if he had capacity to spare, perhaps he should focus on their story, ' you did make two mistakes and that is unacceptable and potentially dangerous.' None of this was of any particular concern to him however, if it came to bluffing he felt he could live with most, but the brief communication that was passed to him from Mr. Reece did cause him some disquiet.

It was a single sheet of typing, no recipient or signatory, but she certified it was for him from Mr. Reece and once he had read it, whom else could it have been from? There were the now customary entreaties to take matters seriously and the hope that he would find his new colleague a boon. Mr. Reece was confident they would make a good team and although he was to concede all matters of security to his new cohort, he was to consider himself still responsible for the overall success of the operation. Obviously Mr Reece did not intend to 'give the farm away' unless results were satisfactory and there was to be no hiding behind delegated or confused accountability.

The item that he found it hard to justify however, was the haste with which it was recommended he set in train arrangements for their 'marriage'. It was suggested that a man with a wife, or about to soon have the responsibility of a family, would be perceived to be a far more predictable and malleable entity than a frivolous bachelor - and far more likely to go unnoticed.

He understood the logic, just not the rush.

Subsequently, he had tried to discuss the subject with Sun and asked if she might be able to 'shed some light' on the matter, perhaps be a little 'illuminating', but he had received the same penetrating stare and a wearied,

"What does it matter if or when two people that don't exist get married?"

It probably didn't in the wonderful wide world of deception and deceit, but it mattered to him and he knew why – marriage was family and family mattered, particularly when you did not have any.

Listlessly he stood and unsteadily sauntered to the hedge at the end of the yard to pee – the French had a few convenient customs – so saving him a visit to the bathroom, he would see what tomorrow had to bring.

She was dressed exactly as she had been when he collected her from the airport save for the pudding basin wig. When he mentioned it she explained that it had been necessary during the journey, but not now.

He asked if she meant when she left London.

"No and it is not now relevant. What have you decided about registering my arrival at the Mairie and the marriage, it will make a difference to the paperwork?"

The Mairie was the village hall and local administrative centre also known as the Hôtel de Ville which insured many tourists tried to book rooms in the town hall – then if you give things silly names what else do you expect – but that was not what had attracted his attention,

"How do you know it will make a difference to the paperwork, have you lived in France?"

"You ask too many questions Timothy."

The way she said the name irritated him.

"I thought we had agreed you would not use that name in return for a profane free zone."

She spoke thoughtfully explaining that in retrospect she believed the abbreviation to be too familiar, lacking the respect afforded by a woman in her position; she would use the full forename.

"What about the swearing?"

His voice sounded petulant even to him.

"You must do as you choose; my motivation is purely a successful outcome to the undertaking."

"What about living in France?"

"No."

He fell silent, not quite sure where to go from there.

"I told you Timothy, you ask too many questions. If you had stopped at 'why do I know about the paperwork' it may have been a little awkward, but you immediately followed it up with a question that could be answered with a simple 'no' – a lack of basic interrogation technique."

"I don't interrogate people." he stated haughtily.

"Obviously."

He was not sure why she irritated him so much or why for instance, it seemed so hard just to go shopping without a confrontation, but he tramped around the supermarket in the nearby town with all the domesticated good grace of a football fan missing the Cup Final. She even managed to annoy him walking back and forth to the store, insisting on staying a respectful pace behind him as she insisted through gritted teeth, would be expected of a new Asian consort. If he thought his feelings at the supermarket were uncomfortable however, they did nothing to prepare him for the excruciating embarrassment at the Mairie.

He had delegated to follow Mr. Reece's requests to the letter, selfishly hoping to nullify any future excuse to deprive him of his remuneration for not following orders. They therefore visited the Mairie on the way back from the supermarket to see the Maire – the mayor, helpfully pronounced the same as the building, but he was unaware if the man was continually pestered for accommodation by doubly confused tourists.

The Maire was not in attendance which was not surprising as in the smaller villages it was a 'part-time' post whilst the Secrétaire de la Mairie was the full time civil servant and professional administrator. In this instance a sympathetic lady of advanced years who was both in attendance and happy to listen. He, true to character did of course not understand, so remained expressionless throughout which was not easy as he listened to his recently arrived betrothed simplistically outline their situation. Peeking from within her all enveloping brown mackintosh, the epitome of oriental submissiveness shyly squinted through her darkened lenses and told how she had arrived in response to the agency's registered needs of their local celibate farmer. They now wished to achieve a state of official union as quickly as possible ere the proximity of their living circumstances arouse the passions of the healthy young man and defeat propriety.

Being a woman and no doubt a good Catholic, the Secrétaire de la Mairie was totally appreciative of the situation and although there would be much to do, 'she would do her best to expedite matters'. Before they departed she rose from her desk and kissed the poor damsel in apparent imminent jeopardy and whispered she should keep her door locked, while during his congratulatory embrace, she quietly voiced over her shoulder that 'he should also be kept away from the wine'.

The atmosphere in the car back to the farm was highly charged and as bad as they had to date experienced – which was no mean feat. Silence reigned until they turned into the drive to the farm, but he knew she had found the episode at the Mairie entertaining.

"You're not very good at this are you?" There was sarcasm in her voice laced with scorn.

"No, but then it's not what I would choose to do for a living."

"Funny, some of your people think you are being paid very well."

"It's not the way I would've wanted it, I don't think there's any option so I don't think it's my fault."

She sighed, "I bet that's what you tell all the girls."

"Bollocks!"

He had driven back to town faster than he should have despite her parting wearied advice not to do anything silly.

Earlier, at the door of the farmhouse he had helped unload the groceries – a distinct 'his and her' mix of fresh food and frozen pre-cooked extravaganzas – leaving the car engine running and briefly explaining that he had some business back in town. Now, having made the telephone call from a booth in the railway station, he was seated in the café across the square from the main entrance waiting for an acquaintance he had not seen for over a month.

They had met by accident.

He had been sauntering around the weekly town market when, looking back at a stall burdened with the type of lady's corsets his grandmother had regularly hung on the line he had stumbled, full length over a wheeled cane shopping cart. Recognising his instinctive 'fucking 'ell' as not the purest *Française* the owner conceded without request that 'his French would be excused' and was he English?

The owner of the shopping cart transpired to be a young American businessman who worked in Paris, but had quite recently bought a property in the town and now commuted to his office, staying overnight in the capital when necessary. Subsequently they had met infrequently but regularly, the arrangement being that if he was in town and saw that the American's car was in attendance at his residence, he would telephone assuming the man would be at home and if so they would take coffee together.

At first it had been purely recreational for both, but as time passed the American began to relate certain problems he had begun to encounter with the authorities. Allegedly the man had come to be aware that the property he had purchased in all good faith and total legitimacy had, unbeknown to him, been coveted for a long time by none other than the town mayor. At the time the property had become available however, the mayor had not been in a position to vie for the purchase, but circumstances had apparently changed and the mayor was making life difficult, presumably in the hope of expediently engineering the property back onto the market.

Initially the American did not believe the allegations confidentially recounted by a mutual acquaintance and who he assumed could well be an antagonist or perhaps even a rival of ostensibly the most powerful bureaucrat in town. But as time went on he began to question this assumption. Mayors in towns are very different to those in small villages. Professional and often very political, they can do much more than block a planning application for some roof lights.

"You look like shit!"

There was no point in prevaricating, after all he was American and looked like shit.

"You better believe it."

Despite the smile and attempt at levity, as the man took the seat opposite he could see his acquaintance from across the Atlantic was in some distress.

"We're heading back to Paris."

It was a shock, he was of the opinion that the American and his wife liked the smaller town and he knew they loved the house.

"What about your wife, you said she'd never been happier since arriving in Europe?"

"Yeah, but that was then."

The café owner arrived to take their order for coffee and brandy.

"We've had three break-in's since I saw you last 'n shit through the letter box 'n the cops just shrug, like their goddam Chief - who just happens to be the Mayor's big buddy! I'd stay and see the arse 'oles off, but they've got to Moira, I can't leave her alone no more. We've gotta go."

The coffee arrived, but not the brandy so he gestured to the café owner that they were missing something and looked questioningly at his soon to be absent friend who shrugged resignedly.

"I have to go with Moira to the store now or they ignore her, even the neighbours don't speak anymore. It's not that they're nasty, they're just frightened, the whole fucking nation's frightened."

The café owner continued to peruse his newspaper patently ignoring the earlier request for the missing brandy.

"Let's see shall we?"

He smashed his fist down on the table and as the café owner looked up called loudly across the bar, "Two more coffees and two brandies - and don't forget this time *Garçon.*"

Garçon was a dangerous word, it could mean waiter or boy; the café owner was in no doubt which he had meant.

"It ain't worth it," the American was reconciled, "an' be careful, drawing attention to yourself when you're with me ain't no great shakes."

They sipped their second coffee after it had been delivered together with the brandy and he felt a little consoled, but their silence extended and he was wondering how he might proceed, for his visit was not without ulterior motive, when the matter was taken from his hands,

"There is one, sure's hell. Now I know, there sure's hell is one."

Even though his drinking partner was leaning forward across the table he had to strain his ears to hear him,

"The Black Book."

His stomach muscles tightened, but he held his blank expression in place.

"I had a visit, this prick told me, Moira and me, we're in it, and the little shit was no freshman. So there is one an' when you're in it, there ain't nothun the bastards can't do and no one ain't gonna help yer, be careful if yer staying fella, it's a lot more Hollywood than yer think."

With that the American gulped the remainder of his brandy, stood and offered his hand,

"Good Luck, Limey. Don't count on the cavalry, especially if it's fucking French." Turned and walked out of the café.

He stayed for a little longer, dropped a note on the table – funny it wasn't really his turn to pay – and walked out of the bar, ignoring the owner who was busily ignoring him and eventually reached the car still deep in thought.

Until now the 'Black Book' had been something he had heard rumours about from various disgruntled foreigners and dissidents, but nothing concrete. Indeed this was nothing concrete, but the source was different, very different. The American was successful and worldly, one could reasonable rely on his testimony; what did he have to lose? If the American wanted to return to Paris, why make up the story, if he did not, why was he returning to Paris? He only hoped for the American's sake the pressures would desist after the move and not pursue him and his wife to the Capital.

Still in uneasy reflection he joined the AutoRoute that would take him clear of the town and the first exit that would take him across country to the village and home. Before he had even completed the curve following the actual exit however, he encountered a police checkpoint. This was not uncommon in France and as in many other countries, it was often about heavy goods vehicles during the day and cars in the evening – after post work imbibing. As it was late afternoon he was surprised to see that there were no lorries parked for inspection, less so that there were no cars. Then as the three saloons that had exited a little in front of him were waved through, he assumed the enforcers of the rules of the road were finished for the day, but no.

As he closed on the first pair of officers one rashly leapt in front of his car waving him to the side and only narrowly avoiding becoming a casualty of his own instigation. There was no politeness, but there never was with the traffic police in France, although he noted these were not the motorcyclists that always hunt in duos, but a contingent of the local Gendarmarie. He was not asked for his 'papers' which was unusual to say the least, but as soon as he had wound down the window a breathalyser was almost forced into his mouth and he was ordered to comply. Out of shear cussedness he pretended not to understand, but very soon it became clear that his inquisitors needed little excuse to detain him in a more permanent fashion and so with a fatuous smile he complied and proved his sobriety, much to his examiners tangible disappointment. Eventually they waved him on and he observed in the rear view mirror that the Gendarmes too had apparently completed their assignment and were about to depart, without at any point during his detainment examining any other vehicle.

He drove carefully home, grateful to the suddenly obnoxious café proprietor for facilitating his clean bill of health at the checkpoint. If the discourtesy in the café and the strange highway control were founded in his connection with the American it was nice to know the conspiracies had proved incompatible. But surely, local bureaucrats could not exploit the forces of law and order for personal gain?

It still seemed extraordinary.

He parked the car and greeted Dog as he scampered to meet him then entered the kitchen with a smile, appreciative of the splendid cooking aroma that greeted him, this evening he would make an effort to be more amenable. He would also be grateful for an alternative perspective on recent events and how they might proceed.

He would make a real effort to be charming – would he never learn?

Chapter 8

It was not pasta this evening nor curry, but some form of Cantonese dish which was nevertheless very tasty and very acceptable. There was a salad that he would not normally bother with, but to show willing he champed his way through the greenery with specious delight.

He waited until the meal was completed and then furnished a detailed account of the events of the afternoon.

"So to be clear….."

He raised his eyes from the glass he had been filling to behold the now familiar expressionless stare that accompanied her words.

"You met this afternoon with an American of all people, who is already under the scrutiny of the authorities and drew attention to yourself by insulting a local café proprietor to the extent whereby he or a third party informed the police. They then mounted an investigation to determine whether or not you were driving whilst under the influence of alcohol. Would you reconcile these actions as those of someone wishing to maintain the consummate 'low profile' as instructed by your superiors?"

She certainly had a way of challenging all he had learned about being charming.

"It was not like that," he tried to keep the 'little boy lost' pleading out of his voice, "I originally met the man by accident and it's a month or more since I saw him last, there could be no perceived obvious relevance to our association."

It was true, from the start quite naturally they had talked about the French and only in recent times had their exchanges dealt with more sinister topics and it was the American that had initially raised the possible existence of a 'Black Book' and bureaucratic conspiracy.

"Surely what occurred this afternoon is not normal and proof to some extent that at best there's illegitimate use of the instruments of state if not outright illegality." He was now really warming to his reasoning, "No police force would react with such alacrity to the whinging of a waiter – who by the way had been perfectly polite up until today."

The expressionless stare continued to consider him, so he was unclear as to the advancement of his argument.

She rose from the table and began to wash-up,

"We shall see, I will include it in my next report and we shall see what London has to say."

"What report?"

"I am to make regular reports concerning security as we are somewhat exposed and to include any other items I think pertinent or that you may want included."

He felt the hollowness begin to build in his stomach, but this time he would control it whatever happened, he would not give her the satisfaction of seeing him annoyed.

"Why don't I make my own report?" He spoke calmly, a perfectly legitimate query.

"Because you don't know how to."

Still calm, just, "I have the telephone contact numbers?"

She came back to the table and so did the expressionless stare, but there was a resignation in her voice, which he found even more irksome than the blank stare,

"The telephone numbers you've been given are 'call home' mechanisms that require someone to come out from

London. Apart from the inconvenience, regular movements by certain personnel onto foreign soil would be noted. Those numbers are normally only for emergency use, hopefully you won't have to use them now I am here."

His annoyance grew, but he was still determined to control it, "So why can't I do whatever it is you do to make a report?"

"I've told you, because you can't. You can't learn overnight the protocols and contact procedures that take over a year to master before they even let you out of the centre.......and in any case, you have enough to think about as it is."

It was reasonable, but no less annoying, "And you will report exactly what I say, no interference, no modifications?"

She sighed, "Exactly as you say, although I would hope we will be able to agree on the content before it is reported."

There was silence.

He refilled his glass and once more she wearily rose from the table.

"Again I am tired so will retire and I would be grateful if in future we might discuss actions like this afternoons' before they take place. I feel I am also obliged to point out that you are regularly drinking over a bottle of wine a night and your physical fitness and judgement will be adversely effected".

Then just before he was able to get his breath to break his promise to himself, "Thank you for being reasonable this evening, I am sure you don't really feel that way. But don't worry, if you refuse to tell me whether you can fight or not, I shall have to find out for myself, which should at least provide you with an outlet for your petulance. Goodnight Timothy."

And with that she was gone to her bed.

Fundamental good government is by the people for the people and in Western democracies, whatever their failings the fundamental is at its most prominent. But there are always failings. The secret services of friend and foe alike act out their charades intent on keeping their respective populace safe and free – and for this there is gratitude.

For government there is less sufferance.

The people are aware that all keepers of the peace have an ultimate master and are instinctively suspicious of politicians with decisive power that are no better or worse than they are – they would like them to be better. Even the oldest democracy in the world, which in the West is almost universally acclaimed as the model to which burgeoning systems of administration should aspire has had problems - aside from all the sporadic conspiracy theories, spurious or otherwise.

Four citizens were imprisoned illegally when the business that they were specifically certified by government to prosecute became embarrassing to that very same organ of state. Only the intervention of an independent and belligerent judiciary brought justice to bear.

France does not enjoy the perpetual tension between the legislature and the judiciary that Britain boasts - despite the enduring attempts of Westminster's Upper House to sway the balance in favour of the legislature. France is a pyramid of power that emanates from Paris and the root cause of the rest of France's antipathy to all things Parisian – not least the Parisians themselves.

.....a republic that feels like a kingdom, where class prejudice abounds and grace and favour are a way of life, where the tax collectors hide their occupation and the police seek safety in numbers - but where everyone is fearful.

The next morning he awoke with a now customary headache and waited until he heard her let Dog out of the kitchen before leaving his bed.

From the first it had become her habit to take the animal for a walk – which was actually a two mile run – as soon as she rose, which to date had always been before him, thus he at least had the bathroom to himself for fifteen minutes or so. He returned to the kitchen and put the kettle on, then hearing the return of the athletes he stepped outside to enquire if she wanted coffee – she apparently never drank tea. Surprisingly she was shutting Dog in the stable and receiving no response from his first enquiry, he ambled across the yard to see what was happening and if he was truly honest to examine more closely the contents of the leotard that had somewhat unexpectedly made a re-appearance.

She turned just as he reached the stables and hit him hard across the face with the back of her hand, immediately recoiling then lunging into his midriff with stiffened fingers and finally repeating her attack on his face with another backhanded slap while his arms were lowered.

"So tell me or show me."

She stood sideways on, gently bouncing on the balls of her feet.

"And if I refuse?" breathlessly, surprised and buying time.

"I will say disparaging things about your dead grandmother and dead parents until you have to."

So she knew all about him and somehow that stung more than the slapping.

He hesitated and her bouncing almost stopped. He wondered if she had reconsidered. The inquisition over perhaps, but it wasn't,

"So who was driving - your Mother or your Father? I suppose it wasn't their fault, never is, is it, always the other person, lorry wasn't it, made a bit of a mess of….."

He dropped into a crouch and rushed as fast as he could, but as she began to speak she had increased the distance between them and it was enough. As he reached her she slipped to the side and an elbow caught him on the side of the head increasing his momentum until he crashed into the stable door. Dog barked encouragingly, no doubt believing it was all a game and he would have freed the animal, but wasn't really sure whose side the dog would take once having become cognisant with the hostilities. He rolled along the stable wall searching for some weapon, but there was nothing, so he ran.

It obviously took her by surprise for she did not catch him until he had reached the hay barn, which although not far was far enough. He ducked behind one off the big round bails from which he fed Perch and the goats whilst they were inside sheltering from the heat of the day and spun round just as she came round after him and almost impaled herself on the pitch fork. He thrust again threateningly and stepped forward as she stumbled backwards to the ground over remnants of the bailing twine - it was then that she pulled the gun.

He did not see where it came from, but it was suddenly there between them pointed up at his face. He very carefully retracted the pitchfork and leant it back against the bail of hay, never loosing her stare.

"May I help you up?"

To his total amazement she began to laugh and although it took some of the shine off the only ascendancy he seemed to have experienced since her arrival it was worth it, she had a lovely laugh and a lovely smile – and she hadn't shot him.

"A bientôt, Madame, merci beaucoup." She put the phone down. Her French was very good and she had achieved what they wanted.

"I made it very clear that we would collect the original application form for me to check because we are going away and although you did your best 'my English fiancé may have made some mistakes'."

He nodded, "Yes, I know, I speak French."

She in turn nodded, "Yes of course, then why don't we ever speak it?"

He sighed, "Because we are English, well at least I am, you remain noncommittal about your ancestry." There was no response and when he looked up the expressionless stare was in place, but the eyes were a little different now, almost as if she saw him.

Following the fracas in the barn they had breakfasted surprisingly amicably after he had first rinsed the blood from his mouth and then taken aspirin for his headache, which she insisted was more to do with wine than wallop. Apparently it wasn't his mastery of any marshal art that interested her, just if he made the right decision 'under fire' and incredibly running away from overwhelming odds was considered correct. He had not 'froze', although the headlong charge had been deemed unenlightened, but understandable and the swift conversion to flight positively applauded. When he explained that he could of course have told her all this, but did not like to be pushed around her retorted 'slapping's OK though?' had made him smile despite himself.

She had now just ended the call following up on the 'lead' that had actually initiated her arrival, the demand for additional information regarding a grant application that he had supposedly submitted, but knew nothing about – the correspondence that included the unknown company name.

"What time are they expecting us?"

He had not heard all the call as the postman had arrived and he had to retrieve the mail through the slit in the driver's window, while at the same time preventing Dog from mounting the bonnet. Fear of the beast however, did not stop the postman from following the letters through the slit with shouts of congratulations on his engagement which seriously loosened his grip on the dog, but the postman was away, spinning his wheels in the gravel.

"I didn't say, not even that it would be today, I thought least said the better."

She was right of course.

They had to gain at least sight of the original application before it was discovered they were aware of its existence. It occurred to him that there would need to have been put in place a method of 'flagging' that would intercept all outbound correspondence and communication and prevent its despatch, a simple internal cut-out. Or perhaps a system that would automatically redirect to an overriding postal address or power of attorney or other recognised agent. If they asked for something to be mailed to them it was likely it would be intercepted as intended, what he already had in his possession he presumed to have been an error, something that slipped through the net – thank goodness for serendipity or 'SNAFU'. Whatever, they now had something to follow up - name, reference and number.

They set off at one o'clock. It was a little over half an hour's journey to the Departmental head office of the Farmers Union who was responsible for the grants and his intention was to be at the desk immediately after lunch. This he assumed would see the junior staff back at their toil whilst their superiors were still munching through their obligatory four courses – he was not disappointed.

Mme. Poirier was at pains to point out that if they waited they would be able to speak to M. Bousse in person upon his return from lunch.

The poor young spectacled creature that appeared to live in her own tent however, became so agitated under the pressure from the arrogant foreigner, who couldn't even speak French would you believe!

The sympathetic Mme. Poirier relented, if they had a train to catch they should really have come in the morning, but at least the poor girl was trying to solve the problems and heaven knows what kind of life she had with this foreign peasant upstart.

They really should stop this 'wife by mail order' business, it was nothing short of certified people trafficking and then there was the sex. God, there were old men running round with young things on their arm that would see them in the ground before their time – it was their own fault of course, but still not natural.

Now the poor petite fille had to listen to the young ox apparently demanding a copy, well at least she could help the enfant déshéritée there – even if it was prohibited, just the one couldn't hurt.

She should keep her door locked at night too for there was certainly no evidence of any rings about, marriage plans or no marriage plans and the young rogue looked far too licentious for Mme. Poirier.

That evening she suggested that perhaps she could prepare something 'quick' while he examined the copy they had obtained from the Farmers Union. He readily agreed and assumed frozen pre-cooked meals were perhaps not to her liking, but then it takes all kinds.

Really there was not much to peruse.

The form was an initial application for a farm building in accordance with the latest generation of grants relating to beef, the missing information was quite insignificant, but in accordance with bureaucratic mentality a box left un-ticked was a box too far, hence the request for additional information. The only slight surprises were that no attempt had been made to copy his normal signature - but then if he was never to see it obviously it was irrelevant - and the amount.

The application was for nearly two hundred thousand Euros.

Chapter 9

They were married on a Monday because it was the postman's day off and he was one of the witnesses. The other was the lady that cleaned the Mairie so was available any morning except weekends. It was a short ceremony, they listened to an extract from the Civil Code, answered 'yes' to the 'do you' queries and were on the road back to the farmhouse within half an hour of the start of proceedings.

He offered to carry her over the threshold, but she ignored him, went directly to her room and shut the door. She did not re-emerge until the evening and the eyes that surveyed him with all the old original animosity were bloodshot as if from crying - were it not such a ridiculous notion. She cooked a meal that for once failed to impress and spoke not at all until she had washed up and was evidently returning to her room, when she hesitated at the door.

"This is not going to be one of those 'touch me and you die' recitations is it?" He grinned, but there was no connection.

"No Timothy, I just want to wish you Good Luck" and the door closed.

He celebrated alone on his wedding night, wrapped in an anorak against an unseasonable autumn chill, even Dog had retired to the shelter of the kitchen and his bed.

Some nuptials!

His grandmother had never said anything about marrying 'one of the girls that wasn't the one for the boy', but then apparently it didn't matter if 'two people that don't exist get married', the problem was he did exist.

This was all he had.

There was no one else for him to be when all this was over. He emptied the bottle into his glass and quaffed it back without hesitation. He couldn't remember if it was half full or half empty when he had started, but he would let the 'pratts' that worry about things like that ponder the puzzle, he only knew it was whisky not wine and if any local newly wed didn't like it, fuck 'em!

Not much had happened for the three previous months.

They had established a routine that allowed them to function without tearing each other apart while at the same time appearing to those around them they were what they purported. She worked around the farm as well as the house and they now had a garden and the beginnings of a vegetable patch, but that would not really blossom – if that's what vegetable patches did – until next year. There were a few specific items secreted in various locations in the hope that they may bear fruit – or whatever they should do – around the festive season, but in any event the farm began to resemble a farm.

Paperwork and documentation trundled back and forth keeping their friend the postman in employment, but there were no more 'errors' from the Farmers Union. On the odd occasion when she had contacted London – as much to remind them of their existence as any thing else - the exhortation was the same, don't rush. So they didn't rush, but it wasn't easy.

They had assimilated all the necessary documentation for their 'Big Day' and had completed the requisite medical checks that confirmed they would not infected one another with any unpleasant social disease or worse and the Mairie was booked for their matrimonial union. During the period that their banns were being read there was a strange happenstance.

Ironically he had acquainted another American during his search for Perch and they had exchanged telephone numbers despite the considerable difference in their taste in equines. The man hailed originally from the great cattle country across the Atlantic, but during a college exchange some thirty years before, had met and married a French student and settled in France, subsequently lecturing in history and art in a well known university.

The now senior lecturer had paid a considerable sum for a traditional American Quarter Horse the like of which were becoming quite popular in France and had had the animal moved following the purchase to an independent livery yard. Upon arrival the proprietor of the yard was suspicious of the condition of the animal and immediately arranged for a veterinary examination and blood tests to be undertaken. These proved the animal had been heavily doped during the purchase procedures and subsequently, once free of the drugs, presented with crippling symptoms that would ultimately prove fatal.

It was an 'open and shut' case, particularly as the man had taken the precaution of insuring against just such a misrepresentation. In fact, the insurers themselves were most confident of an absolute resolution to the dispute – and rapidly.

That had been seven years before.

They had first met purely by coincidence because the man had then been looking for a replacement animal, his original horse eventually having had to be destroyed - judicial contention thus surviving the subject of the dispute. It was a sad and perplexing saga so when the lecturer latterly telephoned and suggested they meet, he willingly agreed.

They met in the café where they had taken coffee on a number of occasions during visits to the yard that rather oddly specialised in both the horse breeds in which they were interested. The American was as calm and composed as many of his countrymen that were born to the vast open spaces and apologised for the intrusion, but having promised to impart how the tale concluded was at pains to honour his pledge.

Although initially adamant that the destruction of the animal would have no effect on the prosecution of their case, the insurance company had suddenly reneged on all that had gone before. This was totally inexplicably, for there had been three court judgements in their client's favour and although all had gone to appeal, it had originally been explained by the insurers that this was no more than a delaying tactic and that they would eventually prevail. Now the insurers had perfunctorily presented the polite quiet man with a judicial ruling discharging them of any responsibilities concerning the case and immunity from any proceedings that may result apropos negligence. The insurers had 'sold out' for immunity from any compensatory action, but who could organise such a legal duplicity?

The quiet man had made one friend within what was a National Insurance organisation who was prepared to speak confidentially in an effort to prevent more money being wasted. It was known that the wife of the original corrupt horse dealer was a Parisian lawyer she being why the appeals had been anticipated, but what was not initially appreciated were the woman's political connections – connections that could bring pressure to bear on commercial enterprise as well as judicial autonomy.

The quiet man had been entered into the 'Black Book'.

He awoke on his first morning of married life with a banging in his head and a banging on the door and he could hardly tell one from the other.

"There is someone here to see you."

His wife shouted through the door from the kitchen and he could hear Dog barking from the stables where he assumed he had been incarcerated. Wondering who could be calling at this hour, he looked at his watch to discover it was late in the morning.

"Who is it?"

"A man from the Ministry."

"What Ministry?" but having pulled on a T-shirt and jeans he had opened the door before she could answer.

"Yes?" he smiled thinly at a man with glasses and clipboard, aware of his own dishevelled appearance.

"He is from the Ministry of Social Integration and has come to measure the rooms."

As a good little wife Sun looked at the floor after completing the translation.

"Why?"

He had never heard of such a Ministry, but that did not mean there wasn't one, France had Ministries for most things.

"He says its standard procedure."

With a view to propriety, he hitched up his jean and tucked in his T-shirt and moved to one of the kitchen unit draws where he kept the papers relating to the house and extracted a thin file. Opening the file on the kitchen table, he selected a copy of the internal plan of the house and handed it to the visitor.

“Tell him he doesn’t have to do any measuring; it’s all there on the plan.”

The man hardly glanced at the plan before returning it to the table as he spoke.

“He says it’s no good, he has to measure the rooms himself.”

Carefully he returned the plan to the file and the file to the draw, then turning, so that he now stood between his interpreter and the man, stared into the latter’s eyes and said,

“Tell him No.”

The man fiddled with his clipboard apparently unused to it not achieving total subjugation.

“He said he is sorry, but it is required.”

The man held his gaze for a little, but then the eyes slid away to his clipboard.

“Tell him don’t be sorry, be careful – then tell him to leave.”

He walked passed the man, the glasses and the clipboard, slipped his feet into his clogs at the door and walked across to the stable.

Dog was still barking as he slid the rope over his head and was slavering on his hind legs by the time he was half way back to the house to see the visitor’s car door slam and the small saloon quickly depart in a spatter of gravel. He memorised the number and wrote in down as soon as he was inside. It was a private registration not an official ministry vehicle.

It had started.

“Would it not have attracted less attention if you had just let him measure the rooms?”

She was obviously unhappy with his actions.

"I don't know, would it? How many married couples do you know that spent their first night sleeping in different beds, let alone different rooms? Anyway, it wasn't an official car and whether there is a Ministry of Integration or whatever it is, or not, he wasn't from it and I think now we have to move fast for once, whatever London says."

He heard his voice rise as he spoke and there was anger that had little to do with the hangover. In fact he did not know what it had to do with, so did not know whether to laugh or scream, when before returning to her room, Sun bowed her head and softly whispered,

"Yes, my husband."

Their stakeout of the Farmers Union head office had lasted nearly two weeks.

Although it only covered the lunchtime period he still found it extremely tedious. It seemed even when he had decided to take action it resulted in more waiting. She of course was quite comfortable and accomplished. She changed her clothing everyday together with glasses, hats and scarves and even seemed to have a variety of gaits to go with the variety of footwear. He tried, but failed to disappear into the woodwork or pavement for that matter and so much of the surveillance had fallen on her shoulders while he drunk much of the coffee.

She had established that what appeared to be the senior staff lunched between one o'clock and two thirty, while the junior staff between twelve thirty and two. Mme. Poirier was back in the front office by two o'clock every day except Wednesday, when for some reason she adopted the management lunch period. This meant that for half an hour in the middle of the week the front office was solely manned by a young girl who had recently passed her driving test, had a boyfriend named Olivier, rode and was learning English.

Sun had gleaned all this from a study of the girl's car - parked in the municipal car park each day - and which she believed would prove enough background to swiftly create a bond and feminine camaraderie. Obviously after only two weeks they could not be sure if every Wednesday was the same, but the next week Sun entered the offices at just after two and was relieved to find she was alone with the young girl.

Her story was quite simple and had worked to a degree before, but like all good 'stings', success would rest in the quality of the performance......

Sun had recently been married only to find that her husband, who was a foreigner and did not speak French, had innocently applied for a number of grants in different named companies, believing it to be an administrative requirement. (He was English – did the girl speak English – really, perhaps they could get together sometime?)

Sun was confident that her new husband had done nothing wrong, but wanted to ensure all was in order and the problem was her husband, who was a farmer and well, not very good with papers, especially ones he couldn't read, had lost some. (He's often out riding when he should be filing – oh, you ride as well – you really must come and see us.)

Sun had been assured his name was on everything, but some of them had company names as well? Sun would be really grateful if the young lady could have a look in the files or run it through the computer or whatever it is they do. Sun really was concerned that they didn't get money they were not entitled to and didn't really want to make a fuss if it could be helped. As she had said only the other day, 'you'll have to take the paperwork a lot more seriously Olivier' – it's his family 'nick-name' after the film – typical farmer, always wanting more! (No, really, amazing, wait 'till I tell him, you really must come and see us - and bring you boyfriend –we can ride and speak English at the same time!)

Oh, and if it would be possible for copies, so that she might take her time checking them, she really would be most grateful.

By the time he watched her exit the offices some senior management were already returning from lunch, but luckily there was no sign of anyone with whom they were acquainted.

He followed her back to the car, then catching up, unlocked the passenger door before moving round to the driver's side and quickly drove away. He did not seek the AutoRoute home, but drove to one of the town's satellite shopping complexes where he parked as near as he could to the entrance to the main concourse. While she surveyed the area around them he examined the copies and found five claims that bore his name, but of which he had no knowledge.

They left the car, he with the file under his arm and entered the precinct, found a large stationers and took further copies of the applications in question purchasing a pack of standard envelopes on the way out. Returning to the car, she addressed five of the envelopes in a variety of hands, but to the same 'import/export' company based in Canary Wharf. He then drove to the main post office and double-parked while she bought international postage stamps valid for the rest of Europe. She stuck one of the stamps to each of the five envelopes and he drove circuitously out of town during which time they posted the envelopes at five different sites including two sub-post offices and then went home.

"So what does it total?"

He had been studying the documents since they had arrived back at the farm.

Along with the original application that he had been sent in error – or really the demand for additional information – the total amount of subsidies that had been applied for in his name and that he knew nothing about, came to just over half a million Euro.

"About four hundred thousand pounds - hardly small change".

He had converted the sum to sterling as he habitually did despite his time abroad, not least because most Euro zone countries still mixed their new community currency with its predecessor, particularly when it mattered. People were very proud to relate the price of a loaf of bread or bottle of wine in Euro, but serious money – for a car or livestock – was still bartered largely in 'old currencies'. This was further exacerbated in France as farm auctions were still traded in the 'old, old currency' – which was about a thousand Francs to the Pound Stirling – very confusing and very French.

"I shall need to report developments to London and inform them there are some things in the post, is there anything else you want me to say?"

She had not wanted him to meet with the second American, but it had not been of any real importance. She had however, voiced serious reservations about his decision to force matters at the Farmers Union office without specific sanction from London. He had justified his decision with reference to the peculiar visit they had received the day following their marriage and that if the powers of darkness were already suspicious and began to take precautions, they would have achieved absolutely nothing, because they had absolutely nothing. He did not actually say in which case he assumed his remuneration would have probably totalled a similar amount, but that was his business and in any event, he had become sick and tired of the waiting and his circumstances in general.

The sham marriage did not sit well with him and he did not totally understand why for they had lived together for three months, although that of itself may have been at the heart of his restlessness. Tension was never far away, but he had begun to enjoy the more mundane times they shared and although he knew she did her best to disguise her femininity, there was only so much that could be hidden within summer garb and certain farming tasks were surprisingly revealing. Ostensibly after the efforts he had made to mollify his language and control the more excesses of his temper he did not seem to bother her, but she had begun to bother him and not in a way for which he was prepared.

"No, just make it clear it was my decision, cool calm and calculated, but mine alone."

He wanted out while he was still in one piece and before she had reason to make good her initial promise.

Chapter 10

The British media is amongst both the best and the worst in the world.

On a good day it is fast, resourceful, investigative and brave, on a bad day it is petty, pernicious, unmerciful and wrong - alas either way, unapologetic.

The destruction of innocents for want of journalistic integrity is unpardonable, but an independent scrutiniser in additional to the judiciary of all governmental procedure is invaluable.

What price such a barb for bureaucratic shenanigans in continental Europe?

She had gone to make her report and would not be back for some hours. He was not aware of the procedure nor did he want to be; not that she would have told him. She had however, told him she wanted internal access to the loft - or granary since it is where the grain had traditionally been stored – which as one space, ran the entire length of the house above the four ground floor rooms. The only existing access was from the external staircase at the end of the house.

Ideally she wished the access to be hidden from any visitors therefore it had to be in her room, which was convenient for two reasons, one it would be immediately available to her and two, there had at an earlier period been an opening. He had noted during his redecorating that there was a metre square area in the ceiling behind the door that had at one time provided access to above, probably by means of a ladder. All he would have to do was reform the opening and bring one of the ladder extensions from the barn and she would have her access.

He completed the work to his satisfaction, but it had been a dusty business and although he had covered as much of the room for which he had plastic sheets, he was still sweeping under the bed when she returned.

"Find anything interesting?"

There was a hard edge to her voice that at first he did not identify.

"No, just cleaning up, I'm afraid it's a bit dusty, but at least you can get up stairs now even if only by ladder."

"And did you get much dust inside the case?"

He had pulled her suitcase from under the bed to better sweep beneath.

"I didn't open the case."

"Are you sure?"

"I would know if I'd opened the case or not".

She moved across the room, picked the case up from the floor and laid it on the bed, hesitating.

"Looking to see if the hair across the catch is broken?" but his sarcasm was wasted.

She finally opened the case and stood to one side, "There are three cameras, one miniature for documents, one long lens for distance and a tourist type that would not attract attention and it would be as well if you acquired some elementary knowledge of their operation."

He was relieved to see the interior of the case was pristine, but less so with its contents.

"These are recording devices and miniature microphones – I assume you already have some knowledge of these although I note you have failed to detect the two I have installed in the kitchen."

It was all very matter of fact and businesslike and all very disagreeable.

"So that you can hear me burn the omelettes?" he chided.

"Timothy, you have not cooked anything for a long time – one wonders if you ever have – but you can start again if you wish? In any case as yet the mics are not activated."

He remained silent for a while, not wishing to tempt fate and find he had to share the cooking again, volunteering to wash-up in lieu was bad enough, but at least he got to eat real food, "And you brought all this with you?"

"No, only the innocent stuff, I received a delivery while making one of the reports."

He had noticed she always left with two bags as well as her purse, the case went on the back seat and a smaller one under it, presumably the case would pass any cursory inspection and there would be deemed no need to look further. It must be a strange life he surmised, but then he now knew it was, he was living it.

"So what did London have to say?" he made an attempt at brightening the moment.

"They may not have agreed with your actions, but it was your decision." She sighed and sat on the bed next to the open case, "I will however, now have only one more 'meet' which they wish to take place within the next two weeks as they feel there is a significant possibility that we may eventually come under at least intermittent surveillance." She sighed again, "So if we want anything we better ask now, all subsequent reports will be telephonic or postal."

He watched her get up, rearrange the items in the case and bend to replace it under the bed.

"What about the stuff we've already put in the post?"

He maintained an upbeat attitude.

"They are pleased, but it is obviously not enough, we are to go on as far as we can collecting as much information as we can and send it back as and when we can."

She stood and walked into the kitchen and lit the gas under the kettle.

"What if something goes wrong, how will they know when to come and get us?"

He had followed her into the kitchen asking the question of her turned back.

"They won't be coming to get us, as you so quaintly put it; we are to make our own way."

It sounded ridiculous.

"What do you mean, we are only three hundred miles from London, they could send a bleeding helicopter?" He was not sure if that was technically possible, but it was not as if they were in the middle of Africa or South America, "this is France and we are only inquiring into some farming fiddle." He felt the hollow feeling in his stomach, but it was not anger this time.

She carried his tea and her coffee to the table and sat down opposite, "And how big do you think this fiddle is? And how far up does it go? How many thick foreign farmers are there like you, let alone the local dimwits - times half a million, how much do you think that comes to?"

She did not rant nor decry.

Her tone reminded him of his grandmother when he had been unable to grasp a transparent certitude, as if talking to a child, then of course his grandmother had been, but by now he thought he had grown up.

"No Timothy they never will come for us – they can't - we are working in a friendly state, an ally. They would sooner send a team to pull someone out of Russia than here. These are some of the most difficult and dangerous operations – and increasingly common. Britain and America have one of the closest ties in the world, but they still do not share all their intelligence, so do you seriously think that with all their resources the Americans don't try and find out what the UK knows?"

She sipped her coffee, eyeing him for signs of comprehension before continuing,

"By comparison one could hardly call the political ties in Europe close – not if you really look – but they are still allies despite everyone being out for as much as they can get. Whatever happens however, one can't afford to embarrass allies and certainly one must never run the risk of being embarrassed oneself, therefore it is all about leverage, none of this will ever go to court, let alone a European tribunal. This is all about strengthening ones hand before you go to the bargaining table and you don't do that by being caught with operatives pursuing clandestine investigations into a friendly power's affairs deep inside that state's borders. This is all about France one day inexplicably supporting a British initiative in Europe or the UN or perhaps providing her significant influence in the Middle East on behalf of British or American interests. No one is going to jail, no one is going to loose their illicit income, no one wants them to - or the leverage dissolves following the court case and our masters would consider that unfortunate."

He had never really taken much interest in politics before, let alone the intricacies of world affairs. During his initiation to 'all things farming', he had of course read and heard much about the disquiet with regard to European agricultural matters, but never linked it with what was now portrayed as tantamount to fictional espionage, but Sun still was not finished.

"Apparently your Common Agricultural Policy doesn't even come under review for a dozen years or more. All that leverage for all that time. No Timothy, they will not come for us and risk the whole thing blowing up in their face. They won't risk a Greenpeace Warrior catastrophe; look what that did for France's image around the world – and who ever cared about New Zealand?"

Vaguely wondering what his old rugby mad physical education teacher would have made of that, he remained silent.

"You don't seriously think they would risk a similar debacle just for our well being do you? I am sorry I have to tell you this so soon, I was instructed to leave it as long as possible, but I think you should know now."

"More tea?"

He fixed two internal brackets to both sides of the doorframe at the top of the outside staircase so that timber bars could be slotted across the inside of the door preventing it opening. He had also finally fitted a bolt to the inside of her door to the lounge, his bedroom, which caused her some amusement, she commenting that 'it hadn't taken long when it wasn't just for her protection', but he was not in the mood. He obviously had had some idea of what he had become involved in, but it was so long since his conversations with Mr. Reece it all seemed somewhat farfetched and he had never imagined he was to be abandoned. As disconcerting as the arrival of Sun had been, it had further bolstered his sense of security, after all that is what she was there for, but even so it all seemed too fantastic, now he was not so sure.

The experiences of the two Americans, the visit of the man from the mysterious ministry and the bogus documents with his name on, but most of all, the money, the sums Sun had propounded were huge and people said that 'where there's muck there's brass', but in his experience it was often just as true the other way round, 'where there's brass there's muck'. Whatever else he may have felt he had certainly begun to take matters seriously now, which at least alleviated his more recent distractions – nothing like a spot of fear to dull the ardour.

"Ready?"

Nearly a fortnight had passed; although she had telephoned for her final 'meet' within a few days of the last somewhat to London's surprise, but it would not have been as big a surprise as when they received his shopping list.

"Yes," he replied, "it's a long time since I've worn a jacket and tie."

She let out the clutch as Dog barked his goodbyes.

"You look very smart Timothy; I only hope you've given them enough time."

"'He who hesitates is lost.'" And with that they continued in silence.

As soon as the car stopped he opened the door, got out and walked into the AutoRoute service station complex while she filled the car with petrol, paid at the kiosk and slowly drove into the car parking area. Here she waited in one of the bays for a few minutes before returning to the AutoRoute, taking the next exit, crossing over the dual carriageways and rejoining headed in the opposite direction.

After entering the service station complex he went immediately to the cloakroom and waited locked in a cubicle until three minutes before the time of his rendezvous, when he exited, crossed the carriageways by use of the pedestrian bridge and arrived at the car park on the other side. Instantly he saw the English registered camping car with the raised bonnet and a man gazing deeply into the engine bay. Eventually the man disappointedly shut the bonnet and after locking the vehicle and checking the tyres, walked unhurriedly into the service station complex of restaurants and shops to no doubt await collection.

He waited a further long five minutes watching the vehicle until those that had been around during the man's engine inspection had departed for sustenance or the open road and then he too unhurriedly, walked over to the camper. He bent to the left hand front wheel and retrieved the two sets of keys from where they had been secreted, walked round to the other side, let himself in the drivers door and was soon on the road in the direction from which he had arrived.

Driving cautiously he pulled into the first AutoRoute rest area where he parked and familiarised himself with the controls of the vehicle from the handbook he found in the glove compartment, including some of the basic amenities the camper had to offer. He also found the shoulder bag that had been left in the toilet and extracted a few items from it including a passport and a pair of horned rim spectacles. Fifteen minutes later he was back on the road and after another thirty, pulled into the courtyard of a caravan centre where he presented himself at the reception desk as the man that had telephoned the day before to reserve an undercover secure parking space.

He confirmed that he had been on his way south with the camper for the winter, when there had been a death in the family and he was returning home immediately by train to join his wife who fortunately was still in England. Her intention had been to fly south to join him once he had arrived, so avoiding the long road journey - she had developed back problems since a riding accident. He did not know how long it would be before he would be back, but he would pay a months money - cash in advance - and would contact them in due course. There was a 'little extra' for all their help – and would they be good enough to telephone for a taxi to take him to the station. For such a nice smart young man they would be only too happy to oblige, especially as he spoke such good French - so unusual for an *Anglais.*

The taxis dropped him outside the booking hall and he carried his shoulder bag first to the bookstall where he bought a paper taking his glasses off to read the smaller print then placing them in his pocket. Loosened his tie as he crossed the station hall and despite the chill in the air, by the time he had scouted the car park and found the car, his jacket was draped over his arm and shoulder bag and he resembled a farmer on a day out in town.

"Everything go OK?"

The car was quite warm where she had had the engine running from time to time and the heater on while waiting.

"No problem."

"Was everything there?"

She was convinced he had not given London enough time.

"As far as I can tell, all my stuff anyway, passports, cash, other odds'n'ends, I don't know what you ordered."

She ignored his terminology as she had during the previous week or so when he insisted on referring to London as if it were some mail order catalogue company.

"But the camper, did they have time to get the camper?"

"Of course," He smiled - you had to take your small victories where you could, "Now we can go on holiday!"

Chapter 11

He had asked for 15,000€ in cash and that's exactly what had been sent.

Their passports showed they might one day be Mr. and Mrs. Mills of Bromley in Kent and he was amused to see that he had aged by two years, but enquiries as to the verity of the similar specific on her document were ignored. He therefore pocketed two thousand of the fifteen, returned all his other items to the shoulder bag and handed it to her for safe keeping.

"What do we do now?"

She slung the bag on her shoulder while enquiring. He was pleased with the day's events, but she seemed less so.

"Wait, that's what we always do." He was disgruntled she was not satisfied with the reaction they had provoked from London, "You cook, I wash up, you go to bed, I drink a bottle of wine and we both wait!"

This time they did not have to wait long, only until breakfast the next day.

They now habitually let Dog loose on the property, only restraining him when they had established who may be visiting or what was causing the animal annoyance and so it was the dog that announced the arrival of another small saloon. As he fought to get the leash around Dog's neck and escort him with typical difficulty to the stable, he noted that this time the vehicle did exhibit an official car registration indicating those inside to be civil servants of some kind. This meant it could have been the

President or the man that delivers sperm, but whoever it was they were paid by the state.

By the time he returned from the stable Sun had already established that the two men bore worrying information with regard to the goats.

"Are they from the Ministry of Goats?"

His witless enquiry produced a blank look from one of the men, but the other involuntary snapped his head round to better observe the origin of the impudence, before sinking back into poorly portrayed unawareness. Sun neglected to translate his query, but when he glanced at her he was sure she too had detected that one of the men understood English, but wished to keep the talent concealed.

It transpired the men were from a department of the Ministry of Agriculture where it had recently come to light that the herd from which he had obtained his goats was infected with a highly contagious and fatal disease, being hereditary, his small herd would also have to be destroyed. There would be some compensation, but there was urgency and the men wished to make arrangements for the collection of the animals. He agreed without argument that the goats could be collected the next day and the two men departed, but not as sanguine as they might have been.

For through Sun, he had asserted most strongly that along with the compensation cheque, he would require from the Ministry a receipt and an official copy of the ruling regarding the obligatory slaughter before he was prepared to let the animals be taken.

"You didn't put up much of a fight." She was surprisingly angry, but he ignored the veiled censure.

"Did you notice one of them obviously spoke English?" she in turn offered no reply, regardless he observed, "We will have to be careful what we say in future – in both languages."

The postman arrived – it was a busy morning.

Dog greeted the man warmly as ever, trying a further copulation with the mail van, but in due time he was able to retrieve his correspondence from the open slit in the drivers door window while insuring the van remained chaste.

There was only one letter and it was more good news. His solicitor regrettably confirmed that the court had upheld the revised decision of the planning authority to reverse their initial positive determination for the approval of two holiday chalets. It had been one of the earlier applications he had made with the assistance and full support of the Marie who was always keen on anything that might bring money to the village – holiday chalets meant holidaymakers with holiday money and probably a lot of it, not least if they were English.

Also small farmers were encouraged to diversify.

This in reality meant do anything that earned them a livelihood and reduced the amount of subsistence they had to seek from the state and ultimately Europe. Small farms were not economically viable and France still had many, many family farmers trying to survive in the face of the unpalatable reality that food production was greater than demand and only the biggest and therefore the cheapest would endure. Rural England had gone through similar turmoil fifty years earlier, albeit without the generous and some would argue misguided aid of a financially obligated greater Europe.

France was terrified that if interventionism ceased and a truly open market was created for her farmers, the resultant 'flat playing field' would run with the blood of the Nation's utter economic ruin. The stakes were high; diversification was the byword, but apparently not for this young farmer.

In response to his request Sun rang and made an appointment for them to see the solicitor that afternoon and Dog barked his customary adieu soon after lunch.

"Tell him I can understand the planning office changing their minds, they are just bureaucrats, but we have a written adjudication from the county court judge herself, finding on our behalf."

They were ensconced in the solicitor's office and her translation was almost perfect.

"So ask him why and how a judge can arbitrarily totally reverse an already published verdict without referral to any court?"

She did as she was bid, but it produced no response save for their solicitor reddening and fidgeting in his chair. There was a long silence that he refused to break and eventually the solicitor closed the file in front of him and pushed it deliberately across the desk before finally speaking. Sun began a simultaneously translation, but nonetheless he initially kept his vacant expression in place.

The solicitor had no comment to make on developments other than to inform them that he no longer was able to represent them and suggested that if they choose to pursue the matter they should approach another law practise. Their self-excused legal representative then sat back in his chair giving the distinct impression that he considered the meeting to be at an end.

He was angry and becoming angrier and perhaps the solicitor perceived his demeanour for finally with both hands raised in a gesture of supplication leaned forward across the desk before confidentially whispering to Sun,

"You must be careful, I strongly urge you not pursue this. I will not repeat this warning, but I really do urge you to forget all about it, now if you'll excuse me?" and with that he stood and walked out of the room.

That evening he ate bread and cheese for dinner – it was just like old times. Sun remained in her room after they had returned from the solicitors and he could not be bothered to bother her. He had been trying to get down to half a bottle of wine a night, but this had definitely been a full bottle day thus, when he awoke early the next morning to the sound of a diesel engine and clanking trailer he was not in the best of moods.

Dog was still in the kitchen striving to break the door down in an attempt to get at the intruders and there was no sign of Sun. He wrestled a rope on the dog and dragged him out to the stables, subsequently returning to greet the two men from the day before and the driver of an elderly Mercedes and even older horse trailer. There was still no sign of Sun and so he struggled with the language to such an extent that the English speaker, finally succumbing to frustration at the lack of progress, explained in the young farmer's mother tongue that they had arrived for the goats.

Language now ceasing to be an obstacle he was able to first ask to see the compensatory cheque, receipt and official judgement as previously discussed. Oddly the man explained that due to an administrative quirk, the compensation could be significantly enhanced if he was prepared to accept cash, but obviously if affairs were to be conducted unofficially, the official documentation would not be forthcoming.

He refused.

He explained that since coming to France he had tried to do everything correctly, it was the English way and he could not change now, he would never rest easy again. Reluctantly the man laid his briefcase on the bonnet of the small saloon and opened it, begrudgingly handing over the three items. A cheque from the Ministry, a receipt for the goats and a document that even to his cursory inspection appeared to have been hastily prepared, but importantly, prepared on official Ministry stationary and with the same signature as that on the cheque.

It did not take long for the four men with the aid of a number of lengths of joined baling twine to act as a mobile corral, to herd the troupe of twenty goats out of the paddock and up the ramp of the trailer. No one seemed interested in staying longer than was necessary and so with a variety of dispositions – the two in the small saloon far less cheerful than the driver of the Mercedes – the little convoy headed down the drive to the open road.

He did not wave his goats goodbye, but he did feel a burning on the back of his neck and when he turned Sun had finally emerged and was gazing at him from the kitchen door. She walked past him without a word and opened the stable door to an excited dog and set off at a pace for her customary morning pursuit of health and beauty.

"I suppose goats are sacred creatures or something up in the hills of Tibet or wherever it is you come from?"

He looked up and really did think this time he had over done it. Her eyes blazed and she did not cross the room so much as one second she was entering the kitchen door and the next was a foot from his face on the other side of the room. She held his eyes for a long moment and then moved to the cooker.

"Sometimes Timothy you are the most stupid of men."

He ignored the not necessarily unique character assessment and spoke reasonably, "You've spent time with the goats and I know you've become fond of them, particularly the youngsters."

There had been three births not long before her arrival.

"So you'll be relieved to hear that they'll live out their full and natural lives."

He couldn't be totally sure as to the animal husbandry ethics of the owner of the Mercedes and trailer, but he seemed a 'good sort' and was certainly pleased with his no doubt very reasonably priced, if not free, instant herd.

"There's no reason to destroy the animals, the paperwork is bogus and it was all a ruse to make this young farmer's life just that little bit harder."

She turned from the lighted cooker her expression still bemused.

"Why did you not say before?"

"I didn't know for sure, but no Ministry official is going to offer more cash instead of more paperwork – not if it's all above board, and in any case, if they were going for slaughter, they would have been collected by the knackerman, not an elderly Mercedes and trailer. I think the goats have found a good home."

She smiled weakly, "But why did you let them go so easily?"

"We have the paperwork in their stead, cheque, receipt, bogus Ministry authorisation, that's what it's all about isn't it, building the case?"

"But you've lost your goats."

Having just recovered a modicum of goodwill he was reluctant to dispense with it, but he could not keep the harshness from his voice.

"Yes and from what you tell me it is likely I'm gonna loose a lot more, but I'm damned if I ain't at least gonna try and keep the animals out of your 'big boy' games. The goats are gone which leaves Perch. Dog could come with us if we get a chance and the bantams can probably look after themselves – because one way or another, one day we're not gonna be here to look after anybody."

It had been another full bottle day so when he woke to hear Sun and Dog depart for their early morning exercise he turned over and pulled the covers over his throbbing head. Sometime later – although it felt like the next minute – there was a knock on his door and Sun asked if he was 'decent'. Mumbling about the inanity of such a ridiculous fashion by which to ascertain if someone was clothed, he climbed out of bed just as she opened the door.

Instantly he was embarrassed by his nudity.

She sniggered and said sorry, but that she had not heard him answer and there was something in the woods that had bothered Dog and she thought they should have a look.

"Right" he muttered.

"Well, aren't you going to get dressed?"

He was standing with the quickly snatched edge of the bed sheet covering his lower torso and could not reach the chair with his clothes without releasing the sheet or dragging it and the duvet off the bed.

"Yes."

Her eyes shone with mocking insolence, "Well?"

"Yes - when I'm left alone." He could feel himself colouring.

"Oh, right, yes of course, I'm sorry." and with a final conspicuous smirk she stepped back into the kitchen and closed the door.

The wood lay in the north-east corner of the farm with the nearest part of its perimeter about three hundred metres from the house and barns. Unlike the two regular morning jogger's circuitous route round the farm, this time they marched directly to the spot that had bothered Dog with the animal straining at the leash and thrilled at the opportunity of another excursion. Once there nothing untoward was apparent until suddenly a dog broke from the cover of the thick scrub and Dog went wild. It took the joint efforts of both of them to restrain the animal and so they did not at first see the two hunters that had followed the stray dog from the wood.

Hunting in France is a very well regulated recreation and even then they manage to kill thirty of each other every year plus half a dozen or so innocent passers by, so to find unauthorised hunters on one's land is unusual and potentially dangerous.

The wood was open to two of the pastures and Perch was allowed access to gain shelter and shade under the fringes of the heavy foliage, much of it evergreen and available throughout the year.

"Ask them what they are doing in my wood."

Sun posed the question and received an answer that was peculiar in the extreme.

The men had been sent because it was rumoured there were animal traps in the wood that were both illegal and dangerous and they were to report on the situation when they returned to the office.

Had they found any traps? – No.

Who had sent them? – Their 'Office'.

Where was the office? – In the 'Town'.

"Tell them I shoot in the wood everyday and I've never come across a trap and that it's very dangerous for them to enter the wood without getting my permission first as I obviously assume there's no one there and tend to shoot accordingly."

He waited on the translation, but noticed it seemed of little interest to the pair of hunters, which was peculiar given the content.

"Tell them in future I will keep an eye out for anything that shouldn't be there and perhaps their office could contact me about the rumours, tell them I don't like rumours."

They watched the pair stride back into the wood with their dog, soon disappearing under the green canopy and behind the enveloping scrub. Allegedly their car was parked on the road the other side of the wood and instinctively he was happier that the pair did not come back passed the farmhouse.

"Did you see the guns they were carrying?" She asked, Dog still on the leash to prevent any covert return to the trees.

"Not really, I was looking at their clothes more than anything."

The truth was he had not taken any notice of their guns as he did not know anything about guns and only a little about clothes, but theirs were quite distinctive.

"They were military carbines, you can purchase them privately, but they are expensive and certainly not a woodsman's first choice."

He smiled despite his anxiety - she did at times have a strange terminology, but continued, "And the clothes were military type fatigues."

His opinions with regards to the fashion outfits evidently redundant he retorted,

"So they've sent in the fucking army!"

Chapter 12

He had thirty-three cartridges of various size shot, but mainly numbers five and eight. It did not however, seem to matter how many little round lead pellets he had in the cardboard cartridge case the clays still flew by unmolested so he assumed there as yet had not been developed a cartridge and gun with sufficient ‘shot’ and ‘spread’ for his ‘eye’. He probably needed a few thousand and 360°.

He placed all the cartridges into his coat pockets took the shotgun out of its mock leather bag and walked into the kitchen.

“Where are you going?” She had a puzzled look on her face.

“To start a war.”

“I thought you said you couldn’t hit anything?” more puzzlement.

“I can’t normally, but I fancy my chances at a ten acre wood from as many feet.”

“Do you think that wise?” She obviously didn’t.

“Probably not, but it’ll make me feel better.”

“Not if they shoot back.” Again she had the last word.

Slamming the kitchen door behind him and calling Dog to heel, which made no difference whatsoever to Dog, he retraced their steps back to the edge of the wood. He paced along the perimeter of the wood where it crossed his land, from the hedge on the right to a neighbour’s barbed wire fence on the left. It measured three hundred and fifty paces. He turned at the fence and counted twenty paces back along the perimeter of the wood and being careful not to hit a large oak almost directly in front, fired into the wood.

Dog yelped with delight while he wished he had remembered his ear protectors, but at least he would not be able to hear the complaints when he returned which reminded him of the type of thing that married men said and really made him angry.

He fired into the wood at every ten paces, ripping holes in the higher scrub and ruining the customary serenity of the tranquil spinney. When he returned to the house, his shoulder ached, he could not hear and even Dog had an excuse for not listening.

"Satisfied?"

"Pardon?"

"Satisfied?"

"Pardon?"

"********!"

Looking at him full face she mouthed one of his favourite single word expletives, but made no sound.

"What did you just say?" He could not help chuckling.

"Ballots, I think we should have a vote before either of us start a war."

Despite his smirking she maintained a perfect poker face, but it still made him laugh.

"C'mon," he said suddenly solemn, "we have to go shopping."

"What for?"

"Some more cartridges."

They were in the car returning from the supermarket and the gunsmiths when she enquired, "Have you thought about what the pair in the wood were doing?"

He had thought about it, but had come to no worthwhile conclusion and before he could confess she went on, "I believe they may have been attempting to establish an observation post, a place from where they could watch the farmhouse, any 'comings and goings' and of course our movements. A 'hide' would be unremarkable in the wood if you stumbled across it, but from the slightly elevated position where they came out; the entire farm buildings would be clearly seen."

"Why?"

Something of the kind had occurred to him, but not the establishment of a fixed position a 'hide' would indeed make any surveillance much more comfortable for the watchers and with added concealment.

"Well, firstly to see if we are working alone or if for example it would be possible to prove any embarrassing third party involvement, remember what I have told you."

He was unconvinced, "Yes, but we're not even sure if anyone knows we're 'working'- whatever that means."

She was undeterred, "OK, so we look at the time line. It's a month since we sent the five copies to London, but another three weeks since we obtained the copy of the initial one sent to you in error. More than enough time for something to have come to light in the Unions Office and if the woman and the young girl were put under pressure they would admit everything."

She continued counting off days on her figures, "Too much has happened too quickly for it to be coincidental, the room measuring man, the goats, the planning and now the hunters or whatever, it's too much."

Satisfied she returned her hands to their normal position, lightly clasped in her lap.

"So as you assure me there'll be no 'embarrassing' visitors, what will they try and achieve, bury us in the woods?"

The remarks carried all his trademark flippancy, but it was really some succour he was seeking.

"No, not unless they think we really have something manifestly incriminating, I believe that all the time they think you are just a lone untutored English farmer, they'll only try to drive you out – make the problem go away, if you're not here you can't be a nuisance."

Not exactly the comfort he was looking for, but it made sense. He parked the car by the kitchen door and they unloaded the shopping before he walked through to get the shotgun.

"Do you really think those two were army?" Now he was not angry he was not brave.

"No," she smiled, "ex-army perhaps, private security or some local villains, there really isn't a lot to choose between them these days, why? Where are you going?"

"To shoot some more holes in the 'hide' – we don't need a ballot for that do we?"

Again not much happened for some weeks.

The man from the Ministry of Integration never returned and nor did the hunters, although he now regularly inspected the wood, but had ceased to shoot it. They complained at the Mairie about the rescinded planning, but only to the extent of an untutored farming family and although there was much shrugged response 'obviously they were sorry, but could not help'. In fact, there was a distinct cooling in the attitude of the Mairie and the few local shopkeepers towards them, which was unfathomable, other than that they were in dispute with the Electricity Board and he had refused to pay the bill, perhaps news of his heresy had spread.

Two months previously he had received the regularly by-monthly bill, but inexplicably it was not in his name. His name was included in the address, but the actual account holder had suddenly changed to the company that appeared on the original application for a farm building grant he had been sent in error. To pay the bill would be to obviously 'accept' that he was the company, the company that had presumably received the grant. It could subsequently be reasonably argued by an adroit advocate that 'accepting' the bill would be 'accepting' ownership of the company that had 'accepted' the grant.

The solution was clear, explain the inaccuracy to the electricity company and arrange for the billing to revert to as it had been for the last eighteen months or more, but they refused. Not initially, there was a great deal of people 'being out of the office' and non-returned phone calls, but in the end they insisted the bill be paid in the form that it had been sent, so he refused. They had now received a number of 'final demands' all of which they responded to by seeking to further justify their case, but to no avail. They even sought to illicit the help of their erstwhile solicitor, assuming this issue would not cause the anxiety their previous had, but he was always out and never returned their calls.

It was all very strange.

“Are you a Christian Timothy?”

Three weeks into December and the weather had turned cold, so they spent most of the time in the kitchen around the wood stove, not bothering to heat the rest of the house.

“Does my vernacular sound like I don’t take the Lord’s name in vain?”

She smiled smugly, “Ah, I assumed you were raised so, you would not know enough to make such a comment if you weren’t, then I shall prepare you a Christmas Dinner which is traditional is it not?”

He grinned, “It’s my Birthday.”

“You should not be so sarcastic or I won’t bother.”

His grin waned a little and he explained, “No, no, it is my Birthday, I was born on the 25th just like Jesus.”

“Not quite like Jesus I fear Timothy. For example I suspect that if you received one big present, you assumed there should have been two and if you received two, that they should have been twice as big. Furthermore you do not strike me as someone who would ‘suffer the little children to come unto him’.”

“I’ve seen enough ‘suffering little children’ Sun.”

They fell into an uncomfortable silence, but eventually as he stood and began to prepare himself for a routine inspection tour of the premises she said quietly, “I’m sorry Timothy, it was thoughtless of me, so now I shall cook you a Birthday Dinner.”

And cook it she did.

They ate at two on the afternoon of his birthday, a meal of surprising authenticity and she was even tempted to toast his health in half a glass of wine.

It was probably the most enjoyable afternoon and evening they had had since her arrival, which was appropriate for at nine o'clock the next morning their electricity supply was cut off.

There is no Boxing Day in France.

The twenty-sixth of December is not a public holiday, but it just as well might have been given the reaction achieved from their telephoned complaint. It appeared the records revealed the bill had not been paid and therefore the supply had been terminated. A visit to the main office resulted in no shift in the electricity-company's position and he found it particularly difficult to maintain his supposed ignorance of the language in the proximity of such absurdity and the smarmy ignoramus that peddled it.

On the way back to the farm he purchased a small generator and the petrol to power it and by that evening he had jury-rigged a supply, via a variety of extension leads, to most of the essential appliances, but it was still inconvenient. Fortunately they cooked by gas and had the wood burner, but more battery torches and candles had to be purchased, although it was the frustration that was hardest to abide.

Thus when he received the six monthly water rates bill, also in the same 'company' name as the electricity bill, he did not bother to wait for developments and changed the water supply to the house from 'mains' to their well water by adding the house to the stable's piping. It was relatively simple as the pump and well water pressure storage cylinder were actually in the house from where the pipes ran onto the stables, one disconnection and one coupling and the job was completed, but they would now use bottled water for cooking and drinking.

"I wonder how long it'll be before they cut the 'phone off?"

It had only just occurred to him. Sun made all the telephone calls, as he did not speak the language, which was probably why it had slipped his mind. He turned from adding another log, carefully closing the doors of the wood burner, the blistering heat of which he had painfully leaned to respect.

"They won't, they'll want to hear what you are planning."

At first he did not understand, and then suddenly it dawned, "You think they'll 'tap' the phone?"

"They already have."

It was New Years Eve, but there had been no suggestion of another festive feast and he felt it risky to raise the subject for fear it was mentioned that technically it was his turn to cook, so he accepted the early evening's simple fare with good grace. Nonetheless he was determined to 'see the New Year in' with conventional optimism and had opened a bottle of fine claret to assist him in his determination and now it would appear it might take two.

"How do you know, why didn't you tell me?"

He could hear her sigh from the table where she sat idly glancing through a magazine by the light of three candles, the generator halted for the night.

"You can hear it on the line and I have a little tester that works quite well - and I did not tell you because you never use the telephone, but now if you do, be careful. They will not cut it off if they think there is some advantage in hearing what we are saying and more importantly, who to."

Once he would have been unreasonably annoyed but not anymore, not until there was enough to be reasonably annoyed about that was, “Any other snippets of information I should know about?”

He noted she smiled where once she may have scowled.

“No, I ‘sweep’ the house and car everyday for ‘bugs’ and have moved a number of items upstairs. Where by the way, I wonder if we could move the large wardrobe, I’ve looked and it comes apart in sections. I wonder if we could re-assemble it adjacent to the hole, so that we can seal it behind us if we retreat there. Push it over the hole if you see what I mean.”

He saw. It was definitely going to be a two-bottle night.

She went back to her magazine and he knew it was not the time to pursue matters further, not least because he was about to open said second bottle which meant the first one had gone.

He gazed at the glowing embers through the soot stained glass of the stove doors and wondered what kind of New Year it would be after this final hour of the old one had passed.

“Oh! Look at the time, I didn’t realise it was so late.”

She stood from the table and patting Dog’s head on the way out wished them both ‘goodnight’.

“Happy New Year.” He tried to sound happier than he felt.

“Oh yes, of course, it’s your New Year isn’t it, Happy New Year Timothy,” and went through his room to her bed.

“’Course it’s our bleedin’ New Year, ain’t it mate?” He sarcastically conferred, dragging Dog into his cockney disparaging, “Don’t they teach ‘em any bleedin’ thing in Tibet.”

Chapter 13

France is a racist country – most countries are.

Despite the striving of many genuinely well meaning sophisticated governments and egalitarian organisations most peoples exhibit preference based on family, tribe, village, town, county, and country. All this before one even considers the most visible form of prejudice – that of colour and potentially the most furious – that of religion.

Most peoples will accept an influx of foreigners to a level whereby the immigrants remain a novel minority, but where the manifestation of alien presence and culture is perceived as a threat to the indigenous way of life there will inevitably be unrest.

No cerebral argument can hold dominion over this basic truth however philosophically desirable. Not now, not today - and governments should always remember they have to legislate for The People as they are, not as they would want them to be. Hope for the best in humanity, but legislate for the worst - but even in this there are dangers.

From her experiences in the Far East and Algeria, France had long perceived a potential threat from the Islamic world. Unlike Britain, for many years she had seen a significant movement of Muslims to the West where, apart from the normal ghetto syndrome synonymous with major migration, she had also seen elements of her civil service and regional administrations come under the control of the new settlers. Add to this the presence of many Muslims within the professions, medical and legal and it is perhaps not surprising that there existed in France an influential intellectual elite that were convinced of an Islamic assault for which draconian measures were essential to protect the status quo. And were it to be that the more innocent fell foul of these imperious powers, it was a small price to pay for the protection of the state.

Liberty, equality and fraternity would have to wait.

Notwithstanding his antipathetic comments on Tibet, a country and peoples of whom he knew nothing and who were probably totally disassociated - Sun and his relationship had changed. Certainly not familiar nor cosy, but amicable and at times perhaps even collaborative – understandable, as she was at pains to point out that they only had each other.

But there was always tension.

He more often that not restricted himself to the reduced wine intake level rode Perch more regularly, as there was now little work to do on the farm and had begun to join in the morning run. At first he only managed part of the circuit and would walk home taking a direct route across the fields, but eventually he managed to complete the mile distance. Satisfied, on the occasion of his first tour, he bent forward hands on knees blowing heavily as she called a tribute over her shoulder and set off with Dog on the second 'fast lap'.

It was clear that she deliberately chose to say nothing about herself, divulging no personal information while at the same time she seemed to have a comprehensive knowledge of his circumstances. He knew, although he did not know why he knew, that this annoyed him significantly. It was as if she were masked in mystery while he stood naked before her – which embarrassingly of course he had once and which certainly did not help.

He had had a similar frustration before his parents had been killed. Being an only child he had been attracted by two older girl's suggestion that they enter into a traditional childhood pact of 'I'll show you mine if you'll show me yours.' Subsequently he felt thoroughly cheated. From the smutty sniggering he assumed the two girls were satisfied with the trade, but for him there had been nothing to see, it was probably the start of his scepticism and wariness of womankind in general!

Nevertheless they muddled along and Dog's life too changed.

Whenever they were absent from the house Dog was shut inside with the full run of the four rooms, thus if ever anyone 'called' while they were absent, it was instantly apparent upon their return. Dog would have torn down a variety of curtains and in some instances the rail as well, in an attempt to consume the visitor. There were unfortunately also additional minor drawbacks like sleeping with the fleas Dog generously deposited on the beds while resting between periods of demolition, but at least they were never burgled.

"So what is this plan you have been working on, Oh Master of Operations?"

It was the only thing that really seemed to bother her apart from his personal shortcomings. She had explained that before her departure she had complained bitterly that a 'split executive field structure' was never desirable and inexplicable as an amateur was involved, but London had insisted. Like any good amateur he offered to abdicate, but she was adamant that they continue as London wished and if things went wrong it would be 'their own fault.' It had occurred to him at the time that it might be

London's fault, but it was their hides, but he said nothing – being only an amateur.

"I wondered if there was someway we could get the actual Union files of the companies that are supposed to be in my name?"

She put down the magazine she had been studying and he noticed it was opened at an advertisement for perfume, which somehow he found totally incongruous.

"You want me to break into the offices of the Farmer's Union and steal some of their files, would you like the computer discs or any hard copies, I am sure I will be able to find both, their can't be that many farmers in France?"

As his grandmother had always said, 'don't tell anyone what you're thinking 'til you've thought it and don't tell anyone what you're doing 'til you've done it.'

"I accept I haven't thought it right through yet and in any case, why would I expect you to be the one to break in anywhere?"

She appraised him with the bored look he found so irksome before replying.

"Have you ever broke' into anywhere? You were in Borstal because you were orphaned not delinquent and every other facility was full, it's dangerous to claim talents you do not possess, Timothy."

He laughed and was almost as surprised at his reaction as she was, "I do beg your pardon, did I tread on the Security Manager's toes and is your black leotard so that you won't be seen at night?"

Touché, it was silly, but it was not unusual for spats like this to flare up if they had no other pressing engagement. Childish as well, but then that had never bothered him, in a contest of juvenile immaturity he would always fancy his chances.

"My toes are fine Timothy and it is sensible to wear dark colours at night if you wish to go undetected, particularly if you are seeking to defeat the alarm systems of what will undoubtedly be a very well defended quasi governmental building. Also bye-the-bye, what you are suggesting would have to be approved by London, any such pre-emptive action and certainly anything blatantly illegal."

He shrugged, "And it would no doubt be the Security Officer that decided if London should be consulted?"

"Of course, who else would be qualified?"

The weather stayed cold for the next few weeks, but very bright and if he put aside the complications of the day it was a wonderful world of crisp mornings, clean air and wintry sunshine.

Just to compensate he had taken up smoking – or at least that is what the villages thought, for most evenings he would now visit the local café-bar to purchase his cigarettes and take the opportunity for a glass of beer or two. Due to his language deficiency he would sit alone, oblivious of what went on around him and the locals nodded sagely amongst themselves that all was not a bed of roses when it came to 'catalogue' wives.

Was this not proof?

The young man had had no need of nicotine and alcohol before her arrival - or to escape for an hour almost every evening. One could only hope that what went on at night made up for it, but they were unconvinced, after all he was English and it was probably not just the language he couldn't manage.

"Anything?"

On his return from the bar he had carried more logs into the kitchen where her routine enquiry had become as common as his chore.

"No, Mme. Daveau has had a baby, Mme. LeLeuch is having a baby and Mme. Trichet wants to have a baby – probably trying right now. Oh and the hunters in the north of the Department managed to bag a dinner lady – apparently she was bringing the baguettes and mulled wine and they mistook her for a stag."

She carried plates to the table, "Will they mount her?"

Happily the childish spats were ever more frequently being replaced with impudent satire.

"I don't know - the proprietress of the bar was not forthcoming as to the hunter's predilection to necrophilia."

They finished the meal and he washed up before rejoining her at the table, "I telephoned the camper storage people to confirm they'd received 'my cheque from England' for the next three months rent."

She nodded, "And?" She had registered there was more to come.

"During the time I was incarcerated, I became aquatinted with a boy who was awaiting charge for transgressing the monopoly and fraud laws - as ridiculous as it seems that an office boy of sixteen could know of such offences let alone how to commit them."

She regarded him with the blank expression he knew so well, but unabashed he continued, "There was obviously confusion with regard to his age and how he was to be indicted, but that aside, it was the circumstances around the actual offence that I believe may be pertinent. Although the files from time to time existed in computerised form they were regularly deleted and only the hard copy, in the old fashion paper and portfolio form were constantly updated. The actual fraud centred on price fixing, the five companies that monopolised the market exchanged information with regard to tenders ensuring all achieved the contracts they wanted at the price they wanted."

It was no earth shattering revelation he was embarked on, some would say not even uncommon, but he was not aware if her comprehensive knowledge of nefarious commercial matters equated to that of the political. As ever her expression gave no clue so he soldered on regardless.

"The Company Directors of those involved met regularly to establish which companies would take which contract, the delegated company would then circulate its tender to the other four 'competitors' who would ensure their own tenders were well in excess. Subsequently these more expensive tenders were circulated to demonstrate to all that everything had been done by those not delegated to win the contract to loose it."

She remained attentive and asked, "Your point being?"

"Wait a moment, I'm coming to that, and we must give the Operations Manager time."

Her expression remained blank, which was the best he could hope for given his cheek, "Eventually the clients – who were often governmental bodies – became suspicious and began to make spot checks at the offices of the companies involved, looking for signs of a conspiracy. In response, each company adopted the practice of storing all incriminating evidence in one place and simply having it removed from the premises as soon as they became aware an inspection was planned - or even in progress. A member of staff was given the responsibility of taking charge of the damning documentation and literally walked out with it, not returning until the next day, having first telephoned to make sure the coast was clear - simple and effective."

He shrugged, as if to underline the efficiency, "Only the sight of a boy leaving an office premises in the middle of the morning with a heavy despatch case by an alert member of the Serious Fraud Squad during an unannounced inspection had defeated the stratagem. In this particular instance the middle manager whose responsibility it had been to make the orderly exit had been sick and so the boy had been instructed to take his place by a panicked executive."

His voice grew harsh, "Sadly the boy was on probation and already had convictions for shop lifting, so was sent to secure accommodation until the affair was resolved - he probably 'went down' and the Directors went to the Caymans."

She sighed, evidently still smarting from his impertinence, "I am deeply touched by your concern for a fellow waif and stray Timothy, but I still fail to see how your rueful tale could have a bearing on our predicament, I was not aware the French SFO works for us."

The words belayed her interest.

"No," he was more assured now, explaining things somehow seemed to help, "but if we could create a panic in the Union Office it just might be that someone would wish to remove any embarrassing evidence. The applications may be on file, but I doubt if the approvals or proof of payments are open to general inspection, they will be secreted somewhere, probably with the beneficiaries of the plot. Remember your friend in reception said that there were no other documents on file, by which she presumably meant computerised and she was surprised to find that only the application form existed in hard copy despite some of the applications being quite old. There are two names on the applications we have seen apart from supposedly mine, the case officer and the Director of the Bureau, one of these two - and I suspect both - must be involved."

She was now openly curious, "But what can we do, we can't just roll up at the offices and demand to inspect their files?"

Nervously he continued with his plan, after all he was only an amateur, "We telephone the Union office and announce that we are officials of a new classified European antifraud squad and will be arriving within the hour to inspect their subsidy records, stand back and see what happens."

She remained motionless looking at him then, "And what if nothing happens?"

"We've lost nothing."

She gave no clue as to her opinion, "And what if either of the men flee the building?"

"We follow them."

Still equivocal, "Then what?"

"We see where they go, make a note of it for another time, telephone the next day to explain we were assigned to another duty at the last minute and for the moment have to postpone the inspection."

She continued her devil's advocacy, "Why won't they just destroy the documents?"

He knew it to be a risk.

"They are high level bureaucrats and not professional villains, they will instinctively not wish to destroy their files which in itself would probably cause them some low level grief at a later date, they won't want to lose face because of lost files. They won't enquire officially after the illusive investigative bureau because that in itself would attract attention and even if they do, what is an illusive bureau all about if not illusive?"

She rose from the table to make coffee, "You could make some of the telephone calls, they obviously wouldn't see you and it would come better from a man in such a chauvinist society, but obviously no calls could be made from here."

They sipped their respective beverages in silence and he was half way through his half bottle allowance before she proclaimed,

"London would have to approve it."

He did not know whether to be pleased or peeved, but he was tired of arguing,

"OK."

She made the telephone call to London the next day from a supermarket in a town they rarely visited. She was asked to call back in an hour, which gave them time to complete the shopping and find the train station from where she made the second call. When she returned to the car he asked if his plan had been approved and she confirmed that it had and she would explain more that evening after dinner. He saw no reason for the delay, but flushed with success over his apparent amateur achievement, he made no argument.

The fire was stoked, dinner was consumed and coffee and tea had been served before she confirmed and expanded on what had briefly been alluded to in the car. He was pleased, but as ever success was never unimpaired for there was a look in her eye that he had come to recognise and he waited for the glad tidings. He had returned the cork to the bottle having again only consumed his self-imposed ration so was surprised when she deliberately reached across the table and carefully eased the protruding cork free again.

"Mr. Reece thinks it would be a good idea if I became pregnant."

"Ah, for fuck sake!"

"Language Timothy, language."

Chapter 14

Like the Gendarmes in France, Jehovah Witnesses present in pairs - Probably because they are no more popular and disdain and discourtesy are easier withstood when shared. The young man and woman, no doubt linked only by their belief in an eventual time of happiness on earth, carried their telltale cheap briefcases apparently full of pamphlets for posterity and brochures for eternal life from house to house around the leafy crescent. Some doors never opened, some only for an instant and some long enough for a brusque dismissal, but the pair were unabashed as all true believers are, content to delight in the joys of God's Earth, the flowers, the shrubs, the gardens, even the houses themselves.

One particularly fine example of recent architectural flamboyance with rendered concrete block and imitation oak they found of specially interest, despite receiving no reply from their repeated knocks. Zealous in their quest for the conversion of all souls they were not to be found derelict in their efforts, diligently searching the grounds for any of life's forsaken, prying wherever possible, but alas, all to no avail. Finally they moved on to the neighbouring property, but there too there was no response and so encountering one last offensive rebuttal from the house opposite, the pair decided to cease their saving for the day and returned to the modest car parked out of sight further round the curve.

In the world of commerce and industry a man with a briefcase is unremarkable, but a man with two is and so earlier that day the man had instantly been noticed. The revolving door rotated slowly, clumsily expelling first two briefcases, clasped respectively by two hands, followed by a nervous looking man in a hurry for which revolving doors were not designed. These typical satchels of the commercially itinerant appeared to be both hefty and heavy from the manner that each was carried by respective straight arms from drooped shoulders.

The man walked steadily along the front of the Farmers Union office building to the executive and managerial car park that extended from the western perimeter wall. Once there he moved to the second block of cars furthest from the building thereby identifying their owners to be of the second tier of distinction, gratefully depositing his double burden in the boot of a new executive saloon well beyond the reasonable expectations of his apparent status.

The man drove erratically paying more attention to the rear view mirrors that the light mid-morning traffic would seem to justify, yet still failed to identify the modest vehicle that followed no doubt as it was being driven by someone skilled in the art of surveillance. Eventually the man arrived without incident at an impressive new property in a quiet part of one of the satellite towns that surrounded the larger central conurbation.

Utilising the remote control the man barely hesitated as he drove through the electric gates turning immediately to the left and down the slope to the double garage built into the basement of the house, habitually parking tight to the overhead garage doors that enclosed the lady of the house's convertible and their motorboat and trailer - the joint reasons for the exclusion of even the new car. Once inside the man blamed the unexpected arrival on confidential matters best dealt with in the privacy of the new study and despite obvious preoccupation with current affairs, was soon enjoying an early lunch in secure and familiar surroundings.

Undoubtedly it was more 'bluff and bluster' from Strasbourg, it had happened before, but no one had actually arrived to investigate, still the chap on the phone had said enough to distinguish himself as a man of 'understanding' - there should be no problem. Not when the local director was aware of the situation and then of course there were the contacts in Paris, more than enough protection, no one would want to loose their 'commissions', why should they?

Care would have to be taken if inspectors suddenly started to appear out of the blue, but their reactions had been simple and effective, they could do it again if necessary. A conversation this evening to see what had transpired at the office and what was to be done next? No, there would be no problem.

The only problem today was avoiding the pestering pair of religious crusaders knocking at the door, it certainly was not the day for soul searching, still if he sat tight long enough they would move on, they always did.

They had worked on the script together. It may only have been for a telephone call, but it was important they got it right. Too trivial a threat and they would create no counteraction, too menacing and there was a considerable risk any evidence would be destroyed and everything would have been wasted – something London was very anxious about. In the end he made the telephone call from the train station in the town, but not before two previous aborted missions.

It was felt imperative that both the signatories that appeared on his applications should be present in the office when the call was received, thereby allowing the two men to immediately confer. This, it was hoped, would reduce to a minimum the risk of irrational panic and with it the chance that the documentation would vanish. It was also essential that their car be parked where the Unions office car park could be watched, as there would not be time to collect it from any other site.

On their first attempt one of the men did not arrive at the office on the day in question and on the second, none of the few parking spaces that would serve their purpose could be secured. Thus he returned home infuriated to have been foiled by an illusive parking space only to be further incensed when told that he probably did not have the necessary patience for the line of work.

The third attempt had proved more productive.

Watching from the café opposite, they observed the two men arrive at the office as normal along with the rest of the staff, took an hour to secure a suitable parking spot, after which it was only a little time before he made the call. He asked to speak to the most senior official in the building, but was naturally referred to a secretary. He thanked her politely for her offer of assistance and downgraded his request to the most senior official in the building that was prepared to talk to him, adding this time that he was en-rout from Strasbourg. On this occasion there was a longer wait, but eventually a man came on the line and somewhat diffidently enquired as to his business.

He explained.

'We are officials of a new European antifraud squad and will be arriving this morning to inspect the approvals and subsidy

payment records and out of courtesy we are telephoning ahead to inform you of our visit.'

'It is of course short notice, but obviously they would understand the need for confidentiality in these matters and it would be appreciated if the whole affair were to be treated as classified.'

'It is so much quicker and easier for all concerned when people are discrete and it allows us to be a lot more 'understanding' in our investigations.'

Forty-nine minutes passed before the man with two briefcases was squeezed uncomfortably out of the revolving doors. Enough time for him to return from the train station to the car and trail after two red herrings she insisted he confirm as such - one escapee illicitly purchasing cigarettes on company time and one poor young girl on a more personal crisis of bodily functions to a pharmacy. He had only just begun to complain about being assigned to snoop into matters periodical when she waved him to silence as the man exited the building and walked to the car park. Shortly the man drove out of the car park to the loud honking of a passing lorry that obviously considered it should have had priority while she began to follow, careful not to provoke any similar noisy protest.

In his opinion she drove sometimes too close and sometimes too distant, but she was oblivious to all his advice, finally commenting that 'she did not tell him how to drink so don't tell her how to drive.' It was apparent the man was nervous from the manner of his driving and consequently it could reasonably be assumed not the easiest quarry to stalk, nonetheless he remained consolatory despite her apparent ungratefulness.

"At times Timothy, you really do act like a spoilt brat – even more than at other times!"

"Bollocks!"

Surely not another character assassination, his plan had worked, what was the problem?

"You interfere in matters in which you have had no tuition or knowledge and become positively puerile when your deficiencies are exposed, perhaps it would be better if you addressed your self-evaluated prodigious talent to Mr. Reece's recent stratagem with regard to my overdue state of parturition? Or should your accent be idiosyncratic of a general lack of tutelage, perhaps I should further elucidate; how am I going to become pregnant in light of your aversion to nudity, in a dark room with my eyes shut?"

They had returned to the farmhouse following their evangelical exertions and his continuing recommendations as to how she should execute her responsibilities following on from his advice during the 'tailing' from the Union offices.

Her outburst was spiteful and probably the first time he had positively identified that she had deliberately set out to hurt him – excluding the two serious slaps in the face. He was not really hurt of course, he never allowed himself to be, but he was upset, which seemed odd because he should have been angry, it was as if he had discovered a flaw in the armour.

"Perhaps you would be kind enough to grant me the benefit of your professionalism and explain to me what the theory behind Mr. Reece's proposal is?"

He had distanced himself, it was in his voice and his eyes and she recognised the shift.

“There are apparently a plethora of grants that are triggered by pregnancy.” She too became business like, “The French government is keen to see as many little Frenchmen as possible enter the world and is prepared to induce the populace to procreation with generous donations to those that have proved fertile. Even pornographic films are allowed on Friday nights to assist with the ambience. Mr. Reece feels it would perhaps create a diversionary tactic and help disguise your other applications if we registered for some family aid and child benefit etc.”

She stared at him for a long time, but he said nothing and was certainly not going to ask any questions, then finally she shrugged and smiled knowingly,

“Of course it would all be a ruse; you wouldn’t really have to take your clothes off.”

He sat in the village café-bar having bought his cigarettes and sipping his chemical cocktail the French call beer, listening intermittently to the conversations within. It was feared the present hunting season would not prove to be a good one so presumably more innocent beasts and bystanders were to survive and reputedly Mme. Trichet – and one would assume her husband - had been successful in their striving to become prospective parents. With surprising alacrity in the opinion of the bar proprietress, but he concluded the couple were most likely spurred on – metaphorically speaking of course - by the late night films.

As satisfying as it was to keep abreast of the story of everyday country folk it was the two strangers sitting in the corner that had caught his attention as soon as he had entered the bar. Their conversation was cloaked from him by the noise of the intervening customers and although he could have chosen a table nearer to their corner, he was afraid to break from his routine and habitual spot in the bar for fear it might draw attention.

The pair was obviously not local, but dressed in the manner of hunters or anglers, albeit he could see no signs of guns or rods. They appeared not to be known to the clientele of the bar and so he assumed they were passing through and they did indeed depart before he had finished his second glass of chilled chemical spill.

As usual on his return from the bar he parked the car and carried extra logs into the kitchen, wondering if after all his unappreciated advice there would be any dinner, but was pleasantly surprised at the smell of cooking as he opened the door.

"Anything?"

Gratefully he deduced all would appear to be normal and so he cheerfully apprised her of the opinions of the locals as to the deficiencies with regard to the present hunting season. Not wishing to tempt fate however, he passed over the successful couplings of Mme. Trichet and spoke vaguely and with little interest about the two strangers until dinner was served. After the meal he washed up and in a genuine effort of recompense for any unwarranted advice he may have proffered, made the coffee and tea.

"I'm sorry you found my comments so annoying, I was only trying to help and I'm well aware of your er...skills and jurisdiction etc, but whatever, I really do think we have had a result."

Given the chance he knew what he wanted to say and had thought about how he might actually say it while he was in the bar, now seemed the right moment and the sooner the better, for he was pleased with the events of the day.

"You want me to tell you what a clever boy you are Timothy and how your plan worked really well?"

He sat opposite her and said nothing but could not keep the smile from his face. The plan had worked and if she must, yes he was a clever boy – certainly for an amateur – and all he wanted was an acknowledgement that they might, just might, be getting somewhere. His Cheshire cat impression did not rile her as his advice on driving had, if fact she too began to smile and grudgingly accepted that things had gone surprisingly well, but what now?

"Steady, steady all in good time, what did they say at the office when you phoned to cancel?"

They had stopped on the way back from their crusading for her to make the call explaining the lack of appearance of the inspectors. When she had returned to the car he had asked if everything was fine and she had answered in the affirmative, but with atmospheric conditions being what they were at the time, he felt lucky to get that much – now things were better.

"C'mon what did they say?"

She shook her head, "What could they say?" then shrugging, "I asked to speak to the secretary to the Director of the Bureau and then asked her to pass on the message. The visit from Strasbourg had had to be cancelled, the gentlemen concerned were very sorry, but would no doubt see them in due course and perhaps it would be as well to remind her boss, politely of course, that it would be better for all concerned if confidentiality was maintained. What was there for her to say? In fact, I don't think she knew anything about it."

He laughed out loud, "Excellent, not bad for an amateur aye?"

She continued to shake her head at his swaggering, "So what now?" reaffirming her curiosity in future machinations.

"All in good time, all in good time." He continued to crow.

"You don't know do you, you've no idea?" She sighed and frowned.

"I've a very good idea, but the last time I spoke before I'd completed my deliberations I believe you were somewhat sceptical and this time I shall wait until I have everything totally finalised."

It was true, both bits, she had criticised him unreasonably for thinking allowed and he did not know exactly what he was going to do, but he was not going to tell her and spoil a rare triumph.

She stood and made to retire to her room, "I still do not believe you know what you are going to do, but regardless I will confess we have had some success at last, today Timothy, has been a good day."

A compliment at last!

"We'll drink to that won't we old fella?"

Although he still had half a bottle of wine left the evening definitely called for something stronger. Contentedly he helped himself to a couple of generous measures of whisky and leaving Dog stretched in front of the stove, walked a little unsteadily to bed, the smile still on his face.

He slept well, the consequence no doubt of a good day and good whisky and would have continued had it not been for the rapping on his door. Each morning, having finished in the bathroom Sun would leave by the external door, walk along the front of the house to the kitchen door let herself in to make coffee and the dog out to make his ablutions.

"Yes?"

He called, but this time remained under the bed covers as the door opened enough for Sun to lean through, "Dog has been out for sometime and has not come back again."

'Again' was being slightly unfair to the animal for he had only gone missing once since her arrival.

When he had first arrived Dog 'went walkabout' on a number of occasions, but recently only the once and that was in pursuit of an amorous liaison with a bitch in an adjoining farm and for which he had been severely chastised by the adjoining farmer. Subsequently the dog had lost all interest in matters carnal and so it was a slight surprise, but he said he would get up and have a look while she set off on her run. A reasonable 'trade off' as late night whiskey and early morning running did not necessarily sit well together.

He looked all round the farm checking a stable door had not accidentally swung to behind the animal, calling as he went which did little for his headache, but regardless there was no response. Sun's run would take her round much of the perimeter of the farm and so the only direction that she would not cover would be the entrance drive - about four hundred metres down to the lane. Knowing this to be on Dog's daily patrol itinerary, where the animal fastidiously marked his territory in time honoured and urinary fashion, he set out a steady walk along the drive.

He was nearing the end, when over the slight rise he spotted Dog stretched out on the edge of the drive about thirty paces from the lane lying with his back toward the house and his shoulders in the longer grass. Dog looked as he had done the night before stretched in front of the stove, totally relaxed and without a care in the world which was how he should have been, for when he reached the animal he saw that the left-hand side of Dog's head had been blown away.

Chapter 15

Perch stepped gingerly onto the barely adequate short ramp and clattered into the small cattle lorry before looking back over his great shoulder with one enormous kind eye.

Not a lot bothered Perch, which after all was why he had bought the horse, plus, the animal knew the lorry as it had been the one he had arrived in many months before. He signed the paper that Sun handed him and shook hands with Perch's chauffeur and breeder who was amazed that the young English man insisted on paying in advance for the two months work to be done with the horse he had originally purchased sometime ago.

The man was pleased to find that since then the Englishman had found himself a French speaking wife making this transaction much easier than the actual purchase, although they had managed it in the end. The man was to take the animal and train it for the true purpose of the breed, to pull a cart or plough. Even today some still earned their livelihoods in this manner, but generally their 'pulling' was now for show, fetes and country festivals, while their owners were enthusiasts or retired old men celebrating a bygone age.

Of this type of equines these were the lucky ones.

In France grants were available for the breeding of heavy horses for slaughter and the table – a significant amount of horsemeat was eaten in France. Technicians from the National Stud would visit the farms and artificially inseminate the mare 'on site', each year the mare would foal and after a further twelve months or so any male foal would go for slaughter, also females if not required for breeding stock. Were Perch to become a fully trained carthorse it would improve the animal's chances of salvation and cheat the knackerman?

It would also depend on whether or not the man could achieve a higher price than that for slaughter when it was time for Perch to be resold, for regardless of his arrangement with the breeder, he knew he would never see the animal again.

Following the discovery of Dog's body he had turned and walked in a similar steady fashion back to the farmhouse. There was no need to hurry; there was nothing to be done for the dog now that demanded haste.

He collected the wheelbarrow from the barn and retraced his steps along the drive. Loading the remains into the barrow was not easy as Dog weighed well over a hundred pounds and the lifeless body was difficult to manipulate, but he did not really notice nor the gore that soiled his corded trousers, only that it was not Dog anymore, Dog had gone.

She was waiting for him as he wheeled the barrow into the yard, but did not speak as he added a spade to his lifeless load and continued passed the house to an area where vegetables had at one time been cultivated. With difficulty he pushed the barrow to the furthest corner and began to dig.

It is surprisingly arduous to dig a grave as those that do it for a living will testify. He toiled for half and hour before he had a hole even remotely worthy of the name and deep enough for the carcass, whereupon he unceremoniously tipped the barrow sideways to deposit its burden. Returning to the barn he found the half bag of lime he remembered had been left over from some rendering he had carried out on the house and soon the bottom of the shallow grave was drenched in white powder oddly camouflaging its content. Without pausing he began to refill the hole completing the task of internment quicker than that of excavation. There was a mound as there always was, but he covered it with the grassy clods he had cut from the surface before digging, so that from only a little distance the prominence was indistinct.

There would be no marker; Dog would be remembered for what he had been, not as a stake in the ground.

He had showered after his exertions in the old vegetable patch and then entered the kitchen where a cup of strong, sweet tea awaited him, a gentle reminder of her efficiency as he did not take sugar, but was indeed shocked. He drank the syrupy liquid without comment and when he eventually did speak it was not concerning the events of the morning.

"I would be grateful if you would ring the breeder from whom I bought Perch, tell him I would like him to collect the animal and take him back for training as he said he would be very happy to do at the time of purchase. Tell him I would like the animal collected as soon as possible as I have to shortly go into hospital and that I am quite prepared to pay for the cost of collection and any inconvenience the short notice might incur."

Similarly without comment she made the call, only briefly first seeking his confirmation that it was acceptable to make the call from the house telephone and surprisingly arrangements were made for the following day – money talks in France as anywhere else, especially in the countryside.

The cattle lorry rattled slowly down the drive and he watched it go with some sadness, but a great deal of anger.

The goats, Dog and Perch all gone, someone would pay.

The chickens were all that was left and he was reasonably confident the birds would be able to fend for themselves for to be precise, they were all Bantams and much more self reliant than the normal domestic bird. Certainly they would be safe enough until some local opportunist neighbour would undoubtedly offer them an alternative home in return for their small, but delicious eggs, for his plan was now quite clear in his mind and there would no room for chickens.

That evening she accompanied him to the bar so that the circumstances surrounding the extraordinary death of their farm dog could be revealed and to solicit any opinions or suggestions as to what or who could have caused the accident. He wanted that they should refer to the incident as an accident despite knowing it was obviously deliberate. Having viewed the injury as he had passed her with the wheelbarrow, Sun had subsequently attempted to venture an opinion as to the weapon and probable silencer that had been utilised, but he had rudely waved her to silence, there would be time for such speculation, but not then.

Everyone was sympathetic, but there were no worthwhile submissions as to the cause or reasoning behind such misfortune and everyone was very confident the accident had not involved a local hunter – strange as no hunter was present so as yet none of them had been asked? As planned Sun then casually enquired after two men that her husband had seen in the café the evening before - her husband thought they were perhaps hunters, but not local?

There was an instant change in the atmosphere.

No one spoke for long seconds and when they did they really said nothing, their eyes as illusive as their tranquillity. No one remembered the men, not even the proprietress, could it be that the husband was mistaken?

It is a strange, but irrefutable fact that if a foreigner does not speak the language of the indigenous population, he is not just considered linguistically deficient, but also mentally deficient. The proprietress smiled understandingly at the poor young women, not actually physically indicating that she thought her new husband was 'gaga', but all but.

He was more interested however, in two of her present customers than opinions as to his coherence, for he knew the two had been installed at their normal table when he had last sat in the bar vainly trying to overhear the strangers. The pair were local farm hands and as his grandmother would have put it 'not the brightest bulbs on the tree.' Garbling a few mangled words of enquiry in their direction his ramblings were easily diverted, but he had come prepared with his French speaking wife, who he engaged to pose a series of unavoidable questions.

Unavoidable but unanswered.

Nevertheless she was able to ascertain that the two apparent strangers of interest to her husband - that were not there - did drive a car with an 'Îlle de France' registration - if of course they had been there, which they were not - but nevertheless confirming they were strangers. Further than that the two clod-hoppers could not say except that the men were never there, but if they had been they were definitely strangers.

Even the proprietress began to shake her head reluctantly conceding that poverty of intellect was not the exclusive domain of foreigners, but by then they had their answers anomalous or not.

After a polite interlude for ‘two large Pastis for the husband and an orange juice for the wife’, she drove them back to the farm in silence, but once inside he suggested that they discuss recent events and possible future action.

“At last, he speaks!”

He considered her without comment.

“You have not said more than a dozen words for nearly two days, not since.......” Her voice trailed off under his fixed gaze and he filled the void.

“It’s my belief we will come under increasing pressure to leave, things designed specifically to drive us out, but I also believe we should stay for the moment at least to see just how far the opposition are prepared to go. I will make the strategic decision if we get that far, but I rely on you to ‘call it’ if you believe our situation to have become unrealistically hazardous. Are you in agreement?”

His tone was reasonable, but there was an underlying menace.

“Yes Timothy.”

She was calm and businesslike, but for the first time felt a little sorry for him as she continued to listen to his uncharacteristic vehemence.

“All the animals are gone now apart from the chickens so we only have ourselves to worry about and I would be grateful if you could explain to me what your suggestions would be were we to come under some form of attack.”

“Like the Alamo?” she smiled, but he ignored her, continuing without pause, “I don’t believe it would be overt or sustained but I do believe it’s possible there could be some attempt to gain entry. At night perhaps to further distress us or even just to ransack the place to see if anything incriminating can be found – possibly even plant something. You will obviously know more about these things than me and so I would like you to consider where we should store the guns etc and whether they should be kept to hand and whatever else you may feel to be of pertinence."

He paused while she watched him reach some private resolution.

"Contrary to apparent popular opinion, I'm not a violent man. Nevertheless it's true I'm able to 'look after myself' to some degree and as we have nothing else to do I would be grateful for any assistance or advice you might be prepared to offer in this area. I believe you were once interested in the 'level of physical support I would be able to offer' and I believe it would be advantageous if you were able to now ascertain this for yourself. Finally, I accept that to date there's been a constant level of antagonism between us for a variety of reasons and I fully accept my share of the responsibility for this. It's said however, that little dogs cease to fight amongst themselves when a big dog comes on the scene and I believe we are now faced with a big dog, if only in Dog's memory I want to give that big dog a bloody nose."

She sat and considered him almost as if for the first time. He was clearly out of his depth and upset, but everything he said was rational and analytically sound. There was no impulsive reaction to what was an obvious considerable reversal and some of the things that he had said could not have been easy, but she had a job to do and her instructions had been quite clear. Should he show signs of any form of breakdown or panic she was to get out with any information she could salvage and protect herself and her masters and if unavoidable, at his expense.

"Would you like something to eat Timothy?"

They were seated at the kitchen table, but while they had been out the fire in the stove had died down so the room was quite chilly.

"No thank you I'm not hungry and anyway I think I'll go to bed."

He stood and paused, not sure why, but she sensed his hesitation and spoke without looking up from her clasped hands.

"Following the loss of Dog I have taken the precaution of fitting some early warning devices around the property and am fairly confident that we would be made aware of any potential intruders unless they were very proficient, I therefore agree we should get a goodnight's sleep and continue tomorrow."

He sighed deeply and made to leave, "Thank you, Sun."

She finally looked up from the table and smiled, slightly uncomfortable.

"There is one thing, I do not believe we should move around alone outside at night and perhaps even be careful during the day, I believe we will have to commute from kitchen to bathroom internally as it were, through each other's rooms, is that OK?"

"Yes if you say so."

"I will always knock of course."

She could not keep the smile out of her voice, but could not see if he too was smiling, although she probably thought not.

French car registration plates identify the Department in which the car has been registered and therefore normally resides. 'Îlle de France' is not a Department, but a Region made up of seven Departments including Paris and a surrounding area of approximately 100 kilometres radius that throughout the rest of France is generally alluded to as 'parisien'.

Much of the antipathy towards Paris and the 'Parisians' stems from the days when the centre of all power and authority resided in Paris – not that long ago and even today, not that really different. Add to this an inherent disposition for deference virgin on capitulation – not a popular word in France - anyone identified to be from the 'capital' with possible authority to match was to be accommodated with some obeisance. To impress on a rural village café owner and a few of her customers that it would be better if the presence of two 'Parisians' was 'omitted' from local discussion would not be difficult.

"I cannot swear to the gun although the men we saw in the wood carried weapons that were perfectly capable, but I am sure it was a 'soft nosed' bullet a 'dumdum' to have done that amount of damage, probably with a silencer"

They had returned from the morning run and completed their workout. He had a fat lip and a sore ear as evidence of her greater speed and she a face full of Perch's recent dung to attest to his unprincipled skirmishing.

"While you consider my conclusions, I would like to shower first for as much as I liked your horse I have no desire to digest his vintage excrement and frankly, although I would understand your 'uneven-handedness' in a real situation, I fail to see the necessity during training."

She had become riled at his artful style of fighting, but it was all he knew; punch, kick, bite, scratch, more like a frightened tart than a marshal art and it worked – 'to a degree'. He would never beat her of course, but he would get her dirty sometimes.

"You hit me!"

Hardly justification for pelting her with horse-shit, but he could not get near her unless he used deception and even then it was usually only to get whacked himself.

"Yes Timothy, but I don't kill you, you wanted some instruction remember? Save the fertiliser frenzy for the real deal."

He smiled thinly despite his aching ear and noted that she chose to exit the kitchen and make her way along to the bathroom outside the house, presumably believing she was free from molestation due to her novel exfoliate. He showered after she had finished in the bathroom and then joined her again in the kitchen for a light breakfast. She of oatmeal flakes and orange juice, he of fried egg sandwiches and tea, but then he did not take sugar and had cut out the fried mushrooms and tomatoes as he was now in training. She winced at the sight of the bright yellow yoke rupturing under his bite and running down his chin, but recounted undaunted.

"All the 'embarrassing' paraphernalia of our investigation I have placed upstairs, only the shotgun would need to be taken up with us if we chose to seek refuge above – which I would recommend if we are harassed. As I have said there's an old heavy wardrobe at the end of the granary that I would like us to move adjacent to the hatch. We could then pull the ladder up behind us, replace the board that at present covers the hole and then tip-over the wardrobe on top. This would make it very difficult for anyone to follow us above from inside and now that the door at the top of the outside stairs is secured, we should be reasonable safe - for a time at least. Should anyone really want to get in of course, they could, but if we believe it's harassment that's intended rather than elimination we should be able to manage.

They will probably try to avoid any 'embarrassment' the same as we and certainly won't want dead bodies laying around – it makes life complicated - so please be careful with the shotgun, better to batter them with 'Perch's poo' rather than pepper them with shot."

She smiled, but he was busy contemplating his second sandwich.

"Should I determine any raid to be unrestrained I will inform you and we will do our best to fight our way out, although if they arrive properly prepared we would be lucky to get away. Or we could capitulate or perhaps I could 'make a run for it while you keep 'em busy' as they say in the movies."

He wiped his mouth on the back of his sleeve something he knew annoyed her, "And where do I tell them my dutiful wife's run off to when they question me? Back to where she came from?"

They stared at each other for a long time before he grinned mockingly and almost whispered, "As if a good 'catalogue' wife would leave her husband in the lurch?"

Then, totally different, almost exuberantly, "Sun, I would be most honoured if you would allow me to take you to dinner next week it's my anniversary?"

He had selected one of the better bottles of claret the restaurant had to offer and was surprised to find he had to forfeit two glasses to his companion in respect of his anniversary. Nevertheless the anniversary itself she was totally bemused he should want to acknowledge.

"And why would you want to celebrate the transgression of 'driving without due care and attention', most men would submit that the little car reversed into the van or forget about it altogether?"

So she knew all about the incident at Dover as well, which itself did not surprise him, but he was surprised at the detail - 'little car' - 'his van'.

"I didn't realise my exploits were so renowned?"

He was not bothered and he certainly did not want to add a sour note to the evening, he just wanted her to know he had noticed.

"I read the files Timothy – particularly when the work is not for those I normally toil and when it's to involve an......"

"Amateur."

He inserted the classification as she faltered then continued, "I understand and it's not a problem for me, I would sooner you be aware of everything so that you may best do your job, although I hope one day you feel able to afford me the same courtesy."

He waited long enough for the comment to be absorbed, then again continued, "After all, it's my life as well and it's that that we are celebrating actually, the start of my new life. Not the most auspicious of starts I'll warrant you, but hopefully things will improve and it'll be a happy and long one – is it to be a long one Sun?"

The question was posed with a grin and in apparent innocence, but there was intensity in his scrutiny and he waited in silence.

"My job is to assist, to do all that I can to achieve a safe and satisfactory conclusion to our assignment that is all, don't forget we are the 'good guys'."

She was serious, though not apologetic and he wondered if she was being totally candid, but for the moment he knew it was the best he would get and for some odd reason he wanted the evening to end well and so said no more.

She drove and he dosed.

The journey home took forty minutes and long before they turned from the lane into the drive the glow could be seen in the dark February sky. Perhaps it was the effects of the claret, but when they reached the farm complex, it was with a sense of measured relief he found that it was the barn and stables that were ablaze and not the farmhouse

Chapter 16

The Pompiers arrived in stages.

First came the chief of the local fire service to explain the others were on their way, then a van with a blue flashing light and the equipment for cutting cars open and finally the fire engine itself, by which time the embers were more conducive to Chestnuts than extinguishers. Being France there was much resigned shrugging only alleviated by the contents of his best whisky bottle and eventually they were left alone to consider the pyrotechnic conclusion to his celebratory dinner.

The Pompiers had used the water from their tender to damp down the extremities of the conflagration ensuring there would be no spread, but then there was not much left for it to spread to apart from the house. He had refused their request for access to the domestic supply for fear they would empty the well and in any event by the time they had arrived there was nothing of the barn and stables left to salvage.

The kitchen smelt of smoke and burnt timber where the door had remained open after their emergency telephone call for assistance and ironically the stove had gone out. Nevertheless the room was still warm which was not surprising given the equivalent of probably twenty years supply of firewood had 'gone up' in as many minutes and as many yards away. He removed the relevant electrical fuses from the board on the wall just inside the door thereby isolating the supply to the barn – just in case the supply was ever turned back on – and threw them both in the bin, turned to the cooker and put the kettle on.

"Coffee?"

She stood by the door watchful.

"You do not seem overly perturbed for someone that has just had their barn burned down?"

He indicated the coffee jar to which she nodded.

"It's not really my barn, is it?"

Before she could answer he effected the question rhetorical, "It has been obvious to me for sometime that whatever the outcome including were we to succeed beyond our wildest dreams, I would never be able to stay here or return here. How could I after incurring the wrath of such a powerful elite?"

He gazed without seeing at the slowly boiling kettle continuing, as if to himself, "If Mr. Reece has been generous in his offer of remuneration it's now apparent it's because he knows I would never be able to collect. If of course I was to be allowed to get far enough that I might try."

As he spoke the last few words he turned his head and looked hard into her eyes, but as ever they were blank.

She took a seat at the table, "Your not becoming paranoid are you Timothy?"

It was her turn to give him no time to answer, "I am not an assassin and your dealings with your masters are your affair not mine, if you have been found wanting in your judgement or have misread the circumstances it is not my fault, you made the deal."

He swore violently at the watched kettle that would not boil, "Like I had a lot of choice."

She stood from the table and crossed to the door, "I applaud you for the fashion in which you have accepted recent reversals Timothy, but please don't 'go all maudlin and self-pitying on me now'. We still have a lot to do – Oh and I think I will pass on the coffee, Goodnight Timothy."

She closed the door behind her and moved across the room, but still heard the coffee cup smash on the wall above the door.

There was a problem with the insurance.

Ominously it was not just with the buildings insurance – that was still under assessment – but it appeared that there was some confusion concerning their social security status. Apparently the Farmers Union were experiencing difficulty securing the details regarding his arrival in France. The reference numbers that he had given were not known to them, it was as if he had never been a member of the Union and certainly his wife had not. Was there any other information that could be forwarded, for at the moment it would appear they had no social security insurance cover – health, pension, accident, in fact, even the right to continually reside in France?

Sun spent many hours over the next few days arguing their case with the Union office and many copies of many documents were posted from the local village post office, but all to no avail, apparently no evidence of their membership could be found at the Union office. The fact that there was clear evidence in the form of all that could reasonably be expected, copies of applications, approvals, membership reference numbers, was all ignored, as if it did not exist. But apparently if the Union office said it did not exist, it didn't – the problem was if it didn't, did they?

"The insurance company says they can't pay out on the barn as it was a farmer's policy and they are informed by the

Union that you are not a farmer, therefor you made a false statement on the policy application and the insurance is automatically nullified."

She was reading from today's pile of 'good-news' letters as he washed his hands after rescuing more 're-burnable' firewood from the remains of the barn.

"We could put in a personal appearance at the Union office, you could swear at them, perhaps even throw dung in someone's face?"

He knew she wanted to visit the Union office and speak to a senior official the like of which would never speak to her on the telephone however much she pleaded with an underling. He understood her frustration, but was very apprehensive about the risk of either of them being identified from the earlier visits to obtain the initial copies of his grant applications – true and false. It may be that now all was known as to their ruse to obtain the copies, but he doubted it and if not it was better it stayed that way, anything to stop anyone over reacting.

"No, we sit tight for the moment."

She said nothing, her displeasure transparent in her handling of the letter opener, "Oh, more good-news," She smiled humourlessly, "The Bank want to see you as you appear to have made a false statement on your account application. It appears you do not work in France and therefore should have had an 'overseas resident's account'."

He persisted with his hand wiping oblivious of their arid condition, but focused on his response.

"Please ring them and explain about the fire and that I will visit as soon as I can, also ask if they would be good enough to prepare copies of all statements since the account was opened.

It's under a couple of years and there won't be that many - make a point of implying ours were destroyed in the fire."

She made a note on the letter and turned to the next, but he distracted her with his next request.

"I would be grateful if you would make us an appointment at the Doctors."

She looked up surprised, "You're not feeling well?"

He shook his head.

"Then what shall I make the appointment for?"

He shrugged slightly apathetic like a real French farmer, "I don't know - what do you normally make appointments at the Doctors for?"

"Sexual problems."

He held her virtuous gaze, his apathy mutating to irritation.

"It's true Timothy, a married couple making an appointment would often be about contraception – or perhaps in this country the lack of it - or those little nasty fungi couples get from time to time, surely a man of your experience must know about things like that?"

There had been more harmony in the dealings between them since his little speech, but this was an area where she would never let an opportunity to cause him discomfiture pass.

"Tell them I have a sore throat and I've not been able to sleep properly since the fire; I just want to see what happens about the insurance."

She sighed, feigning contemplation, "OK, but couldn't I have an 'internal' and you a sperm count, the proprietress at the café will be so disappointed when she finds out in was only a sore throat?"

He ignored her and went back outside to get his hands dirty again.

The lady Doctor took his blood pressure and looked down his throat and advised the wife to assure her husband that there was nothing wrong some antibiotics and rest following the shock of the fire would not put right. Sun in turn informed the Doctor that she had thought the sore throat to be inconsequential, but 'you know what men are' and assured the Doctor with an elaborate wink that she could vouch first hand that there was nothing wrong with his blood pressure.

He sat with an inane smile on his face throughout the whole proceeding as any nincompoop that did not speak the language would, hoping that one day he would have the opportunity to repay his 'wife' in the embarrassment stakes.

At the end of the interview they offered their insurance card to authorise payment and it was refused by the automated system. Three times the Doctor tried and three times it was refused. Finally he paid by cheque wondering how long it would be before that facility was prohibited to them and they drove home.

They did not speak until they were inside when he handed her the bag of three different types of antibiotics the Doctor had supplied them with, suggesting she put it with the other 'emergency stores' in case they might be useful. France has one of the finest medical systems in the world, but if there was one peculiar inclination that he had become almost instantly aware of following a bout of flu soon after his arrival, the excessive prescribing of antibiotics. Often thrice as strong and always thrice as many as in the UK, the tendency led to some very sick septic tanks and some very robust rodents.

He considered raising the subject of her comments to the Doctor, but decided against it, not the most comfortable territory for him.

"How much lead time do we need should we decide to run?"

She was immediately serious.

"I need only the time to pack two suitcases, one to remain with us, the other must be safely disposed of as soon as possible – we must not be caught with it, but there are other considerations. We cannot use the car or our present identities; if at all possible we need to disappear. I should also audit any of your personal effects you intend to leave behind to ensure there is nothing incriminating."

He considered for a moment, but it took no longer, most of his personal effects were not personal.

"I'll put in a corner of my room everything I intend to take, then you can look through the rest – including everything in the house – perhaps you could do it today?"

She asked the obvious, "Are we thinking of leaving then?"

He thought it would soon be time and hoped it was not just his fear, obviously he could not be certain about the timing, but he was certain about the fear.

"I've a feeling it could be quite soon."

She looked at him appraisingly, "What's the feeling like, an afraid feeling?"

He smiled despite the snub, "Definitely."

It was her turn to look amused, but she did not, far from it "Good, no one wants to work with a hero, especially an amateur one, you tend to live longer."

He had never heard her speak with such venom and bitterness. Slightly confused and with his confidence certainly not enhanced, he went to his room and selected the personal effects he intended to flee with, but there weren't many. There was his old guitar and now not so new radio cassette player, but the remainder was easily enclosed in a somewhat smaller suitcase than the one he had needed in Hampshire over two years before, it would appear his life had evolved to a negative degree.

A week passed before they visited the bank and compared with how things were going in general it was a relatively painless exercise. The manager was very polite and explained it was merely a formality that the account be amended to comply with his 'overseas resident' status. It appeared it was not uncommon, apparently people often ticked the wrong box by mistake, but a signature was necessitated to put things right.

The manager was relieved to find the young foreigner quite happy to comply after the situation had been explained to him by his wife, in fact the only thing that seemed to concern the farmer or whatever, was obtaining copies of recent statements – the originals lost in a recent fire. As this was initially all the somewhat dense client could concentrate on the copies were immediately supplied and sure enough the essential signature was obtained and a potentially awkward and distasteful situation averted.

"Are they the same?"

She was driving while he compared the copies of his bank statements with the originals he had secreted in his shoulder bag.

“The numbers are the same, debits, credits and balances, but the monthly standing order to the Union has been changed to an organisation I have never heard of - it has the word ‘agricultural’ in the title, but its not the Union, ergo no subs, no membership.”

They continued in silence for a while and eventually arrived on the outskirts of the village where she took the slight detour that would take them passed the café-bar. This had been their routine for some weeks now whenever passing through and today it proved fruitful.

“Pull past and park fifty metres or so further on.”

She did as she was bidden.

“Walk back and buy me some cigarettes – ‘I’m still not feeling well – bad throat – smoking doesn’t help – Ah men!’ that sought of thing, see if you can get a look, but don’t make them suspect anything.”

She let herself out of the car whispering, “I know my job Timothy.”

He leaned forward and watched her walk back to the bar in the review passenger door mirror, it may of course be a coincidence, but parked outside the café-bar he had spotted a car with a Parisian registration plate.

She was not gone for long and he waited until they were once more on the move.

“Well?”

It appeared that there were two men in the café seated at the same table that he had seen two strangers on the previous occasion.

When later at the farm she had quizzed him in detail as to the exact positioning of the men he had previously seen he did not realise the pertinence until she had explained. Being animals of habit, humans will often stand, sit and even park in the same place - oddly if only having visited a location once before. In general the men fitted his description, but obviously she could not be certain and he most definitely did not want to come face to face and make them aware their presence had been detected.

He sat in deep contemplation staring at the dregs in his mug. Remarkably it had been coffee, he must have said yes at the wrong time, but it did not matter as he had not tasted it anyway, then a thought suddenly struck him, "Are you instructed to inform London when we decided to 'evacuate'?"

She hesitated before answering with her own question, "Would you prefer me not to?"

He joined the game of verbal pin-pong, "Are you prepared to?"

She shrugged and spoke with exaggerated self-ridicule.

"A Security Field Agent's decision, assuming reasonable cause is identified, so what is the reason?"

"Security."

She smiled with fake benevolence at his one word response.

"More please."

He winced, "I don't know exactly when we'll 'go', but it will probably be soon and if London takes some pre-emptive action and we have not gone we'll be severely exposed, plus I don't have a great faith in government departments. My grandmother always told me ‘don’t tell anyone what you’re doing ‘til you’ve done it’.”

She considered him for some while.

“You don’t trust London Timothy that’s clear, you probably don’t trust many people at all, but do you trust me, it’s important, the next phase is likely to be difficult?”

He in turn took his time. He wanted to trust her, no one likes to be afraid alone, but the reality was, as ever, he had little choice - maudlin or otherwise.

“Yes.”

Unimpressed, she could not keep the irritation out of her voice, “Having had to think about it for so long is most unflattering to me Timothy, but now that you have attested to such a belief and at the risk of contravening your granny’s advice, when do we ‘go’?”

He stood up, “We start now.”

Chapter 17

"I'm really sorry it's now such short notice, my wife promised me faithfully she would remember to telephone ahead before I left England."

But he could not really blame her he had gone on to explain, the poor woman had had such a sad time since the death of her Mother and now with her Father taking it so badly. It looked like another year would pass before they would spend time in his adored 'La Belle France'. The receptionist at the caravan centre was very sympathetic and assured him that there would be no problem, people were often coming and going at short notice. She would arrange for all the paperwork to be prepared before his arrival and ensure he and his camper would be on their way back to England without delay, but it was a shame about the holiday, still perhaps later in the year?

He had made the telephone call from the first village on the road to the main town and railway station. Once there he exited the car and entered the booking hall going immediately to the toilets where he combed his hair, counted slowly to ten, donned his spectacles and walked out. Having not met anyone on the way in or overtly interested in his movements, he walked directly to the taxi rank and instructed the driver to take him to the caravan centre. True to her word, once there it took very little time to complete a minimal of paperwork and leaving a generous tip for the inconvenience he had caused, he was soon cautiously exiting the courtyard of the caravan centre to the receptionist's pleasant reminder to 'drive on the right'.

He repeated the journey he had made a few months before, but this time in the opposite direction, exiting the AutoRoute at the same service station complex and parking some distance from the amenities alongside a number of other apparent 'overnight' campers and caravans. He locked the camper after first putting a hand written cardboard sign in the window that announced in English 'collect on Saturday' and walked into the service station complex. This time without hesitation, he crossed the AutoRoute using the pedestrian bridge and walked into the car park where he paused briefly before being collected by the most modest of cars.

When they returned home, there was still enough light left in the day to complete their preparations. She had her two suitcases packed - a small one she would keep and the larger one that must be ditched. These together with his personal effects were hauled above together with the paperwork they had collected and a few basics that would be useful. Half a dozen litre-bottles of water some food and the mattress from his bed – and a bucket, which he had thought of, but she could not bear to!

Before he left that evening for the bar he remarked that it was probably all for nothing but better to be 'safe than sorry' and other such platitudes to which she assured him he was right. It was probably the first time they were both certain that they were seeking to deceive one another, but that is what people often do in times of trepidation, regardless that it rarely works.

It was dark by the time he entered the bar and it was like a scene from a cowboy film, everyone fell instantly silent and just looked at the opened door. Pretending not to notice he walked to the bar and pointed to the cigarette shelf at the back as was his habit, then ordered a beer in his appalling accent. Turning from the bar and ignoring his usual spot he took the table next to four men that were dressed like hunters, bidding them a mangled 'bon-jaw' confirming his paucity of language. He pulled a tattered English newspaper from the inside pocket of his coat and became absorbed in three week old stories of footballers and their wives.

Two of the men had been in the café-bar for most of the day and although it is the tendency for the French to drink little and certainly not often - two thimbles of rosé wine amounting to a good night out - most of the day is a long time. The appearance of an ignorant Englishman was too much for their natural courtesy – already significantly lower than that of the locals because of whence they hailed – and so remarks were bandied back and forth as to their solitary neighbour's character and personage in general.

He of course remained totally oblivious, only once raising his head from the paper and smiling unknowingly at a particularly boisterous exchange. Eventually it was time for him to leave and so standing he returned his glass to the bar, thereby proving conclusively he was from a different country if not a different planet and turning, wished the assemblage a polite 'Oruv-wah'.

She looked almost worried when he entered the kitchen, but it was probably the candle light.

"Anything?"

Yes, this time there was something.

The many months he had painstaking masqueraded as a non-French speaking bucolic oaf had suddenly paid a dividend. He could not be sure if it had been in keeping with some farsighted plan Mr. Reece had conceived, but he could be certain that any alternative benefit could not have been greater.

They came at two o'clock in the morning.

Dog would have warned them if he had still been alive as would the early warning devices she had installed around the property that were now locked in the expendable suitcase, but neither were necessary. Their intentions had been clearly overheard in the café-bar. Even the time and what they might do to the 'slit-eyed bitch' if they got the chance and the 'roast beef' if he bent over long enough, the cause of particularly loud guffaws – 'and look, the silly Pratt was smiling at the thought of it!'

He had taken the first watch from nine until one o'clock, unable in any case to sleep after his experience in the bar, while she on the other hand had been asleep within minutes of stretching out on the mattress. His watch alarm informed him of the change-over hour and her pencil torchlight permitted a smooth and silent transition. He could not envisage achieving any rest and so was astonished to be awoken by a hand over his mouth and a whisper in his ear.

"They have approached from the lane and are obviously overconfident, perhaps the effect of drink, they are not skilled operatives, but potentially dangerous nonetheless, be careful - and don't kill anyone."

Then the hand, the whisper and most of his courage were gone.

He had his tasks, but first he sat up on the mattress and allowed his eyes time to adjust to the dim moonlight that rose into the granary from above the walls that ran the length of the house. Here the roof rafters extended over the walls and created a space equivalent to the depth of the rafter timbers between the tiles on top and the wall underneath. As the extension was perhaps a couple of feet and obviously at the angle of the roof, it did not permit a line of sight into the granary, but ventilation that for the original purpose of the chamber was important for the drying process.

Once acclimatised he moved cautiously to the end of the building opposite that of the external door and took hold of the shotgun, which had been leant against the wall in the corner. He was careful, as he knew the gun to be loaded and checking that the 'safety' was still on, took up his position directly beneath a ventilation aperture about ten inches square and just above head height. There were two of these apertures at each end of the building that he had blocked with polythene film wedged in place within the openings with short lengths of timber. The apertures were inaccessible from outside except with the aid of a ladder – no longer available as the other extension had burnt along with the barn – but he could open them from within by simply pulling out the timber wedges. Then by standing on one of the two kitchen-chairs that had previously been brought up, he would be able to see out of a very tolerable gunport.

He waited.

She was not visible, but he knew she should be by the internal entrance hatch. Again he had used shortish lengths of timber to prop the old wardrobe that had at first been tipped on its long edge and then face down onto the timber supports over the hatch. It rested at less than forty degrees to the horizontal and kicking away the supports would bring it crashing down on top of the board that at present covered the hatch. Before the wardrobe attained its final place it would be possible to clearly hear what was going on downstairs, until of course the hatch was spotted and then the wardrobe had to plunge to protect their eyrie.

He thought he heard noises from outside, but was not sure, then there was the sound of breaking glass and he was sure. The bolts on the kitchen door were slid emitting the tell-tale momentary screech and the door creaked its opening salutation. He was amazed he could hear all this from where he waited at the end of the granary even though he knew all the internal doors to have been left open for such a purpose. There was the noise of breaking crockery from the kitchen and voices, but he could not make out what was being said until, suddenly, they grew louder and it was clear there was a disagreement, as to how the intruders thought they should precede.

Most appeared to favour a mild destruction of the decor and contents to follow the search as instructed, while one was keen to make the acquaintance of the residents. The sound of breaking glass and tumbling furniture suggested the majority view to a large extent had prevailed, but a blow on the underneath of the hatch cover suggested not exclusively. He actually heard another of the kitchen chairs dragged from the room and hoped she was alive to what was afoot, for soon the cover was raised just enough for a torch and the hand holding it to protrude onto the granary floor. With only the added height that a chair would give it was obviously difficult. But the torch and hand did progress a little further into the granary before she kicked the supports away and the wardrobe smashed down on top of them producing an impressive series of screeches worthy of any eyrie.

"Alamo!"

She screamed the word stepping back to cover the wardrobe with the gun. He did not see her move, but could not mistake the signal although he remembered finding the choice of watchword appreciably more amusing at the time than now.

Regardless he stepped up onto the chair, poked the shotgun through the polythene towards the night sky, switched off the safety and yet again wishing he had remembered his ear-protectors, pulled the trigger.

In his enthusiasm not to let the side down – or panic to be more precise – he pulled both triggers, one after the other, nearly dislocating his shoulder and slipping sideways off the chair smashing his watch on the side wall. He was supposed to count to five between each shot, so had already blotted his copybook, but luckily his underwear remained unsullied and it had definitely sounded very impressive, which he was pleased about because at the moment it felt like it was the last thing he would ever hear.

He could not remember how many times he stood on and off the chair, but nearly jumped out of his skin, placing his undergarments in even greater jeopardy, when she touched him on the arm and gestured he terminate his barrage. She asked if he was OK, probably in a whisper, but it was all the same to him for he could hear nothing so he sat down on the chair and began to shake. She gently touched his cheek and indicated that he should take some deep breathes and leaning forward whispered in his ear that he should remain where he was, and 'sit still'. Endorsing her instructions with hand signs she finally began a tour of the granary perimeter - pausing every few paces to listen for noise from outside - regularly moving back to the wardrobe and listening - often for longer periods.

He did not know how long this exercise lasted, he seemed to have lost all sense of time like his shattered watch, but when she finally returned he had stopped shaking, ceased to hyperventilate and could hear again, but not as well as before.

"I think they have gone, but I need to go and check, you must stay here."

"No," his whisper was explosive, "they could still be there, it's too dangerous."

He could not see her clearly, but heard the familiar chuckle.

"Oh Timothy, and I didn't think you cared."

In that one instant he hated her. She was not frightened and he was, it did not matter that this was her world, for the first time he wanted to be an equal, it was a strange feeling.

"Now, you must help me with the wardrobe and the ladder. We will slide the wardrobe off the hatch and lower the ladder. You will then sit behind the wardrobe and wait for me to return. If it's not me, you will fire one warning shot and tell them to leave. If anyone comes up after that you will shoot them, do you understand?"

He nodded, but.

"I thought we didn't want dead bodies lying around?"

"If it's not me that comes up the ladder there will already be dead bodies lying around."

He began to vibrate again, "That's comforting."

They moved the wardrobe, but despite her urging it was not possible to perform the task without a reasonable amount of noise, which he pointed out as the floor was solid, would be much more noticeable below. She shrugged and stood to one side covering the hatch as he lowered the ladder.

"Perhaps we should go together......." He began, but annoyed she waved him to silence.

“I have told you what to do, please do not interfere with me, I know what I am doing, do what I say.” The last few words were spat out and he acquiesced.

She slowly descended the ladder and waited at the bottom for so long he thought perhaps something was amiss then just as he was about to ask he saw her pencil light flicker and she was gone. He sat down and began to count.

Not actually favouring the ‘one little second’ method, he just counted slowly. As he counted he checked off each approximate sixty seconds on his fingers, a minute a finger, not easy when you were holding a loaded shotgun, you just had to remember where your were, but it became more difficult when he ran out of fingers.

So it was over ten minutes.

That seemed a long time to have a quick ‘look see’ to find out if there was anyone about, he started to count from scratch again. When he ran out of fingers this time he began to get seriously worried. Twenty minutes seemed an eternity just to check all was clear.

He started all over again, but half way through whispered ‘bollocks’ to himself and slowly began to descend the ladder.

Chapter 18

Descending a ladder with a loaded shotgun is not easy; trying to manage the feat in silence further enhances the risk of removing ones head with the product of an explosive charge. Eventually achieving *terra firma* intact however, he turned to discover his first mistake; he could see nothing and had forgotten to bring one of the torches. He waited for his eyes to adjust, but as all the shutters were closed it was darker downstairs in the house than in the granary, so unless he waited until morning he would have to move as things were.

The bathroom was the nearest point of access to the outside world and probably the least cluttered – fewer ornaments to break in a bathroom – and so he set off in that direction immediately stumbling over a chair that should not have been there. Hence, sliding his feet instead of stepping, after a few slithers the barrel of the shotgun struck the wall at the side of the bathroom door and he edged carefully through the opening. Continuing his sledding across the tiled floor, he reached the external door and was surprised to find it ajar, thankfully allowing a little light in and indicating he would not be totally blind once outside. He eased the door open further and stood for a little surveying the area in front of the house.

There was no noise and no movement and he did not know what to do, the tranquillity seemed to carry its own menace. Wondering if perhaps sitting upstairs counting was perhaps not as abhorrent as he had initially concluded, he carefully stepped beyond the threshold of the door and edged along the front of the building towards the nearest corner. From the angle of the diffused moonlight leaking through the cloud this end should be in shadow and he thought probably the best place to tarry and ponder his options. Sure enough as soon as he rounded the corner of the house he was obscured in deep shadow and was able to turn and scrutinise the front yard with more assurance.

It was the sensation of not being alone that stirred him, even before he felt the cold round metal barrel touch the back of his neck.

"What the fuck are you doing?"

It was more of a hiss than a whisper and it was very likely he would now have to change his pants, but at least he still had his head on.

"Language Sun, language."

He heard a slow expelling of air and wondered about his head again, but when the whispers came they were rational if incensed.

"You make more noise than an armoured division and just when our friends were thinking of leaving. Now they know at least one of us is out it is likely to rekindle their interest."

Duly chastised he asked the obvious, "Where are they?"

The barn had been built largely of timber, but there was an internal stone corner section of the old stables that remained standing, furthest from the house, about head height and three or four metres on each flank.

"Behind the corner of the stables, three have smoked three cigarettes and whispered profanities and insults to each other and one has suggested it was a shame they couldn't get rid of us like they did the dog."

So, finally, he felt the hollow feeling in his gut build and along with it his courage or to be more accurate according to his grandmother his temper.

"Have they got guns?"

She could not be certain, but had not seen any and although they obviously had access to them and would have taken them on an assignment like the despatching of Dog it was very likely they would not on tonight's errand. Should anything go wrong it would be a very different situation if four trespassers were discovered heavily armed rather than say four drunken strangers losing their way whilst taking a shortcut home from a disco or party?

He looked down at his hands and was almost surprised to see that they were not glowing for he felt incandescent with rage.

"Did you know, unlike the idiotic laws concerning burglary and trespass in the UK, you won't be charged if you shoot an intruder In France – only if you shoot 'em in the back?" And with that he stepped forward out of the shadows lifted the shotgun and fired at the remains of his stables.

Initially he fired twice from the same spot then walked steadily forwards as he reloaded. She may have commented, but the noise of the discharges had debilitated his hearing once more and in any event it would have made no difference. The distance from the corner of the house to the remaining corner of the stables was some fifty metres, but he proceeded at an angle to the spot which would eventually allow him sight along the rear of one of the walls making up the corner. He paced steadily halting each time he had completed his re-loading firing always at the walls themselves, never seeking to hit anything or anyone that ran from the spot, but making it most unpleasant for anyone seeking to maintain a position behind the walls.

He still had what appeared a pocket full of cartridges when he reached a position where he could see along the back of one of the walls forming the corner, but there was no one there. His first frenzy dispelled, he now considered his position, to continue around would place the corner between him and the house and possible in the direction the visitors may have fled. He could not be sure of course that they were not sheltering behind the other wall, but regardless he felt it better to return to the house and so turning strode back the way he had come, never taking his eyes from the target. He adopted the same position just around the corner of the building in the shadows and waited.

"They waited until you were almost in line with the back wall and then made a run for it down the drive, keeping the wall between you and them. One of them was limping so I assume some stray buckshot caught him or perhaps a ricochet."

His ears were still ringing so presumably she was speaking quite loudly.

"Do you think they will come back?"

His voice sounded strange, as if from afar and there was a catch in it that he did not feel - or did he?

"No, they will assume we will call the police and it could become very awkward for them. I think it's over for tonight. Now I think you should go inside and wait by the toilet, you are going to be sick."

He opened his mouth to contest her prognosis, but felt the bile rise in his throat and was only just in time, albeit even then it was the bidet being closer than the pan, but then you can't have everything.

They arrived at the Gendarmerie at nine o'clock to complete their statements with regard to the burglary. There was the usual shrugging and accompanying grimaces – the Gendarmes shrug as much as anyone else in France, particularly when lorry drivers block the roads – but it did not take long. The Gendarmes believed it was probably *romaniche,* the gypsies – who were blamed for half the crime in rural France and therefor obviously never solved or even expected to be – at least they had that in common with the UK. More shrugging suggested the interview was at an end and it occurred to him that it must have been like this on the Maginot Line – lots of shrugging and wincing as the Panzers drove passed. It appeared the only thing the Gendarmes were concerned about was some reports of shooting in the early hours, but they were unable to help them there – obviously they'd had enough to think about at the time with the burglary.

They drove from the police station directly to the village café-bar where there was a distinct lack of strange number-plates and so she entered alone to buy more cigarettes. She also explained about the burglary and how upsetting it had been and that they were going to spend a couple of days with a friend of hers in the north to give her nerves a chance to recover – it really had been most distressing. She related how the Gendarmes had arrived in the early hours following their emergency call and how she had just come from the Gendarmerie having completed the report and what with the fire and all – it really did seem as if everything was against them. After leaving the café they drove back to the house for the last time and checked nothing had been left behind that should not have been.

Prior to telephoning the Gendarmes in the early hours of the morning they had loaded all that was to be taken into the car and parked it away from casual view, although only his guitar and one suitcase was visible on the backseat.

They made some brief modifications to the interior in line with her police report and story of the morning, but it did not really matter now.

"Ready?"

She had hardly spoken to him other than what was minimally required since his one man 'Gunfight at the OK Corral' and he hoped that it was now done and things would gradually improve, but he was wrong.

"I will not comment on the fact that you totally usurped my position and my responsibilities and ignored my instructions in an area for which you have no expertise or training, but I would like to make one thing very clear. I have never seen such a display of shear stupidity and although I'm charged with looking after you, if anything of the kind happens again, you are on your own."

He smiled like a naughty school boy and shrugging – when in Rome.

"You said they didn't have guns."

His smile did nothing to alleviate her hostility, if anything her voice was even harder, "I said I was not certain, I said I had not seen any. Please don't play the little boy lost with me Timothy, in this business one day your temper will get you killed."

She raised her hand as he went to equivocate, "You may still think it's not your business, but I bet it felt like your business last night, now please remember what I've said, if you compromise our situation again I will drop you."

With that she calmly walked to the car and sat in the front passenger seat and waited for him to say goodbye to his farm.

There are many rivers in France and many bridges.

Some of the great watercourses are hundreds of metres wide as they near the end of their journey to the sea, great torrents of fast flowing foaming runoffs from the product of each new years rainy season. Naturally, not all are wide, but still deep enough to be part of the many hundreds of miles of navigable waterways that stretch throughout the country permitting passage from the north to the south, the Atlantic to the Mediterranean. These smaller rivers too have many bridges, but often like the tributaries they span, are quieter, more seclude, less accessible.

They had stopped the car on the middle of the bridge and were now gazing down over the railings into the waters below. Arm in arm they looked like any young couple charmed by the gurgling surge and she turned and waved to the elderly farmer as he piloted his tractor and muck-spreader passed the car.

'What it must be like to be young again' the old man surmised as the tractor turned the corner on the other side of the bridge and began to climb through the dense woodland on either side of the lane.

As soon as the tractor was out of sight he opened the near-side rear door and with some difficulty extracted the heavy suitcase. She helped him lift it onto the handrail and omitting the traditional count of three they pushed the case over into the river below. Not waiting to see how it landed – they were hardly going to go down for it – they got back in the car and were soon well away from such fluvial delights.

They arrived in the main town around lunchtime and dined in a café within a shopping mall they had never visited before. After lunch over coffee, he attended to an urgent script while she visited a supermarket and a number of other stores before returning to find him ready to leave. He helped her carry the shopping bags back to the car where she waited while he returned to the mall and the row of public telephone booths the like of which were becoming ever rarer in the land. He entered the second one he examined not keen on the aroma of urine the first one had exhibited and dialled a now familiar number. This time he asked specifically for the secretary to the Director of the Bureau and when the woman came on the line officiously gave her no opportunity to query anything he said, after all he was from Strasbourg.

'We are the antifraud inspectors that were forced to postpone an earlier visit and are at present travelling and should be arriving late this afternoon could she please inform the gentleman they had spoken to before?'

'We hope to be finished tonight as it is only a cursory review or it may run into tomorrow morning if we find anything unusual, although they hoped not as they were due back in the office tomorrow afternoon for a meeting.'

'It would obviously be a lot quicker and easier for all concerned if they did not find anything odd, could she please pass the message on as he had to rush?'

He walked casually back to the car and opening the boot removed two cheap briefcases placing them on the recently emptied back seat before driving carefully out of the enormous car park. They drove for sometime before he parked in a quiet crescent and in a similar position to that that he had chosen some weeks before. They got out of the car and avoiding the two houses where they had been engaged in devout discussions on their earlier excursion to leafy suburbia, knocked only on the doors of those in need of redemption, but patently against it if the reception they received was definitive.

Unbowed they meandered from rejection to rebuff until finally not long after the owner of a neighbouring rather flamboyant residence arrived home unexpectedly early from work letting himself in through the electric gates, they too tired of their toil and returned to their car parked further round the curve.

He could not remember the last time he had been to the movies. Whenever it was, it most certainly was not the kind of film he was squirming in front of now.

They had had a late, light meal and he had had nothing to drink - which was not easy as most of the last six hours had been spent in a variety of bars as well as the restaurant. It had been her idea to take themselves out of circulation and spend a couple of hours or more at the cinema catching the midnight performance as it is in the early hours it is better not to be seen loitering. A good idea and he had agreed without even considering what the main feature might be, but then he supposed, at this time of night no one really wanted to see the Calvary coming over the hill to the rescue. What with that and the governments hunger for ever-more little Frenchmen he wondered how the illicit pornographic film industry managed with this amount of incursion onto their territory.

She of course was enjoying the interlude.

He had no knowledge as to her taste in films or pornography for that matter, but as ever she was certainly enjoying his discomfiture, which had as much to do with being seated so close to her as the writhing on the screen. It was amazing after living together for over six months he should be so aware of her proximity, it was most confusing, presumably to do with the 'boy-girl at the pictures' scenario, nothing to worry about, but then she touched his leg and he nearly jumped out of his skin. Chuckling almost uncontrollably and gesturing to the screen, he felt her breath on his ear as she leaned towards him and whisper, "Don't worry Timothy, is doesn't always have to take as long as that!"

He hated her again, but at least this time he had a grin on his face - but then it was dark and no one could see.

Chapter 19

He rolled the car to a halt half on and half off the pavement just like some others parked around the crescent. From where he sat he could see the electric gates of the flamboyant residence, but they were still fifty metres or so distant.

He waited.

She had exited the car where the crescent first met the main road and had approached on foot while he had continued passed, entering at the other end and stopping before the house, thus he had no idea where she was at present. The intention was for her to use the neighbouring un-gated drive to get off the road and then climb the wall that divided the gardens of the two properties. It was a six foot wall which she assured him would cause her no problem, but from there it was a matter of luck as to whether their friendly Union manager had locked his boot or car or taken the briefcases inside the house.

They knew the car was customarily left outside the garages, but were not totally certain what had happened to the briefcases. He was of the opinion that the man would not want evidence of his dishonesty soiling his new carpets and the general ambience of his new home, she was not so sure. In any event they both agreed that it was likely that at best she would have to break into the boot of the car and then there was the problem of the car alarm, but she was optimistic it could be done. He just had to wait.

An hour passed.

He had promised faithfully that whatever happened he would not leave the car until she arrived or signalled him, but it was becoming increasingly difficult to sit still despite the events of the previous night. He tried counting, but even with all his fingers unencumbered with firearms it yielded little relief and he had just started to practice counting with his eyes shut for ever increasing periods when there was the unmistakable two tone siren of a car alarm. He immediately started the engine and eased forward down the crescent still with the lights off when suddenly he saw her run out in front of him from the neighbouring drive lugging two briefcases. He accelerated until he was level with her, slowing just enough for her to throw the bags in and jump in after them, before again accelerating away, not turning the car lights on until they were onto the main road.

"Drive carefully."

She said nothing more as she removed her black gloves and ski mask replacing them with her glasses and a berry she had taken to wearing recently. She stuffed the redundant items of clothing and the shoulder bag she had taken into a black bin liner and then wrestled the two briefcases inside as well; topping the plastic sack off with some shirts, blouses and knickers she emptied from a paper bag stored under the seat. She then manhandled the whole into the back passenger foot-well behind the driver's seat, which to all intents and purposes now looked like a bag of dirty laundry – knickers on top. Finally she donned her most unflattering anorak and sat low in the seat looking straight ahead and in the reflection of the headlamps he would have sworn her eyes grew narrower and wider like a good 'catalogue' wife. Only her slightly quickened breathing gave lie to the fact that she was totally serene.

He drove without comment taking the ring road round the town then the exit that would take them to the AutoRoute and which coincidentally was in the direction of the farm which was lucky because as they rounded the exit ramp there was a police road block.

Beside him he felt her stiffen, while he felt strangely assured, “Don’t worry, I haven’t had a drop all night!”

The humour was lost on her so as he slowed, deliberately taking time to reach the flashing blue lights he spoke quietly and quickly.

“We are on our way home from visiting friends in the Paris, we were going to stay, but I panicked because I was worried about looters and wanted to get back to the farm. Do they have any news about the burglary? Make that your first question. I will keep insisting you repeatedly ask it, make them contact our police station if you can, if not why not? I will become agitated. We will have a ‘domestic’ in the car that should amuse them!”

He wound down the window and asked in English before the Gendarme could speak, “Do you have any news yet? Well does he?”

He turned to his wife and she repeated the same question in French. Slightly taken aback the Officer signalled a colleague to join them while asking for his driving licence. He rummaged in his wallet for the document.

“Well do they? Ask them again? They must have some news by now.”

She did as she was bidden, but was answered with a request to state where they were going. She explained about the aborted visit to her friends in Paris, but before she finished her husband again insisted she ask if there was any news of the burglary this time joining in, “Bad man, steal, bad man, you have bad man?”

The Officer shone his torch into the back of the car illuminating what appeared to be a bag of dirty washing, certainly a pair of knickers that had seen better days. Exiting the car at the behest of the Officer he opened the boot while noting the second officer returning to the van. Sure enough, inside were a couple of overnight bags and what looked like an old guitar case which when opened demonstrated its purpose by exposing an old guitar.

"Bad man, you know, telephone village Gendarme."

He blew positively into the breathalyser, confident of a contrary result and so it proved coincidentally around the time his car registration obviously came back on the police van computer proving where they lived even if not that they had been burgled.

"Poor cow, what a nutter!"

The Officer shook his head as he and his colleague watched the car drive away.

"OK?"

He was relieved, but she seemed unreasonably subdued.

"I don't like policeman."

He laughed, louder than he might have due to the release of nervous tension, "I thought you were a policeman."

She sighed deeply, "No Timothy, I am not a policeman."

They drove on in silence until they came to the AutoRoute which he joined heading towards Paris.

"We don't have an alibi now if we are stopped."

She was right it would be unlikely they could bluff there way through another checkpoint driving in the opposite direction.

"I know, but they don't normally stop traffic on the AutoRoute until the toll booths and the camper is parked in the services before the toll and we can still get off this free section of AutoRoute before the toll and head cross country, it's just this bit that's dodgy."

They drove on in silence, but after what seemed an eternity he pulled onto the slip road for the service station complex. Driving slowly once in the parking area, he stopped on the far side of the camper where they quickly unloaded everything from the car on to the tarmac and she drove the car on to the main parking area. By the time she returned he had everything inside the camper with the engine running and they were soon rejoining the AutoRoute, but he changed his original plan and pulled off at the next rest and picnic area, parking as far as he could from the few other vehicles.

It was still not light and the middle of March and even a camper van out of season in the early hours could be conspicuous, it would be better to wait. They drew the curtains and by the glow of one reading light unpacked their few belongings. For the time being the two stolen briefcases were placed in the toilet while almost all their old clothes were dumped in the bin liner along with every other item that might connect them with their recent passed. The camper had been delivered with some clothes and toiletries and to these she added the product of the previous afternoons shopping expedition. Thus they soon had who they once were in the bin liner and who they now were in the wardrobes, Mr. and Mrs. Mills of Bromley in Kent.

The dawn began to glimmer through the thin curtain and he wanted to be on the road as soon as possible, but there were a couple of things before they left. He checked outside, walking through the picnic area to ensure the camper was not overlooked and with his dutiful wife standing over him while he examined the front grill and rear lights of the camper to further hide his actions he changed the vehicles registration plates. Two additional sets had been supplied from London and so he still had one set left, but if the camper had been recorded overnight at the services it would not matter now. That just left the stolen briefcases. These were removed from the toilet and their contents emptied into a couple of the sturdiest of her recently acquired carrier bags, while the briefcases themselves were consigned to the bin liner.

He joined the AutoRoute in a much better frame of mind than he had the last time and took the first exit, then after a few minutes joined a main road that would take them back toward the town the laws of which they had recently contravened. Before too long he spotted a lay-by and an attendant wastebasket accompanied by a number of black sacks, sure sign a rubbish collection was due. He pulled in and without cutting the engine, waited until the road was clear before opening the camper door and adding one extra black, bin liner, comfortably rejoining the road before any other traffic passed.

On the outskirts of the town he joined the ring road completing three sides of the square since leaving the rest and picnic area. This time however, when he reached the AutoRoute, instead of taking the first slip road, which would complete the square by joining the northern carriageway to Paris, he passed onto the second, south to Bordeaux.

All the time they had been on the move since leaving the rest area she had been in the back of the camper with the curtains behind the front driving and passenger seats drawn. Now finally she took her place alongside him, but it was no one he recognised. Foremost there was a smell, true a nice smell and no doubt very expensive, but she had never smelled before. He turned to look at her and there was an instant hoot of complaint from an overtaking car as he swerved beyond his lane.

"Careful Mr. Mills, we haven't come all this way to have an accident now have we?"

Yes the words were condescending, but the tone was not, nor the essence. He risked another glance.

"There will be plenty of time to look at your new wife when we stop Mr. Mills, but I don't think you will be disappointed."

With that she stretched her legs out onto the dashboard, crossing her ankles and sliding her skirt high on her thighs to apply some kind of lotion to the long honey coloured limbs.

He drove on without comment for an hour, only occasionally glancing at the legs.

She read throughout, after replacing the lotion, but leaving the skirt. Firstly she perused the new documents that they had been supplied passports, credit cards, driving licences etc and then the camper handbook from cover to cover, at one point quietly chuckling to herself.

"Where are we going?"

She finally broke the silence, now looking straight ahead through the windscreen and her new designer sunglasses despite the early hour.

"The wrong way."

He had thought of little else - other than the legs - since joining the AutoRoute south. Originally he assumed that if they ran they would make directly for the channel ports and home, but now he needed time to think. He did not know if the roadblock had anything to do with the theft of the briefcases, but even if not, it would soon be clear their proximity to the robbery and continued absence from the farm was suspicious. Not by the police authorities perhaps, but as soon as those at the Farmers Union were aware of the coincidence, which they obviously would be by a combination of the police and their representatives still around the village, their full part in the intrigue would be obvious.

Making directly for the channel ports could then be easily predicted, particularly when their car was found on the northbound carriageway, it would also be assumed they then had a different vehicle and enquiries may lead to the suggestion of a camper. He did not know what kind of resources were available to those who might feel it imperative that they recover the files, but he did know they were considerable - given what had been altered and corrupted to date, very considerable. It would not be difficult to examine every camper returning from the continent at this time of the year and although he was aware that it maybe they did not yet know it was a camper they should be looking for - when it doubt run.

He succinctly informed her of his reasoning trying to give the impression all was under control.

“So you don’t know where you’re going.”

The smell, glasses and legs may have improved, but apparently not the generosity of spirit. He presumed it had been a question, but no, apparently a mere unkind statement of fact for she went on without pause.

“To save you asking….. the briefcases were locked in the boot of the car and although I was able to defeat the mechanical locks there was a secondary laser alarm that I missed.” Then continuing in the same bland monotone, “I would also like to mention that I was impressed with your performance at the roadblock, very commendable and I believe crucial."

At first he said nothing, wondering if his ears were playing tricks with him, then in an attempt at satire that would probably not be appreciated,

"Did that hurt?"

He felt her turn toward him, but stared intensely ahead, his face studiously vacant.

"All in good time Timothy, all in good time. Which reminds me," she picked up the passports, "What are we to call each other?"

Initially he did not understand, but it appeared according to their passports he was Mr. Peter Mills and she was Mrs. Harriet Mills and her concern was whether he would remember to address her by the new name.

"It tends to be something of a 'give away' if you make mistakes with your wife's name, unless of course you're having an affair - and I do hope you're not being unfaithful Peter, I really couldn't bear it?"

He could not help smiling despite the attempt to unsettle him, "Is this the 'all in good time'?"

She suddenly sat upright, removing her legs from the dash and straightening her skirt, "Good gracious me no Peter, not at all," then more thoughtfully, "I think you should refer to me as 'Mrs. Mills'. It's rather 'twee', but not unpopular in some middle class circles for the little wife to be addressed so, OK?"

He nodded as she completed her determinations, "I shall call you Peter and don't worry - your 'all in good time' will come soon enough."

Chapter 20

Bordeaux basked in early springtime sunshine.

They arrived on the outskirts around lunchtime and he drove directly into the centre of town dropping her outside a conspicuous café that they agreed he would pick her up from in three hours. He carried on until the first roundabout which he circled heading back through the town until he found a satellite parking area upon which he locked the camper from the inside and was soon fast asleep on the rear settee. Two and a half hours later he was awoken by his new digital watch she had bought the previous afternoon along with the other shopping and within a few minutes was back on the way to the town centre with a particularly bad taste in his mouth for company.

He was not sure of everything she intended to do, but whatever it was it was expensive as she had asked for another two thousand Euros on the way into the city.

"Don't be so stingy, it's not your money."

She had goaded him and it was true, so he had doubled it and astonished she had laughed out loud, probably for the first time, he just hoped her merriment was not always going to cost so much as they were nearly half way through the kitty.

He crawled up to the café front, but even then almost did not recognise her, if the change before had been appreciable it was now breathtaking. Her hair was different and had dark magenta highlights; the clothes and shoes were expensively different and the sunshades were now St. Tropez as opposed to St. Michael. It was not his wife of course, new or otherwise, but she was right in as much as whoever's wife it was would not be disappointed.

As he stopped she opened the door placing five bulging carrier bags on the floor in front of the passenger seat and climbed in after them, her pleated skirt riding high as she stepped up and sat down.

"Are you coming back down this road?"

He was surprised at the immediate enquiry, but confirmed his intention of circling the roundabout again and passing the café on the opposite side of the road. Then a few seconds late she spoke again.

"Slow down a little, I want you to take the next on the right and stop after about six or seven shops."

He did as he was asked, mesmerised by the long matching magenta fingernails that had miraculously sprouted from the end of each digit.

"There, just there, see it, Maxime Coiffure? They're expecting you, but don't say too much, just act a little embarrassed or something."

He sat where he was for a moment unbelieving. He did not want a hair cut, he probably needed one, but when had that ever had anything to do with it and he certainly did not want some French 'teasy-weasy' champing at his golden locks.

"I don't want a haircut."

He could hear the petulance in his voice, but she was expecting it.

"It doesn't matter what you want, it is a security matter, disguise remember, now go and get yourself tidied up and please don't argue with the man, I have told him exactly what we want."

There was the sound of a horn expressing displeasure at the double-parked foreigner.

"Go on, go on, I will be back in an hour, here or at the café, Oh, and I've already paid, else they wouldn't do it at such short notice, so just leave a tip."

She slid across the central storage locker between the two front seats, worked the handle and almost pushed him out of the door, before slamming it and unsteadily easing into the traffic.

He did not know whether to laugh or cry. Still somewhat dazed and very tired however, he walked along to the barbers, perhaps Maxime's maestro would not be too bad, but as he opened the door and a heavily affected and effeminate young blade minced towards him he knew he would be.

"I have to say Peter you do look extraordinarily smart."

He may look smart but he did not feel it. There was a force eight gale blowing down his neck and Maxime's staff seemed more frightened of the cut-throat razor than he, despite being on the safe side - and he had a number of nicks to prove their trembling disposition. He said nothing until they were parked at a service station courtesy area on the ring road having filled the camper with petrol.

"So what did I get for my money, apart from a budding case of pneumonia?" He was exploring the two bags that he was informed were his, "How do you know they will fit?"

She was busily filling the draws and cupboards with the items she had purchased for herself and their new mobile abode.

"Why should you bother, nothing else did - and don't be such a whiner, just get everything packed away so that when we arrive tonight we look the part – Mr. and Mrs. Mills recently arrived in the Dordogne for their spring holiday. A nice young middle class couple where the man speaks wonderfully good French and the little lady does her best, but fails."

They had discussed that it would be a benefit if their language skill roles were reversed, hopefully adding to the identity change along with the new clothes and hairstyle – or in his case a style.

"How did you get on at Maximes', I hope you didn't say too much?"

Just when he had forgotten about the wind down his collar she had to remind him.

"No Mrs. Mills, I said next to nothing, I was 'embarrassed of Bordeaux' as instructed."

"Excellent," she smiled, "if they remember us it will be for all the wrong reasons. I told them you were a gift from my girlfriends for my birthday, a sort of gigolo, 'stud for a day' all very 'modern woman' these days you know. But that when you turned up you were in such a state I wanted you cleaned up before I could decide what to do with you, if I was going to do anything at all that is."

She said all this as she completed her unpacking then smiling innocently at him, "Ready then?"

While in the town she had booked them into a campsite a hundred kilometres or so east of Bordeaux along the Dordogne, but they needed to be there by seven thirty for the proprietor to see them installed and time was tight. Nevertheless he considered her phoney innocence for many seconds, somehow a little sad that her new elegance had seemed to take her further beyond him, but finally he asked resignedly, "So is this the 'all in good time'?"

She grinned, both impish and refined, "Oh no Peter, your 'all in good time' is yet to come."

"I spoke to London."

The game was over and he was driving quicker than he would have liked to meet the deadline. It was as if for most of the day they had been slightly adjacent to reality, presumably the effects of fatigue and the release of built up tensions, certainly it felt that way to him, but for her of course he never knew.

"You are not going to like it," she continued, giving him no time to comment. "Firstly they were hoping we could have stayed longer," she raised her hand checking his inevitable curse, ".......they should have been consulted before blah, blah, blah, but timing is apparently very important and there is also some dispute as to how things should proceed."

She sighed.

"They didn't actually say it, but it's clear there's some difference of opinion amongst your masters, I've had it before and it is not to be recommended, whatever, we are to remain in France for the time being and London will let us know what they want in due course."

He said nothing after all it was not her fault. Then he thought he must be going soft, it had never been her fault before, but that had not stopped him it must be the perfume.

"Why don't we just post the stuff back?"

She replied cautiously, almost if she was worried about his reaction,

"Specifically forbidden, under any circumstances."

Whatever she may have been worried about did not transpire, in fact nothing happened, he just drove on in silence and soon they were stopped outside the small town of Lalinde asking for directions.

"Nice man."

She observed having watched her new style husband complete the arrangements for an unspecified length of stay, not a problem given the time of year.

"Yes."

He agreed, suddenly tired.

They were parked in a spot that overlooked the river some metres below and had been 'hooked up' to the campsite's power supply the cost of which the 'nice man' was keen to confirm was included in the rental for the position. Watching him wearily join her at the small camper dining table, after ensuring the fridge was functioning and the electric pump for the small sink water supply performed its duty, she stood and took a round cylindrical carton from a secure overhead storage cabinet and placed it on the table.

"Congratulations Timothy and Peter, so far you have done well by any standard, amateur or otherwise, don't drink it all at once."

She then turned and stepped to the end of the camper busying herself making up the bed from the double settees and the sheets and duvet in the storage space beneath. He ceremoniously opened his favourite expensive single malt whisky amazed that she would purchase such an iniquity, let alone the right one. He stood and hesitated, as she turned identifying his quest.

"Oh, up above at the end - even 'catalogue' wives can't think of everything."

He took a step as directed and sure enough inside the top cabinet he discovered a large glass tumbler and was soon relishing the soft fiery liquid of his northern Celtic cousins. The first did nothing to delay the second and it was with a warm feeling slowly emanating from his belly that he considered her latest enquiry.

"If you're looking from the bottom of the bed, do you normally sleep on the left or the right?"

He was tired and had been very sated at the sight of the bottle of whisky, so was confused at the question - he normally slept in the middle, when you were one you did.

She went on while he was deliberating; "Only it makes a difference as to which end I put the pillows."

As beautiful as she was, she should not confuse a truly outstanding malt, "It doesn't matter, do as you wish, I'll sleep on one of the bunks."

She turned from her bed-making and rejoined him at the table, sitting in the opposite single seat, "You did not read all the camper handbook did you?"

He was tired, which sometimes seemed to augment the enjoyment of a good whisky, thus was not overly interested in handbooks and campers. He had read enough for the purposes of driving and storing, the rest he would apparently now have more than sufficient time to contemplate in the days ahead – he said as much.

Undeterred, she continued in a reasonable parody of a car, or indeed caravan salesman.

"This camper is a modified version of a popular design of which only a relatively few customised – and according to the literature 'exclusive' – models were made. It has increased storage space, a separate 'bathroomette' and toilet and although smaller than the original, a generous size dining table for two which we are at present sitting at – and that is the clue. This camper, although based on an original four-berth floor plan, has been modified for just two occupants and has only one bed - a double bed. Now do you sleep on the left or the right?"

His eyes slid from hers to his glass and took in the hands laying lightly one on the other just beyond, the inch long wrapped extensions glistening on the end of each finger in the glow from the overhead lamp.

"I'll sleep on the floor."

His voice had been quiet and she recognised nothing else so exasperated declared, "Look, I'm tired and unlike you I've had no sleep since I can't remember when, so please, what side the damn bed do you want?"

He went to say something, but was too late.

"Oh come on", she was becoming angry, "what side of the bed did you slip into next to your Romany Princess or whatever she was?"

He lifted his eyes and looked at someone he did not recognise, not the face, the smell, the hands, just perhaps the glare. They held each other's gaze for many seconds before she relented and strangely without malice, suddenly enlightened said, "You didn't sleep with her did you. I assumed she wanted to cut your balls off because you used her in bed, but it wasn't like that was it, it wasn't personal. You just got her husband locked up and she wanted some tangible recompense?"

He neither denied nor confirmed, he just sat, his eyes once more dropping to the table.

“Poor old you,” she smiled dismissive, “but we have a job to do and I do not expect you to hamper our chances of success by catching pneumonia or slipping a disc.”

Now more business-like,

“I am a water person so will place the pillows at the end in the direction of the river. I will sleep on the furthest side of the bed under the sheet and you will sleep on the sheet with the duvet over both of us. It is not unusual for people in this line of work to experience these kind of situations.”

His eyes flashed up from the table, “And you’d know all about that?”

Even he was surprised at the venom in his exclamation, but it was too late now, he could not take it back. She stood and replaced the bottle of whisky in the cupboard without asking.

“People that work undercover Peter commonly have normal lives with families and friends and often don’t necessarily like their work colleagues anymore than anybody in any other job, the difference is that if they don’t work together they likely don’t get to go home. Please remember it’s my life as well,” she hesitated, then more conciliatory, “and please don’t sit up all night, you are tired and need sleep.”

Apart from the curtains that stretched across the camper behind the driving area, there was also a pair hung across the centre aisle enclosing the actual bed with enough space between the curtains and the edge in which to disrobe. He waited until he heard the sound of the bed creak as presumably she crawled into it, wrestling with only one thing in mind - did he go and get the whisky? If he did he knew he would likely finish the bottle or probably more likely fall asleep at the table first, but either way he knew neither was the sensible thing to do and he was alive to her summary of their predicament.

Standing, he stepped to the whisky cupboard and opened the door. She just had to speak, one sound, even a sigh and the bottle would be in his hand, but there was nothing. He closed the cupboard and sat back on the edge of the seat at the table and removed his shoes and socks. The aroma was not as expensive as the perfume, but just as pungent and so he laboriously, with no little risk to body if not soul, ran some water into the shower tray and washed his feet as best he could. Finding nothing on which to dry them, he took off his new sweatshirt and undershirt and wiped his feet on the later carefully folding the former and placing it on the other table seat. He then removed his trousers and after more careful folding placed them on top of the sweatshirt, then taking the torch from the shelf next to the cooker reached over and extinguished the light above the table.

Once through the curtains it was clear where he was to repose. The top sheet extended almost to the floor and the corner of the duvet was turned back. He slid as quietly and as gently as he could between the two and lay on his back on the very edge of the bed staring at where he assumed the roof of the camper to be, but which had disappeared as soon as he had turned off the torch. For some while he lay in silence and then bizarrely found himself counting.

Contemplating how odd it was in respect of the last two occasions where he had utilised the procedure, he flinched violently when she spoke.

"Thank you for not revisiting your golden retreat Peter, but if you'll pardon the pun you are quite rigid, I can feel the tension, please just try and relax and you will soon be asleep, we are quite safe for the moment."

Safe was something he did not feel at the moment and he wondered why she was so sanguine about their proximity. Slowly he turned towards her whilst being careful not to move closer.

"Sun?" he spoke quietly with no emotion.

"Mrs. Mills to you." She corrected him and he apologised before carrying on, "This was the other 'all in good time' wasn't it, you'd read about the camper?"

She chuckled.

As far as he could tell through the stygian darkness, she was laying on her back and close, despite the increased size of the camper's modified double bed, nevertheless he continued in the same quiet manner.

"Mrs. Mills, what would you do if Mr. Mills jumped on top of you right now?"

The chuckling stopped, but there was no identifiable apprehension.

"Well let's see," she surmised, "I could join in with enthusiasm or I could kill him."

It was his turn to chuckle as he most carefully rolled back and beyond to face away from his companion.

"A fifty-fifty choice Mrs. Mills, I didn't know you cared, just a few months ago you would only have killed me, to come all this way in such a short time, it must be my charm and boyish good looks."

He sighed elaborately as if embracing sleep, but she could not let it rest, she had to compete even here, "How do you know it isn't ninety-nine per cent to one percent?" Her voice was a little peeved so he could not help be pleased.

"I don't, but then I don't know which way round that would be either, so for the moment I will settle for fifty-fifty."

Now suddenly he was tired, but she apparently was not, "That's ridiculous, how do you know you wouldn't have a ninety-nine per cent chance of annihilation, how do you know things aren't more or less exactly the same as they were before?"

"All in good time Mrs. Mills, all in good time."

She was saying something else in that logical reasoning fashion, but he did not hear it - he was asleep.

Chapter 21

For him the next few days were very much a time for reflection.

He sat for many hours looking out across the river wondering about the events that had led him here both recent and stretching back what seemed a lifetime ago in Germany. She too seemed very introverted in her attitude and they were fortunate that due to the time of the year they had no near neighbours on the site and only waved to the proprietor in passing. The second night passed very much like the first only with added embarrassment after hearing that his 'wife' only ever slept naked, but he was so tired sleep overtook him again almost immediately he rested his head.

The third night however, there was a problem.

Restless, he could not sleep, once touching her with his arm as he stretched and once his body whilst turning. He detected no indication these accidents had been interpreted as anything other than what they were, but it made him uncomfortable and so the next morning they disconnected the electrical umbilical cord and he drove to the local town. Here he bought a single thin camping mattress, a sleeping bag and a tracksuit and did his best to justify his actions.

He was an amateur.

He had not been trained and was only now learning the joys of working undercover, he certainly did not expect, despite their recent sleeping arrangements, he would cause her any problems, but he was uncomfortable with the situation. In future he would sleep in the bag, on the mattress outside the curtains in the aisle, affording her some privacy and with any luck; in the morning he would have his sleeping kit safely hidden away before any prying eyes could view the couple's peculiar sleeping arrangements. At worst he could lay claim to a reoccurring back problem and occasionally even sit inside with the curtains closed and rock the camper from side to side just to show willing if she thought it necessary. She made no protest only to comment that she wondered how many other women that looked like she did 'got turned down when they asked a man to go to bed with them', but nothing more.

He was grateful that there had been no argument for it was hard to truly explain how he felt, although he really did feel uncomfortable about the previous situation while at the same time not being totally confident he may not at some point seek to cause her a problem. Better safe than annihilated, but he could not help noticing she obviously had an awareness of her attractiveness – not all marshal arts and mediocrity then!

Two days later they repeated their excursion to the town where as instructed she again telephoned London the requisite five days having passed as instructed. They had decided to stop for a decent lunch and he could not decide whether to spoil his appetite or suffer the inevitable nervous indigestion following the call, but in the end he plumbed for the latter. Assuming a bottle of claret would help soften any blows, but it did not – because there were no blows.

She had made the call from the train station and returned with the news that she was to telephone again in another five days – London continued to prevaricate.

"C'est la vie!" he shrugged, at least he had escaped the indigestion, but he could see she was uneasy. He was disappointed, as since the resolution of his sleeping dilemma, he was feeling better. The sun continued to shine and he could not help feeling a mite self-satisfied to have such a beautiful woman on his arm – something she had chosen to do to endorse their personas no doubt, but it was very agreeable nonetheless.

She spoke little that evening, but over coffee the next morning – tea had been forgotten – she wanted to talk.

"I am concerned about the difference of opinion in London, as I mentioned before this is never a good situation."

He was not really bothered, it seemed they were safe and he was beginning to enjoy himself, then he remembered that was traditionally never a good sign, so he listened.

"My experience's are that when there is a marked difference of opinion at the top as to how things should proceed it can lead to some faction or other taking arbitrary precipitous action which can endanger the whole outcome of the exercise if not the actual operatives themselves."

She sounded like a politician or a marketing director, full of piss and wind and paid for it. He leaned forward across the table and mimicking adoration and whispered wide eyed, "Mrs. Mills, you are an incredibly attractive wife, but I don't have the slightest clue as to what you are going on about."

She did not laugh or change her expression, but he could see, there was a lot going on behind the eyes. He sat upright, the joke over.

"OK. I'm sorry, but I really don't know what to say, so London doesn't know whether to stick or twist - I can't see what I can do about it or you for that matter?"

She continued to consider him for a long time as if making a decision, while he stared back becoming more familiarly bellicose. Finally she laid her hands on the table in their typical configuration, eight finger tips glistening this time in the early morning sunlight.

"Nothing I have said to you with regard to your position or the project on which we are embarked has been untrue."

She paused, here we go again he thought, but said nothing.

"There are things however, on which I have not expounded. For one, there are those in London that believe it to suit their purpose just as well, if not better, were there to take place a messy well publicised court case that exposed the overall fraudulent operations of the EU. Particularly if this court case originated in France then transferred to the European Court of Appeal. London would lose the bargaining power I have talked about, but there are those that would prefer a quicker 'return', perhaps even prompt a significant reduction in the involvement of the UK in Europe, if not it's withdrawal altogether. From your point of view 'quicker' is very much a comparative term, London would not be bothered how long the French embarrassed themselves in their own courts, which are notoriously long winded and of course Brussels and Strasbourg are not renown for their alacrity. I probably don't need to point out that during this time you would be detained – there would be no bail and it most definitely would be a matter of years, there's the car theft and the shooting, they will say the man was running away even if he wasn't."

Nice to know you can always count on tradition he pondered, but said more positively than he felt, "But what about you. Your people are not gonna let London dump you in a French prison and wash their hands of it, I can understand how I'd be thrown to the wolves, but what about you?"

She said nothing.

He was use to her saying nothing, in total in seemed sometimes as if they had spent half the time since her arrival staring at it each other with varying levels of animosity, what was different this time however, was that she was not staring at him. Eventually she raised her head and he saw a sombre look in her eyes not apologetic more resigned.

"I do not work for your masters, you will remember I have been seconded and my instructions were very clear. Should you show signs of any form of breakdown or panic I am to abort with as much information as I can salvage protecting London and myself, regardless of the repercussions to you."

There was another silence, but this time she did not look away, he grinned, but not with his eyes.

"So I'm not paranoid after all and you're not an assassin, just a Judas – and there's me thinking it was just because I wouldn't sleep with you."

She hit him hard on the side of his face with the back of her hand and for a moment they both thought he was going to hit her back, but he didn't.

"I'm sorry," she sounded almost genuine, "that was for the sleeping bit not the Judas – and I haven't betrayed you, quite the reverse I have just compromised my responsibility, you should be pleased – and wipe the blood off your lip."

She stood up and tore off some kitchen roll from beside the sink placing in on the table, "I am now taking one of the cycles and going to the village for a couple of things. Give some thought while I'm gone as to how and where you wish to go from here and we can discuss it when I get back, but again please remember, this is not a game and if you have any doubts, remember the numbers."

He watched her cycle out of the site on one of the bikes they had hired a couple of days before and remembered how much fun their first ride had been into the woods and the village – dangerous thing enjoyment, almost as bad as optimism.

She had been gone for over half an hour while he sat in one of the folding sun chairs that came with the camper gazing at the waters flowing past wondering if the proprietor's next customers would be in a big blue van with a flashing light on top. Thus it was with an understandable amount of relief he saw her cycle back onto the site and wave at the front office as she passed and him as she neared the camper – professional to the end, 'little wife waves to little husband after visiting the store'.

She climbed inside and immediately put the kettle on, having first marvelled at the efficiency of the stove, which she adjudged to be superior to the one at the farm. Strange she should worry about relative cooker performances with what they were about, perhaps it was how the professionals kept their perspective – shame they did not have more cookers in London.

After a few minutes she carefully exited the camper and walked over to him, "Here, I'm sorry it's only French, but I'll get some proper stuff when we're next at a hypermarket," and handed him a cup of hot colourless tea, "so what have you decided?"

He sipped the tasteless brew wondering how the French managed to take the flavour out of everything and waited for her to join him on the other sun chair. The coffee she brought at least had a smell and perhaps even a taste, but he should not be ungrateful, he was still at liberty and she had cycled to the shops for him and not returned with the Gendarmes.

"As ever and at the risk of sounding 'maudlin' I think you once put it, I don't seem to have a lot of choice. It appears to me it's what you choose to do that matters Mrs. Mills."

In turn she sipped watching the waters ebb by, "Not evading the question are we husband?"

It was a strange time to use the term, was it a ploy, a manoeuvre, is this what it would be like from now on, perpetual suspicion? He thought it, so why not say it?

"It would be silly of me to suggest I am not disappointed by your recent disclosures and worse to pretend I suspected – after all I am an amateur and make no claim to clairvoyance. But before I enthral you with my opinions there is one question I would like you to answer, if you feel able of course." He failed to keep the sarcasm out of his voice, "In your opinion, what might be the strategy of those that would prefer a messy misadventure in the courts?"

There was no vacillation; presumably they were beyond that now.

"Details of our cover and whereabouts would be leaked to the French authorities or at least those that may try and pre-empt the authorities – someone in the Union perhaps - and then the authorities, believe me, it is a tangled web they weave!"

"Cunning devils!" this time he made no attempt to disguise his sarcasm but carried on more reasonably, "I see very little option as I've stated before other than to continue as planned with the risk I might escape with a clean bill of health if not a farm. The only alternative would be for me to run. Presumably then the passport I have now would be made known to the authorities and it would just be a matter of time before I was apprehended, which would no doubt force London's hand and the alternative scheme would be triggered by default."

He leaned forward and placed the cup on the grass at the side of his chair, "And it's here Mrs. Mills where I believe my life is in your hands as they say. Should the 'impatient lobby' in London carry the day or even act precipitously as once again you so quaintly put it, you will undoubtedly be forewarned, if I read the game correctly – mustn't have a borrowed operative detained by the authorities. Plus of course it would not look good in court if the poor persecuted young foreign farmer, whose name had been taken in vain, had a series of James Blunt and Mata Hari's at his 'beck and call'." He reached for the cup again, "So you see Mrs. Mills it really is about what you choose to do, not me – would you help, would you warn me or would the first thing I'd know about it be a heavy knock on the door?"

She may have answered but he thought not, so gave her no opportunity, "Naturally I'm totally unable to predict anything other than the obvious, for I know nothing that might suggest you may act unprofessionally." He exaggerated the word unflatteringly, "I don't know your name, where you come from or who you work for, you've been most diligent in your cloaking. I know somethings, you are comfortable living with someone which would suggest you have done it before and far too much domestically adroit than for it to have been just assignment related – unless of course it was a real marriage thing."

He felt her stiffen, but continued to speak while gazing at the rippling waters, "From my point of view you are an arm of the law. Some fancy department or bureau no doubt, but still part of governmental enforcement, yet not only do you seek to deny your affiliation, you clearly don't like policemen. Then of course there's 'the tears' - all night after the 'wedding'. I'm sure lots of brides cry on their wedding night, out of disappointment probably, but after a fake wedding, that seems most odd."

He was in full flow now, a weakness, once started he did not know when to stop.

"And this morning and my fat lip, you've no concerns one way or another where I sleep and would not deny you have been deceitful, probably expect a citation for it when all of this is over, so why do I have a fat lip? Could it be the correlation of the two? Did we rat on someone we were sleeping with? All a bit too close to home is it?"

He had worked himself up into a considerable huff, but even so sensed the danger. Slowly standing and concentrating only on her cup, he bent down and removed it from her grasp, stepping into the camper and without asking, made more tea and coffee. Once outside again he proffered the refilled cup, which she took without comment and he sat down next to her again. Continuing as if there had been no incident of any moment he asked, his voice conspicuously normal, "Would the real people you work for be interested in any of this, me for example?"

She sipped her coffee and winced as the scorching liquid touched her mouth before answering, "You insult me to the point where you come close to dying at my hands and now you wish me to help you?"

Nice to know his real fear sensors worked even when he was angry, "There's nothing to say you'd win if it's for real," nothing like a little bravado after the event.

"There is no horse shit here, what would you fight with?"

He decided she had had long enough to think about it, "So, would they?"

It was her turn to painstakingly settle her cup on the ground, "I can't think of one reason why they would be, but as it's you I will ask."

She turned to look at him for the first time since they had sat down together, "You do realise that if they agree – and as I say, I can't think why they should - it would mean compromising your allegiance to your own country, some would see that as traitorous?"

He looked back at her, another smile that did not touch his eyes.

"You mean you don't think that if my country decided to sell me out you don't think I'd sell them out first? Oh come now Mrs. Mills, how very amateurish!"

Chapter 22

Politicians lie. The only surprise is that the electorate is surprised.

The definition of the word 'politic' includes admirable correlations like 'judicious' and 'sagacious', but alas more dubious examples like 'expedient' and expressions such as 'fitted to gain the end desired' or 'means of achieving ones end' and of course the damning 'more politic than just'. Electoral surprise is puzzling because the vast majority will have at sometime or another expressed an opinion to the effect that 'they did not think it political to say this or that', meaning they lied. So where is the surprise in a body that takes its name from a descriptive word then lives up to the description?

Democracy was considered by a famous British wartime leader not to be the best form of government just the best anyone had come up with to date, not exactly a resounding endorsement. The alternative can of course be far worse, fascist dictatorships, totalitarian socialism and religious extremism, none particularly attractive to even the modest free thinker. But then there is the various Democratic selection processes designed almost inevitably to exclude anyone of considerable intellect or integrity, but again perhaps this is for the best, perhaps fire has to be fought with fire, if of course you don't happen to 'get in the way'.

Nevertheless it is worrying when once the man considered to be the second most powerful in the UK previously earned a living writing pornography and the most powerful man in the world was a literacy challenged reformed alcoholic and a born again Christian – and these were the 'good guys'!

They left the banks of the Dordogne the next day.

After their discussions of the previous morning he had visited the site office, informed the 'nice man' of their imminent departure plans and paid the bill for the site and the cycles. It was his intention never to stay in the same place for more than a few days at a time and in any event for him the Dordogne had lost its charm. He had received no complaints or otherwise regarding his decision in fact Mrs. Mills had become quite introverted again and very little passed between them before their departure. Thus the only problem he had was where to go, or more specifically, in what direction.

He had considered continuing south and flirted with the idea of the Spanish border, but somehow felt it might attract attention and in any case he knew that although the land borders in most of the EU were easily traversed, it worked both ways. There were of course extradition treaties, but there was also the possibility of more direct action, it did not take much to put someone in the back of a van and drive it through a 'none existent' border check point. His instincts were to stay in France, but also instinctively he wanted to migrate towards his homeland and so he elected to start a loop north. It may also be the least predictable course to take, but whatever - he was more familiar with northern France and the northern European countries - when in doubt run, when in fear run home.

Almost as soon as he left the village he turned off the main route taking a smaller road that eventually carried them a little circuitously to the banks of the Vézère. He tracked this tributary to the Dordogne itself north-east up river for well over an hour before turning north though Hautefort eventually forsaking Aquitaine for the Limousin and after consultation with the *Office de*

Tourisme was comfortable ensconced in a rural camp site outside St.Yrieix-la-Perche.

Three more days passed in what was a polite, but increasingly strained hush, when after another long walk to the town ostensibly for groceries, she asked if she might 'have a word'. It was an absurd way to start a conversation in the light of their enforced inactivity. If they had been who they said they were everything would have been wonderful, the sun shone, but it was not too hot - even for an Englishman - with the countryside resplendent amidst the flush of spring growth, many weeks ahead of its counterpart across the channel.

"My people are not interested in you."

Just like that he thought, so again, why not say it, "Just like that?"

"No, it's worse, they want me out."

They were sitting once again in the sun chairs gazing out this time over green pastures that now did not seem so green anymore and he was wondering whether he should leave the sun chairs behind, perhaps they were bewitched.

"Well," she continued almost apologetically, "not necessarily right now, but certainly if I perceive the confusion in London to become perilous or even if I sense something feels not right."

Three days of near silence and now this, he preferred the silence.

"And they have no interest in me at all?" perhaps he had misheard.

"No, they feel you would be an embarrassment."

"Oh dear, perish the thought," he could not keep the bitterness out of his voice. "So when are you going?" bitterness and fear.

"Trying to get rid of me Mr. Mills?" she almost laughed, but not quite.

"I don't feel like messing about at the minute."

He had tried to sound angry although in control, but there was a catch in his voice, which betrayed his conviction.

"No you wouldn't, I understand, give me time to think, we'll talk again tonight, perhaps we could walk into town for a meal?"

"Last one for the condemned prisoner?" but she had stood and wandered off and left him to consider his options, all none of them.

It was a very different lady to that he had sat opposite at the dinner to celebrate his new life and as much as the latter looked incredible more dazzling - she also appeared decidedly more illusory.

"Now tell me the good news from London."

She had telephoned on the way to the restaurant, but had volunteered no report and he had not quizzed her. They were about to leave and walk back to the camp site after a good meal – steak and chips for him, although they called it something else being France – and he was interested to see if he was due for another. It had been her idea to telephone London before they discussed matters further to get the latest information possible before deciding what to do – again he mentioned he was not so much stuck for choice as just stuck, but made no objection.

She waited until they had left the restaurant and had started the walk home before answering, taking his arm as she did so, "More of the same."

She squeezed his arm as he took breath to blow up and continued,

"Wait, wait, I have asked for a meet, in fact I had to insist, it will be in about a week, I'll telephone again in yet another five days to find out where and when. I have said that you have become aware of certain matters and the whole thing could backfire if they are not careful and that my people will be very displeased if I'm caught up in the net – London won't dare spill the beans while I'm here."

He made no comment and they walked on in silence – more confused than companionable.

She made herself a coffee and he poured himself a whisky and they were seated once more at the camper table before he spoke, "Why?" She shrugged and knew his enquiry had nothing to do with London, "You don't have to stay, you said your people had more or less told you to get out and now you're almost using yourself as a shield, why? You don't owe me, most of the time you don't even like me, why? You're a professional and an 'alright' one I've been assured, so why?"

The smile was that of a beautiful woman that the longer he knew her the less he knew.

"Oh I don't think it's as big a deal as that, anyway it's only another week, at least you know you're safe 'til then."

The statement, as if to confirm that the longer he knew her - the less he knew. What he did know however, was that there was a reprieve. Only for a week perhaps, but they say a week is a long time in politics and it's even longer if you are free rather than fettered.

He returned her almost cheerful goodnight after she had finished her coffee and thanked him for dinner, but it was not until the curtains to the bed area had been drawn for some minutes before it occurred to him that he had not thanked her for his respite. Perhaps he should call out, but that seemed feeble, so perhaps he should step through to thank her face to face, although that seemed too dangerous, as she had once said, not for her, but for him – he poured another drink, he would thank her tomorrow. Tonight he would question the intelligence behind his dictate concerning the alteration to their sleeping arrangements – but then it was probably just the drink talking, although he had to confess, they were his own thoughts.

The next day they moved on again - by passing Limoges and skirting the Monts de Blond, always heading north, through the lakes of the Region de la Brenne and always off the beaten track. Now they stayed only one night in each place, mostly campsites, once in the entrance to a wood when there was no site to be found. It was a pleasant time by any standard, perhaps the imminent arrival of a big dog having its effect on the quarrelling pack pair, but he hoped it was more, he found he was enjoying himself – Oh dear!

"Where shall I say we are?"

They had stopped in the centre of Loches parking near the football stadium and she was about to call London from the post office.

"Indre-et-Loire."

"That's a Department - won't they want more details than that?"

She had not argued just commented.

"Probably, but if they're already here, they can give you an address and we'll go there, if not I suggest they tell us where they'll be in two or three days and we'll meet them there, you can phone again tomorrow to find out what they've arranged."

He too spoke carefully in measured terms seeking no annoyance.

"Mrs. Mills, I've had a very pleasant few days and as I finally remembered to say, I'm very grateful for the reprieve. But, now I have to do it my way, as Frank would say, I'll understand if at any point you choose to get off the carrousel. Should you come under the least pressure from London make it clear that I'll do everything in my power to embarrass them, you can make them aware of the schemes I've discussed if you have to."

They had been quite busy by their recent standards during the drive north. After his awkwardness at trying to say 'thank you' the next morning, while at the same time trying to explain why he had not dared venture beyond the curtain without actually admitting to a reason, which meant there was no reason for not venturing there. She had smiled acknowledgement and they had moved on, albeit he sensed it had not been one of his most impressive shows of nonchalance.

Over the ensuing few days they had divided the Union files and the other material evidence into three lots attempting to make each equally damning. Whether they would ever need three he did not know, but he knew they would at least need two. There were the original and 'doctored' electricity bills, water bills and bank statements. Apportioned were the original demand for additional information he had received in the post, plus the additional copies of the applications he had made and someone else had made on his behalf and of course his actual Union files they had extracted from those taken from the manager's car.

All his personal files he separated and with some difficulty, necessitating the removal of all the strings, he secreted inside his old guitar covering them with a sheet of thin cardboard that best matched the original interior of the instrument. The other three piles were shrunk-wrapped and bound tightly in plastic bags with cellotape and string, all of which they purchased from a supermarket. One packet was then taken to a post office and weighed and the necessary stamps purchased to ensure its safe arrival in the UK plus two other similar quantities of stamps, but nothing was actually mailed.

Once back at the camper the three sets of stamps were stuck to the three parcels, each was addressed in thick black marker pen and they were then hidden throughout the camper. One in the toilet compartment under a waste bin of apparently used toilet paper and one in the storage compartment under the bed, which remained permanently 'made up' as they had no need of the space and the third was stored outside.

He had struggled with the idea for a while, reluctant to hide something outside the camper where it would not be accessible from within, but if the camper was broken into and ransacked they could lose everything. It did not have to be any sophisticated security forces, just some kids or local villains after some petty cash and drug money – they were on English plates and supposedly on holiday, fare game for burglars like themselves.

The camper had external lockable compartments so that the waste, water and gas bottle could be replaced without lugging everything up and into the camper itself. Someone else's shit is a great deterrent even for the earnest of burglars and so the third pile was stored under the tank of many other piles in the locked outside waste tank compartment.

They then turned their attention to anything that was left that could connect them to their earlier incarnation. He had kept the passports, driving licences and credit cards etc in the name of 'Wilkinson' as he thought that they maybe of some use. Now however, he believed that the risk of being caught in possession of alternative papers was not worth any potential future benefit and so they were disposed of along with every personal item that could link them to the farm and their previous life. Obviously much had gone over the bridge and in the rubbish when they had originally left the farm, but this was a total cleansing. Only his guitar had survived and a fading picture of an elderly lady and an even more creased one of a younger couple - but they could have been anybody.

He watched her walk away and wondered if he was to steal another few days and if he did would she stay? She was beautiful and perhaps 'another time another place' as they say, but he did not really think so. It was true she had gone out on a limb for him, but there were times when they had got on quite well, so perhaps it was just a friendly gesture and after all it was only a week. She had never said anymore about his fat lip on the banks of the Dordogne so for all he knew she was probably married or had a 'live in' boyfriend. Probably another bloody James Bond or some such – better concentrate on matters in hand, it's probably just the legs anyway - it was much simpler at the farm with the dungarees and wellies.

He was dozing in the warm sunshine inside the cab of the camper when she returned with more groceries and hopefully good news, he was almost frightened to ask.

"North or South?" It was as near as he could get to a question that mattered. He suddenly did not want the last few days to end.

"They will give me details of the meet tomorrow afternoon at five o'clock our time, but they want you to move west."

"No way," his mind racing, "West is where we've come from."

She waited, again choosing her words carefully, "Not exactly and there maybe some reason for the meet to be in close proximity to the... transgression."

"Why?"

She busied herself replenishing the cupboards with her new purchases as he watched her swivelled in the driver's seat – another thoughtful modification.

"It will be assumed you will be less argumentative when surrounded by the authorities keenest on your apprehension."

He watched her finish her unpacking and waited until she joined him in the passenger seat, "That's straight out of the intimidation chapter of the 'Good Coercion' hand book is it?"

He was serious in essence if not in word, but she laughed out loud.

"If only they knew what they'd conscripted, you're not so much a loose canon Mr. Mills as a bumbling blunderbuss, if I forgot where we are and what we're doing; you're probably one of the most amusing men I've ever met."

There was an awkward silence. She glanced at him, but before their eyes met he looked away.

He was flattered, really pleased - then why was he so angry?

He drove north.

Not actually on the AutoRoute, but still chanced the main roads as he was fairly certain because of the impending meet their details would not have been leaked. He was also driving into camper paradise. For some reason around the famous 24hour racing circuit town of Le Mans there was a plethora of caravan and camper suppliers and rental companies, they would be one of many. Also it was not necessary to enter the town environs, for many people would collect a unit and drive only a few miles before stopping for their first overnight to familiarise themselves with the vehicle and its features. Similarly, because the penalties for late returns were so punitive, many folk would spend their last night close to the rental headquarters for fear they would incur a forfeit if there was a problem on a longer journey back.

After a little under three hours he pulled off a main route for Le Mans into the Forêt de Bercé. It was not an official camping site, but there were many campers settling in for the one night en-route for or returning from more romantic climes and they were just another one of many. True to form, just as he thought they might enjoy a penultimate night her mood changed and although she maintained her polite responses she became withdrawn and preoccupied.

The next day he drove around a little and then found an alternative parking spot still in the same area, which he hoped would still be there when he returned from taking her to the local town post office to make the call to London. They were gone for less than an hour and when they returned there was still the empty land-way where they had resided for the early part of the afternoon. He prepared the evening meal, if salad and boiled eggs qualifies as such and he had also cleared away and washed up before he returned to the table, sat down and waited.

"We are to arrive late afternoon at a camp site in Le Lion-d'Angers apparently it is on the river opposite the National Stud, we check in, the reservation has already been made in the name of 'Mills' and we will be contacted when they are satisfied we're 'clear'."

She spoke as if ordering a pizza - she was back in her world.

"Thank you for the meal Mr. Mills, but as we have a big day tomorrow I think I will retire anything you want to say before I go?"

Obviously a 'dig' about previous awkwardness, but it was said not unkindly.

"You don't call me Peter anymore?"

Silly thing to say, but he did not want her to leave and there was something he wanted to ask without starting a fight if he could.

"No, I thought I could, but I can't, Mr Mills will have to do for the now.......and?"

Was he so transparent these days?

"Who will you be working for tomorrow Mrs. Mills, your people, London or me?"

It was as if she had been expecting the question, but then it was her world.

"I am hoping Mr. Mills that we are able to achieve a situation where there is no conflict between the three, an accommodation I believe it is termed. Why, are you offering me a job as your security officer?"

There was nothing he would have liked more, he was out of his depth and apprehensive, but it was a weakness to show weakness.

"No, I couldn't afford you, I just don't know why you are still here, are we still working together or are you now an infiltrator, am I clutching a viper to my bosom?"

He smiled to try and take the sting out of the words, which seemed an unnecessary courteous, why would she tell him anyway?

"You give the impression Mr Mills, it's been a long time since you've clutched anything to your bosom and at the moment I will confess I don't really know myself, but I will tell you one thing about your fat lip and your perspicacity. I was married and although I did not betray my husband, I did get him killed, so be careful what you wish for when you go to bed."

And the curtains closed like a steel fire door.

Chapter 23

You could not miss the campsite entering the town from the East.

As explained it was on the river opposite the Stud and the road ran alongside both, so he arrived an hour before he had intended, but could not see that it mattered. They were indeed expected and directed to a hard standing along the riverbank, all very pretty and all very 'secluded without being isolated' as the estate agents would have put it. Immediately after once again connecting the camper to the joys of mains electricity, he suggested they take a walk and look round the Stud, giving those that needed to satisfy themselves that they were 'clear' – whatever that was – free reign to complete their task. From the disposition of his wife, he inferred that an instant stroll was not in the Handbook under 'recommended actions on arrival at a prearranged meet' so at least he was pleased about something. Despite her counselling for composure and rapprochement, in general he was angry; it was how he survived in periods of stress.

"You would do well to remember that the people you are to meet are obviously those that have a goal that would be the best option for you or they would not be here."

It had been over breakfast, a surprisingly normal breakfast considering the revelations of the previous evening, but whether they both felt uncomfortable about what had been said or whether it was just he, he did not know, which hardly added to his peace of mind.

"You do at times tend to be a little dismissive in your responses to people and although I know your impudence is a kind of defensive mechanism, not everyone has the time and energy to bother to see below the surface."

They had been looking at the trees seated on the sun chairs - he really must throw the damn things away.

"Decided what side you're on then?"

He had made it a joke - frightened to ask for real.

"Don't be so childish Mr. Mills - and leave the 'chip' at home today, you may need both shoulders free."

A hissed a profanity, but even that annoyed him, she now had him swearing in whispers.

Les Haras Nationaux was impressive, big and beautiful as many of its resident stallions labouring contentedly in the midst of their romantic season.

Some of course would only ever see a mare in passing such were the fraudulent delights of artificial insemination and although the stroll was his idea he had perhaps not picked the most appropriate of venues in view of their circumstances. Nevertheless Mrs. Mills seemed to eventually appreciate the promenade, especially when for a time they joined an official tour party and from the attending guide and technician were made privy to the duties of the 'teaser'. She giggled scandalously while he suggested that it was probably time to "move off on their own again."

They returned to the camper after a couple of hours or so, but there was no sign of life to attest to their 'cleanliness' or otherwise and their only near neighbours were an elderly couple - blue rinse and khaki shorts - for whom one would not modify the initial conclusion. They waited all evening, had a little supper and went to bed - she urging him to stay calm, he bemoaning another wasted teetotal day.

There was a knock on the door.

It had only happened a couple of times before, but she had been very fussy about the procedure for answering any callers – she was to do it. In principle, if there were to be a physical altercation she wanted to be in the open, trapped in the camper aisle would restrict her options and reduce her anticipated advantage. At the time she had also pointed out that it would give him the chance to arm himself with 'a few handfuls of shit' it being his favoured weapon so at least he knew his and Perch's successes still irked.

However, there had never been a knock on the door before while they had been in bed and he was wondering what to do, when the curtains suddenly flew open. Frightened of what he might spy pass over him as he lay in his sleeping bag on the floor of the aisle, he instantly shut his eyes and was therefore not as adroit at removing himself from harms way as was required.

"For goodness sake, look what you're doing."

Not a good start to the day and he was only trying to be respectful, next time perhaps he would point and make animal noises. She had a sheet wrapped around her and opened the door cautiously, her other hand on a steak knife she kept under a tea towel by the sink, he wondered who it was and how long the tucked bath towel style sheet would stay up on its own. Almost as soon as the door was open however, the steak knife was forgotten and the sheet received more support, there was a polite exchange of conversation at the door, which she then closed and turned.

"So if we were beset by intruders you would give them a stern telling off from inside your sleeping bag, is that the plan?"

She was edgy, lovely in the bed sheet, but edgy. He began to extricate himself from his polyester and cotton chrysalis, managing well from over a fortnight's practice.

"You surely don't sleep in the tracksuit as well?"

He ignored her question, but concluded she had no 'peeping tom' tendencies or she would already have known.

"It didn't sound like an invasion from the Republican Guard, so I just laid low." She glared at him, but he continued, reasonably, "Shouldn't you put some clothes on?"

Her eyes widened and she threatened, "D'you want me to drop this sheet?"

Of course he did, but he was not going to admit it and in any case there was a problem, "What's the matter?"

Mollified a little she relented, "I thought we'd have been contacted yesterday and I don't see how the delay is good, it may not be bad, but I don't see how it could be good. And now the old girl next door wants to share their eggs and bacon with us – common practise amongst holiday campers apparently."

He had been in France nearly two years a place where they had eggs and something they thought was bacon, but for a proper English breakfast he could make the world wait. The elderly couple's camper was just across the way and they could easily see the Calvary arrive from there so what would be the harm – and then of course there was the bacon.

"I think we should accept their offer, it might look suspicious if we turn them down particularly if it's a tradition."

She folded her arms and the sheet fell from both shoulders, but remained pinned by her arms across her chest as she cocked her head.

"You are so transparent husband, eternal damnation for an egg sandwich, what possible chance could any poor girl have in the face of competition from a rasher of bacon."

With that she slipped behind the curtains, but not before holding his eyes and squeezing passed him in the aisle, which suddenly seemed much narrower.

"We always come out around this time of the year, made the mistake of coming in August once, disaster, absolute disaster, talk about traffic, unbelievable, d'you know they kill about six hundred of themselves every year just going on their damn holidays, amazing, truly amazing."

Bernard expounded eloquently about his and Auntie's (just call me Auntie everybody does) French holiday experiences, but it did not matter; it was a small price to pay for a truly exceptional English fry-up. It was also Bernard that slightly unusually cooked the breakfast, so one could hardly begrudge him his 'well earned' interval as chief raconteur.

Mr. Mills had eaten twice as much as Mrs. Mills (Auntie thought it was 'enchanting' how some young couples addressed each other like that nowadays) and was on his third cup of 'PG Tips' when Bernard suggested he show the lovely young wife some antique postcards. Bernard had only recently bought a complete set at a local 'flee market' and was totally enthralled with his purchase, they were safely secured in the camper if she would like to 'pop inside and have a deco'?

They had all breakfasted together under their neighbour's awning and although the morning air was fresher than it had been in the south, within the fleecy protection of his sweatshirt it was very pleasant and for that kind of breakfast he would have been happy on an iceberg.

"Did you enjoy your breakfast Mr. Mills?"

He made the characteristic Gallic sign for excellence, forming a circle between thumb and first finger, briefly brushing his lips with other fingers extended.

Auntie chuckled, "Yes, Bernard is a very good cook."

Auntie and he remained sitting outside the camper as the other two scrutinised Bernard's *ancien carte postale.*

"Mr. Reece sends his regards."

Auntie regarded him with considerable interest.

"What, no reaction Mr. Mills, very professinal I'm sure, I was led to believe you were somewhat volatile?"

Why was she never around when he wanted her, not so much to help just to listen, his wife would never believe him when he told her.

Auntie's curiosity continued, "If you're waiting for Mrs. Mills to return, I wonder if that's wise?"

He remained silent, not because of any scholarly negotiating proficiency, he just did not know what to say, but nevertheless it seemed to work, or at least Auntie kept talking.

"It's dangerous to rely too much on alliances formed in the field, pressure clouds judgement, mutual dependency and all that, it's hard enough back in the office. Take Mr Reece and myself, he now has an entirely different strategy to me, luckily I'm his boss, but in this business one has to be so careful."

Perhaps the 'tall dark silent type' ploys had run their course, but still not knowing quite what to say he went for one more allowing an enquiring smile.

"Mrs. Mills won't rejoin us unless you specifically request it, unless of course she now works for you, but should you wish it so to be, I have no objections."

He nodded and after a brief pause Auntie rapped on the side of the camper with Bernard's walking stick, which never seemed to be required to aid Bernard's perambulations and the camper door opened and Mrs. Mills returned to the table. Bernard however, had many duties that needed his attention and although he was often visibly busying himself around the place he ceased to be a part of their confab.

Together with the 'blue rinse' Auntie definitely looked more like a Great Auntie, well into her sixties and with tweeds, mohair and silk neck scarf, she looked every bit everyone's epitome of a maiden Great Aunt. A friend of Miss Marples perhaps and like her 'maybe acquaintance' her eyes were bright and sharp, but hard, slate blue and very hard.

"To save him the bother my dear I shall inform you that I have advised against your engagement in our little chat. You're a lovely woman and he has no experience in these matters and it's so easy even these days to turn a young man's head when living cheek by jowl. He has obviously chosen to ignore my advice. "

He wondered what happened to the tall, dark, silent and professional type, but assumed it was feminine solidarity regardless of the party lines. Auntie had the floor however, and it was evident it was no novelty.

"Mr. Reece and his patrons would be happy to throw you to the wolves Mr. Mills for a quick result – for them that is, not necessarily for you – I believe the young lady will probably have explained this, although technically she should not be cognisant of such information. But as I say, the wiles of beautiful women are still potent even today. I, you will be relieved to hear, favour more or less the original plan, albeit there have necessarily been amendments to ensure I continue to carry a majority of support back at the office. Simplistically, you are to bring all the information, which you have gathered, to the UK on a particular ferry and a particular sailing, which I will specify at some point in the days ahead, but probably around a week before the eighth of May. After that you will be deemed to have completed your task and all passed previous violations will be expunged. How we play the game after that does not concern you, now, do you have any questions? More tea, Bernard could you please put the kettle on?"

Silence had served him well so far this morning and so he sat quietly until he had taken his first sip of Bernard's marvellous brew and even then it was not Auntie to whom he spoke.

"Mrs. Mills," the tone was not sarcastic, but studious, "in the 'Good Coercion Handbook' we were discussing previously, is it recommended you start with the threats or the demands, you appreciate this is all knew to me?" At last he addressed Auntie directly with the self-depreciating end to his statement. The morning still looked mild, but the climate around the table had turned severely chilly.

"Is this your doing young lady?"

Auntie was not happy and presumably all prior suggestions that he may have had autonomy of thought were disingenuous.

"Mrs. Mills has done her job effectively and diligently," he continued before Auntie could interrupt, "We would not be here were it not for her. She has also sought to exert no influence over me other than what I'm certain you would strongly endorse which again is why we are able to be here."

He waited before continuing, but there was no attempted interruption.

"I am prepared to continue as I originally agreed, but expect a remuneration equivalent to that that I was promised. I think it might help you consider my appeal more seriously and assist us to come to some accommodation if I first explain the consequence of failure. There are two packages, already stamped and addressed, one to a particularly anti-European element of the British media, the other to a particularly anti-European element of the British politic. These will be released if we fail to find an agreement or at any time I feel my cause is lost – you obviously will have deduced that we are no longer in possession of the documents. They would be mailed if I call for them so to be."

Auntie was very good, he had no idea what she was thinking, but he plodded on regardless.

"I realise this would play into the hands of your, shall we say 'gainsays', but given what would happen to me, I think you can see that it really is in our interest to come to some understanding. All I require now is a quarter of a million pounds sterling, which I believe would be the value of the farm I was promised, but no one ever expected me to have. Then at the completion of my side of the contract so to speak, an unencumbered identity, visas and free passage to somewhere the other side of the world – the details we can discuss at the time – that's all, after all it's only what I was promised."

Auntie watched him while he drank his tea, it was always difficult dealing with amateurs, eyes bigger than their belly, but there were always the 'families' to lean on - the problem was he had no family or did he?

"Mrs. Mills must be even better in bed than Mrs. Wilkinson if you're going to pay her that much?"

He felt his wife flinch rather than saw it, but he was fine, he wasn't even really angry, he just grinned, just enough.

"The money is to be paid into an orphanage the details of which I will give you before you leave, when I am assured by their accountant that the money has cleared their account I will proceed in accordance with any agreements we make."

Auntie smiled back at him, seeming to come to a determination.

"You drive a hard bargain Mr. Mills, you are not what I expected at all, but in principle I agree to your offer and am happy to assist in your antipodean extravaganza, although as ever there are always a couple of caveats."

He was surprised - Auntie was going to agree.

"One, we will do our best to protect you at our end, but the British government must be seen to have no involvement in this whatsoever – it totally undermines 'nod and wink' diplomacy if everybody's in on it – and two….. It is imperative that the channel crossing is made on precisely the sailing we state – not before or after or any alternative route - or our agreement is rescinded, which would not be good for either party. We will make the reservation, all you need to do is be at the port to collect the tickets and get on the boat, do you understand?"

Yes he understood and said so, but Auntie had not finished.

"I have a new contact number for you Mr. Mills."

Auntie offered him a card, but he gestured to his wife, "Mrs. Mills makes all my calls for me, takes messages all that sort of thing, can't let her people pay her for nothing can we?"

Auntie was unhappy again, "Is that wise Mr. Mills, beautiful women can be devious in this business, surely you are not immune to her charms, unless of course you are homosexual?"

He laughed, genuinely amused. He had experienced many 'confusions' over the last few months which, if nothing else, confirmed he was not gay.

"Come, come Auntie, if it's not broke why fix it? Everything has worked fine to date and so I'd prefer Mrs. Mills to continue handling the contact, after all, I'm really only an amateur, Oh and just one other thing."

There was no chance for Auntie to intercede as he watched her grudgingly hand the card to his wife before continuing, "Could you please make the ferry reservation in the second set of spare number plates, I will at some point change them."

Auntie seemed as upset by being bothered with such trivia as anything else that morning, but to her credit she was alive to the request.

"You will have to give me the registration details then, Mr. Mills."

He smiled at Auntie, almost regretting they had met under such circumstances - she really was quite 'cute'.

"Bernard has them. Well obviously they're not the ones he has jotted down I'm using at the moment, so they'll be the alternative spare set – bound to be on file 'back at the ranch' as they say."

He continued to smile, he could not help himself, but he knew he shouldn't, even in the most insignificant of skirmishes Auntie obviously did not like to be bettered.

Chapter 24

"How did you know he was taking down details of the camper?" They were seated looking across the river watching an occasional early season rental boat chug by - children waving, 'Dad captains for a week' saluting, but Mums still cooking.

Auntie and Bernard had long since departed and the mid afternoon sunshine was quite hot, hot enough for him to wear his new designer base ball cap, he was apparently a 'Boss', but he had misgivings about the legitimacy of such a label. There had been the need for the exchange of minutiae which had been accomplished with elaborate politeness and Bernard was soon at the wheel heading east to presumably join the AutoRoute for Paris and the Channel Ports, holiday curtailed due to brazen car number spotting.

"I saw him with what I thought was a screw driver and was worried in case he had decided to try and break into our poo bucket compartment. Then I realised it was only a pencil and couldn't think of anything else there could be to make a note of."

For sometime she had been lounging back in the chair sunglasses in place, far happier in the strengthening sun than he was ever likely to be.

"You know sometimes I think you have an excrement fetish, which I'm sure Auntie would find most distasteful, not that I think you could probably upset her anymore than you already have." Finally she leaned forward as if to emphasise a point, "And in future I would like to be consulted as to what my people should be asked to allow me to do before you arrange it."

He had asked Auntie to inform 'her people' what a good job she was doing and how her presence was imperative to afford a successful outcome to the mission, they must not worry about her and she would be home soon. He had expected a rebuke and was relieved it was apparently to be so mild.

"You never actually told me Mrs. Mills if you were staying, you didn't even say whose side you were on, just hoping to achieve an 'accommodation', well as far as I can see that's been done."

He rested his case.

Still leaning forward in her chair she said she hoped he was right and was quite happy to continue as before, just repeated she would like to have been asked first, then, "I'm sure Auntie's not normally a field agent. She would not be here if it was not important or someone had insisted she come, I may even know who she is." She sat back again and sighed, "She does not like you Mr. Mills and even if she did - and as much as you won't like me saying it - amateurs have no worth in this world, I advise you to be very careful."

It was his turn to sigh, just when he thought he had made some progress.

"Everyone's always telling me to be careful, Mrs. Mills."

"You often need it Mr. Mills, anyway when and where are we going?"

"East, tonight."

They sat for a couple more hours watching the river flow by. They drank tea and coffee, but said little, there was a lot to think about. He had something of a plan in mind, although if he was honest it was more an escape route, but could see nothing better and he was not as fearful of Auntie as his companion – advantage of being an amateur he supposed. He had asked his good lady if she had spotted anyone 'riding shotgun' for Auntie and she confessed she had not and although it was quite likely there would be some minimal protection in place, it would probably have left along with the principles. Reasonably satisfied, nevertheless he decided to wait until dark before moving on as he did not want to be followed and although it might be no more difficult for the pursuers at night, he felt there was more chance of them being spotted.

Auntie had said that the sailing they were to take would be 'around a week before the eighth of May', a strange way to fix the date, why not 'around the end of April' or 'the beginning of May'? It indicated it was the eighth of May that was pre-eminent and although the date had lost much of its relevance in the UK, in France it continued to be reverently commemorated as '*Victoire1945'* – Victory in Europe, VE Day. For him to it was a pertinent anniversary, his Grandfather had been killed in Germany on the same date, nothing worthy of a gallantry medal, it had apparently been a motor accident, but he was still dead. During the time he had lived with his Grandmother she had told him often about his Grandfather and the short time the pair had had together before the war. The stories were obviously very precious to the elderly lady and had made a big impact on a young boy who had only recently lost both parents. So why was the eighth of May so important to another, albeit very different elderly lady? Perhaps it was just anomalous phraseology and nothing more, it would need thinking about and he would have the time.

According to the anticipated agenda, they would not be due at the channel ports for another three weeks, a reasonable amount of time to cogitate, but he also did not anticipate being idle. At five o'clock he called at the site office to settle their account, returning to prepare the camper for the road again, but they did not depart immediately. After one last cup of tea, he rested on the bed enjoying the deeper foam for a change until after dozing intermittently, she called through the curtains that it was just before ten and within a few minutes they were back on their travels.

He enjoyed driving at night. Less traffic and more professionals – he was beginning to sound like 'them'. Initially he retraced his route of the day before, and then drove around country lanes in ever decreasing circles until he was certain that there was no tail, before joining the AutoRoute for Paris. In total he estimated he would have a journey of six hundred miles with any excursions they may need to make. Obviously Mrs. Mills could do her share, but generally he preferred to drive – she could do the fighting. He drove at a steady sixty miles an hour not wishing to attract attention and they made a first stop around 1am just south of Paris. Then after all he had said about her secretarial skills and personal assistant attributes he spoilt everything and asked for some change to make a telephone call to England.

"So Auntie has had an effect on you after all?"

She was tired and would have appeared insulted if he did not know her better.

"No Mrs. Mills, not one iota, I just want to call a friend."

She carefully selected some coins and supplied her telephone cash card should the booth that accepts coins be broken, which it inevitably was - surprise, surprise - and scribbled her pin number on the back of a serviette.

"I thought you hadn't got any friends." She grumbled after his retreating back, but if he heard he made no sign. Nonetheless he was soon back to confirm the demise of the coin operated booth and also that there had been no one at home.

"At 1am in the morning they're probably in bed."

She really did seem annoyed or was she a little upset?

"Mrs. Mills, it is not 1am in the morning in the UK, it's midnight and they're not in bed, they're not home yet and as I've said, I'm calling a friend."

He lifted the plastic cup of insipid service station tea to his lips the delight further enhanced, as it was now only lukewarm and reasoned as if with an errant child.

"For once you will have to trust me. I'm not attempting to contact any of the people with whom you are acquainted, but I believe there maybe a course of action open to us that could help."

"What?"

She really did seem peculiarly irritated; all he had tried to do was make a phone call.

"If I'm successful as I say, it might help, if not, it won't matter anyway. Except I think it would be better if you didn't know about it then you cannot be censured by my people or yours, after all, you still want a job at the end of all this I'm sure?"

She studied him as she always did when there was latent dissension in the air, "If it's dangerous you're not equipped."

Always nice to know the people around one were not getting carried away with ones capabilities, "It's not dangerous."

Slightly placated she moved to a different tack, "Auntie suggested there maybe a question about your err… orientation, I ask purely from a professional aspect, we've another three weeks or whatever and there's no point sleeping on the floor if there's no need?"

Success for him had always come infrequently and apart from his early life happiness also, thus he could be forgiven at that moment for just beaming broadly across the small plastic table, but alas not by his companion.

"If you don't take that ridiculous smirk off your face, I assure you your next fat lip will reach the Dordogne where the other one started."

He sat back mocking shock and dismay raising his hands in supplication.

"Thank you for your concern Mrs. Mills, but I think it better if I continue on the floor; perhaps Auntie just overestimated the irresistibility of the temptations."

And with that sardonic endorsement to his heterosexuality and by default her limitations as a temptress, he got up from the table while he still could and returned to the phone booths. Again he was soon back and they moved on, but an hour later he stopped at another service station south of Meaux where this time he was gone for longer indicating his call had received a response. When he returned to the camper he explained there was now no hurry and although he did not want to stay at the actual services, suggested they pull into the next rest area for the remainder of the night. This they did, she just managing to bid him a cursory goodnight through gritted teeth.

They breakfasted late the next morning on stale bread and coffee and he drove on for a couple of hours before stopping for lunch. After a more than reasonable meal in the restaurant of an independent chain attached to one of the service centres he drove on again. The AutoRoute had taken them passed Rheims and Metz and they were skirting south of the German border when he stopped again at a rest area for the night. The next morning he entered the town of Sarreguemines, found the train station, collected a number of timetables and had a conversation with a bored ticket clerk before returning to the camper. Here he suggested they use the opportunity to stretch their legs and find somewhere other than a service station in which to eat and discuss his plans for the morrow. She agreed, but made a caustic remark as to her surprise to find she was now part of the inner sanctum then cheered a little as they strolled around the town.

He bought two nondescript rucksacks, which seemed excessive for a few train timetables and once more they enjoyed an agreeable lunch. More than lunch however, he enjoyed some obvious restoration to her morale after what seemed an irrational response to a couple of phone calls, but the ways of the opposite sex were perplexing indeed and it was that 'time of the month'. Something he had again mentioned in all good faith with regard to being prepared for a potentially lengthy time away from pharmaceutical amenities, but she had only fixed him with a malignant glare, which inspired him in future not to be so worldly. In the event, regardless of his initial proposal he waited until they had parked for the night before turning his intentions to the main topic of the day in the hope that his plan may be better received, but inevitably it was not to be.

"You want me to drive this camper round in circles while you go train spotting in Germany, have you completely lost your head or has it been addled by Auntie's flattery."

He smiled, so she had heard some of Auntie's kind words, before Auntie ran out of them of course, he drew a deep breath and reasoned.

"I need to go to Germany and I need for you not to ask me why. You have agreed that if anyone is looking for us – and we know by now at least the operatives of the Union must be - the borders are the most obvious place. If we go into another country we'll have to come back into France or we can't take the ferry to the UK and that'll make it doubly risky, so I've to go by train, they won't be looking for a foot passenger with no luggage."

She began to puff a bit, but there was no actual smoke from her ears so he continued with his rationale.

"Tomorrow we find a good well populated site or a service station where you will go once you have dropped me. You stay there and each evening, you drive pass the pick-up point at six o'clock until I'm back. I expect it to take a day, no more than two."

She remained silent for a bit, presumably a good sign but then, "How can I provide security when you're not even in the same damn country, have you got any idea how it would look on my record if anything happened."

He toyed with the notion of pointing out that if 'anything happened' her record would probably not be foremost in his mind assuming he still had one, but decided against it, he had to do what he intended and so he soldiered on.

"Look, I know to you I'm no better than a big kid, but I can manage a couple of train journeys and I have been in Germany many times, I can speak some of the language and in any case the war 's over and we need to do this."

It sounded totally rational, how could there possibly be a problem, other of course than that he was just as uneasy as she was – and probably a lot more frightened, but he needed to do it and she still needed to challenge it.

"How would I know we need to do this, I'm not allowed to know what it is?"

He had run out of things to say so he said nothing. The silence extended and was hardly companionable, it had become dark in the camper and they now viewed each other through the gloom, neither reaching for a light switch.

"I think I will go to bed Mr. Mills, perhaps you would give me a minute or two and then I would like you to join me."

He began to fidget, but her voice continued cold and detached, "Obviously outside of the duvet, I've been made well aware you're not pestered by temptation, but I would like a final word before your junket tomorrow should you still decide to go."

While he waited, he arranged his bedding on the floor as usual and tried to act as normal as possible - and think it too. Wondering if everyone felt this bad when invited to bed by a beautiful woman - perhaps he was queer? Changing into the tracksuit she liked so much, he slid through the curtains, just managing to make out the edge of the bed and sensed more than saw the form on the far side. He carefully lay down as if on a bed of nails which he hoped it would not prove to be, for his mind was made up and no offers of sexual delights would change it, but as ever in the ways of the heart he was wrong.

"We trained together, where I come from all young people are trained."

It was pitch black now, but as far as he could tell she was also laying on her back facing up toward the ceiling.

"He was the one that enjoyed the training and the excitement. He was very good and therefor selected for special service, I was as well of course, initially only because of my far-eastern appearance, but it was always he that shone, soon achieving a rank and pay on which a married couple could survive. Naturally it's not recommended that people within the service marry each other, but then it's not expressly forbidden either and he was a rising star and there weren't many that looked like me so it was permitted. Before we had worked together on one assignment and that was it – I know deep down you are old fashioned Mr. Mills, but you must remember we are fighting a war and never know what will happen tomorrow. Anyway, ultimately as I say we were married and things were fine, although we often did not see a lot of each other because of different jobs. Until one operation for which I was best suited and I found out later, for which he moved heaven and earth to 'front' – take the lead that is. On the face of it there was no real threat, but that's often where there's most danger."

The duvet moved as she did under it, but he lye still. Rigid he deduced she would term it, but her mind was elsewhere.

"He was undercover at a meet with the opposition and I was the liaison for the snatch squad. Communications were bad and I became almost a staging post for the call to 'go in'. There were two possible sites. He was to ring say the word that coincided to the site where he and the opposition were and I was to pass it on. There would be enough time to get in before his message had been identified and processed by the opposition and they identified there was a leak."

Inside the camper it was very quiet apart from the sound of the occasional heavy truck hauling overnight on the AutoRoute a few dozen yards away, the light of their headlights briefly visible through the curtains.

"As I say communications were bad, so bad in fact that the recording of the call was indefinable even with all the technology they have nowadays, they couldn't make out what he'd said, which was a shame for both of us. When they got to the first site there was no one there and by the time they had moved onto the second there was only him - and he was dead."

She stopped speaking for a time, but did not move or make any other sound and he could not help, even though he could see what was coming.

"Obviously it was a shame for him, he was dead and the shame for me was two fold, I'd called it wrong and lost my husband. Everyone was sympathetic, but I'd lost them one of their best men, it had to be me, who else could it have been, he would hardly make the mistake himself would he, not if his life depended on it?"

There was another silence and he wondered if he was to answer, but he couldn't.

"Do you know, I think if the tapes had been clear, some of them would have wanted to charge me for being reckless with their man, as it being my husband wouldn't have made me more careful, strange, people are very strange......"

Her voice tailed off and he wondered if she had said all that she intended, his sense of inadequacy overwhelming, but he was spared once more for she continued her voice this time a little stronger.

"Its funny, but no one could have wanted those tapes to be clear more than me, you see, I don't think I killed him, I don't know what happened, but I don't think I called it wrong, but I'll never know and that's the worst thing. You see, it may seem odd, but late at night, sometimes if I have any doubt, I would sooner know I had, rather than not know, anything except not knowing."

She moved and he thought she had turned to face him, which was confirmed by the change in the resonance of her voice.

"Now Mr. Mills I am given lesser tasks, those that my people believe me to be better suited for, sometimes loaned out to friendly forces that need someone that looks like me. I sometimes think my people prefer not to see me around, not to be reminded of the loss of a teacher's pet. Now I get jobs like wet nursing amateurs worrying about farmers being paid too much for doing nothing."

There was no malice in her voice, nothing was directed at him, she was just explaining how it was and inexplicably he was not annoyed or upset, but then why should he be, he was still alive.

"So you see Mr. Mills it would be very bad for my career if anything happened to you, but should you decide to go I can't stop you and I won't walk out on you, although I would be really grateful if you were extra careful."

She turned back and he knew the oration was coming to an end, "Do you have any questions Mr. Mills, I'm sorry but I'm suddenly tired."

Dare he, was now the time, he never got these things right? "His name was Peter wasn't it?"

There was a long silence this time and he felt the bed treble, but could have been mistaken. Then she turned away from him so that her voice was no longer clear, but he could still hear, "Bravo Mr. Mills, be careful they don't try and make a detective out of you." There was another small shudder in the bed and just as he thought he might ask more she said quietly, "I shall be asleep soon, it would be nice for me if you did not leave until afterwards."

He said no more.

It was probably an hour before he gently slipped off the bed and into his sleeping bag, long after the reason for tarrying had expired.

He just stayed because he wanted to.

Chapter 25

He did not go to Germany the next day.

They joined the AutoRoute and arrived in the outskirts of Strasbourg by lunchtime finding the railway station quite easily and even determining a place where it would be possible to wait for a few minutes for collection, but then there was a problem. Mrs. Mills was unhappy with the various locations they visited where it was planned she should spend the night or possibly two; they were too busy, too quiet, too far out of town or too close. Eventually he returned to a service station rest area that he believed was the best site they had seen for their purpose and set up for the night.

"There's no point in giving me the evil eye, I said what I think about the camp sites and if I don't think they're right, I don't think they're right!"

Any appeal for succour had long since evaporated, in fact when he had attempted to make some reference to the previous night she had irritably waved a dismissal and if anything now appeared more remote than ever.

"I understand Mrs. Mills and I've adapted accordingly. I've selected what I believe to be the best location and we'll spend the night here to ensure all is well and then you may return tomorrow with confidence. The only slight disadvantage is that I'll now be travelling on Friday the thirteenth, but then that's only if you're superstitious."

He was in the process of preparing a salad for himself, as it was apparent that no one else was going to prepare a meal.

"Would you like something to eat?"

He asked in his most conciliatory tone, but it was not reciprocated she deciding to retire and read.

After he had finished washing up the few items he had soiled, he too retired to his sleeping bag and called at the curtains not to forget that he needed to be at the station by noon, but there was no reply.

Strasbourg was busy and expensive.

Not really surprising with all that money sloshing about he thought, but he would hopefully only be passing through so the coffee he had bought for a small King's Ransom would with luck be the last.

The train journey would be about a hundred miles and he had bought a single ticket not knowing the exact details of the return, but hoping he would. He had watched the camper drive off into the midday traffic with a selection of alien sentiments, none of which helped with regard to the job in hand. He had impressed on her that it was important that she did not make any contact with anyone until he returned - she most definitely must not contact London. This discussion had ended as all others over the last twenty-four hours, her disputing every decision he had made so much so that he sullenly questioned her commitment to the provision of assistance. This guaranteed their ultimately leave-taking had been one of mutual intolerance – he demanding she remember not to make contact with anyone, she treating him to a raised single finger adieu, which from her he had not seen before, but a parking taxis driver found none the less amusing for that.

He boarded the train and found a seat next to the window, resting the rucksack on the floor between his feet. Inside was his overnight toiletries and a clean shirt and shorts, his passport some papers and the other rucksack, folded to make it as small as possible and a screwdriver he had taken from the camper tool kit. He dosed until the guard asked for his ticket, clipped it and handed it back without comment, an hour later he stepped off the train in Mannheim.

There were three addresses of pertinence and he knew them all. More importantly he knew where they were, two of them were hotels and he set out for the lesser. The walk took him nearly half an hour, but his efforts were rewarded and after a brief conversation with the hotel receptionist who contacted one of the rooms and with typical German efficiency, subsequently directed him to his objective. His knock was almost immediately answered - a smiling longhaired, young man greeting him.

"Hi, you must be Bowie."

He was ushered into the modest room, which although he had never been in before, resembled those in the same establishment in which he had spent time on two previous occasions.

"The Chief said you'd be dropping in to see the 'boys' sometime this week, I've arranged for you to stay here for the night, but haven't said anything to them so it'll be a surprise like you want."

The Chief – he was amused the 'boys' manager had achieved another designation for what he had often referred to him as was unprintable. Nevertheless the man had received his telephone call with surprising good grace. Not least he assumed, as all the damaged caused to the van had been repaired in double quick time and without the involvement of the insurance company, apparently it came under some Port Authority jurisdiction – 'a car or something parked in the wrong place making them liable'. His disappearance had obviously been put down to the result of previous misdemeanours and during the call the manager had steered clear of the topic which suited him fine.

He entered the room and put his rucksack down on the unused twin bed and voiced his appreciation, he had discovered by chance he would be in the area at the same time and thought it would be a 'giggle' to drop by, just for the night.

"Not after your old job back then?"

He smiled at the young man, who's name he had been informed was Rod and wondered if his host could possibly understand just how much he did not want his old job back, but in the end decided he probably could not, but tried anyway.

"They're on at nine, are you gonna come down with me beforehand when we do the sound check?"

He could think of nothing else, other than his old job, that he would less rather do, but explained he really did want it to be a surprise so he would pass. In fact, he confessed he did not really want to get involved at all with the performance, obviously he was looking forward to the show, but probably it would be better if he left the 'catching up on old times' until the morning. He assumed after shows the 'boys' would still be a little 'adjacent' as it were, and the frown and raised eyebrows he received, confirmed his conjecture and Rod was pleased to find he had a sympathetic room mate if only for a night.

He rested on the bed after Rod had departed for the sound check and later when he paid his money and stood at the back to take in at least some of the performance he had to admit Rod had appeared to achieve something he had never managed. It really did sound like 'everything was louder than everything else'! By the time Rod returned from his duties as chief nanny he was in bed asleep or at least pretended to be for a late night conversation about bands and equipment he did not relish and sensed there was a tiresome time ahead.

"Bowie, my boy, how's it hanging?"

He had risen quite early and thanked Rod for his hospitality, breakfasting alone in a coffee shop around the corner from the hotel. The 'boys' would not normally be out of bed before noon, but he wanted an element of surprise and so what better than to wake them up – two of them always found that particularly disagreeable. Rod had informed the reception desk of the more opulent hostelry where the 'boys' resided of his surprise visit and he eventually arrived at the hotel around mid morning. Having reported to reception he was escorted to the suite by a bellboy who knocked on the door, but still failed to receive a tip.

"Did you catch the show?"

He had not had time to inform on the suspension of his appendages and true to form, just as he remembered it, the most important thing to the 'boys' was the 'boys'. Three members did in fact rise to the occasion or at least sit up in bed and say how pleased they were to see him, although was it really necessary to come in the middle of the night? They chatted desultorily for a while, but as soon as he saw signs of serious awareness which meant they would soon be reaching for the 'funny fags' he addressed the reason for his visit.

"I have come to ask a favour."

Immediately there was consternation. Favours suggested doing things for other people for no reward and that was not part of the 'boys' philosophy of life.

"It's very simple; I want you to take a package back to England for me. It's perfectly legal, not drugs or any other contraband, just a few papers and to be honest I don't think that's much to ask after what happened with the coke."

There was a lot of avoided eye contact and people suddenly having to go to the bathroom and eventually 'Bassie' was asked his opinion despite still lying completely covered by a duvet. The large bedroom housed four single beds and there was an adjoining lounge, the modified configuration of the suit no doubt in honour of the 'boys' and 'Bassie' had the bed furthest from the lounge. Bassie – he not being bothered that his nickname corresponded to another slightly more competent musician – was the *de fasto* leader of the band. Bassie was also the only one that had not bothered to say sorry about what had happened with the coke regardless of how insincere the apologies might have been he had been grateful for them at the time. If he were to have a problem it would be with Bassie.

At first there was no response from under the duvet, but eventually after a reasonable amount of whining from the others, Bassie rose to grant them the benefit of his wisdom.

"Why should we do anything for you, you don't even bleedin' work for us anymore?"

Bassie came round the end of the bed and stood in front of him as the others gathered nearer, now preferring what they were hearing. He smiled at the bass player and wondered if he still did not sing into his very loud microphone.

"*Quid pro quo* they call it, don't they, tit for tat, I did you a favour now you do me one."

Bassie was unimpressed, "Bollocks to that, piss off, bleedin' roadies, who the bleedin' 'ell d'you think you are?"

There was a silence, but he did not let it develop shrugging and looking sheepish, "You're right, I'm sorry; I hope you didn't mind me asking?" As he spoke he moved towards Bassie to apologise properly, then turned as if to depart, but did not complete the turn. Spinning back, with all the weight of his legs and body behind it, he punched Bassie as hard as he could in the unprotected and unsuspecting stomach.

Bassie made almost no sound, but crumpled on the floor in obvious agony.

"Now gentlemen, I don't think with Bassie, indisposed shall we say, even though there are three of you, you would be silly enough to start any fisticuffs or anything?"

He was confident they would not. They had seen him scrap on a few occasions, but more importantly he had seen them and he knew without Bassie there would be no heroics.

"All I'm asking is that you take a package back to England for me and then you will never hear from me again, if not well let's see……." He spoke as if to a class of ten-year olds, "I know where the drugs come from, the dealers, your suppliers and of course that you do an amount of 'selling on' as you call it, which I believe the authorities term 'dealing' and which they get very upset about."

He waited and watched. Nothing new, they were acquainted with the drug scene, rock stars rarely 'went down' and it was felt by many the 'image' could only be enhanced.

"But there is of course one area where life could get awkward. You'll remember the two young ladies that stayed a couple of years ago, let's see they must be nearly sixteen by now, the trouble is they weren't anything like that at the time." Now he had their attention, "They seemed to enjoy themselves, when I arrived in the morning they were full of it so to speak, but the authorities can't tell the difference between fourteen years and fourteen months, these days it's all Paedophilia. All very difficult for a working band I know, but they really are quite hot on that sort of thing now, people go away for it, even pop stars, in actual fact, one might almost say especially pop stars."

Bassie moaned.

"It's OK Bassie, you'll be alright in a minute just try and pay attention there's a good boy. As I see it your problem is that being 'pretty boy coke heads' life inside is not gonna be good, unless of course you want your arse reamered three times a day. Now," he took the rucksack off his back, opened it and began to extract a few items, "this is the package and it goes in this rucksack." He unfolded the second rucksack and placed the package inside, "With this screwdriver you take the back off one of the speaker cabinets and wedge the rucksack inside, don't tell me you can't because of course I know you can. When you get to the lock-up, you take the rucksack out and you store it amongst the junk in the Orange bin, it's still there is it, no one has tidied it up or something?"

There were nods - it was still there.

The Orange bin was not a dustbin, but a redundant speaker cabinet, the speakers had long since been removed and it was now used as storage for miscellaneous items not in day to day use.

"That's all you have to do, you don't tell anyone about it, not Rod of course like you didn't tell me, but unlike me he will be taking no risk and nor will you, so what's it to be? Bassie what do think, favour or fucked, d'you really never wanna make a noise farting again?"

As he spoke he stamped on Bassie's knee with the bottom of his foot and like the punch he was amazed at how hard he had done it, but it had the desired effect.

"OK, OK." Bassie whispered, but was he convinced?

"One last thing gentlemen, please do not think I'm joking, if you fuck with me I'll see you go down and if the truth won't do it, I'll lie through my fucking teeth."

And with that rather melodramatic rejoinder he tossed the second rucksack on the nearest bed and left the room.

He walked through the hotel lobby unmolested. If he had failed to make an adequate impression it would be the reception desk that would be informed first of the assault. So far so good, but he would not be certain he was in the clear until he was out of the country – the 'boys' might still be wrestling with how the foreign telephone worked. The longer he went unchallenged however, the more likely he would remain so and the 'boys' would complete the task he had set them, if not for the sake of a friend then for the sake of their own arse - literally.

A covert inspection of Rod's key ring had shown that the keys to the lock-up remained the same, for although he had left the keys to the van in Dover, he had retained his set for the lock-up and they matched. If they did as he had asked he would have achieved perhaps some comfort.

The train was on time, on the continent they were rarely anything else and he gratefully took his seat, again by a window. This time his passport was examined along with his ticket, which caused him brief anxiety, but it appeared to be routine and he arrived back in Strasbourg earlier than anticipated, thus had a couple of hours to wait before the rendezvous.

If that is, she arrived?

Chapter 26

Mobile telephones are both a blessing and a curse. To report an emergency - a boon, permanent contact at all times, for a cheating spouse - a nightmare, nowhere to hide, not even for a few hours. But like nearly all modern-day technologies there is a sinister down side - surveillance. In an age when supermarket chains know more about their customers lives than the customers do, it is very burdensome to go unnoticed and inconspicuously.

Mrs. Mills would not use a mobile telephone.

He understood more now her fundamental aversion to the device, but it was the surveillance aspect that really caused her concern. Mobiles could be pinpointed via the transmitters when the number was known and when it was not, it was possible to identify incoming numbers so even the unregistered mobiles were not immune if one knew on what telephones they would call and therefore needed to be scrutinised. Add to that satellite navigational positioning systems that could pin point to within a square metre and her caution could hardly be considered extravagant, no, regardless of the past, Mrs. Mill's mobile phobia was founded in good practice.

It was also at times however, very inconvenient.

He had waited for two hours and rather than growing calmer he was experiencing what he assumed to be a delayed shock to the events of the morning. It was not his way to attack people, even people he did not like and admittedly he did not like Bassie. What troubled him was how hard he had hit the bass player. He had not thought about it at the time, he was just desperate that they do as he asked, which to him seemed a minimal gesture given what had taken place previously. The only argument in their defence was that they were not aware of the whole story concerning his arrest, but even then he was not asking for a lot, he just hoped Bassie was well and the list of indictments against him was not going to grow.

He had thrown caution to the wind and was now on his fourth cup of coffee, the café and similar establishments presumably what the higher denomination Euro notes were printed for, but would soon leave for the rendezvous point. It was too soon, but you never know, perhaps she would be early?

She was not.

He cursed viciously under his breath as he again circled the square sweating beneath his original rucksack which he hoped would demonstrate to any casual observer, he appeared to have the same bags as when he had left. Eventually to his great relief he saw the camper ease into the temporary-parking bay and he forced himself to walk over to it rather than run, which was how he felt. He opened the door, climbed inside and very deliberately put on his seat belt.

"Everything OK?"

There may have been some strangeness in her voice, but he did not really notice, just stared ahead out of the windscreen forcing her to ask again.

"Yes fine," he said eventually and started to shake.

"Just sit still, take some deep breaths and drink your tea."

She had stopped at the first rest area after joining the AutoRoute and it was quite crowded, so they just parked and pulled the curtains as if they were taking a few hours rest during a long journey. The tea was hot and sweet, but thankfully not weak so he assumed she considered his condition not life threatening.

"Do you want to tell me what happened?"

"No." his answer was automatic.

"You ungrateful Bastard!"

He was not accustomed to her casual use of these types of words and it genuinely surprised him and also made him smile, just for a second.

"I hit someone."

"Did they deserve it?" she was offhand, matter of fact, was she laughing at him? "Did you hurt them?"

He took one of the prescribed deep breaths.

"If you're laughing at me I don't care, I hit someone very hard and they were totally defenceless and it's upset me, which I don't quite understand as I don't like the man but then I'm worried in case he's not alright." The little speech seemed to take a lot out of him and he started to shake again.

He swore, "And you could've been a bit early if you'd wanted to!" He was beginning to feel quite unwell.

"It is as potentially hazardous to be early for a rendezvous as it is to be late and at least the person you hit was a man - not that to my knowledge you've ever managed to hit a woman, dirty one occasionally, but never actually hit."

He made as if to comment, but she waved him to silence.

"Now change your clothes and go and lay on the bed and I'll bring you some more tea."

All he had readily available was the tracksuit so he slipped in on over his underpants and went as he had been told to lye down on her bed, stretching, desperately intent on not adopting a foetal position. Knowing he would never be allowed to live it down in the days ahead.

"So what happened?"

She gave him his tea after he had sat up then joined him, sitting with her back rested against the side of the van, her legs stretched down the bed. He told her about the punch.

"Did he go down? Did he make any sound afterwards? Was he conscious? Was he coherent? He answered in the affirmative to all.

"Did he respond to further physical stimuli?"

"Yes," at this rate she could open a nursing home if all else failed.

"How do you know?"

"I stamped on him."

She chuckled, "Don't like doing things by halves do we?"

This time he made no comment.

"It sounds like there will be nothing wrong with your friend once he gets his breath back. It is very hard to kill someone by hitting them where you have explained unless you know what you are doing or are very strong - you are neither, so I shouldn't worry about it – move on. Oh, and while we are on the subject, am I still to be excluded for the reason for all this gratuitous violence?"

He nodded conclusively, finishing his tea, but she carried on unfazed.

"In that case then there's another subject on which I would be grateful if you would elucidate, what is your problem with nudity?"

He was shocked, but then he already was, so what was this all about, make the fat kid sick on doughnuts so he won't eat them anymore?

"Why?"

She carried on in the 'business as usual' manner summarily dismissing his question, "Why not? You won't tell me about why you absconded and we've got to talk about something, so why not the reason for you wearing more clothes in bed than in the woodshed and the panic when I saw you naked?"

"Later."

She was not satisfied, "What'd do you mean, later?"

He lied down, "I'm tired and I think I'll see if I can sleep for a while, I'll tell you later."

"Coward!"

"I know," he was genuinely tired, "anyway, it's none of your business."

"Coward!"

She left the bed and drew the curtains behind her, with any luck he would get some sleep and be back to normal in a few hours, it was always the risk with amateurs, biting off more than they could chew, she must remember to remind him. Still for the moment she had given him something else to think about.

"I wore pyjamas as a kid."

She had rejoined him on the bed. He had slept for nearly two hours, once calling out, but other than that remarkably peacefully considering the state he had worked himself into.

"I only remember one pair now, they were maroon with a gold colour paisley pattern and I was wearing them the night my parents were killed."

It was still only eight o'clock in the evening, but had clouded over and with the curtains of the camper closed it was quite dim inside.

"I was staying with my grandmother when the police came."

He stopped. She did not interrupt, just sat leaning back against the side of the camper on the bed, legs stretched out as before.

"I only wore those pyjamas from then on until the trousers could not be repaired anymore and eventually the top became too small, so I slept with it under the pillow."

There was another pause and then his voice changed.

"And you will be very pleased to hear Mrs. Mills that I never had anymore pyjamas and slept naked from then on, that is until my grandmother died."

She thought for a moment that that was the end of the story, but realised when he spoke again that that had been the end of the boy.

"You learn very quickly in 'care' nudity is not to be recommended."

His voice was hard, no louder but embittered.

"There are the other borders, some of the 'carers' even some of the 'visitors', you learn very quickly 'getting naked' is not good."

He sniggered, but there was no mirth.

"I was OK. I was older than many and I discovered that if you go berserk, it puts people off, they are looking for compliance, appeasement, accommodating attitudes, not trouble-makers or the frenzied."

He was calm now, nearly back to normal and peculiarly she was disappointed.

"So you see Mrs. Mills I've nothing against nudity, I appreciate as an only child I'm not as comfortable or as flamboyant as most, but I'm not against it. Perhaps if you saw where I lived before all this you would understand, even that was not inducible to 'skinny dipping'."

He had lightened the moment and she felt she could interrupt.

"Then why were you so bothered when I came into your room, it was perfectly innocent, why much such a fuss?"

He sniffed. Perhaps she had misread the situation, but there was something here that intrigued her, why she could no think.

"I didn't make a fuss, I just don't see why I have to prance around naked in front of strangers - anyway I didn't like you that much at the time."

Surprised she realised she had found what she was looking for, by default a confession of a reduction in antipathy, it had been easy, but she still was not sure why she had bothered.

"Well, like me or not, I'm going to bed so are you going to stay there for the night or get on the floor?"

There was a hesitation she was sure, but he moved quite quickly to leave her bed.

"Do you want me to get off first or will you be safe climbing over me?"

She was already twisting into a sitting position to allow him to get passed when he bid her a touching goodnight.

"Cow!"

The next morning they were back on the road. They stopped at the first service station for petrol and to check the oil and tyres and then headed west leaving the German border behind. There was no rush as far as making any of the channel ports by the end of the month, but he wanted her to contact London as soon as they could and not from where they were at present. He wanted no risk that anyone should be aware of his trip east. He also wanted to find a place they could wait that would give them reasonable access to all the channel ports as no specific indication had been given as from where they would be directed to sail.

Basically he retraced the route they had taken a few days before on the AutoRoute passed Metz and Rheims, but this time turned south before Paris and arrived by late afternoon in the palace town of Fontainebleau where they comfortably mingled with dozens of other campers. Most of the journey had been made in silence, him concentrating on the driving after waking with what felt like a bad hangover despite having had no drink. He was assured however that this was the consequence of shock and would soon pass which proved to be the case. Indeed it was when he had begun to feel normal again that he broached the subject of his name.

“At the ‘home’ we had a visiting barber.”

He chuckled as if there were at least some amusing interludes while in care.

“The problem was, like many of his profession he was absurdly effeminate and I’m afraid some of us were impolite and his revenge was to make our hair look as if it’d been cut with a variety of implements other than scissors. Thus we drew our nicknames from what those implements might have been, there was ‘Razor’, ‘Mower’ and ‘Chopper’, I was ‘Bowie’, after Jim Bowie’s knife, the American frontiersman.”

She turned to look at him in the seat her voice non-committal, “So you want me to call you Bowie?”

"No," here we go again he thought, "not necessarily, but I thought as we have less than a fortnight to go and there's no one to hear, you can if you want. Regardless of what Auntie says, I don't like this Mr. Mills and Mrs. Mills business, it seems a tad 'effected' as my grandmother would have said."

She made no further comment and continued to look out of the window, so as things were going so well he thought he might take the opportunity to settle one other outstanding issue.

"There is one other item, as things are going so well and if I recall correctly, I believe the correct method of introduction is something like 'nothing I have said to you is untrue but……."

She once more turned toward him, but he was glad his concentration was needed for the road knowing his sarcasm had been a mistake.

"After I was initially marooned at the farm I found it unpleasant, but it was all there was so I just got on with it. I bought some chickens and goats and although I didn't have to make money I could see how a living could be made, not a fortune, but a living and slowly I began to enjoy it."

This was the difficult bit, but it needed to be said.

"A year went by and not much happened. I began to think that I could make a 'go of it' as they say, the locals all thought I was an idiot, but perhaps after everything was over I would get the farm and one day be a farmer. Silly really, I know, but when you're on your own the mind plays games."

He took a deep breath.

"And then you arrived and I knew it was all over. You were a professional, there was no room for you in my little dream you weren't going to stay and if you weren't, obviously nor was I, it had all been a nonsense from the start. Plus I'm afraid, as irrational as it may seem, I resented you for it, there was no one else near enough to blame except you, so I blamed you and for that I am sorry."

He did not expect a rosette or even a pat on the back, but he also did not expect her response, "Tell me about Germany."

"No."

"Not that sorry then!"

The Palace at Fontainebleau was magnificent. It stood in the middle of town almost being half the town and she was desperate to see it before they left. It lived up to everything she had read about and expected, thus she felt the delay well worth while which was gratifying for it had been a mistake. They were not aware of it at the time, in fact to date, they were not aware of any, but then it only takes one.

Chapter 27

He headed for the *Suisse Normande.* 'Norman Switzerland' as it was also known is an area south of the Normandy town of Caen and bordered by the rivers Orne and Dives. It was here that he intended to wait out the remainder of the time before they received instructions regarding the sailing. There were eight major ports that handled ferry crossings from France to England - Calais in the east across the Dover Straits, to Roscoff in the west across the English Channel proper - or *Manche* as it was termed by the French. He would wait equidistant between the two, but it was not for that reason alone.

The eighth of May persisted in influencing his thinking and he reasoned that if Victory in Europe were to play a part it would likely be this area that would be relevant. The northern French ports that included Dunkerque had mixed memories for the two countries, for although the evacuation is now viewed on the north side of the Channel as a heroic retreat, there continues a strong lobby on the south side which believe it to have been an ignominious rout. The Normandy Landings are less contentious and a far safer domain for any mutual commemorations and he would be not much more than an hour's drive from the 'Invasion Coast' and the Beaches of Sword, Juno, Gold, Omaha and Utah.

From Fontainebleau he drove west to the cathedral town of Chartres then Alençon before turning north to Argentan and Falaise eventually stopping for the night at Thury-Harcourt. Here in the *Suisse Normande* they would wait.

The Farmers Union, like all large institutions the world over, was plagued with meetings – committees, conventions, conferences all for the exchange of information or planning or as often, a digression for the management and a treat for the workers. The location of an assemblage can normally attest to the genuine reason for its existence. Early morning in the main office suggests there is some commercial or operation purpose. An overnight stay in a good hotel and a programmed visit to a site of national heritage suggests at least a mixture of work and play - a please and a thank you.

Then of course there is the influence of employee hierarchy to consider. Drivers for example might meet in the Transport Office and lunch in the local diner, while executives in the Boardroom and a 'starred' restaurant or hotel. It was therefore with great delight and just a little smugness that Mme.Poirier discovered her name had been added to the list for the forthcoming conference as a replacement for M. Bousse who had not at all been himself for the last three weeks or more. Her husband would of course complain, but her sister would prepare a meal for him and it was only for one night and whatever he said, she was not going to miss this trip. They were to stay in a particularly nice hotel called the 'Napoleon' of which she had heard exceedingly good reports and she was to at last see the marvellous Palace at Fontainebleau – a wonderful way to start the week.

As it transpired she was not as impressed as perhaps she might have been, but that might have had to do with the after dinner '*digestives*' she had imbibed the previous evening, nevertheless it would have been rude to refuse and after all, one had to get ones moneys worth. It had been while she was seated in the courtyard resting her throbbing head when she experienced a real sense of *déjà vu,* well actually it was the girl, but even then she was really too attractive. Similar to the one there was the fuss about at the office, although of course that poor 'mite' had been much plainer and had that scruffy foreigner as a fiancé or whatever, not like this chap at all, this one was quite smart, casual, but smart. Nonetheless they had arrived in an English camper and she was oriental in appearance and it would give the impression she was on the ball and perhaps they would remember that and not her tripping up the stars on the way to bed.

She had enjoyed herself and the least she could do was report as everyone in the office had confidentially been asked to do, should they come across an Englishman and a far-eastern looking girl. The story was that it was something to do with an accident on a farm and insurance or something, but she believed it was to do with the two that had come into the office that time and then gone missing. She was fairly certain this was not that pair, but it would still look good on her record, if of course anyone ever bothered to notice. Now she just had to walk over and make a note of the vehicle registration.

M. Bousse was not a happy man.

All was not lost of course, there was adequate cover and the disappearance of the Englishman and the girl may be a coincidence and nothing to do with the theft of the papers from the car. It had come to light however, that the pair had been making enquiries and may have obtained some information directly from the office, although everyone denied doing anything irregular except the young girl in reception of course.

There was nothing they could go to the police with other than the actual theft, one had to be careful with the police, they often had there own agenda and obviously the less they knew about the real situation the better. Nevertheless the Union had its own extensive workforce and membership and he had already circulated the licence plate numbers of two possible couples that had been spotted and might be of interest - i.e. an Englishman and a woman of oriental appearance in a camper. Now Mme. Poirier had reported another such sighting and in turn the details would soon be distributed, although whether the recipients would take any notice or not was another matter.

These days all farmers were encouraged to diversify and many set aside a field or paddock for camping – caravans and campers etc. The Union had a register of all these sites and provided some support for a nominal annual subscription, but mainly it was to keep a check on overall development. The problem was that there were as many unregistered sites where farmers chose not to inform the Union, thereby saving the cost and the need to declare the income. All he could do was circulate the licence plate details to those that were on record and hope, but it was really a vain hope, even if anyone wanted the bother, half of them couldn't read or write anyway!

"It's ten days since we saw Auntie."

"Nine."

He corrected her although it was not pertinent; he knew she wanted to contact London for a status report.

"Frightened we'll miss the boat?"

He joked, but she was right of course. Continuing not giving her time to reply, "You can phone from the post office before we go up into the 'mountains' and please if I may be so bold," he became more serious, "all I want to know is the place and time of the boat. I would prefer it if you didn't get into a conversation and if they ask where we are tell 'em Switzerland."

"Yes Master - I have done it before you know."

He made no comment, there was no need, they both knew they were approaching the end of the road - whatever that was – and although there would be an occasional bickering, the big dogs were in sight and the little ones must desist their squabbling.

They had parked overnight in the town car park by the river, specifically for tourists and it was only a short walk to the post office, but even so she was back within a few minutes.

"At present we are scheduled for the night boat from Caen on the thirtieth, but they want us to phone again in five days and then on the thirtieth itself for the confirmation to 'go'."

"Did they ask where we were?"

"Yes."

"What did you say?"

"Switzerland."

"What did they say?"

"I don't know - I hung up."

She gathered her shopping bag and a list from the table.

"Why didn't you get the shopping while you were out?"

From his subconscious he recalled that was her usual practise.

"Then you would not have been sure how long I was on the phone and I know how men complain about women who are always gossippoing on the phone."

The camper door closed behind her and he smiled to himself. It was a generous gesture, representative of a good working relationship perhaps, one pro to another - although he was not a pro of course, but he did appear to be making progress.

M. Laroux stared perplexed at the latest batch of paperwork from the Union.

Forms, accounts, protocols, invoices, newspapers, advertisements and circulars, he did not need a farmhand he needed a secretary - and he was not joking. As much money could be made from shrewd form filling as any other part of farming these days and one had to keep abreast of all variations and modifications in the grants system to maximise the possibilities however arduous the chore. A day would need to be set aside to go through this latest bunch of correspondence he aimlessly sifted through, one item catching his attention as it was not of the usual professional standard all literature seemed to be these days. He had seen something similar recently and he remembered it was about the campsite.

It was a serious source of dissension with M. Laroux for he had registered in all good faith only to find the rascal Gibbet further up the valley had ignored the request from the Union and carried on just as before. No registration, no fees and no tax no doubt – it really did rankle. He would have a wonder up the lane tonight and see if the old fool had any people on his campsite and then he could tell the Union rep about it next time he was in town, although precious little had been done about it last time.

"Funny old boy the farmer, typically piratical, should've been born to the sea not the *bocage,* he said you reminded him of a far eastern princess and I think he's bragging about you right this minute to a neighbour who looks suitably covetous."

Shopping done and secured away they had sedately set out to find a secluded site for the next thirteen nights – annoying how the number kept coming up. After a few false starts and dead ends, they had come across a quite isolated farm site at the end of a lane in one of the ravines along the valley of the River Orne. The local cows did not actually wear bells around their necks in honour of the region's designation, but then the two hundred metres or so the surrounding hills rose probably meant the beasts were too embarrassed to emulate their Swiss cousins.

"Yes it certainly is a lovely spot; do you think you'll miss France Bowie?"

It was the first time she had used the name and it would have been easy to make some wisecrack, but he did not.

They had been on the site for a couple of days now and things had improved between them, Germany appeared to be forgotten and the air - at least to some degree - had been cleared. He thought hard before he answered, for up until recently he most definitely would not have, lately however he was not sure, but it was immaterial anyway. France for him had become a side issue, what he was not sure of now was how to explain what he knew he was going to miss and it would not be long before he had to or let things drift away as usual.

"No, I don't think so. I've leant a lot for a town boy and some of the times have been good, but I don't think I'll miss it as such, I miss Dog and Perch, but there are other fields in other places, if France is closed to me there's always somewhere else."

It was a 'copout' he knew, he could have said more, it was a lovely evening, they were safe, an idyllic setting, you could even hear the river babbling along; he really was very disappointing at times. Nonetheless, judging by the posture and body language he was not as disappointed as their piratical farmer's neighbour who now looked positively nettled at the discussions he was having with their host over the field gate – more quarrels about the subsides no doubt.

By the time he got back M. Laroux had recovered from his irritation, the old fool Gibbet always had that effect on him, but this time it would be worth the hassle. This time he would surely see the old reprobate get his comeuppance. Not only did he have a camper on his unregistered site, it was the very one that the circular had been about, something to do with accidents and assurances, probably some foreigner driving into somebody then driving off.

Still that wasn't important, but when the Union received his letter and leant that he had spotted the camper they were looking for and on an unregistered site, old Gibbet's goose would be well and truly cooked. At first he thought he might ring the Union, but that might look as if he were being vindictive, no he would just send the circular back with a covering note, then no one could accuse him of being a bad neighbour.

Monday mail was always the worst.

Why did so many people wait until the end of the week, then rush off to the post office, was it just to ensure everybody had a desk full of mail on a Monday morning, to get the week off to a 'good' start?

In truth M. Bousse had recently been no happier on the other mornings of the week and although today he had received notification of a sighting of the camper that Mme. Poirier had originally spotted, inevitably everything came with problems. Now he had to get someone to take the young girl from reception to Normandy of all places, to see if she could identify the pair. She had already been away twice on similar local expeditions and people were beginning to wonder about her absences. The girl herself was not going to say anything, he had made it very clear what would happen if she did, disclosing confidential information was a very serious matter, not only could she find herself dismissed, but every likelihood of not finding another position, certainly not in this area.

M. Bousse picked up the telephone to dial the number he had been given by the Director of the Bureau to arrange when the girl was to meet the people that would take her to see the couple in the camper. No doubt they would meet at the station again to ensure no one from the office saw what was going on, all very cloak and dagger, but if it maintained the status quo 'so be it'.

The *Suisse Normande* is renowned for its varying climate. Not dissimilar to southern England, however it is possible to experience continuous days of sunshine even in early spring and before the impressive May blossoms.

His last days in France were such a period.

Mr. and Mrs. Mills enjoyed a surreal week and more surprisingly relaxed camaraderie. They spoke little, but were content nonetheless for that – he thought mischievously perhaps because of it – and although as the days passed the tension grew, it seemed they were at last in concert.

Apart from the sun and the company, he felt there were only two occurrences of note during this period, one was a conversation he had had with Mrs. Mills about anticlimax, which seemed disagreeably par for the course.

"You must prepare yourself for a sense of anticlimax at the end of all this Bowie."

Again he could think of any number of witty ripostes, but for refrained.

"It is very common that what we do will have no natural conclusion like you see in the movies, you must consider it more as 'carrying the ball' for a time as the American would say. You accept it, run with it and pass it on without dropping it – don't expect to feel a sense of achievement or satisfaction at the end of it, our work is not like that."

He could have again said it was not his work, but it would have been churlish and he knew her advice was well meant, although she did not have to worry, he did not think like that, he just wanted what he had wanted from the start - out!

The second incident was more amusing.

M. Gibbet was insistent that Mrs. Mills meet his nephew. The nephew had arrived with another friend and presumably one or other of their girlfriends, but when M. Gibbet had escorted his foreign prize along to his farmhouse it was only the nephew she had met, the other couple remained in the house.

"I noticed you didn't bother to accompany me to meet our friendly pirate's nephew?" she accused upon her return.

Having earlier glared at him over her shoulder while walking arm in arm with M. Gibbet down the field to the farmhouse, but ultimately had not been gone for long.

“What and spoil the old man’s story about how he intends to seduce you?”

She chuckled, “How do you know he says he going to seduce me?”

“He’s French, what else would he say, it’s all they ever think about?”

Her chuckling ended in a theatrical sigh, “Well, it’s nice to know someone thinks about it!”

Chapter 28

Two more nights, he only had two more nights to say something, but what? Probably better to wait until they were back in the UK – now where had he heard that kind of self-advisory procrastination before?

Curiously it also felt that the more normal there time together, the less he felt like raising any questions about what would happen after all this nonsense was over, for it looked at last as if it would end with them all in one piece. He decided he would say something as soon as she returned. It did not have to be anything too definitive, nothing that would case any embarrassment that everyone was so worried about or anything that he could not back out of, just float the idea of what she might be thinking of doing when this was over.

She had gone for a run along the riverbank, he delegating to adopt an 'every other day' modus operandi in view of the sunshine for which he had been duly chastened for his feebleness. London had confirmed everything was still arranged for the thirtieth and unlikely to change, they were just to verify on the day and they would soon be 'home and dry'.

There was a knock on the camper door.

He smiled, she had taken to knocking on returning from shopping or running, feigning consternation that she might happen across him in a state of undress. It was a joke and he was pleased she had taken the trouble to make it such after what he had explained and also that she felt trusted enough to treat an uncomfortable element of his past with a shared humour. He opened the door with a wry grin on his face that most decidedly was not the appropriate expression.

The first punch drove upward into his solar plexus forcing him back against the wardrobe opposite the camper door. He would have crumpled forward, but was held up by his shirt collar long enough for his assailant's knee to strike him agonisingly in the groin and then the floor appeared to rise up and strike him on the side of the head as he was flung sideways. He lay on his side and tried to lift his knees, but the aisle was not wide enough and eventually he realised someone was standing on his ankle which added to, though certainly did not replace, the other tortures.

He first concern was to get some breath into his lungs, but his agenda was not shared and the demands for '*les dossiers*' were dire and malicious. He thought he should perhaps not succumb immediately for fear his inquisitors would become suspicious, but only until the weight on his ankle increased and the pain took precedent over the rest at which point he waved at the bed and the storage locker beneath. The mattress was lifted and thrown back and the locker opened exposing a plastic bag with a few shirts and jumpers stuffed inside covering the package underneath. His ankle received more attention before following his almost screamed clarification, the second intruder was able to ascertain he was moaning the truth and secured the package the pair had been sent to procure.

And then they were gone.

As fast as they had arrived they were suddenly not there. They were replaced however; by the nausea that men joke about with their voices, but never their eyes, not unless that is they have never experienced the delights of crushed testicles. He lay having recovered enough from the blow to his stomach to fully appreciate the waves of nausea that swept over him and he would have cried if it had not hurt so much. Eventually when he thought the pinnacle of his suffering had passed he tried to move only to be overwhelmed by a stabbing sensation, this time in his side. Never having been one for abject torment he decided to sit tight – or to be more precise, lay curled not tight, as there was no room for anything else and that is how she found him.

He did not hear her coming.

She was just suddenly squatting beside him placing her hand on his neck.

"How many?"

It was strange, for all the time they had spent together they had hardly ever touched. Other than when she occasionally took his arm if they were walking in public.

"How many?"

This time it was louder, more urgent, more like the old days – the honeymoon must be over.

"Two, err……. I saw two."

He corrected himself, knowing what a stickler she was for detail when it came to mayhem and mutilation.

"Are you OK?"

"No." he answered, but she was gone.

"Arsehole!" he shouted after her, but it came out like a whisper and brought tears to his eyes from the pain.

"There's no one around now, but with all the wooded ravines it's easy to get near and away if you know what you're doing."

By the time she had returned he had managed a sitting position against the side of the bed and although he seemed to hurt everywhere it was the pain in his side that generated most concern.

"I need to have a look," she edged next to him and replaced the mattress, "can you get up on here?"

"Only with great difficulty and pain and I would rather stay here."

She completely ignored what he had said and bent down to lift his arm over her shoulder and amongst a significant amount of 'whinging and whining' he was manhandled onto the bed. He lay on his back and had begun to feel sick again, which he confessed and she went and got the bin from the toilet.

"Surprised you're interested." He grumbled, willing himself not to vomit.

"If you're referring to securing the area after I got back, it's standard practise and common sense, do you really want them returning while I'm helping you onto the bed?"

He said nothing, looking at the metal bin from the toilet – why was it buckets and bowls always made you feel worse?

"OK, what's the damage?"

He tried to turn and cried out in pain, "I have a pain in my side, well in front on the right hand side, here somewhere." He gingerly fingered the bottom right-hand side of his rib cage.

"Tell me exactly what happened."

He gave a dramatic account of events from the time of the knock on the door until her return, highlighting all agonies and her neglect in glorious Technicolor, which was exactly how he remembered it.

"So you were hit once in the stomach, kneed in the groin and someone stood on your foot?"

As she spoke she removed his shoes and manipulated both ankles, hearing no sound of grinding broken bones, defined as such over his wincing and asked for him to lift his shirt. This he did exposing the lower half of his chest and stomach.

"Do they do this white in gloss finish?" she asked, perfectly serious, "with the body hair you look like a milk bottle with alopechia!"

He said nothing as her fingers prodded at his midriff.

"Now," she moved her hand over the delicate area, "contrary to what the Doctors say, this will hurt."

And it did.

After the swearing had subsided, she wiped the tears from his eyes with the corner of the bed sheet and said she thought he may have cracked a rib, but more likely it was just bruised and there was no serious damage, no lung puncture. It would be painful for a few days, but he would soon be back to normal, she was however impressed with his assailant, he was obviously strong and proficient.

He was very pleased to hear he was to live, but equally unimpressed with her choice of hero and explained thus unequivocally.

"So that leaves the testicles, who's going to check them, you or me?"

The look on his face was a picture as they say and another time and place she could have become hysterical, but if his attacker was as good as it appeared with his fists it was likely he would be equally competent with his knees, it needed to be checked.

She stepped away from the bed and turned around, "You need to stand up and drop your pants." She spoke in a manner of fact fashion not seeking to cause affront, "Make sure everything is loose and can be moved normally without any significant pain, we have to ensure none of the little tubes have become disconnected and of course there should be no blood."

He struggled off the bed and did as he was told, gratefully perceiving no red stains in his underpants. In fact all seemed to be in order other that the understandable dull ache, although there was a distinct overall impression of contraction as if the ensemble involved were as disinclined to violence as their host. He made one last inspection and then looking up reported all was well, only to see she had turned round and was scrutinising with simulated concentration.

"Pervert!" He barked, quickly hoisting his pants.

"And you seem 'pervertly' OK, do you want a cup of tea?" she watched him buckle his belt, "or do you think that's what's at the heart of this incredible shrinking disease you've contracted?"

He ignored the last comment, remaining aloof from such nonsense knowing the diversion intended as an anecdote to his resent trauma – or at least hoping it was.

"No, we have to move on immediately and I'm sorry, but for the minute you will have to organise it."

Instantly she left the camper and packed away all the items they had amassed outside, during the week. Not worrying to much about the tidiness of her packing, piling odds'n'ends into the aisle for the time being only making sure nothing was left behind.

"Do I say anything to Long John Pierre?"

In less than five minutes she had the camper gently easing down the field to the farmhouse.

"No, just pay him and tell him I've a reoccurrence of an intestinal condition and we're going to your Mother's in Paris and don't hang about."

M. Gibbet was not sorry to see them go, but grateful for the tip. The truth was the two men that had insisted he join in a little deception, to see if the English woman was the same one that had stolen their sisters purse, he found quite intimidating. The accents suggested that they came from Paris and it was advisable to keep well clear of the '*parisians*' and he did not know what was going on, but he certainly could not believe that the charming you woman was a thief – only of hearts perhaps?

"Where do I head for?"

He opened the map book, found the appropriate page and placed it on the consul between them.

"East, towards the coast, but as soon as you can, find me an isolated wood or a forest and a land-way or track off the road, Oh and make sure when we stop we're not being followed."

"Shall I fix lunch as well while I'm at it?"

He ignored her again it was his job to be facetious.

"I'm going to lie down, I don't feel so good."

She glanced across from the road ahead, "You OK?"

It sounded almost like she cared, "Yes, fine thank you, I'm just going to try and grow my Willie back!"

"Where are we?"

He had slept for over an hour and had been woken by the camper bumping along a track of some kind.

"St. Sever-Calvados, this is the forest, it's about twenty five miles from the coast. I could have stopped before, but I wanted to be certain we weren't being followed, I am now."

"OK let's get started."

The camper was parked in a forest track well off the road and as importantly, around a corner so that it was not visible. What they had to do would not take long, but it had to be completed beyond the scrutiny of prying eyes.

First he emptied from her suitcase the items that had originally been supplied with the camper; obviously he would replace the licence plates, which would have needed to be done anyway. At the same time he explained the 'stickers and transfers' that attested they had visited a host of UK stately homes and safari parks together with somewhat less gracious seaside resorts, she was to adorn to the rear of the camper. Leaving one for each front wing, the centre of the bonnet and most important of all, six on the door, three on the top and three on the bottom.

There were two magnetic pendants for the top of the dashboard, one flying a plastic Tricolour and ironically the other a Union Jack. A pair of huge fluffy brown and white dice for the central rear view mirror and a large green looking creature that suggested ET did not go home after all, that was to swing in the back window. After replacing the licence plates with the remaining screwdriver from the camper toolbox he used it to prise off all the wheel hubs and hid them behind a tree - for a passing sled enroute for the *Suisse Normande* perhaps?

"Sleds don't have wheels."

He disregarded her lack of empathy for poetic licence and started the camper engine manoeuvring the vehicle off the track alongside and almost touching a medium size Oak that protruded a little beyond its peers. It was necessary for him to climb down from the camper and physically inspect the positioning relative to the tree a couple of times despite the sharp pain in his side, as it was the off-side of the camper that was in question and he had to be precise. He was satisfied when the tree was adjacent to a point behind the rear wheel arch, but in front of the rear light cluster. When he returned to the wheel he forced maximum left hand lock – also a particularly painful exercise - then after increasing the revs, quickly let out the clutch and the camper leapt forward and sideways propelling itself against the tree.

The damage was quite impressive given he had only used medium revs and it was easy to see just how so many campers and caravans carried the badge of a driver who still thought their unit was no longer than a mini - obviously the mysteries of turning circles and fulcrums remaining just that for a surprising number of homes on wheels folk. He repositioned the camper to a more customary position on the track and climbed down for the last time to rub some dirt over the marks that initially suggested the significant dent was recent.

"Very artistic, a kind of Henry Moore of campers are we?"

They both climbed back and he ushered her into the driving seat.

"Not feeling well again?"

"No I feel much better now thank you," he assured her, "but it's all about deception and plausibility and now it will appear much more authentic if the camper's habitual driver is a woman!"

Two hours later they parked in the huge car park at the Le Mont St. Michel. To date he had tended to favour seclusion for there security, but now it was clear the opposition was prepared to use violence he believed they would be safer amidst the masses. Car and campers were not allowed on the island, in reality more of a rocky outcrop from which the steepled abbey rose and so all visiters were herded onto the landing strip of a car park on shore.

They parked and became one of over a hundred nondescript similar mobile bed-sits.

"I'm sorry Mrs. Mills, but now I don't feel so good again, I'm afraid I must ask you to take all this stuff and distribute it outside to make it look as if we've been here for sometime."

He indicated the items lying in the aisle, but she was more concerned with his pale face, "How do you feel?"

There are those men that deny any amount of pain and discomfort and overcome all manner of trials and adversity with stoic indifference – and then there were men like him.

"Apart from the pain in my side I have a headache, still feel sick and sometimes I seem to have double vision."

She had begun to collect things from the aisle.

"Mild concussion, where you bumped your head on the floor."

Bumped was not the word he would have chosen, smashed, battered or bludgeoned, he wondered if she was taking it seriously enough?

"And I'm……. sweating a little."

She stood, arms full of camping accessories, "And what else?"

How did she know there was something else and why did all his troubles with her have to occur south of his belt?

"When I had a pee back at the wood, there was blood in it."

She turned and walked to the door.

"And you've spent the last two hours working yourself into a state and imagining all kinds of things and wondering if your Willie's going to drop off - by the way how did your horticultural efforts go, any improvement?"

He stared at her wondering why he thought he could ever talk to her about anything important or why he would ever want to.

"Did it hurt?"

He shook his head.

"Minor internal bleeding in the duct or urethra, not uncommon amongst fighters if they are not careful, problem with wearing all that 'tackle' on the outside. Now could you open the door for me then go and lay down and try and get over it – someone hit you that's all, he was good, but he still only hit you."

Later she joined him on the bed.

He made a token offer to retire to his sleeping bag, but was easily dissuaded. He was reasonably comfortable, half-asleep and if he was honest, happy not to be alone. The hard floor of the camper held no attraction for him even with the under foam, but that was not the real reason. He thought he had been making progress, but he was patently wrong. Not everyone had what it takes to be a hero, he just hoped he had enough of it to get home and get out.

The way he felt at the minute that was all he could hope for!

Chapter 29

"Does it seem strange waking up in bed next to a beautiful woman Bowie or is it something you're use to?"

He had been awake for sometime, lying on his side watching her face. She slept on her back, her face totally expressionless, serene almost.

"Have you been awake long?" deflecting her question with one of his own.

"Longer than you think and am I not to receive an answer?

He waited, but it did not seem worth the bother of evasion, one way or the other, "It was a while back, I thought there may be something, but there wasn't. She's married now with a couple of kids - and happy, so I'm told."

She did not comment further for a few minutes and then more practically, "I am going to get up now Bowie and you know the attire in which I sleep, so I'm giving you the opportunity to close your eyes."

He still had his eyes closed when she returned with two cups, one coffee one tea.

"You can open your eyes now, I am fully clothed and how are we today?"

He ignored the sarcasm and the sugary tone with which it was delivered.

"I feel better, the headache's gone and I can see straight, there's still a pain in my side, but if I don't pee claret again I'll be fine."

She moved to one side on the edge of the bed, "Then go and pee and come back and tell nurse all about it."

Once more he ignored the disdain and cautiously made his way to the toilet trying to disguise a host of other aches and pains that became apparent as soon as he got off the bed.

"OK?"

He came back and sat on the edge of the bed.

"Well of course it is," she went on answering her own question, "you'd have passed out by now if it wasn't."

She collected the cups and carried them back to the sink, "So what's the plan of campaign Oh Master of Operations, I assume your exposure to the sharp end will now make you much more content back in the strategic planning department at mobile HQ."

He began to chuckle despite the stabbing in his side, "And who's working themselves up into a tizz now, just because their security was breached?"

For a moment he thought she was not going to smile, he even wondered if he was in for another pummelling, but if you 'dish it out you have to be able to take it' and thankfully a wry grin did eventually twitch at her mouth.

"Seriously, what are we going to do?"

"Nothing today - absolutely nothing."

By now the Union would know that their sortie had only managed to recover about a third of the files that had been stolen. Obviously they would make another try for the rest and would start with M. Gibbet. It would be unlikely that the story reported about a trip to Paris and parents because of intestinal problems would be accepted as the truth, particularly if those looking were as proficient as was believed. The two at the farm were probably not Union members, but hired muscle, which suggested the Union was reluctant to go to the police and quite understandably given the circumstances. What would they say 'we sent in some heavies to snatch 'em back, but we didn't get 'em all?'

Should there be an identifiable risk of the files leaving the country however, that may very well change things, but in any event there was a possible 'halfway-house' option that caused him concern.

Customs are not the police.

Most police forces have very little day to day contact with customs, but many farming bodies do, the movement of livestock being a constant catalyst for animal welfare departments like the UK's old Ministry of Agriculture, Fisheries and Food and its replacement DEFRA and the big farming organisations. Often personnel from a variety of these organisations would wait on the same quayside for the same boat to execute their complimentary duties, he knew he had seen them often enough.

French liaisons would be the same if not more intimate. The full resources of the police may not be mobilised against them, but it would be very likely that favours may be asked of customs and it did not help that they had been found 'holed up' an hour from the Normandy coast. That may have been a mistake. He could only hope that they might think he was cleverer than he was and that it was a deception, that they were perhaps intending to attempt a crossing from one of the Pas de Calais ports, after all they were the shortest crossings and the most popular. But with only eight ports the vigil would be thorough, as indeed their disguise needed to be to stand any chance of success.

“We just sit in the camper looking at each other all day?” she demanded.

He had noticed doing nothing was not her style, “Yes, you go onto the Mount if you want to, you won’t be noticed, half the people their will be Japanese, but I shall stay here to complete my recovery and finalise my plans for tomorrow.”

She squinted at him, “I no Yapaneese.”

“I know.”

Then in her more normal dismissive manner, “You have no idea what you’re going to do, do you?”

He smiled, took a pencil and paper from the shelf above the table and sat down. There was an amount of huffing and puffing during the day, but he was grateful that ultimately she chose not to leave the camper and spent the time tidying and preparing a couple of light meals. The tidying would prove worthless once his plan became operational, but he said nothing, people dealt with stress in different ways, look at him he had spent half the morning in the toilet. It had not really helped and how he was going to break the news of his efforts therein caused him as much anxiety as anything else.

“We’ve a busy couple of days ahead of us Mrs. Mills so I think I will have an early night and if it is acceptable, I would like to sleep on the bed as before?”

He seemed to have spent as much time on the statement as he had on the other matters in hand, but she still managed a scornful reply, “Wow! An early night with Bowie, how could a girl resist?”

He sighed resignedly, “Is it OK?”

She did not answer, just nodded her head with a complacent smile. He had already been asleep once when he felt the bed move as she lay down. It was still not dark, but despite the day of inactivity he was tired and just drifting off to sleep again when she spoke, "Good luck, Bowie."

The voice was different, quiet and earnest. She did not often speak like that, but there had been one particular time, he was sure he would be able to remember if he tried, of course, now he had it, it was the day they had been married - and he fell asleep.

They had an eighty-mile journey and the boat sailed at thirty minutes before midnight, although they were due to check in forty-five minutes earlier. The road trip could be completed in a little over two hours, but as ever he had things to do and did not intend to take a direct route. They left the Le Mont St. Michel behind at ten in the morning and made their way via Avranche to the town of St. Lô stopping on the outskirts at a hypermarket; here she would commence her shopping.

"Why me?"

Her complaining he found almost laughable considering the situation.

"Because the vast majority of the items that are to be purchased are normally bought by women. Sometimes by couples I'll grant you, but we do not want to be seen together, therefore you are selected by default."

"You could buy some of these things without drawing attention to yourself."

She really was making a fuss.

"Yes I know, but it would be better if I was not seen if you are going to be seen getting out of the same English registered camper and you have to call London anyway."

She sat studying the list, if he did not know her better he would have said she was sulking.

"What if I can't get 'clear glass gold-rimmed' spectacles?"

She made it sound like he was asking for half a pound of Plutonium.

"Then get the weakest ones they have, they're readily available now in pharmacies and quite cheap – it's not really gold!"

She sighed, "And what do you mean by tinted ones with lenses that make your eyes round?"

She knew exactly what he meant.

"It was a joke."

"'Ballots!'"

He thought his ears were deceiving him.

"What?"

"Ballots, I think we should have ballots about racist insults, after all you've got a couple of things that aren't round anymore."

He sat and waited.

"What if London calls it off?"

He had probably overlooked something, but had anticipated this eventuality, "Say nothing, but we are going tonight whatever happens."

He waited a little longer and then she opened the door and climbed out.

"Don't forget, not too much of the stuff in the same store, not enough to be remarkable."

She mouthed at him through the closed door-window and he wondered just how deficient his hearing was – probably not at all!

"I've got the spectacles, the baby food, orange juice, feeding bottles and the big bin liners the other things we would do better at a specialist baby shop and a hair salon. Oh, and I didn't bother with the little bin liners as we have some - and London said 'go'."

He was driving out of the hypermarket car park and wondering where he would find a baby emporium.

"Did London say anything else?"

"Yes, 'go' and you are to collect the tickets from the Brittany Ferries desk at the port. I briefly informed them of the robbery and they confirmed whatever happens, don't put anything in the post."

He thought for a few moments, "Why all the fuss about the post, we have sent things before?"

She considered his query carefully, "There are machines now that can see, hear and smell. It is possible to impregnate paper or files and for them to be detected by a form of screening. Not everyday stuff and not all the time, but quite possible for example for international mail. If say the official stamp on the grants were detectable it would show up and be investigated. Why was a batch of internal official documents leaving the country?" She paused, "In our business copies are interesting, but the 'real' thing is priceless and the post is not as confidential as people think or you wouldn't have drug runners would you? They'd just 'pop it in the post!'"

Not convinced he again sought elucidation, "Then why did Auntie put up with my nonsense about the package being posted to the newspaper if she knew they wouldn't get there, they paid the money to the home?"

She shrugged, “Because she wouldn’t have what she wanted, would she? Her first concern is to get what she wants, what happens to you is immaterial, good or bad. We are professionals, it’s not personal, she’ll give you all your little triumphs as long as she gets what she wants in the end.”

A strange world he thought continuing on the next leg of their journey.

“Could you put the small bin liners back on the list please, I used all the others up yesterday.”

She made no comment, but amended her paperwork.

The Bayeux Tapestry depicts Duke William’s conquest of England. One in the eye for poor old Harold and he hoped they would fair better than the English king had done almost a thousand years before.

It was not arrows he was worried about however, but being spotted before they had their full disguise in place, nevertheless there was no alternative and so he cruised the *centre ville* until he found a hair salon that from the window display sold wigs. He stopped a hundred metres further on and said he would return and drive past at fifteen-minute intervals. She missed the first two and he was wondering just how long it took to buy a wig when he spotted her on the third pass coming out of a stationers further along.

“I have the wig and the ‘Baby On Board’ sticker and I picked up some different make up.”

She was back in the camper and they were circling the town looking for signs to the shopping centre the hairdressers said boasted a specialist baby store.

“There,” she pointed, “on the by-pass towards Caen.”

He followed her directions and within ten minutes or so they were in yet another shopping centre car park.

"You sure you don't want to be the 'proud Father' this time, shopping for his new born?"

He smiled, "No thank you, I know what's on the list."

This time she did not look back through the camper door window and he could understand how she felt, they were both getting a mite edgy and just wanted it to be over. He thought about her recent word of warning, but 'anticlimax' looked pretty good to him right now.

This time when she advanced on the camper it was not a shopping trolley she was pushing across the car park, but a pram. Once more he could think of no end of witticisms, but instinctively knew that now was not the time. Not even for him. He stepped down from the camper and moved to the door to help her transfer her booty.

"Clothes, blankets, nappies, more feeding bottles and a potty, although how you expect a new born baby to sit on a pot I can't think and of course baby herself."

She proudly held up a lifelike, 'new born baby' size, doll, which when she squeezed it made a sound like a transistor radio being sick.

"And last but not least, baby's chariot itself. Exactly as specified - a wheeled chassis and a superstructure that detaches doubling as a carrycot. All present and correct Captain."

She saluted theatrically.

He disregarded her nautical accolade prompting, "Rubber gloves?"

She held her salute in place, “Rubber gloves and small bin liners also ready and correct Captain, request permission to come aboard?”

The Mulberry harbour was a monument to British ingenuity.

Following the D-Day landings at the start of June 1944, over the next three months more than half a million tons of heavy equipment and supplies were unloaded onto a beachhead without a natural harbour, by way of concrete jetties and pontoons that had been floated across the Channel.

It was late afternoon when he parked the camper along the coast from Arromanches-les-Bains facing the sea and the remnants of Operation Overlord. There was a lot to do, but they had time, being only twenty miles to the port and he intended to arrive no more than an hour before sailing. They ate a light, bland meal on which he was very particular, then all their purchases were unwrapped and the usual excessive amount of cardboard and plastic in which even the most ordinary item now arrived was crammed into a bin liner ready for disposal.

“How long will it take you to put the wig on and makeup etc?”

He was tying the neck of the bin liner.

“An hour or so.”

“An hour!” surprise and a taciturn dispute of the assessment.....

“Do you want round eyes or not?”

Duly chastened he sat and watched the transformation begin.

“Don’t you have anything better to do?”

She was not bothered by his scrutiny just wanted to ensure all was in order.

"Yes, but not 'til later."

Nevertheless he curtailed his study and took his guitar for a walk to the beach. He sat down and laid the canvas case next to him, undoing the front and exposing the old instrument that had served him well over many years. Although he was alone he spoke softly for fear he would be apprehended as a lunatic, voicing thanks for the valiant service and recalling some more mundane episodes as he steadily filled the body with sand and shingle from the beach. When he had finish he wedged the cleaning towel he kept in the case into the sound box on top of the sand preventing any spillage, re-buckled the case and returned to the camper with a very much weightier burden.

"Mrs. Mills, you look truly amazing!"

He meant it. She had long auburn hair, with lighter streaks, tinted wraparound spectacles through which hers eyes peered at him every bit as round as his.

"How do you do that?"

Instinctively she knew to what he was referring, living and working in a 'western' environment he was hardly the first to be astonished at what her make-up and facial contortions could achieve.

"An artistic bent and the ability to maintain a perpetually wide eyed expression."

In truth she was always surprised herself at the possible transformation even though she was only of half-Asian lineage.

"How do you manage the latter?"

"Normally I stick something up my arse!"

He smiled responsively, “That’s definitely the second if not the third naughty word in as many hours Mrs. Mills - is the pressure growing?”

It was not a criticism and not interpreted as such, but was retorted, “And you’ve become more focussed and clinical, you could have made a good field agent if you weren’t such a coward – no offence intended.”

“None taken Mrs. Mills.” The exchange was jocular, tongue in cheek, they were both pondering the night ahead.

“So what now Oh Master of Operations?”

“Now alas Mrs. Mills, we must indulge my alleged fetish.”

Chapter 30

The port of Caen is actually ten miles north of the town at the much smaller seaside resort of Ouistreham. The majority of port traffic would normally use the duel carriageway that runs between the two towns and which gives good access to the Caen ring road and the major routes that fan out south, east and west.

Ouistreham can also however, be approached from the east via a minor coast road, which runs almost directly into the port, by-passing much of the town and the main arterial route from Caen. By this contrivance and good fortune they arrived at the port, presently unscathed and as she wound down the window at the initial check-in booth he perceived, even across the two feet of open air, the woman gag at the stench that exuded from the camper.

Earlier however, things had not been totally devoid of repugnance.....

"I cannot do this Bowie, I'm sorry, I just cannot do it."

"It's OK," his voice was surprisingly considerate, "go and sit in the front, look out to sea and practice nursing little Ruth."

He could well understand why she could not do it; he was finding it hard enough and he was the one with the suppositional fetish. It was an hour before they were due at the port, and he had a dozen disposable nappies laid out in a row along the camper aisle. The glass jars of baby food had been heated and a generous helping applied to each nappy together with an ample splashing of orange juice and hot milk for good measure. Many of the baby clothes, blankets and other paraphernalia had also been spread with the sticky mix and he was relieved that before they had started he had thought to ask her to pack a bag with a selection of their clothes that might escape unblemished.

It was after Mrs. Mills returned from affixing the 'Baby On Board' sticker and he exited the toilet with a number of small bin liners twisted closed at the top that she began to finally doubt his sanity.

"No, no, please tell me that's not what I think it is?"

He stood with three or four bags in each rubber-gloved hand.

"Babies smell of stale milk and shit. Mums get use to it but everybody else would prefer not to, customs and security officers I'm sure are no different, whatever they show on the tele. The people they are looking for – and the need for disguise is that we must assume they are looking – do not have a baby with a severe case of diarrhoea, which might be a symptom of something contagious. By the time we get to the port this camper needs to smell like a cholera epidemic."

"But Bowie, it's disgusting, where did you get it?"

He proudly held up his transparent bags of yellow liquid and the more malleable browns, "All my own work, not all of us were lying around doing nothing yesterday."

"Fuck me, Bowie."

"Now, now Mrs. Mills that's enough of that, we have little Ruth to think about now, so into the front with you and practise that nursing like I told you - baby totally enshrined in the blanket and your shirt open to the waist. When I give the order we want it just like the Grenadier Guards, *tits out party, by the left, out tit* and make sure the nice customs man gets a good distracting eyeful, if it's a woman we'll just have to hope she's gay."

"Please turn the heater off Bowie."

They were parked in a line of campers waiting to go through customs and the heady mixture of baby products and adult by-products was cooking nicely inside the camper. He had been to the reception desk and collected the tickets without incident, but noticed there were more customs personnel around than he would have expected, but then that may be just coincidence.

"All in good time Mrs. Mills, we don't want young Ruthie to get cold, that's why we've got all the windows shut. If you've got a problem poke some more 'Vic' up your nose, but don't fall out of your bra too soon."

He had given her the camphor vapour rub to disguise the overpowering aroma he was cooking up in the camper, which is what they had used in the 'children's home' for similar aromatic crisis.

"I don't wear a bra, but thank you for not noticing it does so much for a girl's confidence."

The lights on the camper in front of them suddenly came on and the gap between the two vehicles widened as it pulled forward. He started the engine and slowly crawled after it.

"Here we go, Good Luck Mrs. Mills."

The customs were politeness personified.

They were sorry to hear about the baby being unwell and after a cursory inspection of their passports they were waved through the checkpoint.

"If you've made me suffer all that I have suffered just for that Bowie, I swear I will see to it they will never be round again."

Just as she was finishing her threat on his manhood, they turned a corner onto the main holding area for embarking vehicles and were waved to an adjacent lane, where two similar vans were being inspected by a group of plain-clothes men.

"OK. Mrs. Mills here we go for real this time, but at least they're all men and remember you don't speak French and speak English with an American accent - Daddy worked there."

He opened his window and said immediately to the man at the door that he thought they had already been through customs. The man was surprised to be addressed so fluently in his own language, but concerned when it was further observed that he was not customs and was there a terrorist problem? Before he could answer the rather superior Englishman was out of the vehicle and stating that if there was any doubt, he would prefer another sailing then proceeded to berate the official with a detailed synopsis of his tale of woe and calamity.

'He had enough on his plate at the moment with a new baby and an intestinal condition that she may have picked up in Spain – he only hoped it was not contagious – diarrhoea is the last thing you need, locked up with in a camper'.

'He could have flown of course, but his wife never would, yet still insisted on visiting his Mother before it was too late'.

'It would not be long now judging by the look of the poor old girl and then he supposed he would have to do the same damn thing all over again for the funeral'.

'Americans! Well she wasn't really, her Father worked over there for most of her childhood and she was raised with all

the paranoia they have out there - and she seemed to have got worse since the baby came along - women!'

'Come inside and have a look, I am quite happy to show you anything you want whatever, anything to stop the bombers that's what I say. Sorry about the smell, we have not been able to get rid of the nappies, had to make a bit of a dash for the port in the end, you forget what a big place France is '.

'Look at this, shit everywhere, it was never like this when I was a kid, I don't know what young Mums are about these days, it was the same when my brother's wife had a baby, shit everywhere.'

'Wash your hands now you have been in the toilet won't you, my wife was sick in there earlier on.'

"Pete, I have to feed Ruthie now, or my tits gonna burst."

The shout came from the front of the camper, passed the piles of rubbish sacks and soiled laundry.

"OK honey!"

'Marvellous, we can't stop it coming out and she wants to put more in, do you want to have a look in her side? If we go out I will open her door, I don't fancy stepping over that lot.'

As he spoke he indicated the pile of plainly soiled and almost effervescing nappies just behind the front seats and making way for the man to descend the steps onto the tarmac outside, quickly followed him while at the same time calling over his shoulder, "By the Left."

He overtook the man as they moved round the bonnet of the camper and opened the passenger door just in time for their inquisitor to get a good view of 'Honey's' left bosom as she tried to thrust the nipple into the blanketed bundle on her lap.

'Honey' was too occupied to notice, but the man wasn't. He would certainly have something to tell the rest of the others about over *pastis* tonight. And she was a good-looking woman. He would have had to do something about the smell though, how could you fancy anyone in that? He waved the camper on and retired immediately to the rest room to wash his hands.

He most certainly did not want a dose of 'Spanish tummy'.

There was a loud clanking as the camper bounced unsteadily off the ramp onto the boat deck. He followed the waved instructions of the loading crew and rolled to rest precisely where indicated. Chocks were placed under the wheels and they were handed a card that informed them which deck and what staircase they would exit by, so that they might return to their vehicle in the morning without getting lost. The stewardess that passed the card through the window winced enough to confirm their disguise was still potent, despite no doubt spending much of her working life dealing with unplanned body evacuations.

"Have I got everything?"

She would have, but was checking.

"Baby in the bottom, extra blankets so no one can pull the covers back and play coochy-coo, milk bottles on top, two dirty nappies for scenting and one clean one to show we care and your bits."

He shut all the windows and vents, climbed down and walked round to help her out with the baby and carrycot.

"Remember it's your pride and joy, don't bang it against the bulkhead or store your duty free in it, you OK on your own?"

She nodded and he reached in for his guitar and with some difficulty rested it onto the deck. He would not lock the camper, he was certain there were those aboard that would have skeleton keys, he would rely on his personal aura of the day before to keep the hounds at bay – two and four footed. If there were dogs on board he believed it would be drugs that they would be trained to find and if their handlers wanted to have a look inside the camper he wished them well. He was fairly confident that they had left the Union thugs behind; it was what awaited them on the other side of the channel that concerned him now.

He had drunk two pints of English beer and felt like he did after breakfast in le Lion-d'Angers.

"Will you have another?"

Strange, she would normally say something similar, but more like 'you will not have another'.

He said as much.

"Your drinking habits have changed Bowie, I believe now you drink as much as the situation dictates, not because you have to." She grinned, "It was just that when you first met me the situation dictated you drunk a lot, a significant amount at times as I remember, but of late you have drunk often very little, sometimes not at all, does that mean you don't care about me anymore Bowie?"

They were relaxing a little, coming back to earth or at least he was, perhaps for her it was the lack of baby bouquet. He ignored the question.

"No, I won't have anymore, we still have a couple of things to do, we'll wait 'till the bar shuts or at least the band finishes, no on can hear the baby's not crying while they're playing and then we'll go for a stroll."

After another half an hour the band announced the 'last number' and like good young parents they stood by the side of the carrycot and shuffled together as the Gladys Knight imitator 'asked for assistance during the hours of imminent darkness'. There were only half a dozen people in the bar when they left and none looked inclined to take a stroll around outside at this time of night and so they were soon alone on one of the promenade decks towards the stern of the ship.

"You first or me?"

He could not make out her face in the light of the moons first quarter despite the thin cloud cover, but he felt her close, closer than ever before somehow.

"I'll go, better baby have as long a life as possible."

He hefted the canvas bag and guitar onto the handrail and with as much force as he could muster pushed it over and away from the ship. Almost before he had time to recover his balance, she had the lighter carrycot with most of its contents on the handrail before it too was condemned to Davie Jones' Locker.

"Come, we have to go now in case someone saw them fall."

She tugged at his sleeve as he dallied looking after his old friend.

"Yes, sorry – and I forgot the sticker," he did not wait to be asked, "Baby Overboard."

They had had 'seats' booked for them for the overnight voyage – you had to book something. Presumably the thinking in London being that if they had got this far it was 'job done' and there was no need to run to the extra expense of a cabin. Whatever, they would only use one. She would sleep in the official reclining seat and he would rough it in the restaurant. Officially one was not allowed to stay in the restaurant overnight, but it had the advantage of having a few corner bench seats where it was possible to lye stretched out, an advantage on the recliners and also there was a lot less snoring – normally only his.

Wherever they were however, it was important they were not together, that way if anyone did remember they had a carrycot, it would be reasonable to assume the other party was in change of it at any given time. It was not imperative to condemn baby to a watery grave along with the guitar and his dossiers, but if they were being watched when they got on the boat it would have appeared very odd if they had left the baby in the camper for the overnight voyage. Similarly he did not want the problem of explaining a 'doll with all the attachments and shit to boot' at the other end. It had not been made clear what would happen at the customs in England it may be they were expected to pass through without assistance, under their own steam as it were. If this were the case, he wanted as little to explain away as possible.

For some peculiar reason he was much happier now that the papers that relating to him personally where at the bottom of the Channel. Odd because they were not in his name or indeed the one he was using at present, but nevertheless he remained gratified no documents now had his signature on them – any of them. He was wondering if he would get a medal and then the bell went to announce the ferry's arrival in Portsmouth and he realised he had been asleep and no doubt as near as he would ever get to a medal.

They had arranged that he would be the first to go down to the camper. Once there he did his best to clean up the mess inside using more of the large bin liners to house the small ones and the nappies. After checking the last remaining package of documents was still safely in the toilet under the now overflowing waste bin recently topped up with nappies, he removed it and placed it in the bottom of a bin liner and piled the last remaining odoriferous debris on top. By the time Mrs. Mills tentatively climbed aboard he had everything 'smelly' tied up in plastic sacks and through wide, open windows and vents was replacing the aroma of effluent with diesel and petrol fumes.

"Ok?" he asked, meaning the atmosphere of the camper.

"If you like women sniggering, men farting and kiddies puking I couldn't have spent a more pleasant time, no wonder they play 'Help Me Make It Through The Night' as their final song."

He chuckled, "I meant the camper?"

"How would I know, my very being is obviously completely permeated with the fetor of your excrement, you certainly know how to show a girl a good time Bowie."

His chuckle expanded to a laugh, "It's just like real married people."

She fixed him with a malevolent glare, "No Bowie, real married people sleep together."

There was the opportunity to draw attention to the fact that they had actually slept together on a number of occasions, but he had a good idea where that would lead and so he let the matter drop.

They were in the last row of vehicles to disembark and even though the boat was not full, this morning it was slow. He was not concerned for it allowed more time for the smell of baby to be expunged and they even had to close the windows before they were overcome by the fumes of impatient drivers and the not uncommon problem of 'premature camper pre-ignition'. An observation he wished he had coached in alternative terminology sensing her head snap toward him, but when she spoke it did not relate to overanxious drivers or lovers.

"Who do you think they were at the port?"

"I don't know," he had given it some thought, but it did not matter now, "health inspectors, animal health or perhaps they were a kosher drugs unit tipped off by the Union, with an under-rider about some official documents as well?"

He deliberated for a little before continuing, "I think more likely one of the former, they didn't seem that experienced at searching for contraband. I also think they did us a favour with the real control officers; they seemed if anything more relaxed than normal presumably because of the second lot. Anyway they never asked for any papers relating to the baby, which was a relief as I was going to have to say we lost them with all the rush and everything like I did at the gate and that was close enough ."

She nodded, "Where I come from they'd be crucified for letting us through."

"Or loaned out to nasty old maiden Aunts!"

It was probably too early for satire, time and choice, she confirmed as much, "You really do make it difficult for people to like you Bowie, is it a gift or are you just really, really stupid?"

He did not answer, but it was nice to know he still ‘had a way’ with the ladies, which would evidently ensure he could stop worrying about ever ‘having it away’ with any of them.

Finally, before carbon monoxide poisoning extinguished all his woes, they were waved forward and with some trepidation he wondered what kind of ‘welcome home’ he was about to receive.

Chapter 31

'Drive on the Left'.

The sign informed him and for once was substantive or he might have forgotten. Not in the port itself, for there was just the one lane and other vehicles to follow, but outside he may have given the drivers on the A3 a nasty surprise and said as much, but was ignored.

The camper crawled along snaking its way towards passport control and customs. Eventually it was their turn, the passport check carried out by a polite middle aged man who came to stand at his window, but from the reaction it was clear they were not totally 'pong free'.

"I wonder which one of us he thinks it is?"

He had accepted the returned passports and wound his window shut before turning to her with the smiled conundrum. She once again ignored him as they crawled a few yards further on before an awaiting customs officer stepped out in front of the camper and waved them toward the row of inspection bays.

"Ah! Voila! Je comprends!"

In the exclamations his voice betrayed all the frustration the preceding months had engendered.

"Careful Bowie," she at last broke her silence, "remember what I've said before, don't upset these people just for the sake of it, you're thinking you've finished the job, they're thinking you're just finished."

They were directed to the furthest inspection bay, furthest but one that is, for in the end bay and stretching back toward the dock, was a convoy of impressive French cars, with senior customs officers and other personages fussing round them like sycophantic uniformed Geisha girls.

As he eased the camper to a halt the door was opened for him and a young man said quietly, "Good morning Mr. and Mrs. Mills, would you be good enough to follow me please?"

He climbed down and waited for her to join him, noting she carried the bag with the hopefully unsoiled clothes.

They followed the young man out of the inspection bay area and around the adjacent warehouse where a car waited to take them to a building on the other side of the port and where they were ushered into a room on the first floor. They waited just long enough for him to begin to swear when the door opened and Auntie and Mr. Reece entered the room and stood by the table at which they were seated.

"Congratulations Mr. Mills for a job well done."

Auntie spoke kind words, but the tone belied any congratulatory conviction.

"We wlll take it from here, your have completed your task and are free to go - Mr. Reece please." Mr. Reece stepped forward and placed a P45 and a thin wad of bank notes on the table while Auntie continued, "This will enable you to gain useful employment in the name of 'Mills'. There is also a small stake of five hundred pounds for immediate expenses - and now I think we are done."

He felt the familiar hollowness in his stomach, but was mindful of recent advice tempering his remarks accordingly, "Was not the arrangement that I receive papers, visa and free passage to the other side of the world upon the successful completion of the job in hand?"

Auntie laughed, it was not an unpleasant sound, but what followed was not so sweet.

"Mr. Mills you do not surely want me to reconsider what's to be done with you?" Auntie was suddenly not laughing anymore, "I don't care about your sad little life and you naive little ways, you had the audacity to try and bargain with me and you're just a little amateur now be on your way, I have work to do."

Auntie made to leave, but he thought it must be worth one last try, he was wrong of course, Auntie became irritated.

"You have cost me money Mr. Mills and I am not calling in any favours on your behalf and anyway, we feel it would be better if for the moment you are where we can keep tabs on you. We created Mr. Mills and we could create a criminal record for him should it prove necessary, if you see what I mean?"

Until now Auntie had been business like and unemotional, but few people are totally devoid of malice.

"And for the record Mr. Mills I will go as far as to confess that you have born the brunt of a ruse, there is not, nor ever has been a disagreement in my department as to how this operation should proceed. The dispute that you were led to believe existed was purely designed to ensure you stayed in France for as long as we wanted you to, despite the added risk. It was of course Mrs. Mills that deceived you, so I can only hope the fringe benefits were worth it."

Auntie smiled disdainfully, satiated by her spite, then turning on her heal ordered, "Search them and the bag and put them on the train to London." Then more conciliatory to Mrs. Mills, "thank you my dear for all your efforts, I believe you have a plane to catch and also I believe your people are keen to have a word with you." And with that she walked out.

As soon as his boss was gone Mr. Reece became instantly animated and most sympathetic, “I’m sorry about that. Auntie has a lot on her plate at the moment, pressure from upstairs as it were, anyway I think you’ve done a really good job, we’ll find the documents easy enough will we?”

He explained they would be found in a bin liner under a pile of shitty nappies, but Mr. Reece accepted the news with no reduction in cordiality, thus he inquired of his inquisitor, “What do they want them for?”

“Err.......”

Mr. Reece was no fool and based on ‘need to know’ Mr. Mills did not.

“Let me guess.”

It was obvious the man was not going to divulge anything, but he could listen.

“There will be, shall we say, some confusion at the inspection bay, someone in the convoy of cars will be rumoured to have brought with them a package of sensitive information concerning fraudulent behaviour within the EU, some virtuous dignitary, an old soldier, war hero, an upstanding politician perhaps. Inspired by a long term gratitude for all that was done over fifty years ago and remorseful for the excesses of Europe in general and his country in particular. A fine gesture triggered by a commemoration ceremony planned for once on this side of the channel. Quite a big affair according to the UK newspapers I read on the boat last night and still a week away, more than enough time for the guests to enjoy their stay and the information in the documents to be analysed.”

Mr.Reece smiled back at him, silent, but with still no diminution in congeniality.

"And what else could you do except accept the information, albeit very embarrassing of course, still perhaps some accommodation could be found some 'quid pro quo', I'm sure someone in that convoy would not want to risk the chance of anyone thinking he was the one that 'bubbled'? Something like that Mr. Reece, I remember someone telling me about this kind of thing a while back and I thought at the time, surely it's usually called 'blackmail' isn't it Mr. Reece?"

"No, no, no Mr. Mills, you have it all wrong, it's just....... diplomacy."

Mr. Reece engaged the services of their young driver to perform the searches and they were soon in the back seat of the car en route for Portsmouth railway station. She went to speak, but he held up his hand and it was not until they were seated on the platform awaiting the train to London before she finally spoke.

"I did not knowingly deceive you, I was led to believe by the telephone contact that there was a dispute about how to proceed, I just want you to know."

There could be some mileage to be made here, he thought, but why does it always have to happen at the wrong time, he grinned, "Does it matter?"

It was true he may have made a run for home if he had thought there were not those that as soon as he set foot near a Channel port would 'shop' him to the authorities. As these people supposedly worked in the same department all his details would be available to them including the camper licence numbers etc. and it had felt safer to stay and 'sit it out' and she had thoroughly endorsed this determination.

They were staring at the platform opposite, not at each other.

"I don't know. If they had asked me it was my job anyway, but they didn't, I just made a wrong call, another one."

"No problem," he was dismissive, hoping it would buy him grace and favour in the hour ahead, "everyone makes mistakes, even me. Only the other day I thought I was wrong then found out I was right all the time, see even Bowie is not infallible."

It was around Liss he felt as prepared as he would ever be and began to fidget.

"You OK?"

She considered him with an appraising eye.

"Yes fine." He lied.

"You don't normally fidget that much unless I'm naked."

She had obviously got over the trauma of offering an apology and consequently forced the middle-aged couple seated opposite each other across the aisle to studiously study one another - although it had been actually possible to see their ears prick. Great, he knew she was trying to lighten the mood after the events of the morning, but for him it was not the time and so when he continued it was in French.

"Is it possible for you to retire from your present employment without repercussions, your not privy to any secrets that would be considered dangerous or anything like that, your people would be prepared to let you go?"

Instantly there was a change, they were back on stony ground. Normally she did not talk about her work unless it was necessary and once confessional thus became instantly cautious even circumspect, but he had expected as much.

"No," she too now spoke in French, "as I have mentioned, they would probably be pleased to see the back of me, why, do you now feel in a position to offer me a job?"

He smiled - they were both aware of his position – here goes he thought, he must be due a result by now.

"It has occurred to me that we've got on remarkably well considering the circumstances, we work well together and have achieved the goal that was set us and I was just wondering if it might not be a good idea to continue as we are as it were."

He was doing fine, better than expected anyway.

"We are Mr. and Mrs. Mills and we are married, albeit not under our own names, but we could have changed our name by deed pole anyway, so we could just carry on as we are. You could resign and we could do something else. You're not appreciated where you are and you're not happy there, why not stay here, we could find ordinary work, lots of people do?"

She regarded him for a long time, "Is this a proposal?"

Make your mind up time, he really did not like these 'yes' or 'no' options.

"Yes."

Done it, he had promised himself he would and he had, he was so relieved and pleased with himself he nearly missed what she was saying.

"The French language is reputedly the most romantic in the world and yet Bowie you have managed somehow to make a proposal of marriage sound like an assessment as to the efficiency of a new vacuum cleaner – I do not feel exactly swept off my feet."

This was the problem with modern women, they wanted their cake and eat it, one minute knocking your teeth down your throat the next all sugar and spice.

"You haven't said no."

She continued to consider him with a pained expression, "And I haven't said yes – and it may have slipped your mind, but you've never even kissed me."

"What ....and get killed?"

"A try would have been nice and not necessarily fatal."

He thought of all the times he might have and wondered why he hadn't for he knew it had little to do with longevity.

She continued, as ever hitting below the belt, "Anyway, we've never had sex, what if we are not compatible?"

Not where he wanted to go at all and she would know that, "I'm a man and you're a woman, that's not a bad start."

"You might be a bad lover?"

"Not much doubt there I'm afraid, but I'll get the hang of it, they're all at it, so it can't be that hard."

His impudence did not appear to be appreciated, but at least she had ignored the opportunity his unfortunate concluding choice of words offered.

"What would Auntie say?"

"It's got nothing to do with them."

He wondered why she had brought Auntie into the debate, but was confident it was only to create more time to think.

"Bowie, all you have in the world is in this bag – and you don't even know what that is as I put it there – you have no prospects other than at anytime there could be a knock on the door from some authority or other. You're not exactly what one might term a 'good catch' are you?"

He could not help smiling it was obviously still going well.

"So that's a 'yes' is it?"

"No, Bowie it is not a 'yes', I will have to think about it."

"That'll do."

And smiling he sat back and watched the Hampshire countryside drift by.

Chapter 32

"You actually lived in there?"

"Yes."

"But it's a factory under a railway line!"

She was obviously not over enamoured with his erstwhile bijou abode, but it had been 'home sweet home' to him and he was naturally defensive.

"It's not like that behind the entrance, that's just for show, like camouflage, it's quite nice in the back."

"But isn't it dark....... and damp?"

"Not if you keep the lights on."

He avoided the other part of the question - he never had managed to solve the problem of the musty smell and the occasional mushroom cluster in the wardrobe.

"If you think I'd ever move into something like that you must be truly mad   in your parlance and persuasion I believe the term would be 'shit for brains'."

He was ecstatic - who could have believed showing her his old haunts would be such a success, "So you're thinking about moving in then?"

"No, I'm still just thinking."

The train had pulled into Waterloo just before midday. She knew the capital fairly well and had not been interested in any sight seeing other than the West End where they had wondered for a while looking at what shows were still running and the latest films.

"Do you spend much time in Soho?"

She had casually asked in her customary effort to draw him into territory where she knew him to be vulnerable, but he just smiled, he had a real sense there was a seismic shift in the air – or perhaps it was too much cappuccino. They had been on their third cup when she had asked to see where he had lived before he had been 'recruited' – she made it sound like he had answered an ad' or walked in off the street to an army centre. Nonetheless he was pleased to agree as he needed to visit the area and could think of no excuse to do so, but before they left the coffee bar he asked, "Should you not contact your people to let them know where you are?"

She considered him for a time before replying, "I hope that wasn't an attempt at a leading question Bowie and the answer is they will know where I am, in London waiting for a flight out and for you, no I'm still thinking."

Soon after they had left the coffee bar, taken a number twenty-four bus south of the river and were at present contemplating his previously vacated castle.

"Come on there's someone I want you to meet."

He took her arm disregarding the theatrical swoon she portrayed at the gesture and marched her out of his 'walk' and along a slightly busier back street to a less than salubrious eating establishment and his earlier second home, 'Bert's Cafe'.

"Bert, Bowie's back an' 'es got a bit-a skirt wiv' 'im."

Betty's voice rang out loud and clear. It carried from counter, through the hatch to the kitchen where Bert resided only ever being seen from neck to naval when he delivered loaded plates to the hatch in response to Betty's commands.

"'E dunno any bleedin' bits-a skirt."

Although other than his once white overall Bert was never seen, his disembodied voice could occasionally be detected if there was confusion over a food order, one sausage and two eggs instead of the opposite for example - or perhaps in the event of a nuclear holocaust. Thus he did not know whether to be honoured or dejected when Bert appeared bent to the hatch to witness the startling circumstance of Bowie with a bird.

"Bert, Betty, this Mrs. Mills."

He made the introductions under the additional scrutiny of late lunchtime diners.

"Oh, it's alright Bert, it's sum-one else's."

He chose a table in the far corner away from the door, which had been his 'almost by right' when he had been between tours and at home. Bert and Betty were truly generous folk that had shown him kindness over the years without smothering their intermittent surrogate son, for at times, that is how they had made him feel and he had often been glad of it.

"Egg, sausage, bubble and beans, two slices and a tea - no sugar," Betty shouted his order toward the hatch without asking, "and for the lady?"

He raised his eyebrows across the chipped Formica table, "Just some toast and a coffee, please." She spoke quietly, but before he had time to turn to the counter with the order.

"Two rounds, one coffee." Betty shouted the order, " sugar love?"

Mrs. Mills shook her head.

"Coffee no sugar."

He leaned forward unnecessarily explaining Betty had phenomenal hearing.

"An' you better beleev it Bowie boy, none of ya 'ankey-pankey' in 'ere wiv marreed ladees."

He grinned, having forgotten Betty's high moral standards.

"It's OK Betty I'm not married now," Mrs Mills called across to their hostess, then more quietly, "not at the moment."

"It's OK Bert, she ain't marreed not now like, but shees finking abart it."

He continued to smile across the table until his meal arrived which he devoured with relish and in silence, paying due homage to one of Bert's outstanding fry-ups. Shortly Betty came over to retrieve their plates and placed another cup of tea in front of him, "More coffee luv?"

Mrs. Mills shook her head and smiled a refusal.

When Betty had retired to her side of the counter he took a deep breath and began what above all else he thought would be the most difficult part of the day.

"I want a favour, just one, aside from everything else we have discussed today just a little thing, that's all."

She eyed him suspiciously, she had watched him growing in confidence and it was not always an advantage, people could become careless or confrontational, she waited.

"I want you to wait hear for me I've something to do, I'll be back in a couple of hours at most, I just want you to wait here....... please."

She clasped her hands on the table in front of her and he could guess what was coming, "And after two hours do you think I will still be here?"

He was neither defensive nor belligerent. He knew she had to come to terms with his proposal about their future and it could not be an easy decision, but felt he had earned the right to pose her the problem.

"Should you decide in the interim your answer is no, you will not be here, if you are here I'll only assume you are still deliberating, nothing more."

Obviously she considered his intended actions inappropriate, "You don't think that what you're intending may tip the balance, perhaps your actions would be better received if you explained what you're going to do?"

"Possibly," he understood how she felt, but if it went wrong she was better off out of it, "but if I cannot be trusted for two hours, what chance for the rest of our lives?"

She continued to stare at him unconvinced, waiting for an explanation.

"Mrs Mills, I accept you think I'm a little old fashioned, but I've never caused you any problems while we've been together and this is only the second time I've asked a favour – I just want you to wait here 'till I get back, that's all, please."

Her stare never changed and she waited a full minute before finally declaring, "Two hours."

He immediately made to leave.

"Err.......shouldn't you at least give the little wife a kiss goodbye?"

He eased back into the chair and returned the stare that had not and he knew would not change, would she always be so combative he wondered as he leaned forward and placed his lips on hers?

"Oy, oy, oy," Betty cried from behind the counter, "Bert, Bowie's gettin' amorous!"

Any reply from the kitchen was lost in the scrape of his chair as he stood and made for the door. He stopped briefly at the counter and asked Betty to keep an eye on his 'bit of skirt' added an order and slipped out of the door without looking back.

He walked quickly to the nearest main thoroughfare and jumped a passing bus that would take him toward the city centre and as soon as the prevalence of taxis suggested he might procure one, he climbed down from the bus and began to hail. After five minutes he was reclining in the backseat of a tradition London cab en route to the Isle of Dogs. He had elected to take a cab there as it was likely he would have to use buses or the tube to return and two hours should be enough, but was not an excessive amount of time.

Inside the cab he had time to reflect on what he was to do, but first thought about the kiss. It had not been returned of course, he never expected it to be, it was simply a statement and he understood. If he had been in the same position after all that had gone on he would not have taken kindly to being left high and dry – if only for two hours. All in a good cause, he tried to convince himself hoping he had not taken on more than he could cope with.

The cab dropped him only a hundred yards from his objective for he had no need to disguise his activities at this end. He walked purposely along the road and turned into the garage lock-up complex without hesitation, taking keys from his pocket and feeling a lot more nervous than hopefully he looked. The padlock opened without resistance in response to the key he had kept from his time as road manager and the only surprise he had when he stepped inside through the Judas gate was that the truck was missing. No reason why it should not be of course, but he had anticipated its presence, no matter, the Orange bin was where he expected to see it and after a few seconds of dread and rising panic, he found the rucksack as prescribed.

He opened it, took out the package and cut the string with a box knife from the garage tool rack and began to sift through the files. There were about thirty, plus some miscellaneous bills and bank statements. He removed the top and bottom files and undoing his belt and trousers, stuffed them up the front of his shirt, tucked it back in his trousers, then re-buckled the belt – he looked as good as new. He then re-wrapped the package as best he could, re-tying the string and making a reasonable job of it before replacing it in the rucksack. Within ten minutes he was outside and walking as before, but this time toward Westferry tube station where he bought a ticket and waited for a west bound train.

He counted the stations he needed to travel on the underground plan and was somewhat dismayed to find it was thirteen, but that included a change of line and so he consoled himself with the notion that it was really two plus eleven. Although he now had no complaints about his prior Friday the thirteenth trip to the Fatherland for it appeared to have born fruit and he hoped Bassie had suffered no long term anguish, but still liked him no better. With five stations to go he estimated he had enough time, but because of the fast developing rush hour and an inexplicable delay outside Westminster he eventually ended his subterranean excursions in mild alarm. There would be no taxis available at this time in the evening and so he ran over Westminster Bridge and was lucky enough to catch a bus along the embankment that put him roughly back on schedule, but he arrived at the road to Bert's Cafe hot and bothered.

There was under ten minutes to go when he turned into the alley fifty yards before the entrance to the café and less by the time he had recognised the correct tradesman's entrance where he had once help unload a new deep fat fryer. More precious seconds had elapsed by the time he knocked on the back door to the café, but thankfully Bert was a man of few words. Thus he was subsequently able to walk through the front door of the café appearing ostensibly exactly the same as when he left with well over a minute to spare.

"Bert, Bowie's back and not before time if you ask me."

There was no response from the kitchen as he made his way to the corner table, but he did not notice – all he saw was that she was still there.

"You look as if you've been running and you smell as if it was a marathon."

He was pleased she was obviously relieved to see him back.

"Can you smell me from there?"

She smiled, patronisingly, "No, but I'm extrapolating from what wafted over when you kissed me, or stumbled while you were getting up, I wasn't really sure which it was."

He didn't care he just smiled and perspired.

"Tea Bowie?" At least Betty cared.

"Yes please, Betty."

Mrs. Mills pushed a plate with a cold sandwich on it across the table in front of him, "I assume this is for you." She said squinting at him ominously.

He said thank you and begun to eat the cold bacon sandwich with innocent relish, "We can go now if you're ready?"

He should not have laughed at her expression, but he could not help it, he felt a little light-headed, perhaps he could do it after all.

"I'm going away for a while Betty, but I'll be back again sometime." He handed the balance of the Euro banknotes over to cover their bill, "Tell Bert he needs to 'change the notes tonight, in the market or somewhere he's not known. There's nothing wrong with 'em, but it would be better, belt and braces sort 'a thing, sorry but I haven't got much Sterling."

Betty pocketed the notes without inspection, "Bowie's orf, Bert, says goodbye."

There was no response from the kitchen and so they closed the door behind them and made their way toward the main road. She waited until they were amidst the hurrying commuters on their frantic daily dash to a railhead and home before making pained polite comment.

"I can only guess at how expensive a plate of the equivalent of a healthy eaters fat and salt consumption for a month would be, but by my estimation you have just paid a little under £3000 for some fried eggs and offal."

He walked on without responding.

"Prudence and careful management of resources are attributes considered by many to be eminently virtuous in a prospective husband Bowie."

He maintained his reticence, now was not the time to explain.

"So what location for my delectation do you have planned for me now, a night amongst the 'winos' and 'meths' drinkers under the arches of some London rail terminus or tube station?"

At least this time he could provide an answer, albeit at a continued cost to his virtuosity as a potential frugal spouse.

“Most definitely not Mrs. Mills, tonight you are to stay at the Hilton!”

Chapter 33

There have traditionally been only two genuinely net contributor states to the European Community, Germany and those diffident, often portrayed as politically awkward isles that make up the United Kingdom.

Within a few years of Mr. and Mrs. Mills sailing north across the Channel, the UK rebuffed pressure to concede its 'rebate' - the term used by Europe for the earlier reduction in contributions the then Prime Minister Margaret Thatcher negotiated in a 'take it or leave it' deal. The 'rebate' – conceived in an effort to lend the UK some increased pecuniary equality - was never well received by the rest of Europe, but sanctioned nonetheless, hardly surprising as who was going to make good the shortfall the lack of UK contributions would have created?

Subsequently, even the remarkably pro European Labour government that followed the Conservatives, balked at the suggestion of restoring the UK liability to original levels and sending even more money to Brussels. Coincidentally at the same European Summit, France agreed to increase her contribution to the community and for the first time, almost equal that of the UK, although because of her enormous agricultural industry, she would continue to take more out than she put in.

Alas, there continued to be no improvement concerning fiscal propriety, no auditors could be found that would 'sign off' the European Unions accounts as a 'true and fair representation' of the organisations financial affairs. Somewhat amazingly there were now many states lined up to join the Union, but then they were all to be net beneficiaries, so maybe it was not so surprising.

For in principle, one may not be too keen on joining a savings club where no adequate records were kept, but then perhaps it would not matter if every year it paid out more than one put in!

The room was big, luxurious and plastic - the 'boys' would have loved it and had in looking like a cross between a launderette and a talcum powder factory in no time.

"I'm going to have a bath Bowie and I shall be gone a long time."

True to her word, it was now over an hour. They had taken the train to Heathrow and probably walked a mile around the airport while he collected a selection of brochures and timetables before finally taking the courtesy bus and booking into the hotel where he paid in advance and in cash. It was difficult to establish which the girls at reception found most suspicious, the fact that they had only an overnight bag between them or that he wanted to pay in cash. There would obviously soon come a time when one would have to pay a premium to pay with anything other than credit – how would the poor old bank robbers manage?

He had also bought a cash card mobile telephone much to Mrs. Mills disgust and that of the sales girl as he insisted on buying the cheapest and not the model that could store the Encyclopaedia Britannica and played Jingle Bells and Bach. Unfortunately the pushy sales girl could not guarantee that the more expensive model would be able to put him in touch with Captain Kirk nor afford 'matter transportation' and so he bought the cheap one.

Mrs. Mills eventually exited the bathroom wrapped in the hotels complimentary towelling dressing gown and although tired and devoid of any cosmetics looked adorable, it was going to be a shame to spoil it.

"Your turn Bowie - and don't worry about taking your time, waltzing round the check-ins has had a rejuvenating effect on your sweat glands."

It seemed as if luxuriating in the bath had done wonders for her morale and who knows what decision he might get if he asked again now - it really was a shame.

"I wonder Mrs. Mills, if you'll be good enough to make a phone call for me?"

She was smiling when he started speaking, but not by the time he had finished. There was a silence which he was obviously expected to fill as she folded her arms and lent back against the dressing table opposite the bed where he had been lazing.

"I would be grateful if you would get Auntie on the phone for me?"

He placed the newly purchased telephone at the bottom of the bed in front of her and sat back.

She looked down at the 'phone as she spoke, "This is not sensible."

All the old antagonism was back, it really was a shame, perhaps he really did not have to do it, but it was too late now. He tried to make it as reasonable as possibly, "I just want what's mine, what they promised me, it's been nearly two years - papers, visas, tickets, that's all."

Lying, that had always been his best suit, but if this worked he might have to re-evaluate - if it worked?

"They will have disconnected the number."

Probably, he had thought as much himself, so it was going to get harder before it got better – always assuming it did.

"Please try."

She picked the phone up from the bed and dialled the number. It amazed him how she carried all these numbers around in her head, he had trouble remembering the number at the flat, but presumably it was the training, the same training that now led her to believe a few abortive attempts would satisfy his needs no doubt.

"As I said, it's been disconnected; it would only have been temporary while we were under control."

"Ah," he raised his eyebrows in acknowledgement, "in that case then, would you please contact your people and ask them to speak to London and get another number for us, as I need to speak to Auntie urgently."

She threw the phone back on the bed and lent back refolding her arms.

"Bowie this is not a game, I have told you before, these are not people you should antagonise, what are you doing, what is the point?"

It was his turn to remain silent.

"You've done something haven't you Bowie, I warn you, if you've done something silly you'll regret it. Auntie is not a nice lady Bowie."

He accepted the harangue, which was becoming an onslaught, silently waiting for the storm to abate.

"It's Germany isn't it, you done something in Germany and why didn't you tell them about the other package in the camper?"

It was a genuine question and she had not just thought of it, but obviously not thought that much about it, perhaps the training said when the jobs over its over, stop thinking about it, but for him the job was not over. Then it dawned.

"Oh God, if you've taken the package to Germany, you'll never get near it, they'll never let you out of the country, you'll be lucky if they ever let you out of jail. Leave it Bowie, walk away."

They were both stubborn and shared feelings of affection and antagonism for one another in equal measure one day perhaps there might even be an impasse, but not today. She snatched up the phone and punched in the number - he had never seen her so angry.

He spoke quickly, "Make it clear to your people you're doing this directly under my urging and that you feel it's in the best interest of everybody, you're only doing your job, that way if it goes wrong you can get out."

She glared at him as never before, but he continued, "Ask them to relay a message to Auntie, 'there has been some confusion over the number of packages and I need to speak to her urgently'; you'll ring back in an hour for a new number."

She spun from where she stood as the call went through, walking over to the window and spoke quietly in the language he did not recognise, although in any event he could hardly hear a word. The call only lasted a minute or two and when she had finished she returned and hurled the phone on the bed before returning to the bathroom and slamming the door, he presumed his bath was to wait and his stink was to linger.

The mobile rang after fifty-three minutes, he knew, he had watched every one expire on the wall clock above the dressing table. He was about to take the phone to the bathroom, but she was out before he had a chance to get off the bed and answered, saying one syllable at the start and one at the end, then threw the mobile back on the bed.

"The original number has been reactivated, but we cannot ring for another half an hour."

She made as if to return to the bathroom, but he interrupted her with a raised hand, "I'm sorry to have involved you and your people, but obviously I couldn't do much without them and," he cut her off before she could comment with another raised hand, "I know it's probably not the best time, but I would be grateful if you could give some more thought to my err.......proposal, I might like an answer sooner rather than later."

He really did think this time she was going to explode and even he was surprised at his cheek and timing, but not at the gritted teeth and hissed response.

"Bowie, there was a time when I hoped one day I might be asked to kick you around a little and then there was a time when I thought that perhaps my dislike was maybe to conceal other feelings that I wasn't prepared to acknowledge. But at this moment, whatever my true feelings for you are, I would really like to kick the shit out of you, just for once, just for me, just because you won't....... ever.......bloody....... listen!"

She picked the phone up from the bed where she had thrown it at exactly the time specified. There had been no conversation after her outburst. He made no wisecracks or apologises no complaints or justifications, on this issue there would be no agreement. She had gone to stand by the window and it was as if they were back at the farm on the day she had arrived, but worse. It was a long half an hour.

"Auntie......."

She offered him the phone the one word identifying who it was at the other end. Then folded her arms, lent back on the dressing table and prepared to listen to him destroy the rest of his life, which was a shame as she suddenly realised she had had her own plans for the rest of his life.

"Hello Auntie, sorry to bother you but there has been a bit of a mix up, you see there were three packages.......yes three....... I know, I don't mean to mess you about and I'm well aware of how upset people get and Mrs. Mills is always telling me to be careful, but it's like it was in 'care', sometimes it's better to be a nuisance and a little shit, unpredictability makes people nervous.......yes I'm sure you're busy Auntie so I'll come straight to the point.......err hang on Auntie, just a minute......."

He did not look at her, but focused on the bathroom door, after this he could have a bath.

"I'm sorry Mrs. Mills, I have to ask you for an answer now?"

She could not believe it. He had taken the phone from his ear and pressed the microphone aperture to his leg, "I really am sorry to hurry you, but I'm on the phone and I need an answer."

"Why.......?" She heard her voice start and was not sure where it was going, but it did not matter because he was talking again.

'Yes' or 'No'.......please Mrs. Mills?"

".......Yes."

She heard the voice again, but it did not sound like her, in fact she wasn't even sure if it was what she had intended to say - did she say yes?

He put the phone to his ear again.

"Sorry about that Auntie, something we had to sort out at this end, anyway back to the plot as it were, it's nothing knew Auntie, just like before really, except the package is in this country now, has been for sometime actually, apparently there may have been some problem with the post so I didn't use it……. anyway, it's here now and obviously could be delivered anywhere, anytime…….no, no, Auntie no need to meet, it's quite simple, if I fail to make the call and all that business……. funny thing is, I had the papers last time, but not this…….now, now Auntie no need for that…….anyway as I was saying, if I continue to make the calls so they know I'm OK, everything will be alright and nothing will get delivered……now, what do I want to ensure I keep making the calls?"

He was going to get married, well I never, he hoped she meant it?

"There's a late evening flight to Sidney tomorrow and I will be at the check-in desk two hours beforehand where I will be provided with tickets and a permanent visas for Mr. and Mrs. Mills…….Oh, by the way we're getting married Auntie err…….well I don't want to appear ungrateful Auntie but I was intending to save that sort of thing for my wife from now on and anyway I'm not sure people of your generation should be using that kind of language?

She would be his wife, I wonder if she had thought of that?

"Anyway that's all I want, obviously birth and marriage certificates can follow on, we can always pick them up from the embassy……. Oh, and in return I will give you a couple of files just to show willing as it were and that the 'diplomacy' is real, I think that's what Mr. Reece called it.......Ah! and one last thing, I nearly forgot, a quarter of a million sterling cleared into Mrs. Mills account by six o'clock tomorrow evening.......now, now, Auntie there's no need to get all flustered, look at it as a wedding present, I'm sure her people will give you the details of her account and in any case, for what you have been able to put before your bosses, it's incredibly good value for money......."

Mind you, he would be her husband that would certainly take some thinking about!

"Now, I have to go, hope to see one of your lads tomorrow then....... don't forget, two hours before the flight.......Oh, and one very last thing, I know you have all those fighting fit chaps around everywhere ready to track people down and all that sort of macho stuff and you probably don't get out much yourself nowadays, but don't worry, I'll make sure you always know where I am, no secrets, although if you ever do come near me again Auntie.......I'll rip your fucking head off!"

After he had laid the phone back on the bed and looked up she was standing with her head in her hands, shaking it gently from side to side.

Chapter 34

The bathroom door exploded open and she leapt over the corner of the bed, only just giving him enough time to put himself between her and the room service waiter. Putting his arm around the young man's shoulders he ushered him to and through the hotel room door out into the corridor, tucked a ten pound note in his breast pocket and winked conspiratorially whilst making muttered references to 'the wrong time of the month'. Once back inside he could see she was still snarling and poised like an advert for a karate nudist camp.

"You have no clothes on."

Her eyes bored into his, but he had no intention of looking anywhere else.

"I am wearing knickers."

True, he thought, but I doubt the waiter would have noticed, and then the poor lad would never have believed he could have been that terrified by a naked lady.

She relaxed a little, "I thought I heard a shot."

He looked away motioning toward the occasional table, "It was the Champagne cork. He asked if he should open it, I said 'yes', there are also some flowers for you and some salmon sandwiches, you've hardly eaten anything all day - can't have a wife too weak to work in the paddy fields."

She almost smiled, but it ended in a frown, "Do you have some pathological condition that makes it impossible for you to complete any compliment or act of human kindness without destroying the gesture as if it might engender an affectionate response that you couldn't cope with?"

He laughed, at himself of course, even if she could not, "I suppose I'm just shy and frightened some lady might try 'n take advantage of me – and can I have a bath soon please?"

After he had blotted his copybook with Auntie there had been an argument about his arbitrary decision making, his pigheadedness, his swearing and his general behaviour that suggested he was perhaps not ready for commitment and wedlock. He responded suggesting that the assessment probably applied to ninety percent of all men that walked down the aisle and even if it was true in his case, which he denied, was it not better to know now than it come as a surprise?

Once again they having not exactly achieved a meeting of minds she had returned to her exile in the bathroom, which was when he had called room service. She walked back into the bathroom for her dressing gown and strolled out again elaborately indicating the facility was vacant, but remarked before he was able to enter, "You have ceased to ask me where I come from. What country I represent etc. and I think it may have some bearing on the future perhaps?"

He lye back on the bed again - he was obviously destined to ferment before he could bath, "I have ceased to ask because it's not important to me now. I have an idea, but I repeat for me it's not important."

He made to move, but should have known better, she was not satisfied with his answer.

"It will be a mixed marriage."

"Yes I know, man and woman, a bit 'old hat', but I believe some still manage it."

She said nothing, but there was the stare again and now even he was finding his odour offensive. Here we go again he thought taking a deep breath.

"The eyes threw me at first, but then it was a place where all young people are trained because there is a constant war, don't celebrate Christmas, slight reaction to the name Ruth and how can anybody not like bacon sandwiches? The only thing I can't figure is the perfect English, I know a lot of people kept the language even after you threw us out, but there's usually an accent or something."

He was tired of arguing. In fact he was tired period, and he hoped she was finished, but he would continue listening whatever.

"English finishing school and then Switzerland. Daddy was a diplomat and met Mummy in the Philippines and they died together in a bombing, ring any bells Bowie?"

It was not said in animosity, quite the opposite.

"I'm sorry, when?"

"I was eighteen."

When was that he wondered and was about to ask, but her question came before he had time to speak.

"What about the children?"

"What children, Fagin's or the Von Trapp's?"

He assumed she would think he was procrastinating, which he was, as he really did not know what she was talking about, but she persisted.

"How will they be brought up?"

First it was his orientation, then his incredible shrinking disease, his questionable ability as a lover and now she was discussing where the kids were going to go to school, he really did feel very tired. Almost staggering to the bathroom he nevertheless said what it was he would only ever say on the subject and the only thing he would strive to achieve whatever ill or well meaning fools might seek to frustrate.

"Happy, I don't care about the rest, just as long as they're brought up happy."

Then to extract himself from a conversation far too intense for his energy level let alone their predicament, "Pardon me for saying, and at the risk of destroying another portentous pontificate, but I think you might be getting a bit 'previous' there Mrs. Mills."

When he came out of the bathroom, he too was wrapped in complementary towelling and had ceased to smell, but the hot suds had done nothing for his alertness. He wandered to the bed, subconsciously noting the room was dim with the onset of nightfall and that his side of the bed had been designated as she was already in the other. He pulled back the covers and was surprised to see his tracksuit folded neatly on the pillow. Involuntarily holding it to his nose he noted it smelled of the camper, nothing worse thank goodness, but he now had hopes for more.

Moving to the bottom of the bed he placed it carefully in the bin under the dressing table then returning to the bed slipped out of the robe and slid into bed and lying on his back as she did, reached across for her hand, squeezing it gently and at the same time sighing as if it was his last breath. There was silence between them as there had been many times before, but this time it was different or at least that is what she thought as she slowly turned her head and asked, "Is this the first night of our honeymoon Bowie?" but he was fast asleep.

He woke not knowing where he was and although he knew whom, was not sure of the name.

"You have slept for twelve hours, missed the first night of your honeymoon, which is a shame 'cause it was a real humdinger!"

She was up, dressed and animated – he felt like shit.

"Why so happy?"

She flung back the drapes and offered to call room service and order breakfast for him, but he said it was too early.

"Today, Bowie you will be in paradise or purgatory and you only have yourself to blame so I shall be an objective observer and cease to be a nuisance to you."

"Yeah, yeah," he grunted, sinking a glass of flat Champagne, but recoiling at the curled fish sandwiches. He struggled out of bed and was halfway across the room before he realised he was naked.

"'Miraclegrow' not working then?"

He would normally have sworn, but he did not, he did not care. Not in a careless way, but there were other things to worry about and she seemed to have made some progress through the night, although it certainly had not been him that had helped her make it.

"Betty told me you were a good boy and she would not like to see you get hurt."

He had showered and sat on the toilet wondering about the coming day until his legs had gone numb and she had peaked in and started giggling. He was now dressed and beginning to wonder if he liked her better, introspective and aggressive, rather than bright and breezy.

"Betty said Bert thought that finding a good woman would be the making of you, did you know they had a child that died of complications from pneumonia when it was still a baby?"

No he did not and he resented her knowing. Is this what marriage was about, being jealous of transport café proprietors?

"Getting nervous?"

She still had the capacity to instantly alienate him, but she was right.

"Yes I am, is that bad or just amateurish?"

Some of her 'joy de vie' evaporated, "It's normal, you have chosen to contest a matter which to you is one of principle and therefore you cannot understand why there needs to be a contest at all. Thus the fact that regardless, there is to be a contest makes you nervous because you obviously don't know the rules of the game and you should be, I have told you before, it is not a game – there are no rules."

He sighed, "Do you think I've missed anything?"

"Oh! Now I'm to be asked for my opinion!" Her voice was mocking, but amused for all that, "Now, after all these months, not to mention the last few weeks when I've almost begged you to be mindful of upsetting the wrong people," her voice hardened, "if it had been in my country you would already be dead."

He did not want an argument, anything but another augment.

"I understand that, but this is not your country, the risk is less."

Her voice remained unyielding, "The threat is less."

Amen to that, he thought, no one was trying to wipe his country from the face of the earth, not at the moment anyway.

"Can you trust Bert?"

She had worked it out. It was not that hard, she had been there, and for her it was now all really quite straightforward.

"Yes and I'd be very grateful if it all goes wrong if you'd leave them out of it, honestly, it has nothing to do with them?"

"Oh dear Bowie, no wonder Betty thinks it will take more than a good woman, I believe her actual words were 'probably need to be a bleedin' saint' - did you really need to ask me that?"

Oddly, rather than walk away she came towards him and touched his cheek, more compassion than affection, but it smothered any irrational possessiveness nonetheless.

"C'mon, it won't be as good as Bert's, but I'll treat you to breakfast, I bet you can do just as much damage to your heart here if you really try!"

The day passed slowly.

Strange because if he was condemned presumably he should savour every minute, but the truth was he just wanted it over – he had begun to doubt his capabilities, it was her fault, he had not been angry all day. They had paid a small fortune to be allowed half a dozen more hours in the hotel room beyond the midday cut off point, but still arrived at the airport far too early and were forced to adjourn to a coffee bar.

"Do they have people watching?"

She sipped her coffee ostensibly totally at ease and at last he envied her the training if nothing else.

"There are two, but it maybe standard airport security; you're demonstrating all the behavioural signs of an impending suicide bomber."

He sniggered and she smiled in response, "That's better; the one thing you cannot afford to show is that you are distressed, we are like all predators, we go for the weakest and the weak spots."

"We?"

She continued to smile as if they were discussing at what restaurant in Manhattan they would eat after they landed.

"It's been my job Bowie, I am neither ashamed nor proud, one way or another you've chosen to make this my last mission, I'm sure you would want me to perform to the best of my ability. The first lesson is to live in the real world, you have proclaimed to the opposition you are strong Bowie, if they now find you are not, you will loose."

That was not exactly how he believed it to be and obviously it showed.

"You may not want to see them as the opposition Bowie, but that is how they see you, I warned you, as I remember you responded with something like 'if my country decided to sell me out I'd sell them out first' or words to that effect."

Not fair.

"I'm not selling them out, I've done what they asked and now I want paying."

She stood up and looked around, "Well, we shall soon find out if your feelings are shared, come, I believe you have an appointment."

"I have identified one observer at the end of the row of check-in desks behind you and Bernard is watching from the balcony, do you want me to wave?"

Amazing, he had tried hard to catch sight of anything unusual, but had spotted nothing.

"Why not? He was good enough to show you his etchings or whatever, it would be rude not to."

She waved and he looked up just in time to see Bernard disappear.

"Someone is approaching you from your left."

He turned and sure enough emerging through a group of confused looking, overweight Americans a man with no luggage halted in front of him with the greeting, "You're about as popular as a dose of penicillin at a pox party!"

He could not help smiling regardless of the lewd salute.

"Mrs. Mills, I'd like you to meet Mr.......err Peashooter, an associate of mine from a couple of years back."

Mrs. Mills nodded, but did not offer her hand.

"Mr. Peashooter my wife, Mrs. Mills."

Mr. Peashooter was taken aback at the announcement, but smiled weakly in acknowledgement prior to a slightly awkward silence, and then Mr. Peashooter found his voice again, "I understand you have something for me?"

"Oh yes of course."

He bent to their bag and extracted the two files that had been placed on top and handed them over. Mr. Peashooter accepted them and vaguely examined them before speaking.

"It would be appreciated if perhaps we could be given all the material now for safe keeping....... as it were....... it would of course make no difference to the arrangements......." He waited, not quite believing Mr. Peashooter would suggest something so patently ridiculous as he remembered him as quite a sensible man and was about to say as much when Mr. Peashooter continued, "Mrs. Mills can verify that the money is in her account and....... you would soon be on your way to the Antipodes......"

He drew breath again to point out the significant flaw in the strategy when viewed from his position, but Mr. Peashooter once again was moved to persist, “Even if you were to just tell us where we could....... Obtain.......or collect the material before you go......”

He really did think he ought to say something, but before he could it was now his normally taciturn wife that was to pre-empt him.

“Mr. Peashooter, it is not your fault, but you must have a word with whoever it is on the other end of your ear-piece or whatever form of receiver you are using, because they are not allowing you the time to effect a normal rhythm of conversation. Thus it is obvious you are but a mouthpiece. You are hesitating so long at times; the messages may just as well be arriving by semaphore.”

Mr. Peashooter regarded Mrs. Mills with an evident lack of affection.

“Also your use of the word ‘Antipodes’ is suspect as we are standing not a dozen yards from a neon sign that says ‘Sidney’, in fact the only time I‘ve heard the word recently was on a campsite in France, perhaps someone in the family is having flash-backs?”

Apparently he was not going to get a word in as immediately she had finished Mr. Peashooter retorted, “So you’ve changed sides then?”

“Not at all Mr. Peashooter,” her voice was icy, “I successfully completed the task I was given and have subsequently resigned. I am now a private citizen again, but I think it worth mentioning that where I come from private citizens are considered very valuable and there is always retaliation.

Obviously there should be no problem between friendly states, but it is worth remembering I am also the widow of a security forces hero. I most definitely would be avenged, whatever our respective masters say."

There was a pause while Mr. Peashooter gazed into space then winced abruptly as if someone had screamed inside his head, which of course they probably had.

"I bought a shotgun like you said." He finally was able to get a few words in while everybody else, visible or not, was taking a break.

"Yes I know." Mr. Peashooter surprised him and apparently it showed, "It's a small world and rumour has it you do not necessarily observe all the basic safety rules as laid down by the gun club regulatory bodies, particularly the bits about firing indiscriminately into woods and wallies." He glanced at his wife, but she was studiously searching the concourse for something or other.

"Here - and don't say we didn't give you anything." Mr. Peashooter held out a pair of flight tickets and a folded document.

"Two things," Mr. Peashooter had taken a strange hold of the lapel of his jacket, from which he had extracted the tickets, as if covering a microphone perhaps, "Good Luck and don't come back." He turned and was soon lost in the crowd.

There were two tickets and one visa carrying both their names. He tucked the visa into his ticket folder, turned to face her and handed her the other. They had begun to call the flight and she bent to pick up the bag, but hesitated when she saw the look on his face.

"There's a night flight out a couple of hours after the Sidney departure, you will have seen the board the same as me, you might even be able to transfer the ticket or something I don't know, but if not it'd just have to come out of the bank."

He smiled uncomfortably, he didn't really want to do this, but he could not face another mistake.

"Cold feet Bowie, you wait 'till I resign then you tell me you're having second thoughts?"

He was surprised, he thought it had been a ploy, "Did you resign, when?"

He was still not certain. "When you were in the bath."

"What about the money?" The money had been for her in case he had messed up her job.

"I don't know, I didn't ask, I only phoned up to resign, does it matter?"

Not to him, he had not been counting on it anyway, but if he were to have responsibilities a stake would be good, "It would be nice to be able to eat when we get there."

She bent for the bag again and this time stood with it held in front of her in both hands.

"C'mon Bowie, don't let Betty down now, be a brave boy."

She turned and led the way to the check-in desk. A few minutes later they were making their way arm in arm along the pierhead toward the plane.

"I'm sorry you felt the need to bring your late husband into all this."

Probably the worst thing he could say given the circumstances, but it had never stopped him before.

"It doesn't matter, he'd be happy to help, anyway he owes me."

He was pleased, there was no rancour or secrecy anymore – perhaps after all the past would not be a problem for them.

"Why?"

"It was him that called it wrong, I know now, I don't know why I know but I do. There were a lot of vested interests that wanted the reputation of their 'star boy' left intact and I guess I just went along with it. In a way deep down I might have been as bad, he really was a star, and it was hard to believe he could have made a mistake, but I know now."

They were almost at the plane.

"Well I'm not sure I can live up to a hero, I mean I can try, but……."

"Cold feet again Bowie?"

"No, No, but romance has never really been my strong point as it were, you know, if there's a problem well, if things don't work as they are or where they are even, we could always, well err…….take them off and try them somewhere else, it's won't be the first time it's been attempted."

She laughed joyously,

"Oh I'm sure that won't be necessary Bowie, I think for the moment we'll find out how well they all work where they're supposed to be before we start thinking about having anything removed."

He followed her through the aircraft door into the cabin.

"Fair enough Mrs. Mills, you're in charge of security."

THE END

Postscript

There can be no real analogy between the exploits of Mr. and Mrs. Mills and the machinations of the European Union – one is fiction. But were an alien vessel to land and little green men alight to consider this narrative, one wonders if they would be able to tell which one it was – especially if they came from a planet with any elemental, auditing heritage?

24015051R00224

Printed in Great Britain
by Amazon